GR...
STORIES: AN ANTHOLOGY
OF TWELVE FAMOUS STO-
RIES AND NOVELETTES

# GREAT MODERN
# *Short Stories*

# GREAT MODERN
# *Short Stories*

*an anthology of twelve
   famous stories and novelettes*

Selected, and with a Foreword
and Biographical Notes,

*by* **Bennett Cerf**

**VINTAGE BOOKS** *A Division of Random House*
NEW YORK

VINTAGE BOOKS EDITION, 1955

ISBN: 0-394-70127-5

# CONTENTS

# FOREWORD

Many years ago, when I chose the twelve superb stories that make up this collection, I predicted that although the contents represented, of course, a very personal taste, the reading public would register emphatic approval, and not even the most carping critic would take exception to the inclusion of a single one of the selections.

For once in my life, at least, I was absolutely right. This collection has proven to be one of the most successful and durable of all the volumes in the Modern Library, its sales increasing every year. The total is now over a million copies. Furthermore, every one of the twelve stories has remained a favorite of critics and the public alike. Three of the authors—Steinbeck, Hemingway, and Faulkner— have since received the Nobel Prize (thus joining Galsworthy and Pearl Buck) and all have been accorded high and enduring places in the history of literature.

Of the twelve, my own favorite four are "Heart of Darkness," "The Apple Tree," "The Snows of Kilimanjaro," and "The Red Pony," but the other eight are almost equally rewarding. Biographical notes have been added at the back of the book. They are up to the minute now, and will be faithfully revised as necessary in future printings. The absence of any pedantic theories on the how and why of great short stories should be another point in the collection's favor.

Publishing, I believe, is the most exciting and satisfying profession in the world. One of its unmatched pleasures is the contemplation of a good book receiving a deserved long life. I am proud, as its publisher, that this anthology of truly great modern short stories has caught the fancy of professors, students, and general bookstore patrons alike.

BENNETT CERF

*Mount Kisco, New York*

*September, 1966*

# Five English Stories

# HEART OF DARKNESS
*by Joseph Conrad*

I

THE *Nellie,* a cruising yawl, swung to her anchor without a flutter of the sails, and was at rest. The flood had made, the wind was nearly calm, and being bound down the river, the only thing for it was to come to and wait for the turn of the tide.

The sea-reach of the Thames stretched before us like the beginning of an interminable waterway. In the offing the sea and the sky were welded together without a joint, and in the luminous space the tanned sails of the barges drifting up with the tide seemed to stand still in red clusters of canvas sharply peaked, with gleams of varnished sprits. A haze rested on the low shores that ran out to sea in vanishing flatness. The air was dark above Gravesend, and farther back still seemed condensed into a mournful gloom, brooding motionless over the biggest, and the greatest, town on earth.

The Director of Companies was our captain and our host. We four affectionately watched his back as he stood in the bows looking to seaward. On the whole river there was nothing that looked half so nautical. He resembled a pilot, which to a seaman is trustworthiness personified. It was difficult to realize his work was not out there in the luminous estuary, but behind him, within the brooding gloom.

Between us there was, as I have already said somewhere, the bond of the sea. Besides holding our hearts together through long periods of separation, it had the effect of making us tolerant of each other's yarns—and even convictions. The Lawyer—the best of old fellows—had, because of his many years and many virtues, the only cushion on deck, and was lying on the only rug. The Accountant had brought out already a box of dominoes, and was toying architecturally with the bones. Marlow sat cross-legged right aft, leaning against the mizzen-mast. He had sunken cheeks, a yellow complexion, a straight back, an ascetic aspect, and, with his arms dropped, the palms of hands outwards, resembled an idol. The director, satisfied the anchor had good hold, made his way aft and sat down amongst us. We exchanged a few words lazily. Afterwards there was silence on board the yacht. For some reason or other we did not begin that game of dominoes. We felt meditative, and fit for nothing but placid staring. The day was ending in a serenity of still and exquisite brilliance. The water shone pacifically; the sky, without a speck, was a benign immensity of unstained light; the very mist on the Essex marshes was like a gauzy and radiant fabric, hung from the wooded rises inland, and draping the low shores in diaphanous folds. Only the gloom to the west, brooding over the upper reaches, became more somber every minute, as if angered by the approach of the sun.

And at last, in its curved and imperceptible fall, the sun sank low, and from glowing white changed to a dull red without rays and without heat, as if about to go out suddenly, stricken to death by the touch of that gloom brooding over a crowd of men.

Forthwith a change came over the waters, and the serenity became less brilliant but more profound. The old river in its broad reach rested unruffled at the decline of day, after ages of good service done to the race that peopled its banks, spread out in the tranquil dignity of a waterway leading to the uttermost ends of the earth. We looked at the venerable stream not in the vivid flush of a short day that comes and departs forever, but in the august light of abiding memories. And indeed nothing is easier for a man who has, as the phrase goes, "followed the sea" with reverence and affection, than to evoke the great spirit of the past upon the lower reaches of the Thames. The tidal current runs to and fro in its unceasing service, crowded with memories of men and ships it had borne to the rest of home or to the battles of the sea. It had known and served all the men of whom the nation is proud, from Sir Francis Drake to Sir John Franklin, knights all, titled and untitled—the knights-errant of the sea. It had borne all the ships whose names are like jewels flashing in the night of time, from the *Golden Hind* returning with her round flanks full of treasure, to be visited by the Queen's Highness and thus pass out of the gigantic tale, to the *Erebus* and *Terror,* bound on other conquests —and that never returned. It had known the ships and the men. They had sailed from Deptford, from Greenwich, from Erith—the adventurers and the settlers; kings' ships and the ships of men on 'Change; captains, admirals, the dark "interlopers" of the Eastern trade, and the commissioned "generals" of East India fleets. Hunters for gold or pursuers of fame, they all had gone out on that stream, bearing the sword, and often the torch, messengers of the might within the land, bearers of a spark from the sacred fire. What greatness had not floated on the ebb of that river into the mystery of an unknown earth! . . . The dreams of men, the seed of commonwealths, the germs of empires.

The sun set; the dusk fell on the stream, and lights began to appear along the shore. The Chapman lighthouse, a three-legged thing erect on a mud-flat, shone strongly. Lights of ships moved in the fairway—a great stir of lights going up and going down. And farther west on the upper reaches the place of the monstrous town was still marked ominously on the sky, a brooding gloom in sunshine, a lurid glare under the stars.

"And this also," said Marlow suddenly, "has been one of the dark places on the earth."

He was the only man of us who still "followed the sea." The worst that could be said of him was that he did not represent his class. He was a seaman, but he was a wanderer, too, while most seamen lead, if one may so express it, a sedentary life. Their minds are of the stay-at-home order, and their home is always with them—the ship; and so is their country—the sea. One ship is very much like another, and the sea is always the same. In the immutability of their surroundings the foreign shores, the foreign faces, the changing immensity of life, glide past, veiled not by a sense of mystery but by a slightly disdainful ignorance; for there is nothing mysterious to a seaman unless it be the sea itself, which is the mistress of his existence and as inscrutable as Destiny. For the rest, after his hours of work, a casual stroll or a casual spree on shore suffices to unfold for him the secret of a whole continent, and generally he finds the secret not worth knowing. The yarns of seamen have a direct simplicity, the whole meaning of which lies within the shell of a cracked nut. But Marlow was not typical (if his propensity to spin yarns be excepted), and to him the meaning of an episode was not inside like a kernel but outside, enveloping the tale which brought it out only as a glow brings out a haze, in the likeness of one of these misty halos that sometimes are made visible by the spectral illumination of moonshine.

His remark did not seem at all surprising. It was just like Marlow. It was accepted in silence. No one took the trouble to grunt even; and presently he said, very slow—

"I was thinking of very old times, when the Romans first came here, nineteen hundred years ago—the other day. . . . Light came out of this river since—you say Knights? Yes; but it is like a running blaze on a plain, like a flash of lightning in the clouds. We live in the flicker—may it last as long as the old earth keeps rolling! But darkness was here yesterday. Imagine the feelings of a commander of a fine—what d'ye call 'em?—trireme in the Mediterranean, ordered suddenly to the north; run overland across the Gauls in a hurry; put in charge of one of these craft the legionaries—a wonderful lot of handy men they must have been, too—used to build, apparently by the hundred, in a month or two, if we may believe what we read. Imagine him here—the very end of the world, a sea the color of lead, a sky the color of smoke, a kind of ship about as rigid as a concertina— and going up this river with stores, or orders, or what you like. Sand-banks, marshes, forests, savages,— precious little to eat fit for a civilized man, nothing but Thames water to drink. No Falernian wine here, no going ashore. Here and there a military camp lost in a wilderness, like a needle in a bundle of hay— cold, fog, tempests, disease, exile, and death,—death skulking in the air, in the water, in the bush. They must have been dying like flies here. Oh, yes—he did it. Did it very well, too, no doubt, and without thinking much about it either, except afterwards to brag of what he had gone through in his time, perhaps. They were men enough to face the darkness. And perhaps he was cheered by keeping his eye on a chance of promotion to the fleet at Ravenna by and by, if he had good friends in Rome and survived the awful climate. Or think of a decent young citizen in a toga—perhaps too much dice, you know— coming out here in the train of some prefect, or tax-gatherer, or trader even, to mend his fortunes. Land in a swamp, march through the woods, and in some inland post feel the savagery, the utter savagery, had closed round him,—all that mysterious life of the wilderness that stirs in the forest, in the jungles, in the hearts of wild men. There's no initiation either into such mysteries. He has to live in the midst of the incomprehensible, which is also detestable. And it has a fascination, too, that goes to work upon him. The fascination of the abomination—you know, imagine the growing regrets, the longing to escape, the powerless disgust, the surrender, the hate."

He paused.

"Mind," he began again, lifting one arm from the elbow, the palm of the hand outwards, so that, with his legs folded before him, he had the pose of a Buddha preaching in European clothes and without a lotus-flower—"Mind, none of us would feel exactly like this. What saves us is efficiency—the devotion to efficiency. But these chaps were not much account, really. They were no colonists; their administration was merely a squeeze, and nothing more, I suspect. They were conquerors, and for that you want only brute force—nothing to boast of, when you have it, since your strength is just an accident arising from the weakness of others. They grabbed what they could get for the sake of what was to be got. It was just robbery with violence, aggravated murder on a great scale, and men going at it blind—as is very proper for those who tackle a darkness. The conquest of the earth, which mostly means the taking it away from those who have a different complexion or slightly flatter noses than ourselves, is not a pretty thing when you look into it too much. What redeems it is the idea only. An idea at the back of it; not a sentimental pretense but an idea; and an unselfish belief in the idea—something you can set up, and bow down before, and offer a sacrifice to. . . ."

He broke off. Flames glided in the river, small green flames, red flames, white flames, pursuing, overtaking, joining, crossing each other—then separating slowly or hastily. The traffic of the great city went on in the deepening night upon the sleepless river. We looked on, waiting patiently—there was nothing else to do till the end of the flood; but it was only after a long silence, when he said, in a hesitating voice, "I suppose you fellows remember I did once turn fresh-water sailor for a bit," that we knew we were fated, before the ebb began to run, to hear one of Marlow's inconclusive experiences.

"I don't want to bother you much with what happened to me personally," he began, showing in this remark the weakness of many tellers of tales who seem so often unaware of what their audience would best like to hear; "yet to understand the effect of it on me you ought to know how I got out there, what I saw, how I went up that river to the place where I first met the poor chap. It was the farthest point of navigation and the culminating point of my experience. It seemed somehow to throw a kind of light on everything about me—and into my thoughts. It was somber enough, too—and pitiful—not extraordinary in any way—not very clear either. No, not very clear. And yet it seemed to throw a kind of light.

"I had then, as you remember, just returned to London after a lot of Indian Ocean, Pacific, China Seas—a regular dose of the East—six years or so, and I was loafing about hindering you fellows in your work and invading your homes, just as though I had got a heavenly mission to civilize you. It was very fine for a time, but after a bit I did get tired of resting. Then I began to look for a ship —I should think the hardest work on earth. But the ships wouldn't even look at me. And I got tired of that game, too.

"Now when I was a little chap I had a passion for maps. I would look for hours at South America, or Africa, or Australia, and lose myself in all the glories of exploration. At that time there were many blank spaces on the earth, and when I saw one that looked particularly inviting on a map (but they all look that) I would put my finger on it and say, When I grow up I will go there. The North Pole was one of these places, I remember. Well, I haven't been there yet, and shall not try now. The glamour's off. Other places were scattered about the Equator, and in every sort of latitude all over the two hemispheres. I have been in some of them, and . . . well, we won't talk about that. But there was one yet—the biggest, the most blank, so to speak —that I had a hankering after.

"True, by this time it was not a blank space any more. It had got filled since my childhood with rivers and lakes and names. It had ceased to be a blank space of delightful mystery—a white patch for a boy to dream gloriously over. It had become a place of darkness. But there was in it one river especially, a mighty big river, that you could see on the map, resembling an immense snake uncoiled, with its head in the sea, its body at rest curving afar over a vast country, and its tail lost in the depths of the land. And as I looked at the map of it in a shop-window, it fascinated me as a snake would a bird—a silly little bird. Then I remembered there was a big concern, a Company for trade on that river. Dash it all! I thought to myself, they can't trade without using some kind of craft on that lot of fresh water—steamboats! Why shouldn't I try to get charge of one? I went on along Fleet Street, but could not shake off the idea. The snake had charmed me.

"You understand it was a Continental concern, that Trading society; but I have a lot of relations living on the Continent, because it's cheap and not so nasty as it looks, they say.

"I am sorry to own I began to worry them. This was already a fresh departure for me. I was not used to getting things that way, you know. I always went my own road and on my own legs where I had a mind to go. I wouldn't have believed it of myself; but, then—you see—I felt somehow I must get there by hook or by crook. So I worried them. The men said 'My dear fellow,' and did nothing. Then—would you believe it?—I tried the women. I, Charlie Marlow, set the women to work—to get a job. Heavens! Well, you see, the notion drove me. I had an

aunt, a dear enthusiastic soul. She wrote: 'It will be delightful. I am ready to do anything, anything for you. It is
a glorious idea. I know the wife of a very high personage
in the Administration, and also a man who has lots of
influence with,' etc., etc. She was determined to make no
end of fuss to get me appointed skipper of a river steamboat, if such was my fancy.

"I got my appointment—of course; and I got it very
quick. It appears the Company had received news that one
of their captains had been killed in a scuffle with the
natives. This was my chance, and it made me the more
anxious to go. It was only months and months afterwards,
when I made the attempt to recover what was left of the
body, that I heard the original quarrel arose from a mis-
understanding about some hens. Yes, two black hens.
Fresleven—that was the fellow's name, a Dane—thought
himself wronged somehow in the bargain, so he went
ashore and started to hammer the chief of the village with
a stick. Oh, it didn't surprise me in the least to hear this,
and at the same time to be told that Fresleven was the
gentlest, quietest creature that ever walked on two legs. No
doubt he was; but he had been a couple of years already
out there engaged in the noble cause, you know, and he
probably felt the need at last of asserting his self-respect
in some way. Therefore he whacked the old nigger merci-
lessly, while a big crowd of his people watched him, thunderstruck, till some man—I was told the chief's son—in
desperation at hearing the old chap yell, made a tentative
jab with a spear at the white man—and of course it went
quite easy between the shoulder-blades. Then the whole
population cleared into the forest, expecting all kinds of
calamities to happen, while, on the other hand, the steamer
Fresleven commanded left also in a bad panic, in charge of
the engineer, I believe. Afterwards nobody seemed to
trouble much about Fresleven's remains, till I got out and
stepped into his shoes. I couldn't let it rest, though; but

when an opportunity offered at last to meet my predecessor, the grass growing through his ribs was tall enough to hide his bones. They were all there. The supernatural being had not been touched after he fell. And the village was deserted, the huts gaped black, rotting, all askew within the fallen enclosures. A calamity had come to it, sure enough. The people had vanished. Mad terror had scattered them, men, women, and children, through the bush, and they had never returned. What became of the hens I don't know either. I should think the cause of progress got them, anyhow. However, through this glorious affair I got my appointment, before I had fairly begun to hope for it.

"I flew around like mad to get ready, and before forty-eight hours I was crossing the Channel to show myself to my employers, and sign the contract. In a very few hours I arrived in a city that always makes me think of a whited sepulcher. Prejudice no doubt. I had no difficulty in finding the Company's offices. It was the biggest thing in the town, and everybody I met was full of it. They were going to run an over-sea empire, and make no end of coin by trade.

"A narrow and deserted street in deep shadow, high houses, innumerable windows with venetian blinds, a dead silence, grass sprouting between the stones, imposing carriage archways right and left, immense double doors standing ponderously ajar. I slipped through one of these cracks, went up a swept and ungarnished staircase, as arid as a desert, and opened the first door I came to. Two women, one fat and the other slim, sat on straw-bottomed chairs, knitting black wool. The slim one got up and walked straight at me—still knitting with down-cast eyes—and only just as I began to think of getting out of her way, as you would for a somnambulist, stood still, and looked up. Her dress was as plain as an umbrella-cover, and she turned round without a word and preceded me into a waiting-room. I gave my name, and looked about. Deal table in the middle, plain chairs all around the walls, on one end a large shining map, marked with all the colors of a rainbow. There was a vast amount of red—good to see at any time, because one knows that some real work is done in there, a deuce of a lot of blue, a little green, smears of orange, and, on the East Coast, a purple patch, to show where the jolly pioneers of progress drink the jolly lager-beer. However, I wasn't going into any of these. I was going into the yellow. Dead in the center. And the river was there—fascinating—deadly—like a snake. Ough! A door opened, a white-haired secretarial head, but wearing a compassionate expression, appeared, and a skinny forefinger beckoned me into the sanctuary. Its light was dim, and a heavy writing-desk squatted in the middle. From behind that structure came out an impression of pale plumpness in a frock-coat. The great man himself. He was five feet six, I should judge, and had his grip on the handle-end of ever so many millions. He shook hands, I fancy, murmured vaguely, was satisfied with my French. *Bon voyage.*

"In about forty-five seconds I found myself again in the waiting-room with the compassionate secretary, who, full of desolation and sympathy, made me sign some document. I believe I undertook amongst other things not to disclose any trade secrets. Well, I am not going to.

"I began to feel slightly uneasy. You know I am not used to such ceremonies, and there was something ominous in the atmosphere. It was just as though I had been let into some conspiracy—I don't know—something not quite right; and I was glad to get out. In the outer room the two women knitted black wool feverishly. People were arriving, and the younger one was walking back and forth introducing them. The old one sat on her chair. Her flat cloth slippers were propped up on a foot-warmer, and a cat reposed on her lap. She wore a starched white affair on her head, had a wart on one cheek, and silver-rimmed spec-

tacles hung on the tip of her nose. She glanced at me
above the glasses. The swift and indifferent placidity of
that look troubled me. Two youths with foolish and
cheery countenances were being piloted over, and she
threw at them the same quick glance of unconcerned wisdom. She seemed to know all about them and about me,
too. An eerie feeling came over me. She seemed uncanny
and fateful. Often far away there I thought of these two,
guarding the door of Darkness, knitting black wool as for a
warm pall, one introducing, introducing continuously to
the unknown, the other scrutinizing the cheery and foolish
faces with unconcerned old eyes. *Ave!* Old knitter of black
wool. *Morituri te salutant.* Not many of those she looked at
ever saw her again—not half, by a long way.

"There was yet a visit to the doctor. 'A simple formality,' assured me the secretary, with an air of taking an
immense part in all my sorrows. Accordingly a young chap
wearing his hat over the left eyebrow, some clerk I suppose,—there must have been clerks in the business, though
the house was as still as a house in a city of the dead—
came from somewhere upstairs, and led me forth. He was
shabby and careless, with inkstains on the sleeves of his
jacket, and his cravat was large and billowy, under a chin
shaped like the toe of an old boot. It was a little too early
for the doctor, so I proposed a drink, and thereupon he
developed a vein of joviality. As we sat over our vermuths
he glorified the Company's business, and by and by I expressed casually my surprise at him not going out there.
He became very cool and collected all at once. 'I am not
such a fool as I look, quoth Plato to his disciples,' he said
sententiously, emptied his glass with great resolution, and
we rose.

"The old doctor felt my pulse, evidently thinking of
something else the while. 'Good, good for there,' he mumbled, and then with a certain eagerness asked me whether
I would let him measure my head. Rather surprised, I said

Yes, when he produced a thing like calipers and got the dimensions back and front and every way, taking notes carefully. He was an unshaven little man in a threadbare coat like a gaberdine, with his feet in slippers, and I thought him a harmless fool. 'I always ask leave, in the interests of science, to measure the crania of those going out there,' he said. 'And when they come back, too?' I asked. 'Oh, I never see them,' he remarked; 'and, moreover, the changes take place inside, you know.' He smiled, as if at some quiet joke. 'So you are going out there. Famous. Interesting, too.' He gave me a searching glance, and made another note. 'Ever any madness in your family?' he asked, in a matter-of-fact tone. I felt very annoyed. 'Is that question in the interests of science, too?' 'It would be,' he said, without taking notice of my irritation, 'interesting for science to watch the mental changes of individuals, on the spot, but . . .' 'Are you an alienist?' I interrupted. 'Every doctor should be—a little,' answered that original, imperturbably. 'I have a little theory which you Messieurs who go out there must help me to prove. This is my share in the advantages my country shall reap from the possession of such a magnificent dependency. The mere wealth I leave to others. Pardon my questions, but you are the first Englishman coming under my observation . . .' I hastened to assure him I was not in the least typical. 'If I were,' said I, 'I wouldn't be talking like this with you.' 'What you say is rather profound, and probably erroneous,' he said, with a laugh. 'Avoid irritation more than exposure to the sun. Adieu. How do you English say, eh? Good-by. Ah! Good-by. Adieu. In the tropics one must before everything keep calm.' . . . He lifted a warning forefinger. . . . '*Du calme, du calme. Adieu.*'

"One thing more remained to do—say good-by to my excellent aunt. I found her triumphant. I had a cup of tea—the last decent cup of tea for many days—and in a room that most soothingly looked just as you would expect a lady's drawing-room to look, we had a long quiet chat by the fireside. In the course of these confidences it became quite plain to me I had been represented to the wife of the high dignitary, and goodness knows to how many more people besides, as an exceptional and gifted creature—a piece of good fortune for the Company—a man you don't get hold of every day. Good heavens! and I was going to take charge of a two-penny-half-penny river-steamboat with a penny whistle attached! It appeared, however, I was also one of the Workers, with a capital—you know. Something like an emissary of light, something like a lower sort of apostle. There had been a lot of such rot let loose in print and talk just about that time, and the excellent woman, living right in the rush of all that humbug, got carried off her feet. She talked about 'weaning those ignorant millions from their horrid ways,' till, upon my word, she made me quite uncomfortable. I ventured to hint that the Company was run for profit.

"'You forget, dear Charlie, that the laborer is worthy of his hire,' she said, brightly. It's queer how out of touch with truth women are. They live in a world of their own, and there has never been anything like it, and never can be. It is too beautiful altogether, and if they were to set it up it would go to pieces before the first sunset. Some confounded fact we men have been living contentedly with ever since the day of creation would start up and knock the whole thing over.

"After this I got embraced, told to wear flannel, be sure to write often, and so on—and I left. In the street—I don't know why—a queer feeling came to me that I was an impostor. Odd thing that I, who used to clear out for any part of the world at twenty-four hours' notice, with less thought than most men give to the crossing of a street, had a moment—I won't say of hesitation, but of startled pause, before this commonplace affair. The best way I can explain it to you is by saying that, for a second or two, I felt as though, instead of going to the center of a continent, I were about to set off for the center of the earth.

"I left in a French steamer, and she called in every blamed port they have out there, for, as far as I could see, the sole purpose of landing soldiers and custom-house officers. I watched the coast. Watching a coast as it slips by the ship is like thinking about an enigma. There it is before you—smiling, frowning, inviting, grand, mean, insipid, or savage, and always mute with an air of whispering, Come and find out. This one was almost featureless, as if still in the making, with an aspect of monotonous grimness. The edge of a colossal jungle, so dark-green as to be almost black, fringed with white surf, ran straight, like a ruled line, far, far away along a blue sea whose glitter was blurred by a creeping mist. The sun was fierce, the land seemed to glisten and drip with steam. Here and there grayish-whitish specks showed up clustered inside the white surf, with a flag flying above them perhaps. Settlements some centuries old, and still no bigger than pinheads on the untouched expanse of their background. We pounded along, stopped, landed soldiers; went on, landed custom-house clerks to levy toll in what looked like a God-forsaken wilderness, with a tin shed and a flag-pole lost in it; landed more soldiers—to take care of the custom-house clerks, presumably. Some, I heard, got drowned in the surf; but whether they did or not, nobody seemed particularly to care. They were just flung out there, and on we went. Every day the coast looked the same, as though we had not moved; but we passed various places—trading places—with names like Gran' Bassam, Little Popo; names that seemed to belong to some sordid farce acted in front of a sinister backcloth. The idleness of a passenger, my isolation amongst all these men with whom I had no point of contact, the oily and languid sea, the uniform somberness of the coast,

seemed to keep me away from the truth of things, within
the toil of a mournful and senseless delusion. The voice
of the surf heard now and then was a positive pleasure,
like the speech of a brother. It was something natural,
that had its reason, that had a meaning. Now and then a
boat from the shore gave one a momentary contact with
reality. It was paddled by black fellows. You could see
from afar the white of their eyeballs glistening. They
shouted, sang; their bodies streamed with perspiration;
they had faces like grotesque masks—these chaps; but
they had bone, muscle, a wild vitality, an intense energy
of movement, that was as natural and true as the surf
along their coast. They wanted no excuse for being there.
They were a great comfort to look at. For a time I would
feel I belonged still to a world of straightforward facts;
but the feeling would not last long. Something would turn
up to scare it away. Once, I remember, we came upon a
man-of-war anchored off the coast. There wasn't even a
shed there, and she was shelling the bush. It appears the
French had one of their wars going on thereabouts. Her
ensign dropped limp like a rag; the muzzles of the long
six-inch guns stuck out all over the low hull; the greasy,
slimy swell swung her up lazily and let her down, swaying her thin masts. In the empty immensity of earth, sky,
and water, there she was, incomprehensible, firing into a
continent. Pop, would go one of the six-inch guns; a
small flame would dart and vanish, a little white smoke
would disappear, a tiny projectile would give a feeble
screech—and nothing happened. Nothing could happen
There was a touch of insanity in the proceeding, a sens
of lugubrious drollery in the sight; and it was not dissipated by somebody on board assuring me earnestly there
was a camp of natives—he called them enemies!—hidden
out of sight somewhere.

"We gave her her letters (I heard the men in that
lonely ship were dying of fever at the rate of three a day)

and went on. We called at some more places with farcical names, where the merry dance of death and trade goes on in a still and earthy atmosphere as of an overheated catacomb; all along the formless coast bordered by dangerous surf, as if Nature herself had tried to ward off intruders; in and out of rivers, streams of death in life, whose banks were rotting into mud, whose waters, thickened into slime, invaded the contorted mangroves, that seemed to writhe at us in the extremity of an impotent despair. Nowhere did we stop long enough to get a particularized impression, but the general sense of vague and oppressive wonder grew upon me. It was like a weary pilgrimage amongst hints for nightmares.

"It was upward of thirty days before I saw the mouth of the big river. We anchored off the seat of the government. But my work would not begin till some two hundred miles farther on. So as soon as I could I made a start for a place thirty miles higher up.

"I had my passage on a little sea-going steamer. Her captain was a Swede, and knowing me for a seaman, invited me on the bridge. He was a young man, lean, fair, and morose, with lanky hair and a shuffling gait. As we left the miserable little wharf, he tossed his head contemptuously at the shore. 'Been living there?' he asked. I said, 'Yes.' 'Fine lot these government chaps—are they not?' he went on, speaking English with great precision and considerable bitterness. 'It is funny what some people will do for a few francs a month. I wonder what becomes of that kind when it goes up-country?' I said to him I expected to see that soon. 'So-o-o!' he exclaimed. He shuffled athwart, keeping one eye ahead vigilantly. 'Don't be too sure,' he continued. 'The other day I took up a man who hanged himself on the road. He was a Swede, too.' 'Hanged himself! Why, in God's name?' I cried. He kept on looking out watchfully. 'Who knows? The sun was too much for him, or the country perhaps.'

"At last we opened a reach. A rocky cliff appeared, mounds of turned-up earth by the shore, houses on a hill, others with iron roofs, amongst a waste of excavations, or hanging to the declivity. A continuous noise of the rapids above hovered over this scene of inhabited devastation. A lot of people, mostly black and naked, moved about like ants. A jetty projected into the river. A blinding sunlight drowned all this at times in a sudden recrudescence of glare. 'There's your Company's station,' said the Swede, pointing to three wooden barrack-like structures on the rocky slope. 'I will send your things up. Four boxes did you say? So. Farewell.'

"I came upon a boiler wallowing in the grass, then found a path leading up the hill. It turned aside for the bowlders, and also for an undersized railway-truck lying there on its back with its wheels in the air. One was off. The thing looked as dead as the carcass of some animal. I came upon more pieces of decaying machinery, a stack of rusty rails. To the left a clump of trees made a shady spot, where dark things seemed to stir feebly. I blinked, the path was steep. A horn tooted to the right, and I saw the black people run. A heavy and dull detonation shook the ground, a puff of smoke came out of the cliff, and that was all. No change appeared on the face of the rock. They were building a railway. The cliff was not in the way or anything; but this objectless blasting was all the work going on.

"A slight clinking behind me made me turn my head. Six black men advanced in a file, toiling up the path. They walked erect and slow, balancing small baskets full of earth on their heads, and the clink kept time with their footsteps. Black rags were wound round their loins, and the short ends behind waggled to and fro like tails. I could see every rib, the joints of their limbs were like knots in a rope; each had an iron collar on his neck, and all were connected together with a chain whose bights swung between them, rhythmically clinking. Another report from the cliff made me think suddenly of that ship of war I had seen firing into a continent. It was the same kind of ominous voice; but these men could by no stretch of imagination be called enemies. They were called criminals, and the outraged law, like the bursting shells, had come to them, an insoluble mystery from the sea. All their meager breasts panted together, the violently dilated nostrils quivered, the eyes stared stonily up-hill. They passed me within six inches, without a glance, with that complete, deathlike indifference of unhappy savages. Behind this raw matter one of the reclaimed, the product of the new forces at work, strolled despondently, carrying a rifle by its middle. He had a uniform jacket with one button off, and seeing a white man on the path, hoisted his weapon to his shoulder with alacrity. This was simple prudence, white men being so much alike at a distance that he could not tell who I might be. He was speedily reassured, and with a large, white, rascally grin, and a glance at his charge, seemed to take me into partnership in his exalted trust. After all, I also was a part of the great cause of these high and just proceedings.

"Instead of going up, I turned and descended to the left. My idea was to let that chain-gang get out of sight before I climbed the hill. You know I am not particularly tender; I've had to strike and to fend off. I've had to resist and to attack sometimes—that's only one way of resisting—without counting the exact cost, according to the demands of such sort of life as I had blundered into. I've seen the devil of violence, and the devil of greed, and the devil of hot desire; but, by all the stars! these were strong, lusty, red-eyed devils, that swayed and drove men—men, I tell you. But as I stood on this hillside, I foresaw that in the blinding sunshine of that land I would become acquainted with a flabby, pretending, weak-eyed devil of a rapacious and pitiless folly. How insidious he could be, too, I was only to find out several months later and a thousand miles farther. For a moment I stood appalled, as though by a warning. Finally I descended the hill, obliquely, towards the trees I had seen.

"I avoided a vast artificial hole somebody had been digging on the slope, the purpose of which I found it impossible to divine. It wasn't a quarry or a sandpit, anyhow. It was just a hole. It might have been connected with the philanthropic desire of giving the criminals something to do. I don't know. Then I nearly fell into a very narrow ravine, almost no more than a scar in the hillside. I discovered that a lot of imported drainage-pipes for the settlement had been tumbled in there. There wasn't one that was not broken. It was a wanton smash-up. At last I got under the trees. My purpose was to stroll into the shade for a moment; but no sooner within than it seemed to me I had stepped into the gloomy circle of some Inferno. The rapids were near, and an uninterrupted, uniform, headlong, rushing noise filled the mournful stillness of the grove, where not a breath stirred, not a leaf moved, with a mysterious sound—as though the tearing pace of the launched earth had suddenly become audible.

"Black shapes crouched, lay, sat between the trees leaning against the trunks, clinging to the earth, half coming out, half effaced within the dim light, in all the attitudes of pain, abandonment, and despair. Another mine on the cliff went off, followed by a slight shudder of the soil under my feet. The work was going on. The work! And this was the place where some of the helpers had withdrawn to die.

"They were dying slowly—it was very clear. They were not enemies, they were not criminals, they were nothing earthly now,—nothing but black shadows of disease and starvation, lying confusedly in the greenish gloom.

Brought from all the recesses of the coast in all the legality of time contracts, lost in uncongenial surroundings, fed on unfamiliar food, they sickened, became inefficient, and were then allowed to crawl away and rest. These moribund shapes were free as air—and nearly as thin. I began to distinguish the gleam of the eyes under the trees. Then, glancing down, I saw a face near my hand. The black bones reclined at full length with one shoulder against the tree, and slowly the eyelids rose and the sunken eyes looked up at me, enormous and vacant, a kind of blind, white flicker in the depths of the orbs, which died out slowly. The man seemed young—almost a boy—but you know with them it's hard to tell. I found nothing else to do but to offer him one of my good Swede's ship's biscuits I had in my pocket. The fingers closed slowly on it and held—there was no other movement and no other glance. He had tied a bit of white worsted round his neck— Why? Where did he get it? Was it a badge—an ornament—a charm—a propitiatory act? Was there any idea at all connected with it? It looked startling round his black neck, this bit of white thread from beyond the seas.

"Near the same tree two more bundles of acute angles sat with their legs drawn up. One, with his chin propped on his knees, stared at nothing, in an intolerable and appalling manner: his brother phantom rested its forehead, as if overcome with a great weariness; and all about others were scattered in every pose of contorted collapse, as in some picture of a massacre or a pestilence. While I stood horror-struck, one of these creatures rose to his hands and knees, and went off on all-fours towards the river to drink. He lapped out of his hand, then sat up in the sunlight, crossing his shins in front of him, and after a time let his woolly head fall on his breastbone.

"I didn't want any more loitering in the shade, and I made haste towards the station. When near the buildings

I met a white man, in such an unexpected elegance of
get-up that in the first moment I took him for a sort
of vision. I saw a high starched collar, white cuffs, a light
alpaca jacket, snowy trousers, a clean necktie, and
varnished boots. No hat. Hair parted, brushed, oiled,
under a green-lined parasol held in a big white hand.
He was amazing, and had a penholder behind his ear.

"I shook hands with this miracle, and I learned he
was the Company's chief accountant, and that all the
book-keeping was done at this station. He had come out
for a moment, he said, 'to get a breath of fresh air.'
The expression sounded wonderfully odd, with its suggestion of sedentary desk-life. I wouldn't have mentioned
the fellow to you at all, only it was from his lips that I
first heard the name of the man who is so indissolubly
connected with the memories of that time. Moreover, I
respected the fellow. Yes; I respected his collars, his vast
cuffs, his brushed hair. His appearance was certainly that
of a hairdresser's dummy; but in the great demoralization
of the land he kept up his appearance. That's backbone.
His starched collars and got-up shirt-fronts were achievements of character. He had been out nearly three years;
and, later, I could not help asking him how he managed
to sport such linen. He had just the faintest blush, and
said modestly, 'I've been teaching one of the native women
about the station. It was difficult. She had a distaste for
the work.' Thus this man had verily accomplished something. And he was devoted to his books, which were in
apple-pie order.

"Everything else in the station was in a muddle,—
heads, things, buildings. Strings of dusty niggers with
splay feet arrived and departed; a stream of manufac-
tured goods, rubbishy cottons, beads, and brass-wire set
into the depths of darkness, and in return came a precious
trickle of ivory.

"I had to wait in the station for ten days—an eternity.

I lived in a hut in the yard, but to be out of the chaos I would sometimes get into the accountant's office. It was built of horizontal planks, and so badly put together that, as he bent over his high desk, he was barred from neck to heels with narrow strips of sunlight. There was no need to open the big shutter to see. It was hot there, too; big flies buzzed fiendishly, and did not sting, but stabbed. I sat generally on the floor, while, of faultless appearance (and even slightly scented), perching on a high stool, he wrote, he wrote. Sometimes he stood up for exercise. When a trucklebed with a sick man (some invalid agent from up-country) was put in there, he exhibited a gentle annoyance. 'The groans of this sick person,' he said, 'distract my attention. And without that it is extremely difficult to guard against clerical errors in this climate.'

"One day he remarked, without lifting his head, 'In the interior you will no doubt meet Mr. Kurtz.' On my asking who Mr. Kurtz was, he said he was a first-class agent; and seeing my disappointment at this information, he added slowly, laying down his pen, 'He is a very remarkable person.' Further questions elicited from him that Mr. Kurtz was at present in charge of a trading post, a very important one, in the true ivory-country, at 'the very bottom of there. Sends in as much ivory as all the others put together. . . .' He began to write again. The sick man was too ill to groan. The flies buzzed in a great peace.

"Suddenly there was a growing murmur of voices and a great tramping of feet. A caravan had come in. A violent babble of uncouth sounds burst out on the other side of the planks. All the carriers were speaking together, and in the midst of the uproar the lamentable voice of the chief agent was heard 'giving it up' tearfully for the twentieth time that day. . . . He rose slowly. 'What a frightful row,' he said. He crossed the room

gently to look at the sick man, and returning, said to me,
'He does not hear.' 'What! Dead?' I asked, startled. 'No,
not yet,' he answered, with great composure. Then, al-
luding with a toss of the head to the tumult in the station-
yard, 'When one has got to make correct entries, one
comes to hate those savages—hate them to the death.'
He remained thoughtful for a moment. 'When you see
Mr. Kurtz,' he went on, 'tell him for me that everything
here'—he glanced at the desk—'is very satisfactory. I
don't like to write to him—with those messengers of ours
you never know who may get hold of your letter—at that
Central Station.' He stared at me for a moment with his
mild, bulging eyes. 'Oh, he will go far, very far,' he began
again. 'He will be a somebody in the Administration before long. They, above—the Council in Europe, you know
—mean him to be.'

"He turned to his work. The noise outside had ceased,
and presently in going out I stopped at the door. In the
steady buzz of flies the homeward-bound agent was lying
flushed and insensible; the other, bent over his books,
was making correct entries of perfectly correct transac-
tions; and fifty feet below the doorstep I could see the
still tree-tops of the grove of death.

"Next day I left that station at last, with a caravan
of sixty men, for a two-hundred-mile tramp.

"No use telling you much about that. Paths, paths,
everywhere; a stamped-in network of paths spreading
over the empty land, through long grass, through burnt
grass, through thickets, down and up chilly ravines, up
and down stony hills ablaze with heat; and a solitude,
a solitude, nobody, not a hut. The population had cleared
out a long time ago. Well, if a lot of mysterious niggers
armed with all kinds of fearful weapons suddenly took
to traveling on the road between Deal and Gravesend,
catching the yokels right and left to carry heavy loads
for them, I fancy every farm and cottage thereabouts

would get empty very soon. Only here the dwellings were gone, too. Still I passed through several abandoned villages. There's something pathetically childish in the ruins of grass walls. Day after day, with the stamp and shuffle of sixty pair of bare feet behind me, each pair under a sixty-lb. load. Camp, cook, sleep, strike camp, march. Now and then a carrier dead in harness, at rest in the long grass near the path, with an empty water-gourd and his long staff lying by his side. A great silence around and above Perhaps on some quiet night the tremor of far-off drums, sinking, swelling, a tremor vast, faint; a sound weird, appealing, suggestive, and wild—and perhaps with as profound a meaning as the sound of bells in a Christian country. Once a white man in an unbuttoned uniform, camping on the path with an armed escort of lank Zanzibaris, very hospitable and festive—not to say drunk. Was looking after the upkeep of the road, he declared. Can't say I saw any road or any upkeep, unless the body of a middle-aged negro, with a bullet-hole in the forehead, upon which I absolutely stumbled three miles farther on, may be considered as a permanent improvement. I had a white companion, too, not a bad chap, but rather too fleshy and with the exasperating habit of fainting on the hot hillsides, miles away from the least bit of shade and water. Annoying, you know, to hold your own coat like a parasol over a man's head while he is coming-to. I couldn't help asking him once what he meant by coming there at all. 'To make money, of course. What do you think?' he said, scornfully. Then he got fever, and had to be carried in a hammock slung under a pole. As he weighed sixteen stone I had no end of rows with the carriers. They jibbed, ran away, sneaked off with their loads in the night—quite a mutiny. So, one evening, I made a speech in English with gestures, not one of which was lost to the sixty pairs of eyes before me, and the next morning I started the hammock off in front all right.

An hour afterwards I came upon the whole concern
wrecked in a bush—man, hammock, groans, blankets,
horrors. The heavy pole had skinned his poor nose. He
was very anxious for me to kill somebody, but there
wasn't the shadow of a carrier near. I remembered the
old doctor—'It would be interesting for science to watch
the mental changes of individuals, on the spot.' I felt I
was becoming scientifically interesting. However, all that
is to no purpose. On the fifteenth day I came in sight of
the big river again, and hobbled into the Central Station.
It was on a back water surrounded by scrub and forest,
with a pretty border of smelly mud on one side, and on
the three others enclosed by a crazy fence of rushes. A
neglected gap was all the gate it had, and the first glance
at the place was enough to let you see the flabby devil
was running that show. White men with long staves in
their hands appeared languidly from amongst the buildings, strolling up to take a look at me, and then retired
out of sight somewhere. One of them, a stout, excitable
chap with black mustaches, informed me with great
volubility and many digressions, as soon as I told him
who I was, that my steamer was at the bottom of the
river. I was thunderstruck. What, how, why? Oh, it was
'all right.' The 'manager himself' was there. All quite
correct. 'Everybody had behaved splendidly! splendidly!'
—'you must,' he said in agitation, 'go and see the general
manager at once. He is waiting!'

"I did not see the real significance of that wreck at
once. I fancy I see it now, but I am not sure—not at
all. Certainly the affair was too stupid—when I think of
it—to be altogether natural. Still. . . . But at the moment
it presented itself simply as a confounded nuisance. The
steamer was sunk. They had started two days before in
a sudden hurry up the river with the manager on board
in charge of some volunteer skipper, and before they had
been out three hours they tore the bottom out of her

on stones, and she sank near the south bank. I asked myself what I was to do there, now my boat was lost. As
a matter of fact, I had plenty to do in fishing my command out of the river. I had to set about it the very next
day. That, and the repairs when I brought the pieces to
the station, took some months.

"My first interview with the manager was curious. He
did not ask me to sit down after my twenty-mile walk
that morning. He was commonplace in complexion, in
feature, in manners, and in voice. He was of middle size
and of ordinary build. His eyes, of the usual blue, were
perhaps remarkably cold, and he certainly could make his
glance fall on one as trenchant and heavy as an ax. But
even at these times the rest of his person seemed to dis-
claim the intention. Otherwise there was only an indefinable, faint expression of his lips, something stealthy—
a smile—not a smile—I remember it, but I can't explain.
It was unconscious, this smile was, though just after he
had said something it got intensified for an instant. It
came at the end of his speeches like a seal applied on
the words to make the meaning of the commonest phrase
appear absolutely inscrutable. He was a common trader,
from his youth up employed in these parts—nothing more.
He was obeyed, yet he inspired neither love nor fear, nor
even respect. He inspired uneasiness. That was it! Uneasiness. Not a definite mistrust—just uneasiness—nothing more. You have no idea how effective such a . . .
a . . . faculty can be. He had no genius for organizing,
for initiative, or for order even. That was evident in
such things as the deplorable state of the station. He had
no learning, and no intelligence. His position had come
to him—why? Perhaps because he was never ill. . . .
He had served three terms of three years out there. . . .
Because triumphant health in the general rout of con-
stitutions is a kind of power in itself. When he went
home on leave he rioted on a large scale—pompously.

Jack ashore—with a difference—in externals only. This
one could gather from his casual talk. He originated nothing, he could keep the routine going—that's all. But he
was great. He was great by this little thing that it was
impossible to tell what could control such a man. He
never gave that secret away. Perhaps there was nothing
within him. Such a suspicion made one pause—for out
there there were no external checks. Once when various
tropical diseases had laid low almost every 'agent' in the
station, he was heard to say, 'Men who come out here
should have no entrails.' He sealed the utterance with
that smile of his, as though it had been a door opening
into a darkness he had in his keeping. You fancied you
had seen things—but the seal was on. When annoyed at
meal-times by the constant quarrels of the white men
about precedence, he ordered an immense round table to
be made, for which a special house had to be built. This
was the station's mess-room. Where he sat was the first
place—the rest were nowhere. One felt this to be his
unalterable conviction. He was neither civil nor uncivil.
He was quiet. He allowed his 'boy'—an overfed young
negro from the coast—to treat the white men, under his
very eyes, with provoking insolence.

"He began to speak as soon as he saw me. I had been
very long on the road. He could not wait. Had to start
without me. The up-river stations had to be relieved.
There had been so many delays already that he did not
know who was dead and who was alive, and how they got
on—and so on, and so on. He paid no attention to my
explanations, and, playing with a stick of sealing-wax,
repeated several times that the situation was 'very grave,
very grave.' There were rumors that a very important
station was in jeopardy, and its chief, Mr. Kurtz, was
ill. Hoped it was not true. Mr. Kurtz was . . . I felt
weary and irritable. Hang Kurtz, I thought. I interrupted
him by saying I had heard of Mr. Kurtz on the coast.

'Ah! So they talk of him down there,' he murmured to himself. Then he began again, assuring me Mr. Kurtz was the best agent he had, an exceptional man, of the greatest importance to the Company; therefore I could understand his anxiety. He was, he said, 'very, very uneasy.' Certainly he fidgeted on his chair a good deal, exclaimed, 'Ah, Mr. Kurtz!' broke the stick of sealing-wax and seemed dumfounded by the accident. Next thing he wanted to know 'how long it would take to.' . . . I interrupted him again. Being hungry, you know, and kept on my feet too, I was getting savage. 'How can I tell?' I said. 'I haven't even seen the wreck yet—some months, no doubt.' All this talk seemed to me so futile. 'Some months,' he said. 'Well, let us say three months before we can make a start. Yes. That ought to do the affair.' I flung out of his hut (he lived all alone in a clay hut with a sort of veranda) muttering to myself my opinion of him. He was a chattering idiot. Afterwards I took it back when it was borne in upon me startlingly with what extreme nicety he had estimated the time requisite for the 'affair.'

"I went to work the next day, turning, so to speak, my back on that station. In that way only it seemed to me I could keep my hold on the redeeming facts of life. Still, one must look about sometimes; and then I saw this station, these men strolling aimlessly about in the sunshine of the yard. I asked myself sometimes what it all meant. They wandered here and there with their absurd long staves in their hands, like a lot of faithless pilgrims bewitched inside a rotten fence. The word 'ivory' rang in the air, was whispered, was sighed. You would think they were praying to it. A taint of imbecile rapacity blew through it all, like a whiff from some corpse. By Jove! I've never seen anything so unreal in my life. And outside, the silent wilderness surrounding this cleared speck on the earth struck me as something great and

invincible, like evil or truth, waiting patiently for the
passing away of this fantastic invasion.

"Oh, these months! Well, never mind. Various things
happened. One evening a grass shed full of calico, cotton
prints, beads, and I don't know what else, burst into a
blaze so suddenly that you would have thought the earth
had opened to let an avenging fire consume all that trash.
I was smoking my pipe quietly by my dismantled steamer,
and saw them all cutting capers in the light, with their
arms lifted high, when the stout man with mustaches
came tearing down to the river, a tin pail in his hand,
assured me that everybody was 'behaving splendidly,
splendidly,' dipped about a quart of water and tore back
again. I noticed there was a hole in the bottom of his
pail.

"I strolled up. There was no hurry. You see the thing
had gone off like a box of matches. It had been hopeless
from the very first. The flame had leaped high, driven
everybody back, lighted up everything—and collapsed.
The shed was already a heap of embers glowing fiercely.
A nigger was being beaten near by. They said he had
caused the fire in some way; be that as it may, he was
screeching most horribly. I saw him, later, for several
days, sitting in a bit of shade looking very sick and trying to recover himself: afterwards he arose and went
out—and the wilderness without a sound took him into
its bosom again. As I approached the glow from the dark
I found myself at the back of two men, talking. I heard
the name of Kurtz pronounced, then the words, 'take
advantage of this unfortunate accident.' One of the men
was the manager. I wished him a good evening. 'Did you
ever see anything like it—eh? it is incredible,' he said,
and walked off. The other man remained. He was a first-
class agent, young, gentlemanly, a bit reserved, with a
forked little beard and a hooked nose. He was stand-
offish with the other agents, and they on their side said

he was the manager's spy upon them. As to me, I had hardly ever spoken to him before. We got into talk, and by and by we strolled away from the hissing ruins. Then he asked me to his room, which was in the main building of the station. He struck a match, and I perceived that this young aristocrat had not only a silver-mounted dressing-case but also a whole candle all to himself. Just at that time the manager was the only man supposed to have any right to candles. Native mats covered the clay walls; a collection of spears, assegais, shields, knives was hung up in trophies. The business intrusted to this fellow was the making of bricks—so I had been informed; but there wasn't a fragment of a brick anywhere in the station, and he had been there more than a year—waiting. It seems he could not make bricks without something, I don't know what—straw, maybe. Anyway, it could not be found there, and as it was not likely to be sent from Europe, it did not appear clear to me what he was waiting for. An act of special creation perhaps. However, they were all waiting—all the sixteen or twenty pilgrims of them—for something; and upon my word it did not seem an uncongenial occupation, from the way they took it, though the only thing that ever came to them was disease —as far as I could see. They beguiled the time by back-biting and intriguing against each other in a foolish kind of way. There was an air of plotting about that station, but nothing came of it, of course. It was as unreal as everything else—as the philanthropic pretense of the whole concern, as their talk, as their government, as their show of work. The only real feeling was a desire to get appointed to a trading-post where ivory was to be had, so that they could earn percentages. They intrigued and slandered and hated each other only on that account,— but as to effectually lifting a little finger—oh, no. By heavens! there is something after all in the world allowing one man to steal a horse while another must not

look at a halter. Steal a horse straight out. Very well.
He has done it. Perhaps he can ride. But there is a way
of looking at a halter that would provoke the most
charitable of saints into a kick.

"I had no idea why he wanted to be sociable, but as
we chatted in there it suddenly occurred to me the fellow
was trying to get at something—in fact, pumping me. He
alluded constantly to Europe, to the people I was supposed to know there—putting leading questions as to my
acquaintances in the sepulchral city, and so on. His little
eyes glittered like mica discs—with curiosity—though he
tried to keep up a bit of superciliousness. At first I was
astonished, but very soon I became awfully curious to
see what he would find out from me. I couldn't possibly
imagine what I had in me to make it worth his while. It
was very pretty to see how he baffled himself, for in truth
my body was full only of chills, and my head had nothing
in it but that wretched steamboat business. It was evident
he took me for a perfectly shameless prevaricator. At last
he got angry, and, to conceal a movement of furious annoyance, he yawned. I rose. Then I noticed a small sketch
in oils, on a panel, representing a woman, draped and
blindfolded, carrying a lighted torch. The background
was somber—almost black. The movement of the woman
was stately, and the effect of the torch-light on the face
was sinister.

"It arrested me, and he stood by civilly, holding an
empty half-pint champagne bottle (medical comforts)
with the candle stuck in it. To my question he said Mr.
Kurtz had painted this—in this very station more than
a year ago—while waiting for means to go to his trading-
post. 'Tell me, pray,' said I, 'who is this Mr. Kurtz?'

"'The chief of the Inner Station,' he answered in a
short tone, looking away. 'Much obliged,' I said, laughing. 'And you are the brickmaker of the Central Station.
Every one knows that.' He was silent for a while. 'He is

a prodigy,' he said at last. 'He is an emissary of pity, and science, and progress, and devil knows what else. We want,' he began to declaim suddenly, 'for the guidance of the cause intrusted to us by Europe, so to speak, higher intelligence, wide sympathies, a singleness of purpose.' 'Who says that?' I asked. 'Lots of them,' he replied. 'Some even write that; and so *he* comes here, a special being as you ought to know.' 'Why ought I to know?' I interrupted, really surprised. He paid no attention. 'Yes. To-day he is chief of the best station, next year he will be assistant-manager, two years more and . . . but I daresay you know what he will be in two years' time. You are of the new gang—the gang of virtue. The same people who sent him specially also recommended you. Oh, don't say no. I've my own eyes to trust.' Light dawned upon me. My dear aunt's influential acquaintances were producing an unexpected effect upon that young man. I nearly burst into a laugh. 'Do you read the Company's confidential correspondence?' I asked. He hadn't a word to say. It was great fun. 'When Mr. Kurtz,' I continued, severely, 'is General Manager, you won't have the opportunity.'

"He blew the candle out suddenly, and we went outside. The moon had risen. Black figures strolled about listlessly, pouring water on the glow, whence proceeded a sound of hissing; steam ascended in the moonlight, the beaten nigger groaned somewhere. 'What a row the brute makes!' said the indefatigable man with the mustaches, appearing near us. 'Serves him right. Transgression—punishment—bang! Pitiless, pitiless. That's the only way. This will prevent all conflagrations for the future. I was just telling the manager. . . ' He noticed my companion, and became crestfallen all at once. 'Not in bed yet,' he said, with a kind of servile heartiness; 'it's so natural. Ha! Danger—agitation.' He vanished. I went on to the river-side, and the other followed me. I heard a scathing

murmur at my ear, 'Heap of muffs—go to.' The pilgrims
could be seen in knots gesticulating, discussing. Several
had still their staves in their hands. I verily believe they
took these sticks to bed with them. Beyond the fence the
forest stood up spectrally in the moonlight, and through
the dim stir, through the faint sounds of that lamentable
courtyard, the silence of the land went home to one's
very heart—its mystery, its greatness, the amazing reality
of its concealed life. The hurt nigger moaned feebly somewhere near by, and then fetched a deep sigh that made
me mend my pace away from there. I felt a hand introducing itself under my arm. 'My dear sir,' said the
fellow, 'I don't want to be misunderstood, and especially
by you, who will see Mr. Kurtz long before I can have
that pleasure. I wouldn't like him to get a false idea of
my disposition. . . .'

"I let him run on, this papier-mâché Mephistopheles,
and it seemed to me that if I tried I could poke my forefinger through him, and would find nothing inside but a
little loose dirt, maybe. He, don't you see, had been plan-
ning to be assistant-manager by and by under the present
man, and I could see that the coming of that Kurtz had
upset them both not a little. He talked precipitately, and
I did not try to stop him. I had my shoulders against the
wreck of my steamer, hauled up on the slope like a carcass
of some big river animal. The smell of mud, of primeval
mud, by Jove! was in my nostrils, the high stillness of
primeval forest was before my eyes; there were shiny
patches on the black creek. The moon had spread over
everything a thin layer of silver—over the rank grass,
over the mud, upon the wall of matted vegetation standing higher than the wall of a temple, over the great river
I could see through a somber gap glittering, glittering, as
it flowed broadly by without a murmur. All this was great,
expectant, mute, while the man jabbered about himself.
I wondered whether the stillness on the face of the im-

mensity looking at us two were meant as an appeal or as
a menace. What were we who had strayed in here? Could
we handle that dumb thing, or would it handle us? I felt
how big, how confoundedly big, was that thing that
couldn't talk, and perhaps was deaf as well. What was
in there? I could see a little ivory coming out from there,
and I had heard Mr. Kurtz was in there. I had heard
enough about it, too—God knows! Yet somehow it didn't
bring any image with it—no more than if I had been told
an angel or a fiend was in there. I believed it in the same
way one of you might believe there are inhabitants in
the planet Mars. I knew once a Scotch sailmaker who
was certain, dead sure, there were people in Mars. If
you asked him for some idea how they looked and behaved, he would get shy and mutter something about
'walking on all-fours.' If you as much as smiled, he would
—though a man of sixty—offer to fight you. I would not
have gone so far as to fight for Kurtz, but I went for
him near enough to a lie. You know I hate, detest, and
can't bear a lie, not because I am straighter than the rest
of us, but simply because it appalls me. There is a taint
of death, a flavor of mortality in lies—which is exactly
what I hate and detest in the world—what I want to for
get. It makes me miserable and sick, like biting something
rotten would do. Temperament, I suppose. Well, I went
near enough to it by letting the young fool there believe
anything he liked to imagine as to my influence in Europe.
I became in an instant as much of a pretense as the rest
of the bewitched pilgrims. This simply because I had a
notion it somehow would be of help to that Kurtz whom
at the time I did not see—you understand. He was just
a word for me. I did not see the man in the name any
more than you do. Do you see him? Do you see the story?
Do you see anything? It seems to me I am trying to
tell you a dream—making a vain attempt, because no
relation of a dream can convey the dream-sensation, that

commingling of absurdity, surprise, and bewilderment in a tremor of struggling revolt, that notion of being captured by the incredible which is of the very essence of dreams. . . ."

He was silent for a while.

". . . No, it is impossible; it is impossible to convey the life-sensation of any given epoch of one's existence—that which makes its truth, its meaning—its subtle and penetrating essence. It is impossible. We live, as we dream —alone. . . ."

He paused again as if reflecting, then added—

"Of course in this you fellows see more than I could then. You see me, whom you know. . . ."

It had become so pitch dark that we listeners could hardly see one another. For a long time already he, sitting apart, had been no more to us than a voice. There was not a word from anybody. The others might have been asleep, but I was awake. I listened, I listened on the watch for the sentence, for the word, that would give me the clew to the faint uneasiness inspired by this narrative that seemed to shape itself without human lips in the heavy night-air of the river.

". . . Yes—I let him run on," Marlow began again, "and think what he pleased about the powers that were behind me. I did! And there was nothing behind me! There was nothing but that wretched, old, mangled steamboat I was leaning against, while he talked fluently about 'the necessity for every man to get on.' 'And when one comes out here, you conceive, it is not to gaze at the moon.' Mr. Kurtz was a 'universal genius,' but even a genius would find it easier to work with 'adequate tools—intelligent men.' He did not make bricks—why, there was a physical impossibility in the way—as I was well aware; and if he did secretarial work for the manager, it was because 'no sensible man rejects wantonly the confidence of his superiors.' Did I see it? I saw it. What more did

I want? What I really wanted was rivets, by heaven! Rivets. To get on with the work—to stop the hole. Rivets I wanted. There were cases of them down at the coast— cases—piled up—burst—split! You kicked a loose rivet at every second step in that station yard on the hillside. Rivets had rolled into the grove of death. You could fill your pockets with rivets for the trouble of stooping down —and there wasn't one rivet to be found where it was wanted. We had plates that would do, but nothing to fasten them with. And every week the messenger, a lone negro, letter-bag on shoulder and staff in hand, left our station for the coast. And several times a week a coast caravan came in with trade goods—ghastly glazed calico that made you shudder only to look at it; glass beads, valued about a penny a quart, confounded spotted cotton handkerchiefs. And no rivets. Three carriers could have brought all that was wanted to set that steamboat afloat.

"He was becoming confidential now, but I fancy my unresponsive attitude must have exasperated him at last, for he judged it necessary to inform me he feared neither God nor devil, let alone any mere man. I said I could see that very well, but what I wanted was a certain quantity of rivets—and rivets were what really Mr. Kurtz wanted, if he had only known it. Now letters went to the coast every week. . . . 'My dear sir,' he cried, 'I write from dictation.' I demanded rivets. There was a way—for an intelligent man. He changed his manner; became very cold, and suddenly began to talk about a hippopotamus; wondered whether sleeping on board the steamer (I stuck to my salvage night and day) I wasn't disturbed. There was an old hippo that had the bad habit of getting out on the bank and roaming at night over the station grounds. The pilgrims used to turn out in a body and empty every rifle they could lay hands on at him. Some even had sat up o' nights for him. All this energy was wasted, though. 'That animal has a charmed life,' he said; 'but you can say this only of brutes in this country. No man—you apprehend me?—no man here bears a charmed life.' He stood there for a moment in the moonlight with his delicate hooked nose set a little askew, and his mica eyes glittering without a wink, then, with a curt good night, he strode off. I could see he was disturbed and considerably puzzled, which made me feel more hopeful than I had been for days. It was a great comfort to turn from that chap to my influential friend, the battered, twisted, ruined, tin-pot steamboat. I clambered on board. She rang under my feet like an empty Huntley & Palmer biscuit-tin kicked along a gutter; she was nothing so solid in make, and rather less pretty in shape, but I had expended enough hard work on her to make me love her. No influential friend would have served me better. She had given me a chance to come out a bit—to find out what I could do. No, I don't like work. I had rather laze about and think of all the fine things that can be done. I don't like work—no man does—but I like what is in the work,—the chance to find yourself. Your own reality—for yourself, not for others—what no other man can ever know. They can only see the mere show, and never can tell what it really means.

"I was not surprised to see somebody sitting aft, on the deck, with his legs dangling over the mud. You see I rather chummed with the few mechanics there were in that station, whom the other pilgrims naturally despised—on account of their imperfect manners, I suppose. This was the foreman—a boiler-maker by trade—a good worker. He was a lank, bony, yellow-faced man, with big intense eyes. His aspect was worried, and his head was as bald as the palm of my hand; but his hair in falling seemed to have stuck to his chin, and had prospered in the new locality, for his beard hung down to his waist. He was a widower with six young children (he had left them in charge of a sister of his to come out there), and the passion of his life was pigeon-flying. He was an enthusiast and a connoisseur. He would rave about pigeons. After work hours he used sometimes to come over from his hut for a talk about his children and his pigeons; at work, when he had to crawl in the mud under the bottom of the steamboat, he would tie up that beard of his in a kind of white serviette he brought for the purpose. It had loops to go over his ears. In the evening he could be seen squatted on the bank rinsing that wrapper in the creek with great care, then spreading it solemnly on a bush to dry.

"I slapped him on the back and shouted, 'We shall have rivets!' He scrambled to his feet exclaiming, 'No! Rivets!' as though he couldn't believe his ears. Then in a low voice, 'You . . . eh?' I don't know why we behaved like lunatics. I put my finger to the side of my nose and nodded mysteriously. 'Good for you!' he cried, snapped his fingers above his head, lifting one foot. I tried a jig. We capered on the iron deck. A frightful clatter came out of that hulk, and the virgin forest on the other bank of the creek sent it back in a thundering roll upon the sleeping station. It must have made some of the pilgrims sit up in their hovels. A dark figure obscured the lighted doorway of the manager's hut, vanished, then, a second or so after, the doorway itself vanished, too. We stopped, and the silence driven away by the stamping of our feet flowed back again from the recesses of the land. The great wail of vegetation, an exuberant and entangled mass of trunks, branches, leaves, boughs, festoons, motionless in the moonlight, was like a rioting invasion of soundless life, a rolling wave of plants, piled up, crested, ready to topple over the creek, to sweep every little man of us out of his little existence. And it moved not. A deadened burst of mighty splashes and snorts reached us from afar, as though an ichthyosaurus had been taking a bath of glitter in the great river. 'After all,' said the boiler-maker in a reasonable tone. 'why shouldn't we get the rivets?' Why not, indeed!

1 did not know of any reason why we shouldn't. 'They'll come in three weeks,' I said, confidently.

"But they didn't. Instead of rivets there came an invasion, an infliction, a visitation. It came in sections during the next three weeks, each section headed by a donkey carrying a white man in new clothes and tan shoes, bowing from that elevation right and left to the impressed pilgrims. A quarrelsome band of footsore sulky niggers trod on the heels of the donkeys; a lot of tents, campstools, tin boxes, white cases, brown bales would be shot down in the courtyard, and the air of mystery would deepen a little over the muddle of the station. Five such installments came, with their absurd air of disorderly flight with the loot of innumerable outfit shops and provision stores, that, one would think, they were lugging, after a raid, into the wilderness for equitable division. It was an inextricable mess of things decent in themselves but that human folly made look like the spoils of thieving.

"This devoted band called itself the Eldorado Exploring Expedition, and I believe they were sworn to secrecy. Their talk, however, was the talk of sordid buccaneers: it was reckless without hardihood, greedy without audacity, and cruel without courage; there was not an atom of foresight or of serious intention in the whole batch of them, and they did not seem aware these things are wanted for the work of the world. To tear treasure out of the bowels of the land was their desire, with no more moral purpose at the back of it than there is in burglars breaking into a safe. Who paid the expenses of the noble enterprise I don't know; but the uncle of our manager was leader of that lot.

"In exterior he resembled a butcher in a poor neighborhood, and his eyes had a look of sleepy cunning. He carried his fat paunch with ostentation on his short legs, and during the time his gang infested the station spoke to no one but his nephew. You could see these two roaming about all day long with their heads close together in an everlasting confab.

"I had given up worrying myself about the rivets. One's capacity for that kind of folly is more limited than you would suppose. I said Hang!—and let things slide. I had plenty of time for meditation, and now and then I would give some thought to Kurtz. I wasn't very interested in him. No. Still, I was curious to see whether this man, who had come out equipped with moral ideas of some sort, would climb to the top after all and how he would set about his work when there."

**II**

"One evening as I was lying flat on the deck of my steamboat, I heard voices approaching—and there were the nephew and the uncle strolling along the bank. I laid my head on my arm again, and had nearly lost myself in a doze, when somebody said in my ear, as it were: 'I am as harmless as a little child, but I don't like to be dictated to. Am I the manager—or am I not? I was ordered to send him there. It's incredible.' . . . I became aware that the two were standing on the shore alongside the forepart of the steamboat, just below my head. I did not move; it did not occur to me to move: I was sleepy. 'It *is* unpleasant,' grunted the uncle. 'He has asked the Administration to be sent there,' said the other, 'with the idea of showing what he could do; and I was instructed accordingly. Look at the influence that man must have. Is it not frightful?' They both agreed it was frightful, then made several bizarre remarks: 'Make rain and fine weather—one man—the Council—by the nose'—bits of absurd sentences that got the better of my drowsiness, so that I had pretty near the whole of my wits about me when the uncle said, 'The climate may do away with this difficulty for you. Is he alone there?' 'Yes,' answered the manager; 'he sent his assistant down the river with a note to me in these terms: "Clear this poor devil out of the country, and don't bother sending more of that sort. I had rather be alone than have the kind of men you can dispose of with me." It was more than a year ago. Can you imagine such impudence!' 'Anything since then?' asked the other, hoarsely. 'Ivory,' jerked the nephew; 'lots of it— prime sort—lots—most annoying, from him.' 'And with that?' questioned the heavy rumble. 'Invoice,' was the reply fired out, so to speak. Then silence. They had been talking about Kurtz.

"I was broad awake by this time, but, lying perfectly at ease, remained still, having no inducement to change my position. 'How did that ivory come all this way?' growled the elder man, who seemed very vexed. The other ex-plained that it had come with a fleet of canoes in charge of an English half-caste clerk Kurtz had with him; that Kurtz had apparently intended to return himself, the sta-tion being by that time bare of goods and stores, but after coming three hundred miles, had suddenly decided to go back, which he started to do alone in a small dugout with four paddlers, leaving the half-caste to continue down the river with the ivory. The two fellows there seemed astounded at anybody attempting such a thing. They were at a loss for an adequate motive. As to me, I seemed to see Kurtz for the first time. It was a distinct glimpse: the dugout, four paddling savages, and the lone white man turning his back suddenly on the headquarters, on relief, on thoughts of home—perhaps; setting his face towards the depths of the wilderness, towards his empty and deso-late station. I did not know the motive. Perhaps he was just simply a fine fellow who stuck to his work for its own sake. His name, you understand, had not been pronounced once. He was 'that man.' The half-caste, who, as far as I could see, had conducted a difficult trip with great pru-dence and pluck, was invariably alluded to as 'that scoundrel.' The 'scoundrel' had reported that the 'man' had been very ill—had recovered imperfectly. . . . The two below me moved away then a few paces, and strolled back and forth at some little distance. I heard: 'Military post—doctor—two hundred miles—quite alone now—unavoidable delays—nine months—no news—strange rumors.' They approached again, just as the manager was saying, 'No one, as far as I know, unless a species of wandering trader—a pestilential fellow, snapping ivory from the natives.' Who was it they were talking about now? I gathered in snatches that this was some man supposed to be in Kurtz's district, and of whom the manager did not approve. 'We will not be free from unfair competition till one of these fellows is hanged for an example,' he said. 'Certainly,' grunted the other; 'get him hanged! Why not? Anything—anything can be done in this country. That's what I say; nobody here, you understand, *here,* can endanger your position. And why? You stand the climate—you outlast them all. The danger is in Europe; but there before I left I took care to—' They moved off and whispered, then their voices rose again. 'The extraordinary series of delays is not my fault. I did my best.' The fat man sighed. 'Very sad.' 'And the pestiferous absurdity of his talk,' continued the other; 'he bothered me enough when he was here "Each station should be like a beacon on the road towards better things, a center for trade, of course, but also for humanizing, improving, instructing." Conceive you—that ass! And he wants to be manager! No, it's—' Here he got choked by excessive indignation, and I lifted my head the least bit. I was surprised to see how near they were--right under me. I could have spat upon their hats. They were looking on the ground, absorbed in thought. The manager was switching his leg with a slender twig: his sagacious relative lifted his head. 'You have been well since you came out this time?' he asked. The other gave a start. 'Who? I? Oh! Like a charm—like a charm. But

the rest—oh, my goodness! All sick. They die so quick,
too, that I haven't the time to send them out of the country
—it's incredible!' 'H'm. Just so,' grunted the uncle. 'Ah!
my boy, trust to this—I say, trust to this.' I saw him ex-
tend his short flipper of an arm for a gesture that took in
the forest, the creek, the mud, the river,—seemed to beckon
with a dishonoring flourish before the sunlit face of the
land a treacherous appeal to the lurking death, to the hidden evil, to the profound darkness of its heart. It was so
startling that I leaped to my feet and looked back at the
edge of the forest, as though I had expected an answer
of some sort to that black display of confidence. You know
the foolish notions that come to one sometimes. The high
stillness confronted these two figures with its ominous
patience, waiting for the passing away of a fantastic
invasion.

"They swore aloud together—out of sheer fright, I believe—then pretending not to know anything of my existence, turned back to the station. The sun was low; and
leaning forward side by side, they seemed to be tugging
painfully uphill their two ridiculous shadows of unequal
length, that trailed behind them slowly over the tall grass
without bending a single blade.

"In a few days the Eldorado Expedition went into the
patient wilderness, that closed upon it as the sea closes
over a diver. Long afterwards the news came that all the
donkeys were dead. I know nothing as to the fate of the
less valuable animals. They, no doubt, like the rest of us,
found what they deserved. I did not inquire. I was then
rather excited at the prospect of meeting Kurtz very soon.
When I say very soon I mean it comparatively. It was just
two months from the day we left the creek when we came
to the bank below Kurtz's station.

"Going up that river was like traveling back to the
earliest beginnings of the world, when vegetation rioted
on the earth and the big trees were kings. An empty

stream, a great silence, an impenetrable forest. The air was warm, thick, heavy, sluggish. There was no joy in the brilliance of sunshine. The long stretches of the waterway ran on, deserted, into the gloom of overshadowed distances. On silvery sandbanks hippos and alligators sunned themselves side by side. The broadening waters flowed through a mob of wooded islands; you lost your way on that river as you would in a desert, and butted all day long against shoals, trying to find the channel, till you thought yourself bewitched and cut off forever from everything you had known once—somewhere—far away—in another existence perhaps. There were moments when one's past came back to one, as it will sometimes when you have not a moment to spare to yourself; but it came in the shape of an unrestful and noisy dream, remembered with wonder amongst the overwhelming realities of this strange world of plants, and water, and silence. And this stillness of life did not in the least resemble a peace. It was the stillness of an implacable force brooding over an inscrutable intention. It looked at you with a vengeful aspect. I got used to it afterwards; I did not see it any more; I had no time. I had to keep guessing at the channel; I had to discern, mostly by inspiration, the signs of hidden banks; I watched for sunken stones; I was learning to clap my teeth smartly before my heart flew out, when I shaved by a fluke some infernal sly old snag that would have ripped the life out of the tin-pot steamboat and drowned all the pilgrims; I had to keep a look-out for the signs of dead wood we could cut up in the night for next day's steaming. When you have to attend to things of that sort, to the mere incidents of the surface, the reality—the reality, I tell you—fades. The inner truth is hidden—luckily, luckily. But I felt it all the same; I felt often its mysterious stillness watching me at my monkey tricks, just as it watches you fellows performing on your respective tight-ropes for —what is it? half-a-crown a tumble—"

"Try to be civil, Marlow," growled a voice, and I knew there was at least one listener awake besides myself.

"I beg your pardon. I forgot the heartache which makes up the rest of the price. And indeed what does the price matter, if the trick be well done? You do your tricks very well. And I didn't do badly either, since I managed not to sink that steamboat on my first trip. It's a wonder to me yet. Imagine a blindfolded man set to drive a van over a bad road. I sweated and shivered over that business considerably, I can tell you. After all, for a seaman, to scrape the bottom of the thing that's supposed to float all the time under his care is the unpardonable sin. No one may know of it, but you never forget the thump—eh? A blow on the very heart. You remember it, you dream of it, you wake up at night and think of it—years after—and go hot and cold all over. I don't pretend to say that steamboat floated all the time. More than once she had to wade for a bit, with twenty cannibals splashing around and pushing. We had enlisted some of these chaps on the way for a crew. Fine fellows—cannibals—in their place. They were men one could work with, and I am grateful to them. And, after all, they did not eat each other before my face: they had brought along a provision of hippo-meat which went rotten, and made the mystery of the wilderness stink in my nostrils. Phoo! I can sniff it now. I had the manager on board and three or four pilgrims with their staves —all complete. Sometimes we came upon a station close by the bank, clinging to the skirts of the unknown, and the white men rushing out of a tumble-down hovel, with great gestures of joy and surprise and welcome, seemed very strange—had the appearance of being held there captive by a spell. The word ivory would ring in the air for a while—and on we went again into the silence, along empty reaches, round the still bends, between the high walls of our winding way, reverberating in hollow claps the ponderous beat of the stern-wheel. Trees, trees, millions of trees, massive, immense, running up high; and at their foot, hugging the bank against the stream, crept the little begrimed steamboat, like a sluggish beetle crawling on the floor of a lofty portico. It made you feel very small, very lost, and yet it was not altogether depressing, that feeling. After all, if you were small, the grimy beetle crawled on —which was just what you wanted it to do. Where the pilgrims imagined it crawled to I don't know. To some place where they expected to get something, I bet! For me it crawled towards Kurtz—exclusively; but when the steam-pipes started leaking we crawled very slow. The reaches opened before us and closed behind, as if the forest had stepped leisurely across the water to bar the way for our return. We penetrated deeper and deeper into the heart of darkness. It was very quiet there. At night sometimes the roll of drums behind the curtain of trees would run up the river and remain sustained faintly, as if hovering in the air high over our heads, till the first break of day. Whether it meant war, peace, or prayer we could not tell. The dawns were heralded by the descent of a chill stillness; the wood-cutters slept, their fires burned low; the snapping of a twig would make you start. We were wanderers on a prehistoric earth, on an earth that wore the aspect of an unknown planet. We could have fancied ourselves the first of men taking possession of an accursed inheritance, to be subdued at the cost of profound anguish and of excessive toil. But suddenly, as we struggled round a bend, there would be a glimpse of rush walls, of peaked grass-roofs, a burst of yells, a whirl of black limbs, a mass of hands clapping, of feet stamping, of bodies swaying, of eyes rolling, under the droop of heavy and motionless foliage. The steamer toiled along slowly on the edge of a black and incomprehensible frenzy. The prehistoric man was cursing us, praying to us, welcoming us —who could tell? We were cut off from the comprehension of our surroundings; we glided past like phantoms, wondering and secretly appalled, as sane men would be before an enthusiastic outbreak in a madhouse. We could not understand because we were too far and could not remember, because we were traveling in the night of first ages, of those ages that are gone, leaving hardly a sign— and no memories.

"The earth seemed unearthly. We are accustomed to look upon the shackled form of a conquered monster, but there—there you could look at a thing monstrous and free. It was unearthly, and the men were— No, they were not inhuman. Well, you know, that was the worst of it—this suspicion of their not being inhuman. It would come slowly to one. They howled and leaped, and spun, and made horrid faces; but what thrilled you was just the thought of their humanity—like yours—the thought of your remote kinship with this wild and passionate uproar. Ugly. Yes, it was ugly enough; but if you were man enough you would admit to yourself that there was in you just the faintest trace of a response to the terrible frankness of that noise. a dim suspicion of there being a meaning in it which you—you so remote from the night of first ages—could comprehend. And why not? The mind of man is capable of anything—because everything is in it, all the past as well as all the future. What was there after all? Joy, fear, sorrow, devotion, valor, rage—who can tell? —but truth—truth stripped of its cloak of time. Let the fool gape and shudder—the man knows, and can look on without a wink. But he must at least be as much of a man as these on the shore. He must meet that truth with his own true stuff—with his own inborn strength. Principles won't do. Acquisitions, clothes, pretty rags—rags that would fly off at the first good shake. No; you want a deliberate belief. An appeal to me in this fiendish row—is there? Very well; I hear; I admit, but I have a voice, too, and for good or evil mine is the speech that cannot be silenced. Of course, a fool, what with sheer fright and fine sentiments, is always safe. Who's that grunting? You wonder I didn't go ashore for a howl and a dance? Well, no —I didn't. Fine sentiments, you say? Fine sentiments, be hanged! I had no time. I had to mess about with white-lead and strips of woolen blanket helping to put bandages on those leaky steam-pipes—I tell you. I had to watch the steering, and circumvent those snags, and get the tin-pot along by hook or by crook. There was surface-truth enough in these things to save a wiser man. And between whiles I had to look after the savage who was fireman. He was an improved specimen; he could fire up a vertical boiler. He was there below me, and, upon my word, to look at him was as edifying as seeing a dog in a parody of breeches and a feather hat, walking on his hind-legs. A few months of training had done for that really fine chap. He squinted at the steam-gauge and at the water-gauge with an evident effort of intrepidity—and he had filed teeth, too, the poor devil, and the wool of his pate shaved into queer patterns, and three ornamental scars on each of his cheeks. He ought to have been clapping his hands and stamping his feet on the bank, instead of which he was hard at work, a thrall to strange witchcraft, full of improving knowledge. He was useful because he had been instructed; and what he knew was this—that should the water in that transparent thing disappear, the evil spirit inside the boiler would get angry through the greatness of his thirst, and take a terrible vengeance. So he sweated and fired up and watched the glass fearfully (with an impromptu charm, made of rags, tied to his arm, and a piece of polished bone, as big as a watch, stuck flatways through his lower lip), while the wooden banks slipped past us slowly, the short noise was left behind, the interminable miles of silence—and we crept on, towards Kurtz. But the snags were thick, the water was treacherous and shallow, the boiler seemed indeed to have a sulky devil in

it, and thus neither that fireman nor I had any time to peer
into our creepy thoughts.

"Some fifty miles below the Inner Station we came upon
a hut of reeds, an inclined and melancholy pole, with the
unrecognizable tatters of what had been a flag of some
sort flying from it, and a neatly stacked woodpile. This
was unexpected. We came to the bank, and on the stack
of firewood found a flat piece of board with some faded
pencil-writing on it. When deciphered it said: 'Wood for
you. Hurry up. Approach cautiously.' There was a signa-
ture, but it was illegible—not Kurtz—a much longer word.
'Hurry up.' Where? Up the river? 'Approach cautiously.'
We had not done so. But the warning could not have been
meant for the place where it could be only found after
approach. Something was wrong above. But what—and
how much? That was the question. We commented ad-
versely upon the imbecility of that telegraphic style. The
bush around said nothing, and would not let us look very
far, either. A torn curtain of red twill hung in the doorway of the hut, and flapped sadly in our faces. The dwelling was dismantled; but we could see a white man had
lived there not very long ago. There remained a rude table
—a plank on two posts; a heap of rubbish reposed in a
dark corner, and by the door I picked up a book. It had
lost its covers, and the pages had been thumbed into a
state of extremely dirty softness; but the back had been
lovingly stitched afresh with white cotton thread, which
looked clean yet. It was an extraordinary find. Its title was,
*An Inquiry into some Points of Seamanship,* by a man
Towser, Towson—some such name—Master in his Majesty's Navy. The matter looked dreary reading enough,
with illustrative diagrams and repulsive tables of figures,
and the copy was sixty years old. I handled this amazing
antiquity with the greatest possible tenderness, lest it
should dissolve in my hands. Within, Towson or Towser
was inquiring earnestly into the breaking strain of ships'

chains and tackle, and other such matters. Not a very enthralling book; but at the first glance you could see there a singleness of intention, an honest concern for the right way of going to work, which made these humble pages, thought out so many years ago, luminous with another than a professional light. The simple old sailor, with his talk of chains and purchases, made me forget the jungle and the pilgrims in a delicious sensation of having come upon something unmistakably real. Such a book being there was wonderful enough; but still more astounding were the notes penciled in the margin, and plainly referring to the text. I couldn't believe my eyes! They were in cipher! Yes, it looked like cipher. Fancy a man lugging with him a book of that description into this nowhere and studying it—and making notes—in cipher at that! It was an extravagant mystery.

"I had been dimly aware for some time of a worrying noise, and when I lifted my eyes I saw the wood pile was gone, and the manager, aided by all the pilgrims, was shouting at me from the river-side. I slipped the book into my pocket. I assure you to leave off reading was like tearing myself away from the shelter of an old and solid friendship.

"I started the lame engine ahead. 'It must be this miserable trader—this intruder,' exclaimed the manager, looking back malevolently at the place we had left. 'He must be English,' I said. 'It will not save him from getting into trouble if he is not careful,' muttered the manager darkly. I observed with assumed innocence that no man was safe from trouble in this world.

"The current was more rapid now, the steamer seemed at her last gasp, the stern-wheel flopped languidly, and I caught myself listening on tiptoe for the next beat of the boat, for in sober truth I expected the wretched thing to give up every moment. It was like watching the last flickers of a life. But still we crawled. Sometimes I would pick out a tree a little way ahead to measure our progress towards Kurtz by, but I lost it invariably before we got abreast. To keep the eyes so long on one thing was too much for human patience. The manager displayed a beautiful resignation. I fretted and fumed and took to arguing with myself whether or no I would talk openly with Kurtz; but before I could come to any conclusion it occurred to me that my speech or my silence, indeed any action of mine, would be a mere futility. What did it matter what any one knew or ignored? What did it matter who was manager? One gets sometimes such a flash of insight. The essentials of this affair lay deep under the surface, beyond my reach, and beyond my power of meddling.

"Towards the evening of the second day we judged ourselves about eight miles from Kurtz's station. I wanted to push on; but the manager looked grave, and told me the navigation up there was so dangerous that it would be advisable, the sun being very low already, to wait where we were till next morning. Moreover, he pointed out that if the warning to approach cautiously were to be followed, we must approach in daylight—not at dusk, or in the dark. This was sensible enough. Eight miles meant nearly three hours' steaming for us, and I could also see suspicious ripples at the upper end of the reach. Nevertheless, I was annoyed beyond expression at the delay, and most unreasonably, too, since one night more could not matter much after so many months. As we had plenty of wood, and caution was the word, I brought up in the middle of the stream. The reach was narrow, straight, with high sides like a railway cutting. The dusk came gliding into it long before the sun had set. The current ran smooth and swift, but a dumb immobility sat on the banks. The living trees, lashed together by the creepers and every living bush of the undergrowth, might have been changed into stone, even to the slenderest twig, to the lightest leaf. It was not sleep—it seemed unnatural, like a state of trance. Not the faintest sound of any kind could be heard. You looked on amazed, and began to suspect yourself of being deaf—then the night came suddenly, and struck you blind as well. About three in the morning some large fish leaped, and the loud splash made me jump as though a gun had been fired. When the sun rose there was a white fog, very warm and clammy, and more blinding than the night. It did not shift or drive; it was just there, standing all round you like something solid. At eight or nine, perhaps, it lifted as a shutter lifts. We had a glimpse of the towering multitude of trees, of the immense matted jungle, with the blazing little ball of the sun hanging over it—all perfectly still—and then the white shutter came down again, smoothly, as if sliding in greased grooves. I ordered the chain, which we had begun to heave in, to be paid out again. Before it stopped running with a muffled rattle, a cry, a very loud cry, as of infinite desolation, soared slowly in the opaque air. It ceased. A complaining clamor, modulated in savage discords, filled our ears. The sheer unexpectedness of it made my hair stir under my cap. I don't know how it struck the others: to me it seemed as though the mist itself had screamed, so suddenly, and apparently from all sides at once, did this tumultuous and mournful uproar arise. It culminated in a hurried outbreak of almost intolerably excessive shrieking, which stopped short, leaving us stiffened in a variety of silly attitudes, and obstinately listening to the nearly as appalling and excessive silence. 'Good God! What is the meaning—' stammered at my elbow one of the pilgrims, —a little fat man, with sandy hair and red whiskers, who wore side-spring boots, and pink pajamas tucked into his socks. Two others remained open-mouthed a whole minute, then dashed into the little cabin, to rush out incontinently and stand darting scared glances, with Winchesters at 'ready' in their hands. What we could see was just the steamer we were on, her outlines blurred as though she

had been on the point of dissolving, and a misty strip of
water, perhaps two feet broad, around her—and that was
all. The rest of the world was nowhere, as far as our eyes
and ears were concerned. Just nowhere. Gone, disappeared; swept off without leaving a whisper or a shadow
behind.

"I went forward, and ordered the chain to be hauled in
short, so as to be ready to trip the anchor and move the
steamboat at once if necessary. 'Will they attack?' whispered an awed voice. 'We will be all butchered in this
fog,' murmured another. The faces twitched with the
strain, the hands trembled slightly, the eyes forgot to wink.
It was very curious to see the contrast of expressions of
the white men and of the black fellows of our crew, who
were as much strangers to that part of the river as we,
though their homes were only eight hundred miles away.
The whites, of course, greatly discomposed, had besides a
curious look of being painfully shocked by such an outrageous row. The others had an alert, naturally interested
expression; but their faces were essentially quiet, even
those of the one or two who grinned as they hauled at the
chain. Several exchanged short, grunting phrases, which
seemed to settle the matter to their satisfaction. Their
headman, a young, broad-chested black, severely draped
in dark-blue fringed cloths, with fierce nostrils and his
hair all done up artfully in oily ringlets, stood near me.
'Aha!' I said, just for good fellowship's sake. 'Catch 'em,'
he snapped, with a bloodshot widening of his eyes and a
flash of sharp teeth—'catch 'im. Give 'im to us.' 'To you,
eh?' I asked; 'what would you do with them?' 'Eat 'im!'
he said, curtly, and, leaning his elbow on the rail, looked
out into the fog in a dignified and profoundly pensive attitude. I would no doubt have been properly horrified, had
it not occurred to me that he and his chaps must be very
hungry: that they must have been growing increasingly
hungry for at least this month past. They had been en-

gaged for six months (I don't think a single one of them
had any clear idea of time, as we at the end of countless
ages have. They still belonged to the beginnings of time—
had no inherited experience to teach them as it were)
and of course, as long as there was a piece of paper
written over in accordance with some farcical law or other
made down the river, it didn't enter anybody's head to
trouble how they would live. Certainly they had brought
with them some rotten hippo-meat, which couldn't have
lasted very long, anyway, even if the pilgrims hadn't, in
the midst of a shocking hullabaloo, thrown a considerable
quantity of it overboard. It looked like a high-handed proceeding; but it was really a case of legitimate self-defense.
You can't breathe dead hippo waking, sleeping, and eating, and at the same time keep your precarious grip on
existence. Besides that, they had given them every week
three pieces of brass wire, each about nine inches long;
and the theory was they were to buy their provisions with
that currency in river-side villages You can see how *that*
worked. There were either no villages, or the people were
hostile, or the director, who like the rest of us fed out of
tins, with an occasional old he-goat thrown in, didn't want
to stop the steamer for some more or less recondite reason.
So, unless they swallowed the wire itself, or made loops
of it to snare the fishes with, I don't see what good their
extravagant salary could be to them. I must say it was
paid with a regularity worthy of a large and honorable
trading company. For the rest, the only thing to eat—
though it didn't look eatable in the least—I saw in their
possession was a few lumps of some stuff like half-cooked
dough, of a dirty lavender color, they kept wrapped in
leaves, and now and then swallowed a piece of, but so
small that it seemed done more for the looks of the thing
than for any serious purpose of sustenance. Why in the
name of all the gnawing devils of hunger they didn't go
for us—they were thirty to five—and have a good tuck-in

for once, amazes me now when I think of it. They were
big powerful men, with not much capacity to weigh the
consequences, with courage, with strength, even yet,
though their skins were no longer glossy and their muscles
no longer hard. And I saw that something restraining, one
of those human secrets that baffle probability, had come
into play there. I looked at them with a swift quickening
of interest—not because it occurred to me I might be
eaten by them before very long, though I own to you that
just then I perceived—in a new light, as it were—how
unwholesome the pilgrims looked, and I hoped, yes, I positively hoped, that my aspect was not so—what shall I say?
—so—unappetizing: a touch of fantastic vanity which
fitted well with the dream-sensation that pervaded all my
days at that time. Perhaps I had a little fever, too. One
can't live with one's finger everlastingly on one's pulse.
I had often 'a little fever,' or a little touch of other things
—the playful paw-strokes of the wilderness, the preliminary trifling before the more serious onslaught which came
in due course. Yes; I looked at them as you would on any
human being, with a curiosity of their impulses, motives,
capacities, weaknesses, when brought to the test of an inexorable physical necessity. Restraint! What possible restraint? Was it superstition, disgust, patience, fear—or
some kind of primitive honor? No fear can stand up to
hunger, no patience can wear it out, disgust simply does
not exist where hunger is; and as to superstition, beliefs,
and what you may call principles, they are less than chaff
in a breeze. Don't you know the devilry of lingering starvation, its exasperating torment, its black thoughts, its
somber and brooding ferocity? Well, I do. It takes a man
all his inborn strength to fight hunger properly. It's really
easier to face bereavement, dishonor, and the perdition
of one's soul—than this kind of prolonged hunger. Sad,
but true. And these chaps, too, had no earthly reason for
any kind of scruple. Restraint! I would just as soon have

expected restraint from a hyena prowling amongst the corpses of a battlefield. But there was the fact facing me —the fact dazzling, to be seen, like the foam on the depths of the sea, like a ripple on an unfathomable enigma, a mystery greater—when I thought of it—than the curious, inexplicable note of desperate grief in this savage clamor that had swept by us on the river-bank, behind the blind whiteness of the fog.

"Two pilgrims were quarreling in hurried whispers as to which bank. 'Left.' 'No, no; how can you? Right, right, of course.' 'It is very serious,' said the manager's voice behind me; 'I would be desolated if anything should happen to Mr. Kurtz before we came up.' I looked at him, and had not the slightest doubt he was sincere. He was just the kind of man who would wish to preserve appearances. That was his restraint. But when he muttered something about going on at once, I did not even take the trouble to answer him. I knew, and he knew, that it was impossible. Were we to let go our hold of the bottom, we would be absolutely in the air—in space. We wouldn't be able to tell where we were going to—whether up or down stream, or across—till we fetched against one bank or the other,—and then we wouldn't know at first which it was. Of course I made no move. I had no mind for a smash-up. You couldn't imagine a more deadly place for a shipwreck. Whether drowned at once or not, we were sure to perish speedily in one way or another. 'I authorize you to take all the risks,' he said, after a short silence. 'I refuse to take any,' I said, shortly; which was just the answer he expected, though its tone might have surprised him. 'Well, I must defer to your judgment. You are captain,' he said, with marked civility. I turned my shoulder to him in sign of my appreciation, and looked into the fog. How long would it last? It was the most hopeless look-out. The approach to this Kurtz grubbing for ivory in the wretched bush was beset by as many dangers as though he had been

an enchanted princess sleeping in a fabulous castle. 'Will
they attack, do you think?' asked the manager, in a confidential tone.

"I did not think they would attack, for several obvious reasons. The thick fog was one. If they left the
bank in their canoes they would get lost in it, as we would
be if we attempted to move. Still, I had also judged the
jungle of both banks quite impenetrable—and yet eyes
were in it, eyes that had seen us. The river-side bushes
were certainly very thick; but the undergrowth behind
was evidently penetrable. However, during the short lift
I had seen no canoes anywhere in the reach—certainly
not abreast of the steamer. But what made the idea of
attack inconceivable to me was the nature of the noise—
of the cries we had heard. They had not the fierce character boding immediate hostile intention. Unexpected,
wild, and violent as they had been, they had given me
an irresistible impression of sorrow. The glimpse of the
steamboat had for some reason filled those savages with
unrestrained grief. The danger, if any, I expounded, was
from our proximity to a great human passion let loose.
Even extreme grief may ultimately vent itself in violence
—but more generally takes the form of apathy. . . .

"You should have seen the pilgrims stare! They had
no heart to grin, or even to revile me: but I believe they
thought me gone mad—with fright, maybe. I delivered
a regular lecture. My dear boys, it was no good bothering. Keep a look-out? Well, you may guess I watched
the fog for the signs of lifting as a cat watches a mouse;
but for anything else our eyes were of no more use to us
than if we had been buried miles deep in a heap of cotton-
wool. It felt like it, too—choking, warm, stifling. Besides,
all I said, though it sounded extravagant, was absolutely true to fact. What we afterwards alluded to as an
attack was really an attempt at repulse. The action was
very far from being aggressive—it was not even de-

fensive, in the usual sense: it was undertaken under the
stress of desperation, and in its essence was purely pro-
tective.

"It developed itself, I should say, two hours after
the fog lifted, and its commencement was at a spot,
roughly speaking, about a mile and a half below Kurtz's
station. We had just floundered and flopped round a bend,
when I saw an islet, a mere grassy hummock of bright
green, in the middle of the stream. It was the only thing
of the kind; but as we opened the reach more, I perceived it was the head of a long sandbank, or rather
of a chain of shallow patches stretching down the middle
of the river. They were discolored, just awash, and the
whole lot was seen just under the water, exactly as a
man's backbone is seen running down the middle of his
back under the skin. Now, as far as I did see, I could go
to the right or to the left of this. I didn't know either
channel, of course. The banks looked pretty well alike,
the depth appeared the same; but as I had been informed
the station was on the west side, I naturally headed for
the western passage.

"No sooner had we fairly entered it than I became
aware it was much narrower than I had supposed. To the
left of us there was the long uninterrupted shoal, and
to the right a high, steep bank heavily overgrown with
bushes. Above the bush the trees stood in serried ranks.
The twigs overhung the current thickly, and from distance
to distance a large limb of some tree projected rigidly
over the stream. It was then well on in the afternoon,
the face of the forest was gloomy, and a broad strip of
shadow had already fallen on the water. In this shadow
we steamed up—very slowly, as you may imagine. I
sheered her well inshore—the water being deepest near the
bank, as the sounding-pole informed me.

"One of my hungry and forbearing friends was sounding in the bows just below me. This steamboat was

exactly like a decked scow. On the deck, there were two
little teak-wood houses, with doors and windows. The
boiler was in the fore-end, and the machinery right astern.
Over the whole there was a light roof, supported on
stanchions. The funnel projected through that roof, and
in front of the funnel a small cabin built of light planks
served for a pilot-house. It contained a couch, two campstools, a loaded Martini-Henry leaning in one corner, a
tiny table, and the steering-wheel. It had a wide door
in front and a broad shutter at each side. All these were
always thrown open, of course. I spent my days perched
up there on the extreme fore-end of that roof, before the
door. At night I slept, or tried to, on the couch. An
athletic black belonging to some coast tribe, and educated by my poor predecessor, was the helmsman. He
sported a pair of brass earrings, wore a blue cloth wrapper
from the waist to the ankles, and thought all the world
of himself. He was the most unstable kind of fool I had
ever seen. He steered with no end of a swagger while you
were by; but if he lost sight of you, he became instantly
the prey of an abject funk, and would let that cripple
of a steamboat get the upper hand of him in a minute.

"I was looking down at the sounding-pole, and feeling
much annoyed to see at each try a little more of it stick
out of that river, when I saw my poleman give up the
business suddenly, and stretch himself flat on the deck,
without even taking the trouble to haul his pole in. He
kept hold on it though, and it trailed in the water. At the
same time the fireman, whom I could also see below me,
sat down abruptly before his furnace and ducked his head.
I was amazed. Then I had to look at the river mighty
quick, because there was a snag in the fairway. Sticks, little
sticks, were flying about—thick: they were whizzing before my nose, dropping below me, striking behind me
against my pilot-house. All this time the river, the shore,
the woods, were very quiet—perfectly quiet. I could only

hear the heavy splashing thump of the stern-wheel and the patter of these things. We cleared the snag clumsily. Arrows, by Jove! We were being shot at! I stepped in quickly to close the shutter on the land-side. That fool-helmsman, his hands on the spokes, was lifting his knees high, stamping his feet, champing his mouth, like a reined-in horse. Confound him! And we were staggering within ten feet of the bank. I had to lean right out to swing the heavy shutter, and I saw a face amongst the leaves on the level with my own, looking at me very fierce and steady; and then suddenly, as though a veil had been removed from my eyes, I made out, deep in the tangled gloom, naked breasts, arms, legs, glaring eyes,—the bush was swarming with human limbs in movement, glistening, of bronze color. The twigs shook, swayed, and rustled, the arrows flew out of them, and then the shutter came to. 'Steer her straight,' I said to the helmsman. He held his head rigid, face forward; but his eyes rolled, he kept on lifting and setting down his feet gently, his mouth foamed a little. 'Keep quiet!' I said in a fury. I might just as well have ordered a tree not to sway in the wind. I darted out. Below me there was a great scuffle of feet on the iron deck; confused exclamations; a voice screamed, 'Can you turn back?' I caught sight of a V-shaped ripple on the water ahead. What? Another snag! A fusillade burst out under my feet. The pilgrims had opened with their Winchesters, and were simply squirting lead into that bush. A deuce of a lot of smoke came up and drove slowly forward. I swore at it. Now I couldn't see the ripple or the snag either. I stood in the doorway, peering, and the arrows came in swarms. They might have been poisoned, but they looked as though they wouldn't kill a cat. The bush began to howl. Our wood-cutters raised a warlike whoop; the report of a rifle just at my back deafened me. I glanced over my shoulder, and the pilot-house was yet full of noise and smoke when I made a dash at the wheel. The fool-nigger had dropped everything to throw the shutter open and let off that Martini-Henry. He stood before the wide opening, glaring, and I yelled at him to come back, while I straightened the sudden twist out of that steamboat. There was no room to turn even if I had wanted to, the snag was somewhere very near ahead in that confounded smoke, there was no time to lose, so I just crowded her into the bank—right into the bank, where I knew the water was deep.

"We tore slowly along the overhanging bushes in a whirl of broken twigs and flying leaves. The fusillade below stopped short, as I had foreseen it would when the squirts got empty. I threw my head back to a glinting whizz that traversed the pilot-house, in at one shutter-hole and out at the other. Looking past that mad helmsman, who was shaking the empty rifle and yelling at the shore, I saw vague forms of men running bent double, leaping, gliding, distinct, incomplete, evanescent. Something big appeared in the air before the shutter, the rifle went overboard, and the man stepped back swiftly, looked at me over his shoulder in an extraordinary, profound, familiar manner, and fell upon my feet. The side of his head hit the wheel twice, and the end of what appeared a long cane clattered round and knocked over a little camp-stool. It looked as though after wrenching that thing from somebody ashore he had lost his balance in the effort. The thin smoke had blown away, we were clear of the snag, and looking ahead I could see that in another hundred yards or so I would be free to sheer off, away from the bank; but my feet felt so very warm and wet that I had to look down. The man had rolled on his back and stared straight up at me; both his hands clutched that cane. It was the shaft of a spear that, either thrown or lunged through the opening, had caught him in the side just below the ribs; the blade had gone in out of sight, after making a frightful gash; my shoes were full; a pool

ot blood lay very still, gleaming dark-red under the wheel;
his eyes shone with an amazing luster. The fusillade burst
out again. He looked at me anxiously, gripping the spear
like something precious, with an air of being afraid I
would try to take it away from him. I had to make an
effort to free my eyes from his gaze and attend to steering. With one hand I felt above my head for the line of
the steam whistle, and jerked out screech after screech
hurriedly. The tumult of angry and warlike yells was
checked instantly, and then from the depths of the woods
went out such a tremulous and prolonged wail of mournful fear and utter despair as may be imagined to follow the
flight of the last hope from the earth. There was a great
commotion in the bush; the shower of arrows stopped, a
few dropping shots rang out sharply—then silence, in
which the languid beat of the stern-wheel came plainly
to my ears. I put the helm hard a-starboard at the moment
when the pilgrim in pink pajamas, very hot and agitated,
appeared in the doorway. 'The manager sends me—' he
began in an official tone, and stopped short. 'Good God!'
he said, glaring at the wounded man.

"We two whites stood over him, and his lustrous and
inquiring glance enveloped us both. I declare it looked
as though he would presently put to us some question in
an understandable language; but he died without uttering a sound, without moving a limb, without twitching
a muscle. Only in the very last moment, as though in
response to some sign we could not see, to some whisper
we could not hear, he frowned heavily, and that frown
gave to his black death-mask an inconceivably somber,
brooding, and menacing expression. The luster of inquiring
glance faded swiftly into vacant glassiness. 'Can you
steer?' I asked the agent eagerly. He looked very dubious;
but I made a grab at his arm, and he understood at once
I meant him to steer whether or no. To tell you the
truth, I was morbidly anxious to change my shoes and

socks. 'He is dead,' murmured the fellow, immensely impressed. 'No doubt about it,' said I, tugging like mad at the shoe-laces. 'And by the way, I suppose Mr. Kurtz is dead as well by this time.'

"For the moment that was the dominant thought. There was a sense of extreme disappointment, as though I had found out I had been striving after something altogether without a substance. I couldn't have been more disgusted if I had traveled all this way for the sole purpose of talking with Mr. Kurtz. Talking with . . . I flung one shoe overboard, and became aware that that was exactly what I had been looking forward to—a talk with Kurtz. I made the strange discovery that I had never imagined him as doing, you know, but as discoursing. I didn't say to myself, 'Now I will never see him,' or 'Now I will never shake him by the hand,' but, 'now I will never hear him.' The man presented himself as a voice. Not of course that I did not connect him with some sort of action. Hadn't I been told in all the tones of jealousy and admiration that he had collected, bartered, swindled, or stolen more ivory than all the other agents together? That was not the point. The point was in his being a gifted creature, and that of all his gifts the one that stood out preëminently, that carried with it a sense of real presence, was his ability to talk, his words—the gift of expression, the bewildering, the illuminating, the most exalted and the most contemptible, the pulsating stream of light, or the deceitful flow from the heart of an impenetrable darkness.

"The other shoe went flying unto the devil-god of that river. I thought, by Jove! it's all over. We are too late; he has vanished—the gift has vanished, by means of some spear, arrow, or club. I will never hear that chap speak after all,—and my sorrow had a startling extravagance of emotion, even such as I had noticed in the howling sorrow of these savages in the bush. I couldn't have felt more lonely desolation somehow, had I been robbed of a belief or had missed my destiny in life. . . . Why do you sigh in this beastly way, somebody? Absurd? Well, absurd. Good Lord! mustn't a man ever— Here, give me some tobacco." . . .

There was a pause of profound stillness, then a match flared, and Marlow's lean face appeared, worn, hollow, with downward folds and drooped eyelids, with an aspect of concentrated attention; and as he took vigorous draws at his pipe, it seemed to retreat and advance out of the night in the regular flicker of the tiny flame. The match went out.

"Absurd!" he cried. "This is the worst of trying to tell. . . . Here you all are, each moored with two good addresses, like a hulk with two anchors, a butcher round one corner, a policeman round another, excellent appetites, and temperature normal—you hear—normal from year's end to year's end. And you say, Absurd! Absurd be—exploded! Absurd! My dear boys, what can you expect from a man who out of sheer nervousness had just flung overboard a pair of new shoes! Now I think of it, it is amazing I did not shed tears. I am, upon the whole, proud of my fortitude. I was cut to the quick at the idea of having lost the inestimable privilege of listening to the gifted Kurtz. Of course I was wrong. The privilege was waiting for me. Oh, yes, I heard more than enough. And I was right, too. A voice. He was very little more than a voice. And I heard—him—it—this voice—other voices— all of them were so little more than voices—and the memory of that time itself lingers around me, impalpable, like a dying vibration of one immense jabber, silly, atrocious, sordid, savage, or simply mean, without any kind of sense. Voices, voices—even the girl herself—now—"

He was silent for a long time.

"I laid the ghost of his gifts at last with a lie," he began, suddenly. "Girl! What? Did I mention a girl? Oh,

she is out of it—completely. They—the women I mean
—are out of it—should be out of it. We must help them
to stay in that beautiful world of their own, lest ours gets
worse. Oh, she had to be out of it. You should have heard
the disinterred body of Mr. Kurtz saying, 'My Intended.'
You would have perceived directly then how completely
she was out of it. And the lofty frontal bone of Mr.
Kurtz! They say the hair goes on growing sometimes, but
this—ah—specimen, was impressivly bald. The wilderness
had patted him on the head, and, behold, it was like a
ball—an ivory ball; it had caressed him, and—lo!—he had
withered; it had taken him, loved him, embraced him, got
into his veins, consumed his flesh, and sealed his soul
to its own by the inconceivable ceremonies of some devil-
ish initiation. He was its spoiled and pampered favorite.
Ivory? I should think so. Heaps of it, stacks of it. The
old mud shanty was bursting with it. You would think
there was not a single tusk left either above or below the
ground in the whole country. 'Mostly fossil,' the manager
had remarked, disparagingly. It was no more fossil than
I am; but they call it fossil when it is dug up. It appears
these niggers do bury the tusks sometimes—but evidently
they couldn't bury this parcel deep enough to save the
gifted Mr. Kurtz from his fate. We filled the steamboat
with it, and had to pile a lot on the deck. Thus he could
see and enjoy as long as he could see, because the appreciation of this favor had remained with him to the last.
You should have heard him say, 'My ivory.' Oh, yes, I
heard him. 'My Intended, my ivory, my station, my river,
my—' everything belonged to him. It made me hold my
breath in expectation of hearing the wilderness burst into
a prodigious peal of laughter that would shake the fixed
stars in their places. Everything belonged to him—but that
was a trifle. The thing was to know what he belonged to,
how many powers of darkness claimed him for their own.
That was the reflection that made you creepy all over.

It was impossible—it was not good for one either—trying to imagine. He had taken a high seat amongst the devils of the land—I mean literally. You can't understand. How could you?—with solid pavement under your feet, surrounded by kind neighbors ready to cheer you or to fall on you, stepping delicately between the butcher and the policeman, in the holy terror of scandal and gallows and lunatic asylums—how can you imagine what particular region of the first ages a man's untrammeled feet may take him into by the way of solitude—utter solitude without a policeman—by the way of silence—utter silence, where no warning voice of a kind neighbor can be heard whispering of public opinion? These little things make all the great difference. When they are gone you must fall back upon your own innate strength, upon your own capacity for faithfulness. Of course you may be too much of a fool to go wrong—too dull even to know you are being assaulted by the powers of darkness. I take it, no fool ever made a bargain for his soul with the devil: the fool is too much of a fool, or the devil too much of a devil—I don't know which. Or you may be such a thunderingly exalted creature as to be altogether deaf and blind to anything but heavenly sights and sounds. Then the earth for you is only a standing place—and whether to be like this is your loss or your gain I won't pretend to say. But most of us are neither one nor the other. The earth for us is a place to live in, where we must put up with sights, with sounds, with smells, too, by Jove!— breathe dead hippo, so to speak, and not be contaminated. And there, don't you see? your strength comes in, the faith in your ability for the digging of unostentatious holes to bury the stuff in—your power of devotion, not to yourself, but to an obscure, back-breaking business. And that's difficult enough. Mind, I am not trying to excuse or even explain—I am trying to account to myself for—for—Mr. Kurtz—for the shade of Mr. Kurtz. This

initiated wraith from the back of Nowhere honored me
with its amazing confidence before it vanished altogether.
This was because it could speak English to me. The
original Kurtz had been educated partly in England, and
—as he was good enough to say himself—his sympathies
were in the right place. His mother was half-English, his
father was half-French. All Europe contributed to the
making of Kurtz; and by and by I learned that, most
appropriately, the International Society for the Suppression of Savage Customs had intrusted him with the making
of a report, for its future guidance. And he had written
it, too. I've seen it. I've read it. It was eloquent, vibrating
with eloquence, but too high-strung, I think. Seventeen
pages of close writing he had found time for! But this
must have been before his—let us say—nerves, went
wrong, and caused him to preside at certain midnight
dances ending with unspeakable rites, which—as far as I
reluctantly gathered from what I heard at various times—
were offered up to him—do you understand?—to Mr.
Kurtz himself. But it was a beautiful piece of writing.
The opening paragraph, however, in the light of later information, strikes me now as ominous. He began with
the argument that we whites, from the point of develop-
ment we had arrived at, 'must necessarily appear to them
[savages] in the nature of supernatural beings—we approach them with the might as of a deity,' and so on,
and so on. 'By the simple exercise of our will we can exert
a power for good practically unbounded,' etc. etc. From
that point he soared and took me with him. The peroration
was magnificent, though difficult to remember, you know.
It gave me the notion of an exotic Immensity ruled by an
august Benevolence. It made me tingle with enthusiasm.
This was the unbounded power of eloquence—of words—
of burning noble words. There were no practical hints to
interrupt the magic current of phrases, unless a kind of
note at the foot of the last page, scrawled evidently much

later, in an unsteady hand, may be regarded as the exposition of a method. It was very simple, and at the end of that moving appeal to every altruistic sentiment it blazed at you, luminous and terrifying, like a flash of lightning in a serene sky: 'Exterminate all the brutes!' The curious part was that he had apparently forgotten all about that valuable postscriptum, because, later on, when he in a sense came to himself, he repeatedly entreated me to take good care of 'my pamphlet' (he called it), as it was sure to have in the future a good influence upon his career. I had full information about all these things, and, besides, as it turned out, I was to have the care of his memory. I've done enough for it to give me the indisputable right to lay it, if I choose, for an everlasting rest in the dustbin of progress, amongst all the sweepings and, figuratively speaking, all the dead cats of civilization. But then, you see, I can't choose. He won't be forgotten. Whatever he was, he was not common. He had the power to charm or frighten rudimentary souls into an aggravated witch-dance in his honor; he could also fill the small souls of the pilgrims with bitter misgivings: he had one devoted friend at least, and he had conquered one soul in the world that was neither rudimentary nor tainted with self-seeking. No; I can't forget him, though I am not prepared to affirm the fellow was exactly worth the life we lost in getting to him. I missed my late helmsman awfully,—I missed him even while his body was still lying in the pilot-house. Perhaps you will think it passing strange this regret for a savage who was no more account than a grain of sand in a black Sahara. Well, don't you see, he had done something, he had steered; for months I had him at my back—a help—an instrument. It was a kind of partnership. He steered for me—I had to look after him, I worried about his deficiencies, and thus a subtle bond had been created, of which I only became aware when it was suddenly broken. And the intimate profundity of that look he gave me when he received his hurt remains to this day in my memory—like a claim of distant kinship affirmed in a supreme moment.

"Poor fool! If he had only left that shutter alone. He had no restraint, no restraint—just like Kurtz—a tree swayed by the wind. As soon as I had put on a dry pair of slippers, I dragged him out, after first jerking the spear out of his side, which operation I confess I performed with my eyes shut tight. His heels leaped together over the little door-step; his shoulders were pressed to my breast; I hugged him from behind desperately. Oh! he was heavy, heavy; heavier than any man on earth, I should imagine. Then without more ado I tipped him overboard. The current snatched him as though he had been a wisp of grass, and I saw the body roll over twice before I lost sight of it forever. All the pilgrims and the manager were then congregated on the awning-deck about the pilot-house, chattering at each other like a flock of excited magpies, and there was a scandalized murmur at my heartless promptitude. What they wanted to keep that body hanging about for I can't guess. Embalm it, maybe. But I had also heard another, and a very ominous, murmur on the deck below. My friends the wood-cutters were likewise scandalized, and with a better show of reason— though I admit that the reason itself was quite inadmissible. Oh, quite! I had made up my mind that if my late helmsman was to be eaten, the fishes alone should have him. He had been a very second-rate helmsman while alive, but now he was dead he might have become a first-class temptation, and possibly cause some startling trouble. Besides, I was anxious to take the wheel, the man in pink pajamas showing himself a hopeless duffer at the business.

"This I did directly the simple funeral was over. We were going half-speed, keeping right in the middle of the stream, and I listened to the talk about me. They had given up Kurtz, they had given up the station; Kurtz was dead,

and the station had been burnt—and so on—and so on.
The red-haired pilgrim was beside himself with the thought
that at least this poor Kurtz had been properly avenged.
'Say! We must have made a glorious slaughter of them
in the bush. Eh? What do you think? Say?' He positively
danced, the bloodthirsty little gingery beggar. And he had
nearly fainted when he saw the wounded man! I could
not help saying, 'You made a glorious lot of smoke, anyhow.' I had seen, from the way the tops of the bushes
rustled and flew, that almost all the shots had gone too
high. You can't hit anything unless you take aim and fire
from the shoulder; but these chaps fired from the hip
with their eyes shut. The retreat, I maintained—and I
was right—was caused by the screeching of the steam-
whistle. Upon this they forgot Kurtz, and began to howl
at me with indignant protests.

"The manager stood by the wheel murmuring confiden-
tially about the necessity of getting well away down the
river before dark at all events, when I saw in the distance
a clearing on the river-side and the outlines of some sort
of building. 'What's this?' I asked. He clapped his hands
in wonder. 'The station!' he cried. I edged in at once, still
going half-speed.

"Through my glasses I saw the slope of a hill interspersed with rare trees and perfectly free from undergrowth. A long decaying building on the summit was half
buried in the high grass; the large holes in the peaked
roof gaped black from afar; the jungle and the woods
made a background. There was no enclosure or fence
of any kind; but there had been one apparently, for near
the house half-a-dozen slim posts remained in a row,
roughly trimmed, and with their upper ends ornamented
with round carved balls. The rails, or whatever there had
been between, had disappeared. Of course the forest surrounded all that. The river-bank was clear, and on the
water-side I saw a white man under a hat like a cart-

wheel beckoning persistently with his whole arm. Examining the edge of the forest above and below, I was almost certain I could see movements—human forms gliding here and there. I steamed past prudently, then stopped the engines and let her drift down. The man on the shore began to shout, urging us to land. 'We have been attacked,' screamed the manager. 'I know—I know. It's all right,' yelled back the other, as cheerful as you please. 'Come along. It's all right. I am glad.'

"His aspect reminded me of something I had seen—something funny I had seen somewhere. As I maneuvered to get alongside, I was asking myself, 'What does this fellow look like?' Suddenly I got it. He looked like a harlequin. His clothes had been made of some stuff that was brown holland probably, but it was covered with patches all over, with bright patches, blue, red, and yellow, —patches on the back, patches on the front, patches on elbows, on knees; colored binding around his jacket, scarlet edging at the bottom of his trousers; and the sunshine made him look extremely gay and wonderfully neat withal, because you could see how beautifully all this patching had been done. A beardless, boyish face, very fair, no features to speak of, nose peeling, little blue eyes, smiles and frowns chasing each other over that open countenance like sunshine and shadow on a wind-swept plain. 'Look out, captain!' he cried; 'there's a snag lodged in her last night.' What! Another snag? I confess I swore shamefully. I had nearly holed my cripple, to finish off that charming trip. The harlequin on the bank turned his little pug-nose up to me. 'You English?' he asked, all smiles. 'Are you?' I shouted from the wheel. The smiles vanished, and he shook his head as if sorry for my disappointment. Then he brightened up. 'Never mind!' he cried, encouragingly. 'Are we in time?' I asked. 'He is up there,' he replied, with a toss of the head up the hill, and becoming gloomy all of a sudden. His face was like the autumn sky, overcast one moment and bright the next.

"When the manager, escorted by the pilgrims, all of them armed to the teeth, had gone to the house this chap came on board. 'I say, I don't like this. These natives are in the bush,' I said. He assured me earnestly it was all right. 'They are simple people,' he added; 'well, I am glad you came. It took me all my time to keep them off.' 'But you said it was all right,' I cried. 'Oh, they meant no harm,' he said; and as I stared he corrected himself, 'Not exactly.' Then vivaciously, 'My faith, your pilot-house wants a clean-up!' In the next breath he advised me to keep enough steam on the boiler to blow the whistle in case of any trouble. 'One good screech will do more for you than all your rifles. They are simple people,' he repeated. He rattled away at such a rate he quite overwhelmed me. He seemed to be trying to make up for lots of silence, and actually hinted, laughing, that such was the case. 'Don't you talk with Mr. Kurtz?' I said. 'You don't talk with that man—you listen to him,' he exclaimed with severe exaltation. 'But now—' He waved his arm, and in the twinkling of an eye was in the uttermost depths of despondency. In a moment he came up again with a jump, possessed himself of both my hands, shook them continuously, while he gabbled: 'Brother sailor . . . honor . . . pleasure . . . delight . . . introduce myself . . . Russian . . . son of an arch-priest . . . Government of Tambov. . . . What? Tobacco! English tobacco; the excellent English tobacco! Now, that's brotherly. Smoke? Where's a sailor that does not smoke?'

"The pipe soothed him, and gradually I made out he had run away from school, had gone to sea in a Russian ship; ran away again; served some time in English ships; was now reconciled with the arch-priest. He made a point of that. 'But when one is young one must see things, gather experience, ideas; enlarge the mind.' 'Here!' I interrupted. 'You can never tell! Here I met Mr Kurtz,' he

said, youthfully solemn and reproachful. I held my tongue
after that. It appears he had persuaded a Dutch trading-
house on the coast to fit him out with stores and goods,
and had started for the interior with a light heart, and
no more idea of what would happen to him than a baby.
He had been wandering about that river for nearly two
years alone, cut off from everybody and everything. 'I
am not so young as I look. I am twenty-five,' he said. 'At
first old Van Shuyten would tell me to go to the devil,'
he narrated with keen enjoyment; 'but I stuck to him,
and talked and talked, till at last he got afraid I would
talk the hind-leg off his favorite dog, so he gave me some
cheap things and a few guns, and told me he hoped he
would never see my face again. Good old Dutchman, Van
Shuyten. I've sent him one small lot of ivory a year ago,
so that he can't call me a little thief when I get back.
I hope he got it. And for the rest I don't care. I had
some wood stacked for you. That was my old house.
Did you see?'

"I gave him Towson's book. He made as though he
would kiss me, but restrained himself. 'The only book
I had left, and I thought I had lost it,' he said, looking
at it ecstatically. 'So many accidents happen to a man
going about alone, you know. Canoes get upset sometimes
—and sometimes you've got to clear out so quick when the
people get angry.' He thumbed the pages. 'You made notes
in Russian?' I asked. He nodded. 'I thought they were
written in cipher.' I said. He laughed, then became serious. 'I had lots of trouble to keep these people off,' he
said. 'Did they want to kill you?' I asked. 'Oh, no!' he
cried, and checked himself. 'Why did they attack us?' I
pursued. He hesitated, then said shamefacedly, 'They don't
want him to go.' 'Don't they? I said, curiously. He nodded
a nod full of mystery and wisdom. 'I tell you,' he cried,
this man has enlarged my mind.' He opened his arms

wide, staring at me with his little blue eyes that were
perfectly round."

### III

"I LOOKED at him, lost in astonishment. There he was
before me, in motley, as though he had absconded from
a troupe of mimes, enthusiastic, fabulous. His very existence was improbable, inexplicable, and altogether bewildering. He was an insoluble problem. It was inconceivable how he had existed, how he had succeeded in
getting so far, how he had managed to remain—why he
did not instantly disappear. 'I went a little farther,' he
said, 'then still a little farther—till I had gone so far that
I don't know how I'll ever get back. Never mind. Plenty
time. I can manage. You take Kurtz away quick—quick—
I tell you.' The glamour of youth enveloped his parti-
colored rags, his destitution, his loneliness, the essential
desolation of his futile wanderings. For months—for
years—his life hadn't been worth a day's purchase;
and there he was gallantly, thoughtlessly alive, to all appearance indestructible solely by the virtue of his few
years and of his unreflecting audacity. I was seduced into
something like admiration—like envy. Glamour urged him
on, glamour kept him unscathed. He surely wanted nothing
from the wilderness but space to breathe in and to push
on through. His need was to exist, and to move onwards
at the greatest possible risk, and with a maximum of
privation. If the absolutely pure, uncalculating, unprac-
tical spirit of adventure had ever ruled a human being,
it ruled this be-patched youth. I almost envied him the
possession of this modest and clear flame. It seemed to
have consumed all thought of self so completely, that
even while he was talking to you, you forgot that it was
he—the man before your eyes—who had gone through
these things. I did not envy him his devotion to Kurtz,
though. He had not meditated over it. It came to him

and he accepted it with a sort of eager fatalism. I must say that to me it appeared about the most dangerous thing in every way he had come upon so far.

"They had come together unavoidably, like two ships becalmed near each other, and lay rubbing sides at last. I suppose Kurtz wanted an audience, because on a certain occasion, when encamped in the forest, they had talked all night, or more probably Kurtz had talked. 'We talked of everything,' he said, quite transported at the recollection. 'I forgot there was such a thing as sleep. The night did not seem to last an hour. Everything! Everything! . . . Of love, too.' 'Ah, he talked to you of love!' I said, much amused. 'It isn't what you think,' he cried, almost passionately. 'It was in general. He made me see things—things.'

"He threw his arms up. We were on deck at the time, and the headman of my wood-cutters, lounging near by, turned upon him his heavy and glittering eyes. I looked around, and I don't know why, but I assure you that never, never before, did this land, this river, this jungle, the very arch of this blazing sky, appear to me so hopeless and so dark, so impenetrable to human thought, so pitiless to human weakness. 'And, ever since, you have been with him, of course?' I said.

"On the contrary. It appears their intercourse had been very much broken by various causes. He had, as he informed me proudly, managed to nurse Kurtz through two illnesses (he alluded to it as you would to some risky feat), but as a rule Kurtz wandered alone far in the depths of the forest. 'Very often coming to this station, I had to wait days and days before he would turn up,' he said. 'Ah, it was worth waiting for!—sometimes.' 'What was he doing? exploring or what?' I asked. 'Oh, yes, of course'; he had discovered lots of villages, a lake, too—he did not know exactly in what direction; it was dangerous to inquire too much—but mostly his expedi-

tions had been for ivory. 'But he had no goods to trade
with by that time,' I objected. 'There's a good lot of
cartridges left even yet,' he answered, looking away. 'To
speak plainly, he raided the country,' I said. He nodded.
'Not alone, surely!' He muttered something about the
villages round that lake. 'Kurtz got the tribe to follow
him, did he?' I suggested. He fidgeted a little. 'They
adored him,' he said. The tone of these words was so
extraordinary that I looked at him searchingly. It was
curious to see his mingled eagerness and reluctance to
speak of Kurtz. The man filled his life, occupied his
thoughts, swayed his emotions. 'What can you expect?'
he burst out; 'he came to them with thunder and lightning, you know—and they had never seen anything like
it—and very terrible. He could be very terrible. You
can't judge Mr. Kurtz as you would an ordinary man.
No, no, no! Now—just to give you an idea—I don't mind
telling you, he wanted to shoot me, too, one day—but I
don't judge him.' 'Shoot you!' I cried. 'What for?' 'Well,
I had a small lot of ivory the chief of that village near
my house gave me. You see I used to shoot game for
them. Well, he wanted it, and wouldn't hear reason. He
declared he would shoot me unless I gave him the ivory
and then cleared out of the country, because he could do
so, and had a fancy for it, and there was nothing on earth
to prevent him killing whom he jolly well pleased. And
it was true, too. I gave him the ivory. What did I care!
But I didn't clear out. No, no. I couldn't leave him. I had
to be careful, of course, till we got friendly again for a
time. He had his second illness then. Afterwards I had
to keep out of the way; but I didn't mind. He was living
for the most part in those villages on the lake. When he
came down to the river, sometimes he would take to me,
and sometimes it was better for me to be careful. This
man suffered too much. He hated all this, and somehow
he couldn't get away. When I had a chance I begged him

to try and leave while there was time; I offered to go back with him. And he would say yes, and then he would remain; go off on another ivory hunt; disappear for weeks; forget himself amongst these people—forget himself—you know.' 'Why! he's mad,' I said. He protested indignantly. Mr. Kurtz couldn't be mad. If I had heard him talk, only two days ago, I wouldn't dare hint at such a thing. . . . I had taken up my binoculars while we talked, and was looking at the shore, sweeping the limit of the forest at each side and at the back of the house. The consciousness of there being people in that bush, so silent, so quiet—as silent and quiet as the ruined house on the hill—made me uneasy. There was no sign on the face of nature of this amazing tale that was not so much told as suggested to me in desolate exclamations, completed by shrugs, in interrupted phrases, in hints ending in deep sighs. The woods were unmoved, like a mask—heavy, like the closed door of a prison—they looked with their air of hidden knowledge, of patient expectation, of unapproachable silence. The Russian was explaining to me that it was only lately that Mr. Kurtz had come down to the river, bringing along with him all the fighting men of that lake tribe. He had been absent for several months—getting himself adored, I suppose—and had come down unexpectedly, with the intention to all appearance of making a raid either across the river or down stream. Evidently the appetite for more ivory had got the better of the—what shall I say?—less material aspirations. However he had got much worse suddenly. 'I heard he was lying helpless, and so I came up—took my chance,' said the Russian. 'Oh, he is bad, very bad.' I directed my glass to the house. There were no signs of life, but there was the ruined roof, the long mud wall peeping above the grass, with three little square window-holes, no two of the same size; all this brought within reach of my hand, as it were. And then I made

a brusque movement, and one of the remaining posts of
that vanished fence leaped up in the field of my glass.
You remember I told you I had been struck at the distance by certain attempts at ornamentation, rather remarkable in the ruinous aspect of the place. Now I had
suddenly a nearer view, and its first result was to make
me throw my head back as if before a blow. Then I went
carefully from post to post with my glass, and I saw my
mistake. These round knobs were not ornamental but
symbolic; they were expressive and puzzling, striking
and disturbing—food for thought and also for vultures
if there had been any looking down from the sky; but at
all events for such ants as were industrious enough to
ascend the pole. They would have been even more im-
pressive, those heads on the stakes, if their faces had not
been turned to the house. Only one, the first I had made
out, was facing my way. I was not so shocked as you may
think. The start back I had given was really nothing but
a movement of surprise. I had expected to see a knob
of wood there, you know. I returned deliberately to the
first I had seen—and there it was, black, dried, sunken.
with closed eyelids,—a head that seemed to sleep at the
top of that pole, and with the shrunken dry lips showing
a narrow white line of the teeth, was smiling, too, smiling
continuously at some endless and jocose dream of that
eternal slumber.

"I am not disclosing any trade secrets. In fact, the
manager said afterwards that Mr. Kurtz's methods had
ruined the district. I have no opinion on that point, but
I want you clearly to understand that there was nothing
exactly profitable in these heads being there. They only
showed that Mr. Kurtz lacked restraint in the gratifica·
tion of his various lusts, that there was something want·
ing in him—some small matter which, when the pressing
need arose, could not be found under his magnificent
eloquence. Whether he knew of this deficiency himself I

can't say. I think the knowledge came to him at last—
only at the very last. But the wilderness had found him
out early, and had taken on him a terrible vengeance for
the fantastic invasion. I think it had whispered to him
things about himself which he did not know, things of
which he had no conception till he took counsel witn this
great solitude—and the whisper had proved irresistibly
fascinating. It echoed loudly within him because he was
hollow at the core. . . . I put down the glass, and the
head that had appeared near enough to be spoken to
seemed at once to have leaped away from me into inac-
cessible distance.

"The admirer of Mr. Kurtz was a bit crestfallen. In
a hurried indistinct voice he began to assure me he had
not dared to take these—say, symbols—down. He was not
afraid of the natives; they would not stir till Mr. Kurtz
gave the word. His ascendancy was extraordinary. The
camps of these people surrounded the place, and the
chiefs came every day to see him. They would crawl. . . .
'I don't want to know anything of the ceremonies used
when approaching Mr. Kurtz,' I shouted. Curious, this
feeling that came over me that such details would be
more intolerable than those heads drying on the stakes
under Mr. Kurtz's windows. After all, that was only a
savage sight, while I seemed at one bound to have been
transported into some lightless region of subtle horrors,
where pure, uncomplicated savagery was a positive relief,
being something that had a right to exist—obviously—
in the sunshine. The young man looked at me with surprise. I suppose it did not occur to him that Mr. Kurtz
was no idol of mine. He forgot I hadn't heard any of
these splendid monologues on, what was it? on love, justice, conduct of life—or what not. If it had come to
crawling before Mr. Kurtz, he crawled as much as the
veriest savage of them all. I had no idea of the condi-
tions, he said: these heads were the heads of rebels. I

shocked him excessively by laughing. Rebels! What would
be the next definition I was to hear? There had been
enemies, criminals, workers—and these were rebels. Those
rebellious heads looked very subdued to me on their
sticks. 'You don't know how such a life tries a man like
Kurtz,' cried Kurtz's last disciple. 'Well, and you?' I said.
'I! I! I am a simple man. I have no great thoughts. I
want nothing from anybody. How can you compare me
to . . . ?' His feelings were too much for speech, and
suddenly he broke down. 'I don't understand, he groaned.
'I've been doing my best to keep him alive, and that's
enough. I had no hand in all this. I have no abilities. There
hasn't been a drop of medicine or a mouthful of invalid
food for months here. He was shamefully abandoned.
A man like this, with such ideas. Shamefully! Shamefully! I—I—haven't slept for the last ten nights. . . .

"His voice lost itself in the calm of the evening. The
long shadows of the forest had slipped downhill while
we talked, had gone far beyond the ruined hovel, beyond
the symbolic row of stakes. All this was in the gloom
while we down there were yet in the sunshine, and the
stretch of the river abreast of the clearing glittered in a
still and dazzling splendor, with a murky and overshadowed bend above and below. Not a living soul was
seen on the shore. The bushes did not rustle.

"Suddenly round the corner of the house a group of
men appeared, as though they had come up from the
ground. They waded waist-deep in the grass, in a compact body, bearing an improvised stretcher in their midst.
Instantly, in the emptiness of the landscape, a cry arose
whose shrillness pierced the still air like a sharp arrow
flying straight to the very heart of the land; and, as if
by enchantment, streams of human beings—of naked
human beings—with spears in their hands, with bows,
with shields, with wild glances and savage movements,
were poured into the clearing by the dark-faced and pen-

sive forest. The bushes shook, the grass swayed for a time, and then everything stood still in attentive immobility.

"'Now, if he does not say the right thing to them we are all done for,' said the Russian at my elbow. The knot of men with the stretcher had stopped, too, halfway to the steamer, as if petrified. I saw the man on the stretcher sit up, lank and with an uplifted arm, above the shoulders of the bearers. 'Let us hope that the man who can talk so well of love in general will find some particular reason to spare us this time,' I said. I resented bitterly the absurd danger of our situation, as if to be at the mercy of that atrocious phantom had been a dishonoring necessity. I could not hear a sound, but through my glasses I saw the thin arm extended commandingly, the lower jaw moving, the eyes of that apparition shining darkly far in its bony head that nodded with grotesque jerks. Kurtz—Kurtz—that means short in German—don't it? Well, the name was as true as everything else in his life—and death. He looked at least seven feet long. His covering had fallen off, and his body emerged from it pitiful and appalling as from a winding-sheet. I could see the cage of his ribs all astir, the bones of his arm waving. It was as though an animated image of death carved out of old ivory had been shaking its hand with menaces at a motionless crowd of men made of dark and glittering bronze. I saw him open his mouth wide—it gave him a weirdly voracious aspect, as though he had wanted to swallow all the air, all the earth, all the men before him. A deep voice reached me faintly. He must have been shouting. He fell back suddenly. The stretcher shook as the bearers staggered forward again, and almost at the same time I noticed that the crowd of savages was vanishing without any perceptible movement of retreat, as if the forest that had ejected these beings so suddenly had drawn them in again as the breath is drawn in a long aspiration.

"Some of the pilgrims behind the stretcher carried his arms—two shot-guns, a heavy rifle, and a light revolver-carbine—the thunderbolts of that pitiful Jupiter. The manager bent over him murmuring as he walked beside his head. They laid him down in one of the little cabins—just a room for a bedplace and a camp-stool or two, you know. We had brought his belated correspondence, and a lot of torn envelopes and open letters littered his bed. His hand roamed feebly amongst these papers. I was struck by the fire of his eyes and the composed languor of his expression. It was not so much the exhaustion of disease. He did not seem in pain. This shadow looked satiated and calm, as though for the moment it had had its fill of all the emotions.

"He rustled one of the letters, and looking straight in my face said, 'I am glad.' Somebody had been writing to him about me. These special recommendations were turning up again. The volume of tone he emitted with out effort, almost without the trouble of moving his lips, amazed me. A voice! a voice! It was grave, profound, vibrating, while the man did not seem capable of a whisper. However, he had enough strength in him—factitious no doubt—to very nearly make an end of us, as you shall hear directly.

"The manager appeared silently in the doorway; I stepped out at once and he drew the curtain after me. The Russian, eyed curiously by the pilgrims, was staring at the shore. I followed the direction of his glance.

"Dark human shapes could be made out in the distance, flitting indistinctly against the gloomy border of the forest, and near the river two bronze figures, leaning on tall spears, stood in the sunlight under fantastic head-dresses of spotted skins, warlike and still in statuesque repose. And from right to left along the lighted shore moved a wild and gorgeous apparition of a woman.

"She walked with measured steps, draped in striped

and fringed cloths, treading the earth proudly, with a
slight jingle and flash of barbarous ornaments. She carried her head high; her hair was done in the shape of a
helmet; she had brass leggings to the knee, brass wire
gauntlets to the elbow, a crimson spot on her tawny cheek,
innumerable necklaces of glass beads on her neck; bizarre
things, charms, gifts of witch-men, that hung about her,
glittered and trembled at every step. She must have had
the value of several elephant tusks upon her. She was
savage and superb, wild-eyed and magnificent; there was
something ominous and stately in her deliberate progress.
And in the hush that had fallen suddenly upon the whole
sorrowful land, the immense wilderness, the colossal body
of the fecund and mysterious life seemed to look at her,
pensive, as though it had been looking at the image of its
own tenebrous and passionate soul.

"She came abreast of the steamer, stood still, and faced
us. Her long shadow fell to the water's edge. Her face
had a tragic and fierce aspect of wild sorrow and of
dumb pain mingled with the fear of some struggling, half-
shaped resolve. She stood looking at us without a stir,
and like the wilderness itself, with an air of brooding
over an inscrutable purpose. A whole minute passed, and
then she made a step forward. There was a low jingle,
a glint of yellow metal, a sway of fringed draperies, and
she stopped as if her heart had failed her. The young fellow by my side growled. The pilgrims murmured at my
back. She looked at us all as if her life had depended upon
the unswerving steadiness of her glance. Suddenly she
opened her bared arms and threw them up rigid above
her head, as though in an uncontrollable desire to touch
the sky, and at the same time the swift shadows darted
out on the earth, swept around on the river, gathering
the steamer into a shadowy embrace. A formidable silence
hung over the scene.

"She turned away slowly, walked on, following the

bank, and passed into the bushes to the left. Once only her eyes gleamed back at us in the dusk of the thickets before she disappeared.

"'If she had offered to come aboard I really think I would have tried to shoot her,' said the man of patches, nervously. 'I have been risking my life every day for the last fortnight to keep her out of the house. She got in one day and kicked up a row about those miserable rags I picked up in the storeroom to mend my clothes with. I wasn't decent. At least it must have been that, for she talked like a fury to Kurtz for an hour, pointing at me now and then. I don't understand the dialect of this tribe. Luckily for me, I fancy Kurtz felt too ill that day to care, or there would have been mischief. I don't understand. . . . No—it's too much for me. Ah, well, it's all over now.'

"At this moment I heard Kurtz's deep voice behind the curtain: 'Save me!—save the ivory, you mean. Don't tell me. Save *me!* Why, I've had to save you. You are interrupting my plans now. Sick! Sick! Not so sick as you would like to believe. Never mind. I'll carry my ideas out yet—I will return. I'll show you what can be done. You with your little peddling notions—you are interfering with me. I will return. I . . .'

"The manager came out. He did me the honor to take me under the arm and lead me aside. 'He is very low, very low,' he said. He considered it necessary to sigh, but neglected to be consistently sorrowful. 'We have done all we could for him—haven't we? But there is no disguising the fact, Mr. Kurtz has done more harm than good to the Company. He did not see the time was not ripe for vigorous action. Cautiously, cautiously—that's my principle. We must be cautious yet. The district is closed to us for a time. Deplorable! Upon the whole, the trade will suffer. I don't deny there is a remarkable quantity of ivory—mostly fossil. We must save it, at all events—

but look how precarious the position is—and why? Because the method is unsound.' 'Do you,' said I, looking
at the shore, 'call it "unsound method"?' 'Without doubt,'
he exclaimed, hotly. 'Don't you?' . . . 'No method at
all,' I murmured after a while. 'Exactly,' he exulted. 'I
anticipated this. Shows a complete want of judgment. It
is my duty to point it out in the proper quarter.' 'Oh,'
said I, 'that fellow—what's his name?—the brickmaker,
will make a readable report for you.' He appeared confounded for a moment. It seemed to me I had never
breathed an atmosphere so vile, and I turned mentally to
Kurtz for relief—positively for relief. 'Nevertheless I
think Mr. Kurtz is a remarkable man,' I said with
emphasis. He started, dropped on me a cold heavy glance,
said very quietly, 'he *was*,' and turned his back on me
My hour of favor was over; I found myself lumped
along with Kurtz as a partisan of methods for which the
time was not ripe: I was unsound! Ah! but it was something to have at least a choice of nightmares.

"I had turned *to* the wilderness really, not to Mr.
Kurtz, who, I was ready to admit, was as good as buried
And for a moment it seemed to me as if I also were
buried in a vast grave full of unspeakable secrets. I felt
an intolerable weight oppressing my breast, the smell of
the damp earth, the unseen presence of victorious cor-
ruption, the darkness of an impenetrable night. . . . The
Russian tapped me on the shoulder. I heard him mumbling
and stammering something about 'brother seaman—
couldn't conceal—knowledge of matters that would affect
Mr. Kurtz's reputation.' I waited. For him evidently Mr.
Kurtz was not in his grave; I suspect that for him Mr.
Kurtz was one of the immortals. 'Well!' said I at last,
'speak out. As it happens, I am Mr. Kurtz's friend—in
a way.'

"He stated with a good deal of formality that had we
not been 'of the same profession,' he would have kept the

matter to himself without regard to consequences. 'He suspected there was an active ill will towards him on the part of these white men that—' 'You are right,' I said, remembering a certain conversation I had overheard. 'The manager thinks you ought to be hanged.' He showed a concern at this intelligence which amused me at first. 'I had better get out of the way quietly,' he said, earnestly. 'I can do no more for Kurtz now, and they would soon find some excuse. What's to stop them? There's a military post three hundred miles from here.' 'Well, upon my word,' said I, 'perhaps you had better go if you have any friends amongst the savages near by.' 'Plenty,' he said. 'They are simple people—and I want nothing, you know.' He stood biting his lip, then: 'I don't want any harm to happen to these whites here, but of course I was thinking of Mr. Kurtz's reputation—but you are a brother seaman and—' 'All right,' said I, after a time. 'Mr. Kurtz's reputation is safe with me.' I did not know how truly I spoke.

"He informed me, lowering his voice, that it was Kurtz who had ordered the attack to be made on the steamer. 'He hated sometimes the idea of being taken away—and then again. . . . But I don't understand these matters. I am a simple man. He thought it would scare you away— that you would give it up, thinking him dead. I could not stop him. Oh, I had an awful time of it this last month.' 'Very well,' I said. 'He is all right now.' 'Ye-e-es,' he muttered, not very convinced apparently. 'Thanks,' said I; 'I shall keep my eyes open.' 'But quiet—eh?' he urged, anxiously. 'It would be awful for his reputation if anybody here— I promised a complete discretion with great gravity. 'I have a canoe and three black fellows waiting not very far. I am off. Could you give me a few Martini-Henry cartridges?' I could, and did, with proper secrecy. He helped himself, with a wink at me, to a handful of my tobacco. 'Between sailors—you know—good English tobacco.' At the door of the pilot-house he turned round—'I say, haven't you a pair of shoes you could spare?' He raised one leg. 'Look.' The soles were tied with knotted strings sandal-wise under his bare feet. I rooted out an old pair, at which he looked with admiration before tucking them under his left arm. One of his pockets (bright red) was bulging with cartridges, from the other (dark blue) peeped 'Towson's Inquiry,' etc., etc. He seemed to think himself excellently well equipped for a renewed encounter with the wilderness. 'Ah! I'll never, never meet such a man again. You ought to have heard him recite poetry—his own, too, it was, he told me. Poetry!' He rolled his eyes at the recollection of these delights. 'Oh, he enlarged my mind!' 'Good-by,' said I. He shook hands and vanished in the night. Sometimes I ask myself whether I had ever really seen him—whether it was possible to meet such a phenomenon! . . .

"When I woke up shortly after midnight his warning came to my mind with its hint of danger that seemed, in the starred darkness, real enough to make me get up for the purpose of having a look round. On the hill a big fire burned, illuminating fitfully a crooked corner of the station-house. One of the agents with a picket of a few of our blacks, armed for the purpose, was keeping guard over the ivory; but deep within the forest, red gleams that wavered, that seemed to sink and rise from the ground amongst confused columnar shapes of intense blackness, showed the exact position of the camp where Mr. Kurtz's adorers were keeping their uneasy vigil. The monotonous beating of a big drum filled the air with muffled shocks and a lingering vibration. A steady droning sound of many men chanting each to himself some weird incantation came out from the black, flat wall of the woods as the humming of bees comes out of a hive, and had a strange narcotic effect upon my half-awake senses. I believe I dozed off leaning over the rail, till an abrupt burst of yells, an overwhelming outbreak of a pent-up and mysterious frenzy, woke me up in a bewildered wonder. It was cut short all at once, and the low droning went on with an effect of audible and soothing silence. I glanced casually into the little cabin. A light was burning within, but Mr. Kurtz was not there.

"I think I would have raised an outcry if I had be-lieved my eyes. But I didn't believe them at first—the thing seemed so impossible. The fact is I was completely unnerved by a sheer blank fright, pure abstract terror, unconnected with any distinct shape of physical danger. What made this emotion so overpowering was—how shall I define it?—the moral shock I received, as if something altogether monstrous, intolerable to thought and odious to the soul, had been thrust upon me unexpectedly. This lasted of course the merest fraction of a second, and then the usual sense of commonplace, deadly danger, the pos-sibility of a sudden onslaught and massacre, or something of the kind, which I saw impending, was positively wel-come and composing. It pacified me, in fact, so much, that I did not raise an alarm.

"There was an agent buttoned up inside an ulster and sleeping on a chair on deck within three feet of me. The yells had not awakened him; he snored very slightly; I left him to his slumbers and leaped ashore. I did not be-tray Mr. Kurtz—it was ordered I should never betray him—it was written I should be loyal to the nightmare of my choice. I was anxious to deal with this shadow by my-self alone,—and to this day I don't know why I was so jealous of sharing with any one the peculiar blackness of that experience.

"As soon as I got on the bank I saw a trail—a broad trail through the grass. I remember the exultation with which I said to myself, 'He can't walk—he is crawling on all-fours—I've got him.' The grass was wet with dew. I strode rapidly with clenched fists. I fancy I had some

vague notion of falling upon him and giving him a drub
bing. I don't know. I had some imbecile thoughts. The
knitting old woman with the cat obtruded herself upon my
memory as a most improper person to be sitting at the
other end of such an affair. I saw a row of pilgrims squirting lead in the air out of Winchesters held to the hip. I
thought I would never get back to the steamer, and imagined myself living alone and unarmed in the woods to
an advanced age. Such silly things—you know. And I
remember I confounded the beat of the drum with the
beating of my heart, and was pleased at its calm regularity.

"I kept to the track though—then stopped to listen.
The night was very clear; a dark blue space, sparkling
with dew and starlight, in which black things stood very
still. I thought I could see a kind of motion ahead of me.
I was strangely cocksure of everything that night. I actually left the track and ran in a wide semicircle (I verily
believe chuckling to myself) so as to get in front of that
stir, of that motion I had seen—if indeed I had seen anything. I was circumventing Kurtz as though it had been a
boyish game.

"I came upon him, and, if he had not heard me coming, I would have fallen over him, too, but he got up in
time. He rose, unsteady, long, pale, indistinct, like a vapor
exhaled by the earth, and swayed slightly, misty and silent
before me; while at my back the fires loomed between the
trees, and the murmur of many voices issued from the
forest. I had cut him off cleverly; but when actually con-
fronting him I seemed to come to my senses, I saw the
danger in its right proportion. It was by no means over
yet. Suppose he began to shout? Though he could hardly
stand, there was still plenty of vigor in his voice. 'Go
away—hide yourself,' he said, in that profound tone. It
was very awful. I glanced back. We were within thirty
yards from the nearest fire. A black figure stood up, strode
on long black legs, waving long black arms, across the

glow. It had horns—antelope horns, I think—on its head.
Some sorcerer, some witch-man, no doubt: it looked fiend-
like enough. 'Do you know what you are doing?' I whispered. 'Perfectly,' he answered, raising his voice for that
single word: it sounded to me far off and yet loud, like
a hail through a speaking-trumpet. If he makes a row we
are lost, I thought to myself. This clearly was not a case
for fisticuffs, even apart from the very natural aversion
I had to beat that Shadow—this wandering and tormented
thing. 'You will be lost,' I said—'utterly lost.' One gets
sometimes such a flash of inspiration, you know. I did
say the right thing, though indeed he could not have been
more irretrievably lost than he was at this very moment,
when the foundations of our intimacy were being laid—
to endure—to endure—even to the end—even beyond.

" 'I had immense plans,' he muttered irresolutely. 'Yes,'
said I; 'but if you try to shout I'll smash your head
with—' There was not a stick or a stone near. 'I will
throttle you for good,' I corrected myself. 'I was on the
threshold of great things,' he pleaded, in a voice of longing, with a wistfulness of tone that made my blood run
cold. 'And now for this stupid scoundrel—' 'Your success
in Europe is assured in any case,' I affirmed, steadily. I
did not want to have the throttling of him, you understand
—and indeed it would have been very little use for any
practical purpose. I tried to break the spell—the heavy,
mute spell of the wilderness—that seemed to draw him to
its pitiless breast by the awakening of forgotten and brutal
instincts, by the memory of gratified and monstrous passions. This alone, I was convinced, had driven him out to
the edge of the forest, to the bush, towards the gleam of
fires, the throb of drums, the drone of weird incantations;
this alone had beguiled his. unlawful soul beyond the
bounds of permitted aspirations. And, don't you see, the
terror of the position was not in being knocked on the
head—though I had a very lively sense of that danger,

too—but in this, that I had to deal with a being to whom I could not appeal in the name of anything high or low. I had, even like the niggers, to invoke him—himself—his own exalted and incredible degradation. There was nothing either above or below him, and I knew it. He had kicked himself loose of the earth. Confound the man! he had kicked the very earth to pieces. He was alone, and I before him did not know whether I stood on the ground or floated in the air. I've been telling you what we said—repeating the phrases we pronounced—but what's the good? They were common everyday words—the familiar, vague sounds exchanged on every waking day of life. But what of that? They had behind them, to my mind, the terrific suggestiveness of words heard in dreams, of phrases spoken in nightmares. Soul! If anybody had ever struggled with a soul, I am the man. And I wasn't arguing with a lunatic either. Believe me or not, his intelligence was perfectly clear—concentrated, it is true, upon himself with horrible intensity, yet clear; and therein was my only chance—barring, of course, the killing him there and then, which wasn't so good, on account of unavoidable noise. But his soul was mad. Being alone in the wilderness, it had looked within itself, and, by heavens! I tell you, it had gone mad. I had—for my sins, I suppose—to go through the ordeal of looking into it myself. No eloquence could have been so withering to one's belief in mankind as his final burst of sincerity. He struggled with himself, too. I saw it,—I heard it. I saw the inconceivable mystery of a soul that knew no restraint, no faith, and no fear, yet struggling blindly with itself. I kept my head pretty well; but when I had him at last stretched on the couch, I wiped my forehead, while my legs shook under me as though I had carried half a ton on my back down that hill. And yet I had only supported him, his bony arm clasped round my neck—and he was not much heavier than a child.

"When next day we left at noon, the crowd, of whose

presence behind the curtain of trees I had been acutely conscious all the time, flowed out of the woods again, filled the clearing, covered the slope with a mass of naked, breathing, quivering, bronze bodies. I steamed up a bit, then swung downstream, and two thousand eyes followed the evolutions of the splashing, thumping, fierce river-demon beating the water with its terrible tail and breathing black smoke into the air. In front of the first rank, along the river, three men, plastered with bright red earth from head to foot, strutted to and fro restlessly. When we came abreast again, they faced the river, stamped their feet, nodded their horned heads, swayed their scarlet bodies; they shook towards the fierce river-demon a bunch of black feathers, a mangy skin with a pendent tail—something that looked like a dried gourd; they shouted periodically together strings of amazing words that resembled no sounds of human language; and the deep murmurs of the crowd, interrupted suddenly, were like the responses of some satanic litany.

"We had carried Kurtz into the pilot-house: there was more air there. Lying on the couch, he stared through the open shutter. There was an eddy in the mass of human bodies, and the woman with helmeted head and tawny cheeks rushed out to the very brink of the stream. She put out her hands, shouted something, and all that wild mob took up the shout in a roaring chorus of articulated, rapid, breathless utterance.

"'Do you understand this?' I asked.

"He kept on looking out past me with fiery, longing eyes, with a mingled expression of wistfulness and hate. He made no answer, but I saw a smile, a smile of indefinable meaning, appear on his colorless lips that a moment after twitched convulsively. 'Do I not?' he said slowly, gasping, as if the words had been torn out of him by a supernatural power.

"I pulled the string of the whistle, and I did this be-

cause I saw the pilgrims on deck getting out their rifles
with an air of anticipating a jolly lark. At the sudden
screech there was a movement of abject terror through
that wedged mass of bodies. 'Don't! don't you frighten
them away,' cried some one on deck disconsolately. I
pulled the string time after time. They broke and ran, they
leaped, they crouched, they swerved, they dodged the flying terror of the sound. The three red chaps had fallen
flat, face down on the shore, as though they had been shot
dead. Only the barbarous and superb woman did not so
much as flinch, and stretched tragically her bare arms after
us over the somber and glittering river.

"And then that imbecile crowd down on the deck started
their little fun, and I could see nothing more for smoke.

"The brown current ran swiftly out of the heart of
darkness, bearing us down towards the sea with twice the
speed of our upward progress; and Kurtz's life was running swiftly, too, ebbing, ebbing out of his heart into the
sea of inexorable time. The manager was very placid, he
had no vital anxieties now, he took us both in with a com-
prehensive and satisfied glance: the 'affair' had come off
as well as could be wished. I saw the time approaching
when I would be left alone of the party of 'unsound
method.' The pilgrims looked upon me with disfavor. I
was, so to speak, numbered with the dead. It is strange
how I accepted this unforeseen partnership, this choice of
nightmares forced upon me in the tenebrous land invaded
by these mean and greedy phantoms.

"Kurtz discoursed. A voice! a voice! It rang deep to
the very last. It survived his strength to hide in the magnificent folds of eloquence the barren darkness of his
heart. Oh, he struggled! he struggled! The wastes of his
weary brain were haunted by shadowy images now—images of wealth and fame revolving obsequiously round
his unextinguishable gift of noble and lofty expression.

My Intended, my station, my career, my ideas—these were the subjects for the occasional utterances of elevated sentiments. The shade of the original Kurtz frequented the bedside of the hollow sham, whose fate it was to be buried presently in the mold of primeval earth. But both the diabolic love and the unearthly hate of the mysteries it had penetrated fought for the possession of that soul satiated with primitive emotions, avid of lying fame, of sham distinction, of all the appearances of success and power.

"Sometimes he was contemptibly childish. He desired to have kings meet him at railway stations on his return from some ghastly Nowhere, where he intended to accomplish great things. 'You show them you have in you something that is really profitable, and then there will be no limits to the recognition of your ability,' he would say. 'Of course you must take care of the motives—right motives—always.' The long reaches that were like one and the same reach, monotonous bends that were exactly alike, slipped past the steamer with their multitude of secular trees looking patiently after this grimy fragment of another world, the forerunner of change, of conquest, of trade, of massacres, of blessings. I looked ahead—piloting. 'Close the shutter,' said Kurtz suddenly one day; 'I can't bear to look at this.' I did so. There was a silence. 'Oh, but I will wring your heart yet!' he cried at the invisible wilderness.

"We broke down—as I had expected—and had to lie up for repairs at the head of an island. This delay was the first thing that shook Kurtz's confidence. One morning he gave me a packet of papers and a photograph—the lot tied together with a shoestring. 'Keep this for me,' he said. 'This noxious fool' (meaning the manager) 'is capable of prying into my boxes when I am not looking.' In the afternoon I saw him. He was lying on his back with closed eyes, and I withdrew quietly, but I heard him mutter, 'Live rightly, die, die. . . .' I listened. There was nothing more. Was he rehearsing some speech in his sleep, or was it a fragment of a phrase from some newspaper article? He had been writing for the papers and meant to do so again, 'for the furthering of my ideas. It's a duty.'

"His was an impenetrable darkness. I looked at him as you peer down at a man who is lying at the bottom of a precipice where the sun never shines. But I had not much time to give him, because I was helping the engine-driver to take to pieces the leaky cylinders, to straighten a bent connecting-rod, and in other such matters. I lived in an infernal mess of rust, filings, nuts, bolts, spanners, hammers, ratchet-drills—things I abominate, because I don't get on with them. I tended the little forge we fortunately had aboard; I toiled wearily in a wretched scrap-heap—unless I had the shakes too bad to stand.

"One evening coming in with a candle I was startled to hear him say a little tremulously, 'I am lying here in the dark waiting for death.' The light was within a foot of his eyes. I forced myself to murmur, 'Oh, nonsense!' and stood over him as if transfixed.

"Anything approaching the change that came over his features I have never seen before, and hope never to see again. Oh, I wasn't touched. I was fascinated. It was as though a veil had been rent. I saw on that ivory face the expression of somber pride, of ruthless power, of craven terror—of an intense and hopeless despair. Did he live his life again in every detail of desire, temptation, and surrender during that supreme moment of complete knowledge? He cried in a whisper at some image, at some vision —he cried out twice, a cry that was no more than a breath—

" 'The horror! The horror!'

"I blew the candle out and left the cabin. The pilgrims were dining in the mess-room, and I took my place opposite the manager, who lifted his eyes to give me a questioning glance, which I successfully ignored. He leaned back, serene, with that peculiar smile of his sealing the un-expressed depths of his meanness. A continuous shower of small flies streamed upon the lamp, upon the cloth, upon our hands and faces. Suddenly the manager's boy put his insolent black head in the doorway, and said in a tone of scathing contempt—

" 'Mistah Kurtz—he dead.'

"All the pilgrims rushed out to see. I remained, and went on with my dinner. I believe I was considered brutally callous. However, I did not eat much. There was a lamp in there—light, don't you know—and outside it was so beastly, beastly dark. I went no more near the remarkable man who had pronounced a judgment upon the adventures of his soul on this earth. The voice was gone. What else had been there? But I am of course aware that next day the pilgrims buried something in a muddy hole.

"And then they very nearly buried me.

"However, as you see, I did not go to join Kurtz there and then. I did not. I remained to dream the nightmare out to the end, and to show my loyalty to Kurtz once more. Destiny. My destiny! Droll thing life is—that mysterious arrangement of merciless logic for a futile purpose. The most you can hope from it is some knowledge of your-self—that comes too late—a crop of unextinguishable regrets. I have wrestled with death. It is the most unex-citing contest you can imagine. It takes place in an im-palpable grayness, with nothing underfoot, with nothing around, without spectators, without clamor, without glory, without the great desire of victory, without the great fear of defeat, in a sickly atmosphere of tepid skepticism, without much belief in your own right, and still less in that of your adversary. If such is the form of ultimate wisdom, then life is a greater riddle than some of us think it to be. I was within a hair's breadth of the last oppor-tunity for pronouncement, and I found with humiliation that probably I would have nothing to say. This is the reason why I affirm that Kurtz was a remarkable man. He had something to say. He said it. Since I had peeped over the edge myself, I understand better the meaning of his stare, that could not see the flame of the candle, but was wide enough to embrace the whole universe, piercing enough to penetrate all the hearts that beat in the darkness. He had summed up—he had judged. 'The horror!' He was a remarkable man. After all, this was the expression of some sort of belief; it had candor, it had conviction, it had a vibrating note of revolt in its whisper, it had the appalling face of a glimpsed truth—the strange commingling of desire and hate. And it is not my own extremity I remember best—a vision of grayness without form filled with physical pain, and a careless contempt for the evanescence of all things—even of this pain itself. No! It is his extremity that I seem to have lived through. True, he had made that last stride, he had stepped over the edge, while I had been permitted to draw back my hesitating foot. And perhaps in this is the whole difference; perhaps all the wisdom, and all truth, and all sincerity, are just compressed into that inappreciable moment of time in which we step over the threshold of the invisible. Perhaps! I like to think my summing-up would not have been a word of careless contempt. Better his cry—much better. It was an affirmation, a moral victory paid for by innumerable defeats, by abominable terrors, by abominable satisfactions. But it was a victory! That is why I have remained loyal to Kurtz to the last, and even beyond, when a long time after I heard once more, not his own choice, but the echo of his magnificent eloquence thrown to me from a soul as translucently pure as a cliff of crystal.

"No, they did not bury me, though there is a period of time which I remember mistily, with a shuddering wonder, like a passage through some inconceivable world that had no hope in it and no desire. I found myself back in the sepulchral city resenting the sight of people hurrying through the streets to filch a little money from each other, to devour their infamous cookery, to gulp their unwholesome beer, to dream their insignificant and silly dreams. They trespassed upon my thoughts. They were intruders whose knowledge of life was to me an irritating pretense, because I felt so sure they could not possibly know the things I knew. Their bearing, which was simply the bearing of commonplace individuals going about their business in the assurance of perfect safety, was offensive to me like the outrageous flauntings of folly in the face of a danger it is unable to comprehend. I had no particular desire to enlighten them, but I had some difficulty in restraining myself from laughing in their faces, so full of stupid importance. I daresay I was not very well at that time. I tottered about the streets—there were various affairs to settle—grinning bitterly at perfectly respectable persons. I admit my behavior was inexcusable, but then my temperature was seldom normal in these days. My dear aunt's endeavors to 'nurse up my strength' seemed altogether beside the mark. It was not my strength that wanted nursing, it was my imagination that wanted soothing. I kept the bundle of papers given me by Kurtz, not knowing exactly what to do with it. His mother had died lately, watched over, as I was told, by his Intended. A clean-shaved man, with an official manner and wearing gold-rimmed spectacles, called on me one day and made inquiries, at first circuitous, afterwards suavely pressing, about what he was pleased to denominate certain 'documents.' I was not surprised, because I had had two rows with the manager on the subject out there. I had refused to give up the smallest scrap out of that package, and I took the same attitude with the spectacled man. He became darkly menacing at last, and with much heat argued that the Company had the right to every bit of information about its 'territories.' And said he, 'Mr. Kurtz's knowledge of unexplored regions must have been necessarily extensive and peculiar—owing to his great abilities and to the deplorable circumstances in which he had been placed: therefore—' I assured him Mr. Kurtz's knowledge, however extensive, did not bear upon the problems of commerce or administration. He invoked then the name of science. 'It would be an incalculable loss if,' etc., etc. I offered him the report on the 'Supression of Savage Customs,' with the postscriptum torn off. He took it up eagerly, but ended by sniffing at it with an air of contempt. 'This is not what we had a right to expect,' he remarked. 'Expect nothing else,' I said. 'There are only private letters.' He withdrew upon some threat of legal proceedings, and I saw him no more; but another fellow, calling himself Kurtz's cousin, appeared two days later, and was anxious to hear all the details about his dear relative's last moments. Incidentally he gave me to understand that Kurtz had been essentially a great musician. There was the making of an immense success,' said the man, who was an organist, I believe, with lank gray hair flowing over a greasy coat-collar. I had no reason to doubt his statement; and to this day I am unable to say what was Kurtz's profession, whether he ever had any—which was the greatest of his talents. I had taken him for a painter who wrote for the papers, or else for a journalist who could paint—but even the cousin (who took snuff during the interview) could not tell me what he had been—exactly. He was a universal genius—on that point I agreed with the old chap, who thereupon blew his nose noisily into a large cotton handkerchief and withdrew in senile agitation, bearing off some family letters and memoranda without importance. Ultimately a journalist anxious to know something of the fate of his 'dear colleague' turned up. This visitor informed me Kurtz's proper sphere ought to have been politics 'on the popular side.' He had furry straight eyebrows, bristly hair cropped short, an eye-glass on a broad ribbon, and, becoming expansive confessed his opinion that Kurtz really couldn't write a bit—'but heavens! how that man could talk. He electrified large meetings. He had faith—don't you see?—he had the faith. He could get himself to believe anything—anything. He would have been a splendid leader of an extreme party.' 'What party?' I asked. 'Any party,' answered the other. 'He was an—an—extremist.' Did I not think so? I assented. Did I know, he asked, with a sudden flash of curiosity, 'what it was that had induced him to go out there?' 'Yes,' said I, and forthwith handed him the famous Report for publication, if he thought fit. He glanced through it hurriedly, mumbling all the time, judged 'it would do,' and took himself off with this plunder.

"Thus I was left at last with a slim packet of letters and the girl's portrait. She struck me as beautiful—I mean she had a beautiful expression. I know that the sunlight can be made to lie, too, yet one felt that no manipulation of light and pose could have conveyed the delicate shade of truthfulness upon those features. She seemed ready to listen without mental reservation, without suspicion, without a thought for herself. I concluded I would go and give her back her portrait and those letters myself. Curiosity? Yes; and also some other feeling perhaps. All that had been Kurtz's had passed out of my hands: his soul, his body, his station, his plans, his ivory, his career. There remained only his memory and his Intended—and I wanted to give that up, too, to the past, in a way—to surrender personally all that remained of him with me to that oblivion which is the last word of our common fate. I don't defend myself. I had no clear perception of what it was I really wanted. Perhaps it was an impulse of unconscious loyalty, or the fulfillment of one of those ironic necessities that lurk in the facts of human existence. I don't know. I can't tell. But I went.

"I thought his memory was like the other memories

of the dead that accumulate in every man's life—a vague impress on the brain of shadows that had fallen on it in their swift and final passage; but before the high and ponderous door, between the tall houses of a street as still and decorous as a well-kept alley in a cemetery, I had a vision of him on the stretcher, opening his mouth voraciously, as if to devour all the earth with all its mankind. He lived then before me; he lived as much as he had ever lived—a shadow insatiable of splendid appearances, of frightful realities; a shadow darker than the shadow of the night, and draped nobly in the folds of a gorgeous eloquence. The vision seemed to enter the house with me —the stretcher, the phantom-bearers, the wild crowd of obedient worshipers, the gloom of the forests, the glitter of the reach between the murky bends, the beat of the drum, regular and muffled like the beating of a heart—the heart of a conquering darkness. It was a moment of triumph for the wilderness, an invading and vengeful rush which, it seemed to me, I would have to keep back alone for the salvation of another soul. And the memory of what I had heard him say afar there, with the horned shapes stirring at my back, in the glow of fires, within the patient woods, those broken phrases came back to me, were heard again in their ominous and terrifying simplicity. I remembered his abject pleading, his abject threats, the colossal scale of his vile desires, the meanness, the torment, the tempestuous anguish of his soul. And later on I seemed to see his collected languid manner, when he said one day, 'This lot of ivory now is really mine. The Company did not pay for it. I collected it myself at a very great personal risk. I am afraid they will try to claim it as theirs though. H'm. It is a difficult case. What do you think I ought to do—resist? Eh? I want no more than justice.' . . . He wanted no more than justice—no more than justice. I rang the bell before a mahogany door on the first floor, and while I waited he seemed to stare at me out of the glassy panel—stare with that wide and immense stare embracing, condemning, loathing all the universe. I seemed to hear the whispered cry, 'The horror! The horror!'

"The dusk was falling. I had to wait in a lofty drawing-room with three long windows from floor to ceiling that were like three luminous and bedraped columns. The bent gilt legs and backs of the furniture shone in indistinct curves. The tall marble fireplace had a cold and monumental whiteness. A grand piano stood massively in a corner; with dark gleams on the flat surfaces like a somber and polished sarcophagus. A high door opened—closed. I rose.

"She came forward, all in black, with a pale head, floating towards me in the dusk. She was in mourning. It was more than a year since his death, more than a year since the news came; she seemed as though she would remember and mourn forever. She took both my hands in hers and murmured, 'I had heard you were coming.' I noticed she was not very young—I mean not girlish. She had a mature capacity for fidelity, for belief, for suffering. The room seemed to have grown darker, as if all the sad light of the cloudy evening had taken refuge on her forehead. This fair hair, this pale visage, this pure brow, seemed surrounded by an ashy halo from which the dark eyes looked out at me. Their glance was guileless, profound, confident, and trustful. She carried her sorrowful head as though she were proud of that sorrow, as though she would say, I—I alone know how to mourn him as he deserves. But while we were still shaking hands, such a look of awful desolation came upon her face that I perceived she was one of those creatures that are not the playthings of Time. For her he had died only yesterday. And, by Jove! the impression was so powerful that for me, too, he seemed to have died only yesterday—nay, this very minute. I saw her and him in the same instant of time—his death and her sorrow—I saw her sorrow in the very moment of his death. Do you understand? I saw them together—I heard them together. She had said, with a deep catch of the breath, 'I have survived' while my strained ears seemed to hear distinctly, mingled with her tone of despairing regret, the summing up whisper of his eternal condemnation. I asked myself what I was doing there, with a sensation of panic in my heart as though I had blundered into a place of cruel and absurd mysteries not fit for a human being to behold. She motioned me to a chair. We sat down. I laid the packet gently on the little table, and she put her hand over it. . . . 'You knew him well,' she murmured, after a moment of mourning silence.

" 'Intimacy grows quickly out there,' I said. 'I knew him as well as it is possible for one man to know another.'

" 'And you admired him,' she said. 'It was impossible to know him and not to admire him. Was it?'

" 'He was a remarkable man,' I said, unsteadily. Then before the appealing fixity of her gaze, that seemed to watch for more words on my lips, I went on, 'It was impossible not to—'

" 'Love him,' she finished eagerly, silencing me into an appalled dumbness. 'How true! how true! But when you think that no one knew him so well as I! I had all his noble confidence. I knew him best.'

" 'You knew him best,' I repeated. And perhaps she did. But with every word spoken the room was growing darker, and only her forehead, smooth and white, remained illumined by the unextinguishable light of belief and love.

" 'You were his friend,' she went on. 'His friend,' she repeated, a little louder. 'You must have been, if he had given you this, and sent you to me. I feel I can speak to you—and oh! I must speak. I want you—you have heard his last words—to know I have been worthy of him. . . . It is not pride. . . . Yes! I am proud to know I understood him better than any one on earth—he told me so himself. And since his mother died I have had no one— no one—to—to—'

"I listened. The darkness deepened. I was not even sure he had given me the right bundle. I rather suspect he wanted me to take care of another batch of his papers which, after his death, I saw the manager examining under the lamp. And the girl talked, easing her pain in the certitude of my sympathy; she talked as thirsty men drink. I had heard that her engagement with Kurtz had been disapproved by her people. He wasn't rich enough or something. And indeed I don't know whether he had not been a pauper all his life. He had given me some reason to infer that it was his impatience of comparative poverty that drove him out there.

"'. . . Who was not his friend who had heard him speak once?' she was saying. 'He drew men towards him by what was best in them.' She looked at me with intensity. 'It is the gift of the great,' she went on, and the sound of her low voice seemed to have the accompaniment of all the other sounds, full of mystery, desolation, and sorrow, I had ever heard—the ripple of the river, the soughing of the trees swayed by the wind, the murmurs of the crowds, the faint ring of incomprehensible words cried from afar, the whisper of a voice speaking from beyond the threshold of an eternal darkness. 'But you have heard him! You know!' she cried.

"'Yes, I know,' I said with something like despair in my heart, but bowing my head before the faith that was in her, before that great and saving illusion that shone with an unearthly glow in the darkness, in the triumphant darkness from which I could not have defended her—from which I could not even defend myself.

"'What a loss to me—to us!'—she corrected herself with beautiful generosity; then added in a murmur, 'To the world.' By the last gleams of twilight I could see the glitter of her eyes, full of tears—of tears that would not fall.

"'I have been very happy—very fortunate—very proud,' she went on. 'Too fortunate. Too happy for a little while. And now I am unhappy for—for life.'

"She stood up; her fair hair seemed to catch all the remaining light in a glimmer of gold. I rose, too.

"'And of all this,' she went on, mournfully, 'of all his promise, and of all his greatness, of his generous mind, of his noble heart, nothing remains—nothing but a memory. You and I—'

"'We shall always remember him,' I said, hastily.

"'No!' she cried. 'It is impossible that all this should be lost—that such a life should be sacrificed to leave nothing—but sorrow. You know what vast plans he had. I knew of them, too—I could not perhaps understand—but others knew of them. Something must remain. His words, at least, have not died.'

"'His words will remain,' I said.

"'And his example,' she whispered to herself. 'Men looked up to him—his goodness shone in every act. His example—'

"'True,' I said; 'his example, too. Yes, his example. forgot that.'

"'But I do not. I cannot—I cannot believe—not yet. I cannot believe that I shall never see him again, that nobody will see him again, never, never, never.'

"She put out her arms as if after a retreating figure, stretching them black and with clasped pale hands across the fading and narrow sheen of the window. Never see him! I saw him clearly enough then. I shall see this eloquent phantom as long as I live, and I shall see her, too, a tragic and familiar Shade, resembling in this gesture another one, tragic also, and bedecked with powerless charms, stretching bare brown arms over the glitter of the infernal stream, the stream of darkness. She said suddenly very low, 'He died as he lived.'

"'His end,' said I, with dull anger stirring in me, 'was in every way worthy of his life.''

"'And I was not with him,' she murmured. My anger subsided before a feeling of infinite pity.

"'Everything that could be done—' I mumbled.

"'Ah, but I believed in him more than any one on earth —more than his own mother, more than—himself. He needed me! Me! I would have treasured every sigh, every word, every sign, every glance.'

"I felt like a chill grip on my chest. 'Don't,' I said, in a muffled voice.

"'Forgive me. I—I—have mourned so long in silence —in silence. . . . You were with him—to the last? I think of his loneliness. Nobody near to understand him as I would have understood. Perhaps no one to hear. . . .'

"'To the very end,' I said, shakily. 'I heard his very last words. . . .' I stopped in a fright.

"'Repeat them,' she murmured in a heart-broken tone. 'I want—I want—something—something—to—live with.'

"I was on the point of crying at her, 'Don't you hear them?' The dusk was repeating them in a persistent whisper all around us, in a whisper that seemed to swell menacingly like the first whisper of a rising wind. 'The horror! The horror!'

"'His last word—to live with,' she insisted. 'Don't you understand I loved him—I loved him—I loved him!'

"I pulled myself together and spoke slowly.

"'The last word he pronounced was—your name.'

"I heard a light sigh and then my heart stood still, stopped dead short by an exulting and terrible cry, by the cry of inconceivable triumph and of unspeakable pain. 'I knew it—I was sure!' . . . She knew. She was sure. I heard her weeping; she had hidden her face in her hands. It seemed to me that the house would collapse before I could escape, that the heavens would fall upon my head. But nothing happened. The heavens do not fall for such a trifle. Would they have fallen, I wonder, if I had rendered Kurtz that justice which was his due? Hadn't he said he wanted only justice? But I couldn't. I could not tell her. It would have been too dark—too dark altogether. . . ."

Marlow ceased, and sat apart, indistinct and silent, in the pose of a meditating Buddha. Nobody moved for a time. "We have lost the first of the ebb," said the Director, suddenly. I raised my head. The offing was barred by a black bank of clouds, and the tranquil waterway leading to the uttermost ends of the earth flowed somber under an overcast sky—seemed to lead into the heart of an immense darkness.

# THE APPLE-TREE
## by John Galsworthy

"The Apple-tree, the singing, and the gold."
            —Murray's *Hippolytus of Euripides.*

On their silver-wedding day Ashurst and his wife
were motoring along the outskirts of the moor, intending
to crown the festival by stopping the night at Torquay,
where they had first met. This was the idea of Stella
Ashurst, whose character contained a streak of sentiment.
If she had long lost the blue-eyed, flower-like charm, the
cool slim purity of face and form, the apple-blossom
coloring, which had so swiftly and so oddly affected
Ashurst twenty-six years ago, she was still at forty-three
a comely and faithful companion, whose cheeks were
faintly mottled, and whose gray-blue eyes had acquired a
certain fullness.

It was she who had stopped the car where the common
rose steeply to the left, and a narrow strip of larch and
beech, with here and there a pine, stretched out towards the
valley between the road and the first long high hill of the
full moor. She was looking for a place where they might
lunch, for Ashurst never looked for anything; and this,
between the golden furze and the feathery green larches
smelling of lemons in the last sun of April—this, with a
view into the deep valley and up to the long moor heights,
seemed fitting to the decisive nature of one who sketched
in water-colors, and loved romantic spots. Grasping her
paint box, she got out.

"Won't this do, Frank?"

Ashurst, rather like a bearded Schiller, gray in the
wings, tall, long-legged, with large remote gray eyes which

sometimes filled with meaning and became almost beautiful, with nose a little to one side, and bearded lips just
open—Ashurst, forty-eight, and silent, grasped the luncheon basket, and got out too.

"Oh! Look, Frank! A grave!"

By the side of the road, where the track from the top
of the common crossed it at right angles and ran through
a gate past the narrow wood, was a thin mound of turf,
six feet by one, with a moorstone to the west, and on it
some one had thrown a blackthorn spray and a handful of
bluebells. Ashurst looked, and the poet in him moved. At
cross-roads—a suicide's grave! Poor mortals with their
superstitions! Whoever lay there, though, had the best of
it, no clammy sepulcher among other hideous graves
carved with futilities—just a rough stone, the wide sky,
and wayside blessings! And, without comment, for he had
learned not to be a philosopher in the bosom of his family,
he strode away up on to the common, dropped the luncheon basket under a wall, spread a rug for his wife to sit
on—she would turn up from her sketching when she was
hungry—and took from his pocket Murray's translation
of the "Hippolytus." He had soon finished reading of
"The Cyprian" and her revenge, and looked at the sky
instead. And watching the white clouds so bright against
the intense blue, Ashurst, on his silver-wedding day,
longed for—he knew not what. Maladjusted to life—man's
organism! One's mode of life might be high and scrupu-
lous, but there was always an undercurrent of greediness,
a hankering, and sense of waste. Did women have it too?
Who could tell? And yet, men who gave vent to their
appetites for novelty, their riotous longings for new adventures, new risks, new pleasures, these suffered, no
doubt, from the reverse side of starvation, from surfeit.
No getting out of it—a maladjusted animal, civilized
man! There could be no garden of his choosing, of "the

Apple-tree, the singing, and the gold," in the words of that lovely Greek chorus, no achievable elysium in life, or lasting haven of happiness for any man with a sense of beauty—nothing which could compare with the captured loveliness in a work of art, set down forever, so that to look on it or read was always to have the same precious sense of exaltation and restful inebriety. Life no doubt had moments with that quality of beauty, of unbidden flying rapture, but the trouble was, they lasted no longer than the span of a cloud's flight over the sun; impossible to keep them with you, as Art caught beauty and held it fast. They were fleeting as one of the glimmering or golden visions one had of the soul in nature, glimpses of its remote and brooding spirit. Here, with the sun hot on his face, a cuckoo calling from a thorn tree, and in the air the honey savor of gorse—here among the little fronds of the young fern, the starry blackthorn, while the bright clouds drifted by high above the hills and dreamy valleys —here and now was such a glimpse. But in a moment it would pass—as the face of Pan, which looks round the corner of a rock, vanishes at your stare. And suddenly he sat up. Surely there was something familiar about this view, this bit of common, that ribbon of road, the old wall behind him. While they were driving he had not been taking notice—never did; thinking of far things or of nothing—but now he saw! Twenty-six years ago, just at this time of year, from the farmhouse within half a mile of this very spot he had started for that day in Torquay whence it might be said he had never returned. And a sudden ache beset his heart; he had stumbled on just one of those past moments in his life, whose beauty and rapture he had failed to arrest, whose wings had fluttered away into the unknown; he had stumbled on a buried memory, a wild sweet time, swiftly choked and ended. And, turning on his face, he rested his chin on his hands, and stared at the short grass where the little blue milk-wort was growing. . . .

And this is what he remembered.

I

On the first of May, after their last year together at college, Frank Ashurst and his friend Robert Garton were on a tramp. They had walked that day from Brent, intending to make Chagford, but Ashurst's football knee had given out, and according to their map they had still some seven miles to go. They were sitting on a bank beside the road, where a track crossed alongside a wood, resting the knee and talking of the universe, as young men will. Both were over six feet, and thin as rails; Ashurst pale, idealistic, full of absence; Garton queer, round-the-corner, knotted, curly, like some primeval beast. Both had a literary bent; neither wore a hat. Ashurst's hair was smooth, pale, wavy, and had a way of rising on either side of his brow, as if always being flung back; Garton's was a kind of dark unfathomed mop. They had not met a soul for miles.

"My dear fellow," Garton was saying, "pity's only an effect of self-consciousness; it's a disease of the last five thousand years. The world was happier without."

Ashurst, following the clouds with his eyes, answered:

"It's the pearl in the oyster, anyway."

"My dear chap, all our modern unhappiness comes from pity. Look at animals, and Red Indians, limited to feeling their own occasional misfortunes; then look at ourselves —never free from feeling the toothaches of others. Let's get back to feeling for nobody, and have a better time."

"You'll never practice that."

Garton pensively stirred the hotch-potch of his hair.

"To attain full growth, one mustn't be squeamish. To

starve oneself emotionally's a mistake. All emotion is to the good—enriches life."

"Yes, and when it runs up against chivalry?"

"Ah! That's so English! If you speak of emotion the English always think you want something physical, and are shocked. They're afraid of passion, but not of lust—oh no!—so long as they can keep it secret."

Ashurst did not answer; he had plucked a blue floweret, and was twiddling it against the sky. A cuckoo began calling from a thorn tree. The sky, the flowers, the songs of birds! Robert was talking through his hat! And he said:

"Well, let's go on, and find some farm where we can put up." In uttering those words, he was conscious of a girl coming down from the common just above them. She was outlined against the sky, carrying a basket, and you could see that sky through the crook of her arm. And Ashurst, who saw beauty without wondering how it could advantage him, thought: 'How pretty!' The wind, blowing her dark frieze skirt against her legs, lifted her battered peacock tam-o'-shanter; her grayish blouse was worn and old, her shoes were split, her little hands rough and red, her neck browned. Her dark hair waved untidy across her broad forehead, her face was short, her upper lip short, showing a glint of teeth, her brows were straight and dark, her lashes long and dark, her nose straight; but her gray eyes were the wonder—dewy as if opened for the first time that day. She looked at Ashurst—perhaps he struck her as strange, limping along without a hat, with his large eyes on her, and his hair flung back. He could not take off what was not on his head, but put up his hand in a salute, and said:

"Can you tell us if there's a farm near here where we could stay the night? I've gone lame."

"There's only our farm near, sir." She spoke without shyness, in a pretty, soft, crisp voice.

"And where is that?"

"Down here, sir."

"Would you put us up?"

"Oh! I think we would."

"Will you show us the way?"

"Yes, sir."

He limped on, silent, and Garton took up the catechism.

"Are you a Devonshire girl?"

"No, sir."

"What then?"

"From Wales."

"Ah! I *thought* you were a Celt; so it's not your farm?"

"My aunt's, sir."

"And your uncle's?"

"He is dead."

"Who farms it, then?"

"My aunt, and my three cousins."

"But your uncle was a Devonshire man?"

"Yes, sir."

"Have you lived here long?"

"Seven years."

"And how d'you like it after Wales?"

"I don't know, sir."

"I suppose you don't remember?"

"Oh, yes! But it is different."

"I believe you!"

Ashurst broke in suddenly:

"How old are you?"

"Seventeen, sir."

"And what's your name?"

"Megan David."

"This is Robert Garton, and I am Frank Ashurst. We wanted to get on to Chagford."

"It is a pity your leg is hurting you."

Ashurst smiled, and when he smiled his face was rather beautiful.

Descending past the narrow wood, they came on the

farm suddenly—a long, low, stone-built dwelling with casement windows, in a farmyard where pigs and fowls and an old mare were straying. A short steep-up grass hill behind was crowned with a few Scotch firs, and in front, an old orchard of apple-trees, just breaking into flower, stretched down to a stream and a long wild meadow. A little boy with oblique dark eyes was shepherding a pig, and by the house door stood a woman, who came towards them. The girl said:

"It is Mrs. Narracombe, my aunt."

"Mrs. Narracombe, my aunt," had a quick, dark eye, like a mother wild-duck's, and something of the same snaky turn about her neck.

"We met your niece on the road," said Ashurst; "she thought you might perhaps put us up for the night."

Mrs. Narracombe, taking them in from head to heel, answered:

"Well, I can, if you don't mind one room. Megan, get the spare room ready, and a bowl of cream. You'll be wanting tea, I suppose."

Passing through a sort of porch made by two yew trees and some flowering-currant bushes, the girl disappeared into the house, her peacock tam-o'-shanter bright athwart that rosy-pink and the dark green of the yews.

"Will you come into the parlor and rest your leg? You'll be from college, perhaps?"

"We were, but we've gone down now."

Mrs. Narracombe nodded sagely.

The parlor, brick-floored, with bare table and shiny chairs and sofa stuffed with horsehair, seemed never to have been used, it was so terribly clean. Ashurst sat down at once on the sofa, holding his lame knee between his hands, and Mrs. Narracombe gazed at him. He was the only son of a late professor of chemistry, but people found a certain lordliness in one who was often so sublimely unconscious of them.

"Is there a stream where we could bathe?"

"There's the strame at the bottom of the orchard, but sittin' down you'll not be covered!"

"How deep?"

"Well, 'tis about a foot and a half, maybe."

"Oh! That'll do fine. Which way?"

"Down the lane, through the second gate on the right, an' the pool's by the big apple-tree that stands by itself. There's trout there, if you can tickle them."

"They're more likely to tickle us!"

Mrs. Narracombe smiled. "There'll be the tea ready when you come back."

The pool, formed by the damming of a rock, had a sandy bottom; and the big apple-tree, lowest in the orchard, grew so close that its boughs almost overhung the water: it was in leaf, and all but in flower—its crimson buds just bursting. There was not room for more than one at a time in that narrow bath, and Ashurst waited his turn, rubbing his knee and gazing at the wild meadow, all rocks and thorn trees and field flowers, with a grove of beeches beyond, raised up on a flat mound. Every bough was swinging in the wind, every spring bird calling, and a slanting sunlight dappled the grass. He thought of Theocritus, and the river Cherwell, of the moon, and the maiden with the dewy eyes; of so many things that he seemed to think of nothing; and he felt absurdly happy.

## II

During a late and sumptuous tea with eggs to it, cream and jam, and thin, fresh cakes touched with saffron, Garton descanted on the Celts. It was about the period of the Celtic awakening, and the discovery that there was Celtic blood about this family had excited one who believed that he was a Celt himself. Sprawling on a horsehair chair, with a hand-made cigarette dribbling from the corner of his curly lips, he had been plunging his cold pin-points of eyes into Ashurst's and praising the refinement of the Welsh. To come out of Wales into England was like the change from china to earthenware! Frank, as a d——d Englishman, had not of course perceived the exquisite refinement and emotional capacity of that Welsh girl! And, delicately stirring in the dark mat of his still wet hair, he explained how exactly she illustrated the writings of the Welsh bard Morgan-ap-Something in the twelfth century.

Ashurst, full length on the horsehair sofa, and jutting far beyond its end, smoked a deeply-colored pipe, and did not listen, thinking of the girl's face when she brought in a relay of cakes. It had been exactly like looking at a flower, or some other pretty sight in Nature—till, with a funny little shiver, she had lowered her glance and gone out, quiet as a mouse.

"Let's go to the kitchen," said Garton, "and see some more of her."

The kitchen was a white-washed room with rafters, to which were attached smoked hams; there were flower-pots on the window-sill, and guns hanging on nails, queer mugs, china and pewter, and portraits of Queen Victoria. A long, narrow table of plain wood was set with bowls and spoons, under a string of high-hung onions; two sheep-dogs and three cats lay here and there. On one side of the recessed fireplace sat two small boys, idle, and good as gold; on the other sat a stout, light-eyed, red-faced youth with hair and lashes the color of the tow he was running through the barrel of a gun; between them Mrs. Narra-combe dreamily stirred some savory-scented stew in a large pot. Two other youths, oblique-eyed, dark-haired, rather sly-faced, like the two little boys, were talking together and lolling against the wall; and a short, elderly, clean-shaven man in corduroys, seated in the window, was con-ning a battered journal. The girl Megan seemed the only active creature—drawing cider and passing with the jugs from cask to table. Seeing them thus about to eat, Garton said:

"Ah! If you'll let us, we'll come back when supper's over," and without waiting for an answer they withdrew again to the parlor. But the color in the kitchen, the warmth, the scents, and all those faces, heightened the bleakness of their shiny room, and they resumed their seats moodily.

"Regular gypsy type, those boys. There was only one Saxon—the fellow cleaning the gun. That girl is a very subtle study psychologically."

Ashurst's lips twitched. Garton seemed to him an ass just then. Subtle study! She was a wild flower. A creature it did you good to look at. Study!

Garton went on:

"Emotionally she would be wonderful. She wants awakening."

"Are you going to awaken her?"

Garton looked at him and smiled. "How coarse and English you are!" that curly smile seemed saying.

And Ashurst puffed his pipe. Awaken her! This fool had the best opinion of himself! He threw up the window and leaned out. Dusk had gathered thick. The farm buildings and the wheel-house were all dim and bluish, the apple-trees but a blurred wilderness; the air smelled of wood smoke from the kitchen fire. One bird going to bed later than the others was uttering a half-hearted twitter, as though surprised at the darkness. From the stable came the snuffle and stamp of a feeding horse. And away over there was the loom of the moor, and away and away the shy stars which had not as yet full light, pricking white through the deep blue heavens. A quavering owl hooted. Ashurst drew a deep breath. What a night to wander out in! A padding of unshod hoofs came up the lane, and three dim, dark shapes passed—ponies on an evening march. Their heads, black and fuzzy, showed above the gate. At the tap of his pipe, and a shower of little sparks, they shied round and scampered. A bat went fluttering past, uttering its almost inaudible "chip, chip." Ashurst held out his hand; on the upturned palm he could feel the dew. Suddenly from overhead he heard little burring boys' voices, little thumps of boots thrown down, and another voice, crisp and soft—the girl's putting them to bed, no doubt; and nine clear words: "No, Rick, you can't have the cat in bed"; then came a skirmish of giggles and gurgles, a soft slap, a laugh so low and pretty that it made him shiver a little. A blowing sound, and the glim of the candle which was fingering the dusk above, went out; silence reigned. Ashurst withdrew into the room and sat down; his knee pained him, and his soul felt gloomy.

"You go to the kitchen," he said; "I'm going to bed."

III

For Ashurst the wheel of slumber was wont to turn noiseless and slick and swift, but though he seemed sunk in sleep when his companion came up, he was really wide awake; and long after Garton, smothered in the other bed of that low-roofed room, was worshiping darkness with his upturned nose, he heard the owls. Barring the discomfort of his knee, it was not unpleasant—the cares of life did not loom large in night watches for this young man. In fact he had none; just enrolled a barrister, with literary aspirations, the world before him, no father or mother, and four hundred a year of his own. Did it matter where he went, what he did, or when he did it? His bed, too, was hard, and this preserved him from fever. He lay, sniffing the scent of the night which drifted into the low room through the open casement close to his head. Except for a definite irritation with his friend, natural when you have tramped with a man for three days, Ashurst's memories and visions that sleepless night were kindly and wistful and exciting. One vision, specially clear and unreasonable, for he had not even been conscious of noting it, was the face of the youth cleaning the gun; its intent, stolid, yet startled uplook at the kitchen doorway, quickly shifted to the girl carrying the cider jug. This red, blue-eyed, light-lashed, tow-haired face stuck as firmly in his memory as the girl's own face, so dewy and simple. But at last, in the square of darkness through the uncurtained casement, he saw day coming, and heard one hoarse and sleepy caw. Then followed silence, dead as ever, till the song of a blackbird, not properly awake, adventured into the hush. And, from staring at the framed brightening light, Ashurst fell asleep.

Next day his knee was badly swollen; the walking tour was obviously over. Garton, due back in London on the morrow, departed at midday with an ironical smile which left a scar of irritation—healed the moment his loping figure vanished round the corner of the steep lane. All day Ashurst rested his knee, in a green-painted wooden chair on the patch of grass by the yew-tree porch, where the sunlight distilled the scent of stocks and gillyflowers, and a ghost of scent from the flowering-currant bushes. Beatifically he smoked, dreamed, watched.

A farm in spring is all birth—young things coming out of bud and shell, and human beings watching over the process with faint excitement feeding and tending what has been born. So still the young man sat, that a mother-goose, with stately cross-footed waddle, brought her six yellow-necked gray-backed goslings to strop their little beaks against the grass blades at his feet. Now and again Mrs. Narracombe or the girl Megan would come and ask if he wanted anything, and he would smile and say: "Nothing, thanks. It's splendid here." Towards tea-time they came out together, bearing a long poultice of some dark stuff in a bowl, and after a long and solemn scrutiny of his swollen knee, bound it on. When they were gone, he thought of the girl's soft "Oh!"—of her pitying eyes, and the little wrinkle in her brow. And again he felt that unreasoning irritation against his departed friend, who had talked such rot about her. When she brought out his tea, he said:

"How did you like my friend, Megan?"

She forced down her upper lip, as if afraid that to smile was not polite. "He was a funny gentleman; he made us laugh. I think he is very clever."

"What did he say to make you laugh?"

"He said I was a daughter of the bards. What are they?"

"Welsh poets, who lived hundreds of years ago."

"Why am I their daughter, please?"

"He meant that you were the sort of girl they sang about."

She wrinkled her brows. "I think he likes to joke. Am I?"

"Would you believe me, if I told you?"

"Oh, yes."

"Well, I think he was right."

She smiled.

And Ashurst thought: "You *are* a pretty thing!"

"He said, too, that Joe was a Saxon type. What would that be?"

"Which is Joe? With the blue eyes and red face?"

"Yes. My uncle's nephew."

"Not your cousin, then?"

"No."

"Well, he meant that Joe was like the men who came over to England about fourteen hundred years ago, and conquered it."

"Oh! I know about them; but is he?"

"Garton's crazy about that sort of thing; but I must say Joe does look a bit Early Saxon."

"Yes."

That "yes" tickled Ashurst. It was so crisp and graceful, so conclusive, and politely acquiescent in what was evidently Greek to her.

"He said that all the other boys were regular gypsies. He should not have said that. My aunt laughed, but she didn't like it, of course, and my cousins were angry. Uncle was a farmer—farmers are not gypsies. It is wrong to hurt people."

Ashurst wanted to take her hand and give it a squeeze, but he only answered:

"Quite right, Megan. By the way, I heard you putting the little ones to bed last night."

She flushed a little. "Please to drink your tea—it is getting cold. Shall I get you some fresh?"

"Do you ever have time to do anything for yourself?"

"Oh, yes."

"I've been watching, but I haven't seen it yet."

She wrinkled her brows in a puzzled frown, and her color deepened.

When she was gone, Ashurst thought: "Did she think I was chaffing her? I wouldn't for the world!" He was at that age when to some men "Beauty's a flower," as the poet says, and inspires in them the thoughts of chivalry. Never very conscious of his surroundings, it was some time before he was aware that the youth whom Garton had called "a Saxon type" was standing outside the stable door; and a fine bit of color he made in his soiled brown velvetcords, muddy gaiters, and blue shirt; red-armed, red-faced, the sun turning his hair from tow to flax; immovably stolid, persistent, unsmiling he stood. Then, seeing Ashurst looking at him, he crossed the yard at that gait of the young countryman always ashamed not to be slow and heavy-dwelling on each leg, and disappeared round the end of the house towards the kitchen entrance. A chill came over Ashurst's mood. Clods! With all the good will in the world, how impossible to get on terms with them! And yet—see that girl! Her shoes were split, her hands rough; but—what was it? Was it really her Celtic blood, as Garton had said?—she was a lady born, a jewel, though probably she could do no more than just read and write!

The elderly, clean-shaven man he had seen last night in the kitchen had come into the yard with a dog, driving the cows to their milking. Ashurst saw that he was lame.

"You've got some good ones there!"

The lame man's face brightened. He had the upward look in his eyes which prolonged suffering often brings.

"Yeas; they'm praaper buties; gude milkers tu."

"I bet they are."

" 'Ope as yure leg's better, zurr."

"Thank you, it's getting on."

The lame man touched his own: "I know what 'tes, meself; 'tes a main worritin' thing, the knee. I've a 'ad mine bad this ten year."

Ashurst made the sound of sympathy which comes so readily from those who have an independent income, and the lame man smiled again.

"Mustn't complain, though—they mighty near 'ad it off."

"Ho!"

"Yeas; an' compared with what 'twas, 'tis almost so gude as nu."

"They've put a bandage of splendid stuff on mine."

"The maid she picks et. She'm a gude maid wi' the flowers. There's folks zeem to know the healin' in things. My mother was a rare one for that. 'Ope as yu'll zune be better, zurr. Goo ahn, therr!"

Ashurst smiled. "Wi' the flowers!" A flower herself.

That evening, after his supper of cold duck, junket, and cider, the girl came in.

"Please, auntie says—will you try a piece of our May-day cake?"

"If I may come to the kitchen for it."

"Oh, yes! You'll be missing your friend."

"Not I. But are you sure no one minds?"

"Who would mind? We shall be very pleased."

Ashurst rose too suddenly for his stiff knee, staggered
and subsided. The girl gave a little gasp, and held out
her hands. Ashurst took them, small, rough, brown;
checked his impulse to put them to his lips, and let her
pull him up. She came close beside him, offering her
shoulder. And leaning on her he walked across the room.
That shoulder seemed quite the pleasantest thing he had
ever touched. But he had presence of mind enough to
catch his stick out of the rack, and withdraw his hand
before arriving at the kitchen.

That night he slept like a top, and woke with his knee
of almost normal size. He again spent the morning in his
chair on the grass patch, scribbling down verses; but
in the afternoon he wandered about with the two little
boys Nick and Rick. It was Saturday, so they were early
home from school; quick, shy, dark little rascals of seven
and six, soon talkative, for Ashurst had a way with children. By four o'clock they had shown him all their methods
of destroying life, except the tickling of trout; and
with breeches tucked up, lay on their stomachs over the
trout stream, pretending they had this accomplishment
also. They tickled nothing, of course, for their giggling
and shouting scared every spotted thing away. Ashurst,
on a rock at the edge of the beech clump, watched them,
and listened to the cuckoos, till Nick, the elder and less
persevering, came up and stood beside him.

"The gypsy bogle zets on that stone," he said.

"What gypsy bogle?"

"Dunno; never zeen 'e. Megan zays 'e zets there; an'
old Jim zeed 'e once. 'E was zettin' there naight afore our
pony kicked-in father's 'ead. 'E plays the viddle."

"What tune does he play?"

"Dunno."

"What's he like?"

" 'E's black. Old Jim zays 'e's all over 'air. 'E's a praaper
bogle. 'E don' come only at naight." The little boy's

oblique dark eyes slid round. "D'yu think 'e might want to take me away? Megan's feared of 'e."

"Has she seen him?"

"No. She's not afeared o' yu."

"I should think not. Why should she be?"

"She zays a prayer for yu."

"How do you know that, you little rascal?"

"When I was asleep, she said: 'God bless us all, an' Mr. Ashes.' I 'eard 'er whisperin'."

"You're a little ruffian to tell what you hear when you're not meant to hear it!"

The little boy was silent. Then he said aggressively:

"I can skin rabbets. Megan, she can't bear skinnin' 'em. I like blood."

"Oh! you do; you little monster!"

"What's that?"

"A creature that likes hurting others."

The little boy scowled. "They'm only dead rabbets, what us eats."

"Quite right, Nick. I beg your pardon."

"I can skin frogs, tu."

But Ashurst had become absent. "God bless us all, and Mr. Ashes!" And puzzled by that sudden inaccessibility, Nick ran back to the stream where the giggling and shouts again uprose at once.

When Megan brought his tea, he said:

"What's the gypsy bogle, Megan?"

She looked up, startled.

"He brings bad things."

"Surely you don't believe in ghosts?"

"I hope I will never see him."

"Of course you won't. There aren't such things. What old Jim saw was a pony."

"No! There are bogles in the rocks; they are the men who lived long ago."

"They aren't gypsies, anyway; those old men were dead long before gypsies came."

She said simply: "They are all bad."

"Why? If there are any, they're only wild, like the rabbits. The flowers aren't bad for being wild; the thorn trees were never planted—and you don't mind them. I shall go down at night and look for your bogle, and have a talk with him."

"Oh, no! Oh, no!"

"Oh, yes! I shall go and sit on his rock."

She clasped her hands together: "Oh, please!"

"Why! What does it matter if anything happens to me?"

She did not answer; and in a sort of pet he added:

"Well, I daresay I shan't see him, because I suppose I must be off soon."

"Soon?"

"Your aunt won't want to keep me here."

"Oh, yes! We always let lodgings in summer."

Fixing his eyes on her face, he asked:

"Would you like me to stay?"

"Yes."

"I'm going to say a prayer for *you* to-night!"

She flushed crimson, frowned, and went out of the room. He sat cursing himself, till his tea was stewed. It was as if he had hacked with his thick boots at a clump of bluebells. Why had he said such a silly thing? Was he just a towny college ass like Robert Garton, as far from understanding this girl?

## IV

Ashurst spent the next week confirming the restoration of his leg, by exploration of the country within easy reach. Spring was a revelation to him this year. In a kind of intoxication he would watch the pink-white buds of some backward beech tree sprayed up in the sunlight against the deep blue sky, or the trunks and limbs of the few Scotch firs, tawny in violent light, or again on the moor, the gale-bent larches which had such a look of life when the wind streamed in their young green, above the rusty black underboughs. Or he would lie on the banks, gazing at the clusters of dog-violets, or up in the dead bracken, fingering the pink, transparent buds of the dew-berry, while the cuckoos called and yaffles laughed, or a lark, from very high, dripped its beads of song. It was certainly different from any spring he had ever known, for spring was within him, not without. In the daytime he hardly saw the family; and when Megan brought in his meals she always seemed too busy in the house or among the young things in the yard to stay talking long. But in the evenings he installed himself in the window seat in the kitchen, smoking and chatting with the lame man Jim, or Mrs. Narracombe, while the girl sewed, or moved about, clearing the supper things away. And sometimes with the sensation a cat must feel when it purrs, he would become conscious that Megan's eyes—those dew-gray eyes—were fixed on him with a sort of lingering soft look which was strangely flattering.

It was on Sunday week in the evening, when he was lying in the orchard listening to a blackbird and com-posing a love poem, that he heard the gate swing to, and saw the girl come running among the trees, with the red-cheeked, stolid Joe in swift pursuit. About twenty yards away the chase ended, and the two stood fronting each other, not noticing the stranger in the grass—the boy pressing on, the girl fending him off. Ashurst could see her face, angry, disturbed; and the youth's—who would have thought that red-faced yokel could look so distraught! And painfully affected by that sight, he jumped up. They saw him then. Megan dropped her hands, and shrank behind a tree-trunk; the boy gave an angry grunt, rushed at the bank, scrambled over and vanished. Ashurst went slowly up to her. She was standing quite still, biting her lip—very pretty, with her fine, dark hair blown loose about her face, and her eyes cast down.

"I beg your pardon," he said.

She gave him one upward look, from eyes much dilated; then, catching her breath, turned away. Ashurst followed

"Megan!"

But she went on; and taking hold of her arm, he turned her gently round to him.

"Stop and speak to me."

"Why do you beg my pardon? It is not to me you should do that."

"Well, then, to Joe."

"How dare he come after me?"

"In love with you, I suppose."

She stamped her foot.

Ashurst uttered a short laugh. "Would you like me to punch his head?"

She cried with sudden passion:

"You laugh at me—you laugh at us!"

He caught hold of her hands, but she shrank back, till her passionate little face and loose dark hair were caught among the pink clusters of the apple blossom. Ashurst raised one of her imprisoned hands and put his lips to it. He felt how chivalrous he was, and superior to that clod Joe—just brushing that small, rough hand with his mouth! Her shrinking ceased suddenly; she seemed to tremble towards him. A sweet warmth overtook Ashurst from top to toe. This slim maiden, so simple and fine and pretty, was pleased, then, at the touch of his lips. And, yielding to a swift impulse, he put his arms round her, pressed her to him, and kissed her forehead. Then he was frightened—she went so pale, closing her eyes, so that the long, dark lashes lay on her pale cheeks; her hands, too, lay inert at her sides. The touch of her breast sent a shiver through him. "Megan!" he sighed out, and let her go. In the utter silence a blackbird shouted. Then the girl seized his hand, put it to her cheek, her heart, her lips, kissed it passionately, and fled away among the mossy trunks of the apple-trees, till they hid her from him.

Ashurst sat down on a twisted old tree growing almost along the ground, and, all throbbing and bewildered, gazed vacantly at the blossom which had crowned her hair—those pink buds with one white open apple star. What had he done? How had he let himself be thus stampeded by beauty—or—just the spring! He felt curiously happy, all the same; happy and triumphant, with shivers running through his limbs, and a vague alarm. This was the beginning of—what? The midges bit him, the dancing gnats tried to fly into his mouth, and all the spring around him seemed to grow more lovely and alive; the songs of the cuckoos and the blackbirds, the laughter of the yaffles, the level-slanting sunlight, the apple blossom which had crowned her head—! He got up from the old trunk and strode out of the orchard, wanting space, an open sky, to get on terms with these new sensations. He made for the moor, and from an ash tree in the hedge a magpie flew out to herald him.

Of man—at any age from five years on—who can say he has never been in love? Ashurst had loved his partners at his dancing class; loved his nursery governess; girls in school-holidays; perhaps never been quite out of love, cherishing always some more or less remote admiration. But this was different, not remote at all. Quite a new sensation; terribly delightful, bringing a sense of completed manhood. To be holding in his fingers such a wild flower, to be able to put it to his lips, and feel it tremble with delight against them! What intoxication, and—embarrassment! What to do with it—how met her next time? His first caress had been cool, pitiful:

but the next could not be, now that, by her burning little kiss on his hand, by her pressure of it to her heart, he knew that she loved him. Some natures are coarsened by love bestowed on them; others, like Ashurst's, are swayed and drawn, warmed and softened, almost exalted, by what they feel to be a sort of miracle.

And up there among the tors he was racked between the passionate desire to revel in this new sensation of spring fulfilled within him, and a vague but very real uneasiness. At one moment he gave himself up completely to his pride at having captured this pretty, trustful, dewy-eyed thing! At the next he thought with factitious solemnity: "Yes, my boy! But look out what you're doing! You know what comes of it!"

Dusk dropped down without his noticing—dusk on the carved, Assyrian-looking masses of the rocks. And the voice of Nature said: "This is a new world for you!" As when a man gets up at four o'clock and goes out into a summer morning, and beasts, birds, trees stare at him and he feels as if all had been made new.

He stayed up there for hours, till it grew cold, then groped his way down the stones and heather roots to the road, back into the lane, and came again past the wild meadow to the orchard. There he struck a match and looked at his watch. Nearly twelve! It was black and unstirring in there now, very different from the lingering, bird-befriended brightness of six hours ago! And suddenly he saw this idyll of his with the eyes of the outer world—had mental vision of Mrs. Narracombe's snake-like neck turned, her quick dark glance taking it all in, her shrewd face hardening; saw the gypsy-like cousins coarsely mocking and distrustful; Joe stolid and furious; only the lame man, Jim, with the suffering eyes, seemed tolerable to his mind. And the village pub!—the gossiping matrons he passed on his walks; and then— his own friends—Robert Garton's smile when he went off that morning ten days ago; so ironical and know-ing! Disgusting! For a minute he literally hated this earthly, cynical world to which one belonged, willy-nilly. The gate where he was leaning grew gray, a sort of shim-mer passed before him and spread into the bluish dark-ness. The moon! He could just see it over the bank behind; red, nearly round—a strange moon! And turning away, he went up the lane which smelled of the night and cow-dung and young leaves. In the straw-yard he could see the dark shapes of cattle, broken by the pale sickles of their horns, like so many thin moons, fallen ends-up. He unlatched the farm gate stealthily. All was dark in the house. Muffling his footsteps, he gained the porch, and, blotted against one of the yew trees, looked up at Megan's window. It was open. Was she sleeping, or lying awake perhaps disturbed—unhappy at his absence? An owl hooted while he stood there peering up, and the sound seemed to fill the whole night, so quiet was all else, save for the never-ending murmur of the stream running below the orchard. The cuckoos by day, and now the owls—how wonderful they voiced this troubled ecstasy within him! And suddenly he saw her at her window, looking out. He moved a little from the yew tree, and whispered: "Megan!" She drew back, vanished, reap-peared, leaning far down. He stole forward on the grass patch, hit his shin against the green-painted chair, and held his breath at the sound. The pale blur of her stretched-down arm and face did not stir; he moved the chair, and noiselessly mounted it. By stretching up his arm he could just reach. Her hand held the huge key of the front door, and he clasped that burning hand with the cold key in it. He could just see her face, the glint of teeth between her lips, her tumbled hair. She was still dressed —poor child, sitting up for him, no doubt! "Pretty Megan!" Her hot, roughened fingers clung to his; her face had a strange, lost look. To have been able to reach

it—even with his hand! The owl hooted, a scent of sweet-
briar crept into his nostrils. Then one of the farm dogs
barked; her grasp relaxed, she shrank back.

"Good night, Megan!"

"Good night, sir!" She was gone! With a sigh he
dropped back to earth, and, sitting on that chair, took
off his boots. Nothing for it but to creep in and go to
bed; yet for a long while he sat unmoving, his feet
chilly in the dew, drunk on the memory of her lost,
half-smiling face, and the clinging grip of her burning
fingers, pressing the cold key into his hand.

### v

He awoke feeling as if he had eaten heavily overnight,
instead of having eaten nothing. And far off, unreal,
seemed yesterday's romance! Yet it was a golden morning.
Full spring had burst at last—in one night the "goldie-
cups," as the little boys called them, seemed to have made
the field their own, and from his window he could see
apple blossoms covering the orchard as with a rose and
white quilt. He went down almost dreading to see Megan;
and yet, when not she but Mrs. Narracombe brought in
his breakfast, he felt vexed and disappointed. The woman's
quick eye and snaky neck seemed to have a new alacrity
this morning. Had she noticed?

"So you an' the moon went walkin' last night, Mr.
Ashurst! Did ye have your supper anywheres?"

Ashurst shook his head.

"We kept it for you, but I suppose you was too busy in
your brain to think o' such a thing as that?"

Was she mocking him, in that voice of hers, which still
kept some Welsh crispness against the invading burr of
the West Country? If she knew! And at that moment he
thought: "No, no; I'll clear out. I won't put myself in
such a beastly false position."

But, after breakfast, the longing to see Megan began and increased with every minute, together with fear lest something should have been said to her which had spoiled everything. Sinister that she had not appeared, not given him even a glimpse of her! And the love poem, whose manufacture had been so important and absorbing yesterday afternoon under the apple-trees, now seemed so paltry that he tore it up and rolled it into pipe spills. What had he known of love, till she seized his hand and kissed it! And now—what did he not know? But to write of it seemed mere insipidity! He went up to his bedroom to get a book, and his heart began to beat violently, for she was in there making the bed. He stood in the doorway watching; and suddenly, with turbulent joy, he saw her stoop and kiss his pillow, just at the hollow made by his head last night. How let her know he had seen that pretty act of devotion? And yet if she heard him stealing away, it would be even worse. She took the pillow up, holding it as if reluctant to shake out the impress of his cheek, dropped it, and turned round.

"Megan!"

She put her hands up to her cheeks, but her eyes seemed to look right into him. He had never before realized the depth and purity and touching faithfulness in those dew-bright eyes, and he stammered:

"It was sweet of you to wait up for me last night."

She still said nothing, and he stammered on:

"I was wandering about on the moor; it was such a jolly night. I—I've just come up for a book."

Then, the kiss he had seen her give the pillow afflicted him with sudden headiness, and he went up to her. Touching her eyes with his lips, he thought with queer excitement: "I've done it! Yesterday all was sudden—anyhow; but now—I've done it!" The girl let her forehead rest against his lips, which moved downwards till they reached hers. That first real lover's kiss—strange, wonderful, still almost innocent—in which heart did it make the most disturbance?

"Come to the big apple-tree to-night, after they've gone to bed. Megan—promise!"

She whispered back: "I promise!"

Then, scared at her white face, scared at everything, he let her go, and went downstairs again. Yes! he had done it now! Accepted her love, declared his own! He went out to the green chair as devoid of a book as ever; and there he sat staring vacantly before him, triumphant and remorseful, while under his nose and behind his back the work of the farm went on. How long he had been sitting in that curious state of vacancy he had no notion when he saw Joe standing a little behind him to the right. The youth had evidently come from hard work in the fields. and stood shifting his feet, breathing loudly, his face colored like a setting sun, and his arms, below the rolled-up sleeves of his blue shirt, showing the hue and furry sheen of ripe peaches. His red lips were open, his blue eyes with their flaxen lashes stared fixedly at Ashurst, who said ironically:

"Well, Joe, anything I can do for you?"

"Yeas."

"What, then?"

"Yu can goo away from yere. Us don' want yu."

Ashurst's face, never too humble, assumed its most lordly look.

"Very good of you, but, do you know, I prefer the others should speak for themselves."

The youth moved a pace or two nearer, and the scent of his honest heat afflicted Ashurst's nostrils.

"What d'yu stay yere for?"

"Because it pleases me."

"'Twon't please yu when I've bashed yure head in!"

"Indeed! When would you like to begin that?"

Joe answered only with the loudness of his breathing,

but his eyes looked like those of a young and angry bull.
Then a sort of spasm seemed to convulse his face.

'Megan don' want yu."

A rush of jealousy, of contempt, and anger with this
thick, loud-breathing rustic got the better of Ashurst's
self-possession; he jumped up and pushed back his chair.

"You can go to the devil!"

And as he said those simple words, he saw Megan in the
doorway with a tiny brown spaniel puppy in her arms.
She came up to him quickly:

"It's eyes are blue!" she said.

Joe turned away; the back of his neck was literally
crimson.

Ashurst put his finger to the mouth of the little brown
bullfrog of a creature in her arms. How cozy it looked
against her!

"It's fond of you already. Ah! Megan, everything is
fond of *you*."

"What was Joe saying to you, please?"

"Telling me to go away, because you didn't want me
here."

She stamped her foot; then looked up at Ashurst. At
that adoring look he felt his nerves quiver, just as if he
had seen a moth scorching its wings.

"To-night!" he said. "Don't forget!"

"No." And smothering her face against the puppy's
little fat, brown body, she slipped back into the house.

Ashurst wandered down the lane. At the gate of the
wild meadow he came on the lame man and his cows.

"Beautiful day, Jim!"

"Ah! 'Tes brave weather for the grass. The ashes be
later than th' oaks this year. 'When th' oak before th'
ash—' "

Ashurst said idly: "Where were you standing when
you saw the gypsy bogle, Jim?"

"It might be under that big apple-tree, as you might say."

"And you really do think it was there?"

The lame man answered cautiously:

"I shouldn't like to say rightly that *'twas* there. 'Twas in my mind as 'twas there."

"What do you make of it?"

The lame man lowered his voice.

"They du zay old master, Mist' Narracombe, come o' gypsy stock. But that's tellin'. They'm a wonderful people, yu know, for claimin' their own. Maybe they knu 'e was goin', and sent this feller along for company. That's what I've a-thought about it."

"What was he like?"

" 'E 'ad 'air all over 'is face, an' goin' like this, he was, zame as if 'e 'ad a viddle. They zay there's no such thing as bogles, but I've a-zeen the 'air on this dog standin' up of a dark naight, when I couldn' zee nothin', meself."

"Was there a moon?"

"Yeas, very near full, but 'twas on'y just risen, gold-like be'ind them trees."

"And you think a ghost means trouble, do you?"

The lame man pushed his hat up; his aspiring eyes looked at Ashurst more earnestly than ever.

" 'Tes not for me to zay that—but 'tes they bein' so unrestin'-like. There's things us don' understand, that's zartin, for zure. There's people that zee things, tu, an' others that don't never zee nothin'. Now, our Joe—yu might putt anything under 'is eyes an' 'e'd never see it; and them other boys, tu, they'm rattlin' fellers. But yu· take an' putt our Megan where there's suthin', she'll zee it, an' more tu, or I'm mistaken."

"She's sensitive, that's why."

"What's that?"

"I mean, she feels everything."

"Ah! She'm very lovin'-'earted."

Ashurst, who felt color coming into his cheeks, held out his tobacco pouch.

"Have a fill, Jim?"

"Thank 'ee, sir. She'm one in an 'underd, I think."

"I expect so," said Ashurst shortly, and folding up his pouch, walked on.

"Lovin'-'earted!" Yes! And what was he doing? What were his intentions—as they say—towards this loving-hearted girl? The thought dogged him, wandering through fields bright with buttercups, where the little red calves were feeding, and the swallows flying high. Yes, the oaks were before the ashes, brown-gold already; every tree in different stage and hue. The cuckoos and a thousand birds were singing; the little streams were very bright. The ancients believed in a golden age, in the garden of the Hesperides! . . . A queen wasp settled on his sleeve. Each queen wasp killed meant two thousand fewer wasps to thieve the apples which would grow from that blossom in the orchard; but who, with love in his heart, could kill anything on a day like this? He entered a field where a young red bull was feeding. It seemed to Ashurst that he looked like Joe. But the young bull took no notice of this visitor, a little drunk himself, perhaps, on the singing and the glamour of the golden pasture, under his short legs. Ashurst crossed out unchallenged to the hillside above the stream. From that slope a tor mounted to its crown of rocks. The ground there was covered with a mist of blue-bells, and nearly a score of crab-apple trees were in full bloom. He threw himself down on the grass. The change from the buttercup glory and oak-goldened glamour of the fields to this ethereal beauty under the gray tor filled him with a sort of wonder; nothing the same, save the sound of running water and the songs of the cuckoos. He lay there a long time, watching the sunlight wheel till the crab-trees threw shadows over the bluebells, his only companions a few wild bees. He was not quite sane, thinking of that morning's kiss, and of to-night under the apple-tree. In such a spot as this, fauns and dryads surely lived; nymphs, white as the crab-apple blossom, retired within those trees; fauns, brown as the dead bracken, with pointed ears, lay in wait for them. The cuckoos were still calling when he woke, there was the sound of running water; but the sun had couched behind the tor, the hillside was cool, and some rabbits had come out. "To-night!" he thought. Just as from the earth everything was pushing up, unfolding under the soft insistent fingers of an unseen hand, so were his heart and senses being pushed, unfolded. He got up and broke off a spray from a crab-apple tree. The buds were like Megan—shell-like, rose-pink, wild, and fresh; and so, too, the opening flowers, white, and wild, and touching. He put the spray into his coat. And all the rush of the spring within him escaped in a triumphant sigh. But the rabbits scurried away.

## VI

It was nearly eleven that night when Ashurst put down the pocket "Odyssey" which for half an hour he had held in his hands without reading, and slipped through the yard down to the orchard. The moon had just risen, very golden, over the hill, and like a bright, powerful, watching spirit peered through the bars of an ash tree's half-naked boughs. In among the apple-trees it was still dark, and he stood making sure of his direction, feeling the rough grass with his feet. A black mass close behind him stirred with a heavy grunting sound, and three large pigs settled down again close to each other, under the wall. He listened. There was no wind, but the stream's burbling whispering chuckle had gained twice its daytime strength. One bird, he could not tell what, cried "Pip—pip," "Pip—pip," with perfect monotony; he could hear a night-jar spinning very far off; an owl hooting. Ashurst moved a step or two, and again halted, aware of a dim living whiteness all round his head. On the dark unstirring trees innumerable flowers and buds all soft and blurred were being bewitched to life by the creeping moonlight. He had the oddest feeling of actual companionship, as if a million white moths or spirits had floated in and settled between dark sky and darker ground, and were opening and shutting their wings on a level with his eyes. In the bewildering, still, scentless beauty of that moment he almost lost memory of why he had come to the orchard. The flying glamour which had clothed the earth all day had not gone now that night had fallen, but only changed into this new form. He moved on through the thicket of stems and boughs covered with that live powdering whiteness, till he reached the big apple-tree. No mistaking that, even in the dark, nearly twice the height and size of any other, and leaning out towards the open meadows and the stream. Under the thick branches he stood still again, to listen. The same sounds exactly, and a faint grunting from the sleepy pigs. He put his hands on the dry, almost warm tree trunk, whose rough mossy surface gave forth a peaty scent at his touch. Would she come—would she? And among these quivering, haunted, moon-witched trees he was seized with doubts of everything! All was unearthly here, fit for no earthly lovers; fit only for god and goddess, faun and nymph—not for him and this little country girl. Would it not be almost a relief if she did not come? But all the time he was listening. And still that unknown bird went "Pip—pip," "Pip—pip," and there rose the busy chatter of the little trout stream, whereon the moon was flinging glances through the bars of her tree-prison. The blossom on a level with his eyes seemed to grow more living every moment, seemed with its mysterious white beauty more and more a part of his suspense. He plucked a fragment and held it close—three blossoms. Sacrilege to pluck fruit-tree blossom—soft, sacred, young blossom—and throw it

away! Then suddenly he heard the gate close, the pigs
stirring again and grunting; and leaning against the trunk,
he pressed his hands to its mossy sides behind him. and
held his breath. She might have been a spirit threading the
trees, for all the noise she made! Then he saw her quite
close—her dark form part of a little tree, her white face
part of its blossom; so still, and peering towards him. He
whispered: "Megan!" and held out his hands. She ran
forward, straight to his breast. When he felt her heart
beating against him, Ashurt knew to the full the sensations
of chivalry and passion. Because she was not of his world,
because she was so simple and young and headlong, adoring and defenseless, how could he be other than her pro-
tector in the dark! Because she was all simple Nature and
beauty, as much a part of this spring night as was the
living blossom, how should he not take all that she would
give him—how not fulfill the spring in her heart and his!
And torn between these two emotions he clasped her close,
and kissed her hair. How long they stood there without
speaking he knew not. The stream went on chattering, the
owls hooting, the moon kept stealing up and growing
whiter; the blossom all round them and above brightened
in suspense of living beauty. Their lips had sought each
other's, and they did not speak. The moment speech began
all would be unreal! Spring has no speech, nothing but
rustling and whispering. Spring has so much more than
speech in its unfolding flowers and leaves, and the coursing
of its streams, and in its sweet restless seeking! And sometimes spring will come alive, and, like a mysterious
Presence, stand, encircling lovers with its arms, laying on
them the fingers of enchantment, so that, standing lips to
lips, they forget everything but just a kiss. While her
heart beat against him, and her lips quivered on his,
Ashurst felt nothing but simple rapture—Destiny meant
her for his arms, Love could not be flouted! But when
their lips parted for breath, division began again at once.

Only, passion now was so much the stronger, and he sighed:

"Oh! Megan! Why did you come?"

She looked up, hurt, amazed.

"Sir, you asked me to."

"Don't call me 'sir,' my pretty sweet."

"What should I be callin' you."

"Frank."

"I could not. Oh, no!"

"But you love me—don't you?"

"I could not help lovin' you. I want to be with you that's all."

"All!"

So faint that he hardly heard, she whispered:

"I shall die if I can't be with you."

Ashurst took a mighty breath.

"Come and be with me, then!"

"Oh!"

Intoxicated by the awe and rapture in that "Oh!" he went on, whispering:

"We'll go to London. I'll show you the world. And I *will* take care of you, I promise, Megan. I'll never be a brute to you!"

"If I can be with you—that is all."

He stroked her hair, and whispered on:

"To-morrow I'll go to Torquay and get some money, and get you some clothes that won't be noticed, and then we'll steal away. And when we get to London, soon perhaps, if you love me well enough, we'll be married."

He could feel her hair shiver with the shake of her head.

"Oh, no! I could not. I only want to be with you!"

Drunk on his own chivalry, Ashurst went on murmuring:

"It's I who am not good enough for you. Oh! Megan, when did you begin to love me?"

"When I saw you in the road, and you looked at me. The first night I loved you; but I never thought you would want me."

She slipped down suddenly to her knees, trying to kiss his feet.

A shiver of horror went through Ashurst; he lifted her up bodily and held her fast—too upset to speak.

She whispered: "Why won't you let me?"

"It's I who will kiss your feet!"

Her smile brought tears into his eyes. The whiteness of her moonlit face so close to his, the faint pink of her opened lips, had the living, unearthly beauty of the apple blossom.

And then, suddenly, her eyes widened and stared past him painfully; she writhed out of his arms, and whispered: "Look!"

Ashurst saw nothing but the brightened stream, the furze faintly gilded, the beech trees glistening, and behind them all the wide loom of the moonlit hill. Behind him came her frozen whisper: "The gypsy bogle!"

"Where?"

"There—by the stone—under the trees!"

Exasperated, he leapt the stream, and strode towards the beech clump. Prank of the moonlight! Nothing! In and out of the bowlders and thorn trees, muttering and cursing, yet with a kind of terror, he rushed and stumbled. Absurd! Silly! Then he went back to the apple-tree. But she was gone; he could hear a rustle, the grunting of the pigs, the sound of a gate closing. Instead of her, only this old apple-tree! He flung his arms round the trunk. What a substitute for her soft body; the rough moss against his face—what a substitute for her soft cheek; only the scent, as of the woods, a little the same! And above him, and around, the blossoms, more living, more moonlit than ever, seemed to glow and breathe.

## VII

Descending from the train at Torquay station, Ashurst wandered uncertainly along the front, for he did not know this particular queen of English watering-places. Having little sense of what he had on, he was quite unconscious of being remarkable among its inhabitants, and strode along in his rough Norfolk jacket, dusty boots, and battered hat, without observing that people gazed at him rather blankly. He was seeking a branch of his London bank, and having found one, found also the first obstacle to his mood. Did he know any one in Torquay? No. In that case, if he would wire to his bank in London they would be happy to oblige him on receipt of the reply. That suspicious breath from the matter-of-fact world somewhat tarnished the brightness of his visions. But he sent the telegram.

Nearly opposite to the post office he saw a shop full of ladies' garments, and examined the window with strange sensations. To have to undertake the clothing of his rustic love was more than a little disturbing. He went in. A young woman came forward; she had blue eyes and a faintly puzzled forehead. Ashurst stared at her in silence.

"Yes, sir?"

"I want a dress for a young lady."

The young woman smiled. Ashurst frowned—the peculiarity of his request struck him with sudden force.

The young woman added hastily:

"What style would you like—something modish?"

"No. Simple."

"What figure would the young lady be?"

"I don't know; about two inches shorter than you, I should say."

"Could you give me her waist measurement?"

Megan's waist!

"Oh! anything usual!"

"Quite!"

While she was gone he stood disconsolately eyeing the models in the window, and suddenly it seemed to him incredible that Megan—his Megan—could ever be dressed save in the rough tweed skirt, coarse blouse, and tam-o'-shanter cap he was wont to see her in. The young woman had come back with several dresses in her arms, and Ashurst eyed her laying them against her own modish figure. There was one whose color he liked, a dove-gray, but to imagine Megan clothed in it was beyond him. The young woman went away, and brought some more. But on Ashurst there had now come a feeling of paralysis. How choose? She would want a hat too, and shoes, and gloves; and, suppose, when he had got them all, they commonized her, as Sunday clothes always commonized village folk! Why should she not travel as she was? Ah? But conspicuousness would matter; this was a serious elopement. And, staring at the young woman, he thought: "I wonder if she guesses, and thinks me a blackguard?"

"Do you mind putting aside that gray one for me?" he said desperately at last. "I can't decide now; I'll come in again this afternoon."

The young woman sighed.

"Oh! certainly. It's a very tasteful costume. I don't think you'll get anything that will suit your purpose better."

"I expect not," Ashurst murmured, and went out.

Freed again from the suspicious matter-of-factness of the world, he took a long breath, and went back to visions. In fancy he saw the trustful, pretty creature who was going to join her life to his; saw himself and her stealing forth at night, walking over the moor under the moon, he with his arm around her, and carrying her new garments, till, in some far-off wood, when dawn was coming, she would slip off her old things and put on these, and an early train at a distant station would bear them away

on their honeymoon journey, till London swallowed them
up, and the dreams of love came true.

"Frank Ashurst! Haven't seen you since Rugby, old
chap!"

Ashurst's frown dissolved; the face, close to his own,
was blue-eyed, suffused with sun—one of those faces
where sun from within and without join in a sort of luster.
And he answered:

"Phil Halliday, by Jove!"

"What are you doing here?"

"Oh! nothing. Just looking round, and getting some
money. I'm staying on the moor."

"Are you lunching anywhere? Come and lunch with
us; I'm here with my young sisters. They've had measles."

Hooked in by that friendly arm Ashurst went along,
up a hill, down a hill, away out of the town, while the
voice of Halliday, redolent of optimism as his face was
of sun, explained how "in this moldy place the only
decent things were the bathing and boating," and so on,
till presently they came to a crescent of houses a little
above and back from the sea, and into the center one—
an hotel—made their way.

"Come up to my room and have a wash. Lunch'll be
ready in a jiffy."

Ashurst contemplated his visage in a looking-glass.
After his farmhouse bedroom, the comb and one spare
shirt *régime* of the last fortnight, this room littered with
clothes and brushes was a sort of Capua; and he thought:
"Queer—one doesn't realize—" But what—he did not
quite know.

When he followed Halliday into the sitting-room for
lunch, three faces, very fair and blue-eyed, were turned
suddenly at the words: "This is Frank Ashurst—my
young sisters."

Two were indeed young, about eleven and ten. The
third was perhaps seventeen, tall and fair-haired too, with

pink-and-white cheeks just touched by the sun, and eyebrows, rather darker than the hair, running a little upwards from her nose to their outer points. The voices
of all three were like Halliday's, high and cheerful; they
stood up straight, shook hands with a quick movement,
looked at Ashurst critically, away again at once, and
began to talk of what they were going to do in the afternoon. A regular Diana and attendant nymphs! After the
farm this crisp, slangy, eager talk, this cool, clean, off-
hand refinement, was queer at first, and then so natural
that what he had come from became suddenly remote.
The names of the two little ones seemed to be Sabina
and Freda; of the eldest, Stella.

Presently the one called Sabina turned to him and
said:

"I say, will you come shrimping with us?—it's awful
fun!"

Surprised by this unexpected friendliness, Ashurst
murmured:

"I'm afraid I've got to get back this afternoon."

"Oh!"

"Can't you put it off?"

Ashurst turned to the new speaker, Stella, shook his
head, and smiled. She was very pretty! Sabina said re-
gretfully: "You might!" Then the talk switched off to
caves and swimming.

"Can you swim far?"

"About two miles."

"Oh!"

"I say!"

"How jolly!"

The three pairs of blue eyes, fixed on him, made him
conscious of his new importance. The sensation was agreeable. Halliday said:

"I say, you simply must stop and have a bathe. You'd
better stay the night."

"Yes, do!"

But again Ashurst smiled and shook his head. Then suddenly he found himself being catechized about his physical achievements. He had rowed—it seemed—in his college boat, played in his college football team, won his college mile, and he rose from table a sort of hero. The two little girls insisted that he must see "their" cave, and they set forth chattering like magpies, Ashurst between them, Stella and her brother a little behind. In the cave, damp and darkish like any other cave, the great feature was a pool with possibility of creatures which might be caught and put into bottles. Sabina and Freda, who wore no stockings on their shapely brown legs, exhorted Ashurst to join them in the middle of it, and help sieve the water. He too was soon bootless and sockless. Time goes fast for one who has a sense of beauty, when there are pretty children in a pool and a young Diana on the edge, to receive with wonder anything you can catch! Ashurst never had much sense of time. It was a shock when, pulling out his watch, he saw it was well past three. No cashing his check to-day—the bank would be closed before he could get there. Watching his expression, the little girls cried out at once:

"Hurrah! Now you'll have to stay!"

Ashurst did not answer. He was seeing again Megan's face, when at breakfast he had whispered: "I'm going to Torquay, darling, to get everything; I shall be back this evening. If it's fine we can go to-night. Be ready." He was seeing again how she quivered and hung on his words. What would she think? Then he pulled himself together, conscious suddenly of the calm scrutiny of this other young girl, so tall and fair and Diana-like, at the edge of the pool, of her wondering blue eyes under those brows which slanted up a little. If they knew what was in his mind—if they knew that this very night he had meant—! Well, there would be a little sound of disgust, and he would be alone in the cave. And with a curious mixture of anger, chagrin, and shame, he put his watch back into his pocket and said abruptly:

"Yes; I'm dished for to-day."

"Hurrah! Now you can bathe with us."

It was impossible not to succumb a little to the contentment of these pretty children, to the smile on Stella's lips, to Halliday's "Ripping, old chap! I can lend you things for the night!" But again a spasm of longing and remorse throbbed through Ashurst, and he said moodily:

"I must send a wire!"

The attractions of the pool palling, they went back to the hotel. Ashurst sent his wire, addressing it to Mrs. Narracombe: "Sorry, detained for the night, back to-morrow." Surely Megan would understand that he had too much to do; and his heart grew lighter. It was a lovely afternoon, warm, the sea calm and blue, and swimming his great passion; the favor of these pretty children flattered him, the pleasure of looking at them, at Stella, at Halliday's sunny face; the slight unreality, yet extreme naturalness of it all—as of a last peep at normality before he took this plunge with Megan! He got his borrowed bathing dress, and they all set forth. Halliday and he undressed behind one rock, the three girls behind another. He was first into the sea, and at once swam out with the bravado of justifying his self-given reputation. When he turned he could see Halliday swimming along shore, and the girls flopping and dipping, and riding the little waves, in the way he was accustomed to despise, but now thought pretty and sensible, since it gave him the distinction of the only deep-water fish. But drawing near, he wondered if they would like him, a stranger, to come into their splashing group; he felt shy, approaching that slim nymph. Then Sabina summoned him to teach her to float, and between them the little girls kept him so busy that he had no time even to notice whether

Stella was accustomed to his presence, till suddenly he heard a startled sound from her. She was standing submerged to the waist, leaning a little forward, her slim white arms stretched out and pointing, her wet face puckered by the sun and an expression of fear.

"Look at Phil! Is he all right? Oh, look!"

Ashurst saw at once that Phil was not all right. He was splashing and struggling out of his depth, perhaps a hundred yards away; suddenly he gave a cry, threw up his arms, and went down. Ashurst saw the girl launch herself towards him, and crying out: "Go back, Stella! Go back!" he dashed out. He had never swum so fast, and reached Halliday just as he was coming up a second time. It was a case of cramp, but to get him in was not difficult, for he did not struggle. The girl, who had stopped where Ashurst told her to, helped as soon as he was in his depth, and once on the beach they sat down one on each side of him to rub his limbs, while the little ones stood by with scared faces. Halliday was soon smiling. It was—he said—rotten of him, absolutely rotten! If Frank would give him an arm, he could get to his clothes all right now. Ashurst gave him the arm, and as he did so caught sight of Stella's face, wet and flushed and tearful, all broken up out of its calm; and he thought: "I called her Stella! Wonder if she minded?"

While they were dressing, Halliday said quietly:

"You saved my life, old chap!"

"Rot!"

Clothed, but not quite in their right minds, they went up all together to the hotel and sat down to tea, except Halliday, who was lying down in his room. After some slices of bread and jam, Sabina said:

"I say, you know, you *are* a brick!" And Freda chimed in:

"Rather!"

Ashurst saw Stella looking down; he got up in con-

fusion, and went to the window. From there he heard
Sabina mutter: "I say, let's swear blood bond. Where's
your knife, Freda?" and out of the corner of his eye
he could see each of them solemnly prick herself, squeeze
out a drop of blood and dabble on a bit of paper. He
turned and made for the door.

"Don't be a stoat! Come back!" His arms were seized;
imprisoned between the little girls he was brought back
to the table. On it lay a piece of paper with an effigy
drawn in blood, and the three names Stella Halliday,
Sabina Halliday, Freda Halliday—also in blood, running
towards it like the rays of a star. Sabina said:

"That's you. We shall have to kiss you, you know."

And Freda echoed:

"Oh! Blow—Yes!"

Before Ashurst could escape, some wettish hair dangled
against his face, something like a bite descended on his
nose, he felt his left arm pinched, and other teeth softly
searching his cheek. Then he was released, and Freda said:

"Now, Stella."

Ashurst, red and rigid, looked across the table at a red
and rigid Stella. Sabina giggled; Freda cried:

"Buck up—it spoils everything!"

A queer, ashamed eagerness shot through Ashurst; then
he said quietly:

"Shut up, you little demons!"

Again Sabina giggled.

"Well, then, she can kiss her hand, and you can put it
against your nose. It *is* on one side!"

To his amazement the girl did kiss her hand and stretch
it out. Solemnly he took that cool, slim hand and laid it to
his cheek. The two little girls broke into clapping, and
Freda said:

"Now, then, we shall have to save your life at any
time; that's settled. Can I have another cup, Stella, not
so beastly weak?"

Tea was resumed, and Ashurst, folding up the paper, put it in his pocket. The talk turned on the advantages of measles, tangerine oranges, honey in a spoon, no lessons, and so forth. Ashurst listened, silent, exchanging friendly looks with Stella, whose face was again of its normal sun-touched pink and white. It was soothing to be so taken to the heart of this jolly family, fascinating to watch their faces. And after tea, while the two little girls pressed seaweed, he talked to Stella in the window seat and looked at her water-color sketches. The whole thing was like a pleasurable dream; time and incident hung up, importance and reality suspended. To-morrow he would go back to Megan, with nothing of all this left save the paper with the blood of these children, in his pocket. Children! Stella was not quite that—as old as Megan! Her talk—quick, rather hard and shy, yet friendly—seemed to flourish on his silences, and about her there was something cool and virginal—a maiden in a bower. At dinner, to which Halliday, who had swallowed too much sea water, did not come, Sabina said:

"I'm going to call you Frank."

Freda echoed:

"Frank, Frank, Franky."

Ashurst grinned and bowed.

"Every time Stella calls you Mr. Ashurst, she's got to pay a forfeit. It's ridiculous."

Ashurst looked at Stella, who grew slowly red. Sabina giggled; Freda cried:

"She's 'smoking'—'smoking!'—Yah!"

Ashurst reached out to right and left, and grasped some fair hair in each hand.

"Look here," he said, "you two! Leave Stella alone, or I'll tie you together!"

Freda gurgled:

"Ouch! You *are* a beast!"

Sabina murmured cautiously:

"*You* call *her* Stella, you see!"

"Why shouldn't I? It's a jolly name!"

"All right; we give you leave to!"

Ashurst released the hair. Stella! What would she call him—after this? But she called him nothing; till at bed-time he said, deliberately:

"Good night, Stella!"

"Good night, Mr.—Good night, Frank! It *was* jolly of you, you know!"

"Oh—that! Bosh!"

Her quick, straight handshake tightened suddenly, and as suddenly, became slack.

Ashurst stood motionless in the empty sitting-room. Only last night, under the apple-tree and the living blossoms, he had held Megan to him, kissing her eyes and lips. And he gasped, swept by that rush of remembrance. To-night it should have begun—his life with her who only wanted to be with him! And now, twenty-four hours and more must pass, because—of not looking at his watch! Why had he made friends with this family of innocents just when he was saying good-by to innocence, and all the rest of it? "But I mean to marry her," he thought; "I told her so!"

He took a candle, lighted it, and went to his bedroom, which was next to Halliday's. His friend's voice called as he was passing:

"Is that you, old chap? I say, come in."

He was sitting up in bed, smoking a pipe and reading. "Sit down a bit."

Ashurst sat down by the open window.

"I've been thinking about this afternoon, you know," said Halliday rather suddenly. "They say you go through all your past. I didn't. I suppose I wasn't far enough gone."

"What did you think of?"

Halliday was silent for a little, then said quietly:

"Well, I did think of one thing—rather odd—of a girl at Cambridge that I might have—you know; I was glad I hadn't got her on my mind. Anyhow, old chap, I owe it to you that I'm here; I should have been in the big dark by now. No more bed, or baccy; no more anything. I say, what d'you suppose happens to us?"

Ashurst murmured:

"Go out like flames, I expect."

"Phew!"

"We may flicker, and cling about a bit, perhaps."

"H'm! I think that's rather gloomy. I say, I hope my young sisters have been decent to you?"

"Awfully decent."

Halliday put his pipe down, crossed his hands behind his neck, and turned his face towards the window.

"They're not bad kids!" he said.

Watching his friend, lying there, with that smile, and the candle-light on his face, Ashurst shuddered. Quite true! He might have been lying there with no smile, with all that sunny look gone out forever! He might not have been lying there at all, but "sanded" at the bottom of the sea, waiting for resurrection on the—ninth day, was it? And that smile of Halliday's seemed to him suddenly something wonderful, as if in it were all the difference between life and death—the little flame—the all! He got up, and said softly:

"Well, you ought to sleep, I expect. Shall I blow out?"

Halliday caught his hand.

"I can't say it, you know; but it must be rotten to be dead. Good night, old boy!"

Stirred and moved, Ashurst squeezed the hand, and went downstairs. The hall door was still open, and he passed out on to the lawn before the Crescent. The stars were bright in a very dark blue sky, and by their light some lilacs had that mysterious color of flowers by night which no one can describe. Ashurst pressed his face against a spray; and before his closed eyes Megan started up, with the tiny brown spaniel pup against her breast. "I thought of a girl that I might have—you know. I was glad I hadn't got her on my mind!" He jerked his head away from the lilac, and began pacing up and down over the grass, a gray phantom coming to substance for a moment in the light from the lamp at either end. He was with her again under the living, breathing whiteness of the blossom, the stream chattering by, the moon glinting steel-blue on the bathing-pool; back in the rapture of his kisses on her upturned face of innocence and humble passion, back in the suspense and beauty of that pagan night. He stood still once more in the shadow of the lilacs. Here the sea, not the stream, was Night's voice; the sea with its sigh and rustle; no little bird, no owl, no nightjar called or spun; but a piano tinkled, and the white houses cut the sky with solid curve, and the scent from the lilacs filled the air. A window of the hotel, high up, was lighted; he saw a shadow move across the blind. And most queer sensations stirred within him, a sort of churning, and twining, and turning of a single emotion on itself, as though spring and love, bewildered and confused, seeking the way, were baffled. This girl, who had called him Frank, whose hand had given his that sudden little clutch, this girl so cool and pure—what would *she* think of such wild, unlawful loving? He sank down on the grass, sitting there cross-legged, with his back to the house, motionless as some carved Buddha. Was he really going to break through innocence, and steal? Sniff the scent out of a wild flower, and—perhaps—throw it away? "Of a girl at Cambridge that I might have—you know!" He put his hands to the grass, one on each side, palms downwards, and pressed; it was just warm still—the grass, barely moist, soft and firm and friendly. "What am I going to do?" he thought. Perhaps Megan was at her window, looking out at the blossom, thinking of him! Poor little Megan! "Why not?"

he thought. "I love her! But do I—really love her? or do I only want her because she is so pretty, and loves me? What am I going to do?" The piano tinkled on, the stars winked; and Ashurst gazed out before him at the dark sea, as if spellbound. He got up at last, cramped and rather chilly. There was no longer light in any window. And he went in to bed.

VIII

Out of a deep and dreamless sleep he was awakened by the sound of thumping on the door. A shrill voice called:

"Hi! Breakfast's ready."

He jumped up. Where was he—? Ah!

He found them already eating marmalade, and sat down in the empty place between Stella and Sabina, who, after watching him a little, said:

"I say, do buck up; we're going to start at half-past nine."

"We're going to Berry Head, old chap; you *must* come!"

Ashurst thought: "Come! Impossible. I shall be getting things and going back." He looked at Stella. She said quickly:

"Do come!"

Sabina chimed in:

"It'll be no fun without you."

Freda got up and stood behind his chair.

"You've got to come, or else I'll pull your hair!"

Ashurst thought: "Well—one day more—to think it over! One day more!" And he said:

"All right! You needn't tweak my mane!"

"Hurrah!"

At the station he wrote a second telegram to the farm and then—tore it up; he could not have explained why From Brixham they drove in a very little wagonette

There, squeezed between Sabina and Freda, with his knees touching Stella's, they played "Up Jenkins"; and the gloom he was feeling gave way to frolic. In this one day more to think it over, he did not want to think! They ran races, wrestled, paddled—for to-day nobody wanted to bathe—they sang catches, played games, and ate all they had brought. The little girls fell asleep against him on the way back, and his knees still touched Stella's in the wagonette. It seemed incredible that thirty hours ago he had never set eyes on any of those three flaxen heads. In the train he talked to Stella of poetry, discovering her favorites, and telling her his own with a pleasing sense of superiority; till suddenly she said, rather low:

"Phil says you don't believe in a future life, Frank. I think that's dreadful."

Disconcerted, Ashurst muttered:

"I don't either believe or not believe—I simply don't know."

She said quickly:

"I couldn't bear that. What would be the use of living?"

Watching the frown of those pretty oblique brows. Ashurst answered:

"I don't believe in believing things because one wants to."

"But why should one *wish* to live again, if one isn't going to?"

And she looked full at him.

He did not want to hurt her, but an itch to dominate pushed him on to say:

"While one's alive one naturally wants to go on living forever; that's part of being alive. But it probably isn't anything more."

"Don't you believe in the Bible at all, then?"

Ashurst thought: "Now I shall really hurt her!"

"I believe in the Sermon on the Mount, because it's beautiful and good for all time."

"But don't you believe Christ was divine?"

He shook his head.

She turned her face quickly to the window, and there sprang into his mind Megan's prayer, repeated by little Nick: "God bless us all, and Mr. Ashes!" Who else would ever say a prayer for him, like her who at this moment must be waiting—waiting to see him come down the lane? And he thought suddenly: "What a scoundrel I am!"

All that evening this thought kept coming back; but, as is not unusual, each time with less poignancy, till it seemed almost a matter of course to be a scoundrel. And—strange!—he did not know whether he was a scoundrel if he meant to go back to Megan, or if he did not mean to go back to her.

They played cards till the children were sent off to bed, then Stella went to the piano. From over on the window seat, where it was nearly dark, Ashurst watched her between the candles—that fair head on the long, white neck bending to the movement of her hands. She played fluently, without much expression; but what a picture she made, the faint golden radiance, a sort of angelic atmosphere—hovering about her! Who could have passionate thoughts or wild desires in the presence of that swaying, white-clothed girl with the seraphic head? She played a thing of Schumann's called *"Warum?"* Then Halliday brought out a flute, and the spell was broken. After this they made Ashurst sing, Stella playing him accompaniments from a book of Schumann songs, till, in the middle of *"Ich grolle nicht,"* two small figures clad in blue dressing-gowns crept in and tried to conceal themselves beneath the piano. The evening broke up in confusion, and what Sabina called "a splendid rag."

That night Ashurst hardly slept at all. He was thinking, tossing and turning. The intense domestic intimacy of these last two days, the strength of this Halliday atmosphere, seemed to ring him round, and make the farm and Megan

—even Megan—seem unreal. Had he really made love to her—really promised to take her away to live with him? He must have been betwiched by the spring, the night, the apple blossom! The notion that he was going to make her his mistress—that simple child not yet eighteen—now filled him with a sort of horror, even while it still stung and whipped his blood. He muttered to himself: "It's awful, what I've done—awful!" And the sound of Schumann's music throbbed and mingled with his fevered thoughts, and he saw again Stella's cool, white, fair-haired figure and bending neck, the queer, angelic radiance about her. "I must have been—I must be—mad!" he thought. "What came into me? Poor little Megan!" "God bless us all, and Mr. Ashes!" "I want to be with you—only to be with you!" And burying his face in his pillow, he smothered down a fit of sobbing. Not to go back was awful! To go back—more awful still!

Emotion, when you are young, and give real vent to it, loses its power of torture. And he fell asleep, thinking: "What was it—a few kisses—all forgotten in a month!"

Next morning he got his check cashed, but avoided the shop of the dove-gray dress like the plague; and, instead, bought himself some necessaries. He spent the whole day in a queer mood, cherishing a kind of sullenness against himself. Instead of the hankering of the last two days, he felt nothing but a blank—all passionate longing gone, as if quenched in that outburst of tears. After tea Stella put a book down beside him, and said shyly:

"Have you read that, Frank?"

It was Farrar's "Life of Christ." Ashurst smiled. Her anxiety about his beliefs seemed to him comic, but touching. Infectious, too, perhaps, for he began to have an itch to justify himself, if not to convert her. And in the evening, when the children and Halliday were mending their shrimping nets, he said:

"At the back of orthodox religion, so far as I can see,

there's always the idea of reward—what you can get for being good; a kind of begging for favors. I think it all starts in fear."

She was sitting on the sofa making reefer knots with a bit of string. She looked up quickly:

"I think it's much deeper than that."

Ashurst felt again that wish to dominate.

"You think so," he said; "but wanting the *quid pro quo* is about the deepest thing in all of us! It's jolly hard to get to the bottom of it!"

She wrinkled her brows in a puzzled frown.

"I don't think I understand."

He went on obstinately:

"Well, think, and see if the most religious people aren't those who feel that this life doesn't give them all they want. I believe in being good because to be good is good in itself."

"Then you do believe in being good?"

How pretty she looked now—it was easy to be good with her! And he nodded and said:

"I say, show me how to make that knot!"

With her fingers touching his, in maneuvering the bit of string he felt soothed and happy. And when he went to bed he willfully kept his thoughts on her, wrapping himself in her fair, cool sisterly radiance, as in some garment of protection.

Next day he found they had arranged to go by train to Totness, and picnic at Berry Pomeroy Castle. Still in that resolute oblivion of the past, he took his place with them in the landau beside Halliday, back to the horses. And, then, along the sea front, nearly at the turning to the railway station, his heart almost leaped into his mouth. Megan—Megan herself!—was walking on the far pathway, in her old skirt and jacket and her tan-o'-shanter, looking up into the faces of the passers-by. Instinctively he threw his hand up for cover, then made a feint of clearing dust out of his eyes; but between his fingers he could see her still, moving, not with her free country step, but wavering, lost-looking, pitiful—like some little dog which has missed its master and does not know whether to run on, to run back—where to run. How had she come like this?—what excuse had she found to get away?—what did she hope for? But with every turn of the wheels bearing him away from her, his heart revolted and cried to him to stop them, to get out, and go to her! When the landau turned the corner to the station he could stand it no more, and opening the carriage door, muttered: "I've forgotten something! Go on—don't wait for me! I'll join you at the castle by the next train!" He jumped, stumbled, spun round, recovered his balance, and walked forward, while the carriage with the astonished Hallidays rolled on.

From the corner he could only just see Megan, a long way ahead now. He ran a few steps, checked himself, and dropped into a walk. With each step nearer to her, further from the Hallidays, he walked more and more slowly. How did it alter anything—this sight of her? How make the going to her, and that which must come of it, less ugly? For there was no hiding it—since he had met the Hallidays he had become gradually sure that he would not marry Megan. It would only be a wild love-time, a troubled, remorseful, difficult time—and then—well, then he would get tired, just because she gave him everything, was so simple, and so trustful, so dewy. And dew—wears off! The little spot of faded color, her tam-o'-shanter cap, wavered on far in front of him; she was looking up into every face, and at the house windows. Had any man ever such a cruel moment to go through? Whatever he did, he felt he would be a beast. And he uttered a groan which made a nursemaid turn and stare. He saw Megan stop and lean against the sea-wall, looking at the sea; and he too stopped. Quite likely she had never seen the sea before, and even in her distress could not resist that sight. "Yes—

she's seen nothing," he thought; "everything's before her.
And just for a few weeks' passion, I shall be cutting her
life to ribbons. I'd better go and hang myself rather than
do it!" And suddenly he seemed to see Stella's calm eyes
looking into his, the wave of fluffy hair on her forehead
stirred by the wind. Ah! it would be madness, would mean
giving up all that he respected, and his own self-respect.
He turned and walked quickly back towards the station.
But memory of that poor, bewildered little figure, those
anxious eyes searching the passers-by, smote him too hard
again, and once more he turned towards the sea. The cap
was no longer visible; that little spot of color had vanished
in the stream of the noon promenaders. And impelled by
the passion of longing, the dearth which comes on one
when life seems to be whiling something out of reach, he
hurried forward. She was nowhere to be seen; for half an
hour he looked for her; then on the beach flung himself
face downward in the sand. To find her again he knew he
had only to go to the station and wait till she returned
from her fruitless quest, to take her train home; or to take
train himself and go back to the farm, so that she found
him there when she returned. But he lay inert in the sand,
among the indifferent groups of children with their spades
and buckets. Pity at her little figure wandering, seeking,
was well-nigh merged in the spring-running of his blood;
for it was all wild feeling now—the chivalrous part, what
there had been of it, was gone. He wanted her again
wanted her kisses, her soft, little body, her abandonment,
all her quick, warm, pagan emotion; wanted the wonderful
feeling of that night under the moon-lit apple boughs;
wanted it all with a horrible intensity, as the faun wants
the nymph. The quick chatter of the little bright trout-
stream, the dazzle of the buttercups, the rocks of the old
"wild men"; the calling of the cuckoos and yaffles, the
hooting of the owls; and the red moon peeping out of the
velvet dark at the living whiteness of the blossom; and

her face just out of reach at the window, lost in its love-look; and her heart against his, her lips answering his, under the apple-tree—all this besieged him. Yet he lay inert. What was it which struggled against pity and this feverish longing, and kept him there paralyzed in the warm sand? Three flaxen heads—a fair face with friendly blue-gray eyes, a slim hand pressing his, a quick voice speaking his name—"So you do believe in being good?" Yes, and a sort of atmosphere as of some old walled-in English garden, with pinks, and cornflowers, and roses, and scents of lavender and lilac—cool and fair, untouched, almost holy—all that he had been brought up to feel was clean and good. And suddenly he thought: "She might come along the front again and see me!" and he got up and made his way to the rock at the far end of the beach. There, with the spray biting into his face, he could think more coolly. To go back to the farm and love Megan out in the woods, among the rocks, with everything around wild and fitting—that, he knew, was impossible, utterly. To trans-plant her to a great town, to keep, in some little flat or rooms, one who belonged so wholly to Nature—the poet in him shrank from it. His passion would be a mere sensu-ous revel, soon gone; in London, her very simplicity, her lack of all intellectual quality, would make her his secret plaything—nothing else. The longer he sat on the rock, with his feet dangling over a greenish pool from which the sea was ebbing, the more clearly he saw this; but it was as if her arms and all of her were slipping slowly, slowly down from him, into the pool, to be carried away out to sea; and her face looking up, her lost face with beseeching eyes, and dark, wet hair—possessed, haunted, tortured him! He got up at last, scaled the low rock-cliff, and made his way down into a sheltered cove. Perhaps in the sea he could get back his control—lose this fever! And stripping off his clothes, he swam out. He wanted to tire himself so that nothing mattered, and swam recklessly, fast and far;

then suddenly, for no reason, felt afraid. Suppose he could
not reach shore again—suppose the current set him out—
or he got cramps, like Halliday! He turned to swim in. The
red cliffs looked a long way off. If he were drowned they
would find his clothes. The Hallidays would know; but
Megan perhaps never—they took no newspaper at the
farm. And Phil Halliday's words came back to him again.
"A girl at Cambridge I might have— Glad I haven't got
her on my mind!" And in that moment of unreasoning
fear he vowed he would not have her on his mind. Then
his fear left him; he swam in easily enough, dried himself
in the sun, and put on his clothes. His heart felt sore, but
no longer ached; his body cool and refreshed.

When one is as young as Ashurst, pity is not a violent
emotion. And, back in the Hallidays' sitting-room, eating
a ravenous tea, he felt much like a man recovered from
fever. Everything seemed new and clear; the tea, the but·
tered toast, and jam tasted absurdly good; tobacco had
never smelt so nice. And walking up and down the empty
room, he stopped here and there to touch or look. He took
up Stella's work-basket, fingered the cotton reels and a
gayly colored plait of sewing silks, smelt at the little bag
filled with wood-roffe she kept among them. He sat down
at the piano, playing tunes with one finger, thinking: "To-
night she'll play; I shall watch her while she's playing;
it does me good to watch her." He took up the book, which
still lay where she had placed it beside him, and tried to
read. But Megan's little, sad figure began to come back at
once, and he got up and leaned in the window, listening to
the thrushes in the Crescent gardens, gazing at the sea;
dreamy and blue below the trees. A servant came in and
cleared the tea away, and he still stood, inhaling the evening air, trying not to think. Then he saw the Hallidays
coming through the gate of the Crescent, Stella a little in
front of Phil and the children, with their baskets, and instinctively he drew back. His heart, too sore and discom-

fited, shrank from this encounter, yet wanted its friendly
solace—bore a grudge against this influence, yet craved its
cool innocence, and the pleasure of watching Stella's face.
From against the wall behind the piano he saw her come
in and stand looking a little blank as though disappointed;
then she saw him and smiled, a swift, brilliant smile which
warmed yet irritated Ashurst.

"You never came after us, Frank."

"No; I found I couldn't."

"Look! We picked such lovely late violets!" She held
out a bunch. Ashurst put his nose to them, and there
stirred within him vague longings, chilled instantly by a
vision of Megan's anxious face lifted to the faces of the
passers-by.

He said shortly: "How jolly!" and turned away. He
went up to his room, and, avoiding the children, who were
coming up the stairs, threw himself on his bed, and lay
there with his arms crossed over his face. Now that he felt
the die really cast, and Megan given up, he hated himself,
and almost hated the Hallidays and their atmosphere of
healthy, happy English homes. Why should they have
chanced here, to drive away first love—to show him that he
was going to be no better than a common seducer? What
right had Stella, with her fair, shy beauty, to make him
know for certain that he would never marry Megan; and,
tarnishing it all, bring him such bitterness of regretful
longing and such pity? Megan would be back by now,
worn out by her miserable seeking—poor little thing!—
expecting, perhaps, to find him there when she reached
home. Ashurst bit at his sleeve, to stifle a groan of remorseful longing. He went to dinner glum and silent, and
his mood threw a dinge even over the children. It was a
melancholy, rather ill-tempered evening, for they were all
tired; several times he caught Stella looking at him with a
hurt, puzzled expression, and this pleased his evil mood.
He slept miserably; got up quite early, and wandered out.

He went down to the beach. Alone there with the serene, the blue, the sunlit sea, his heart relaxed a little. Conceited fool—to think that Megan would take it so hard! In a week or two she would almost have forgotten! And he—well, he would have the reward of virtue! A good young man! If Stella knew, she would give him her blessing for resisting that devil she believed in; and he uttered a hard laugh. But slowly the peace and beauty of sea and sky, the flight of the lonely seagulls, made him feel ashamed. He bathed, and turned homewards.

In the Crescent gardens Stella herself was sitting on a camp stool, sketching. He stole up close behind. How fair and pretty she was, bent diligently, holding up her brush, measuring, wrinkling her brows.

He said gently:

"Sorry I was such a beast last night, Stella."

She turned round, startled, flushed very pink, and said in her quick way:

"It's all right. I knew there was something. Between friends it doesn't matter, does it?"

Ashurst answered:

"Between friends—and we are, aren't we?"

She looked up at him, nodded vehemently, and her upper teeth gleamed again in that swift, brilliant smile.

Three days later he went back to London, traveling with the Hallidays. He had not written to the farm. What was there he could say?

On the last day of April in the following year he and Stella were married. . . .

Such were Ashurst's memories, sitting against the wall among the gorse, on his silver-wedding day. At this very spot, where he had laid out the lunch, Megan must have stood outlined against the sky when he had first caught sight of her. Of all queer coincidences! And there moved in him a longing to go down and see again the farm and the orchard, and the meadow of the gypsy bogle. It would not take long; Stella would be an hour yet, perhaps.

How well he remembered it all—the little crowning group of pine trees, the steep-up grass hill behind! He paused at the farm gate. The low stone house, the yew-tree porch, the flowering currants—not changed a bit; even the old green chair was out there on the grass under the window, where he had reached up to her that night to take the key. Then he turned down the lane, and stood leaning on the orchard gate—gray skeleton of a gate, as then. A black pig even was wandering in there among the trees. Was it true that twenty-six years had passed, or had he dreamed and awakened to find Megan waiting for him by the big apple-tree? Unconsciously he put up his hand to his grizzled beard and brought himself back to reality. Opening the gate, he made his way down through the docks and nettles till he came to the edge, and the old apple-tree itself. Unchanged! A little more of the gray-green lichen, a dead branch or two, and for the rest it might have been only last night that he had embraced that mossy trunk after Megan's flight and inhaled its woody savor, while above his head the moonlit blossom had seemed to breathe and live. In that early spring a few buds were showing already; the blackbirds shouting their songs, a cuckoo calling, the sunlight bright and warm. Incredibly the same—the chattering trout-stream, the narrow pool he had lain in every morning, splashing the water over his flanks and chest; and out there in the wild meadow the beech clump and the stone where the gypsy bogle was supposed to sit. And an ache for lost youth, a hankering, a sense of wasted love and sweetness, gripped Ashurst by the throat. Surely, on this earth of such wild beauty, one was meant to hold rapture to one's heart, as this earth and sky held it! And yet, one could not!

He went to the edge of the stream, and, looking down at the little pool, thought: "Youth and spring! What has

become of them all, I wonder?" And then, in sudden fear
of having this memory jarred by human encounter, he
went back to the lane, and pensively retraced his steps to
the cross-roads.

Beside the car an old, gray-bearded laborer was leaning
on a stick, talking to the chauffeur. He broke off at once,
as though guilty of disrespect, and, touching his hat, prepared to limp on down the lane.

Ashurst pointed to the narrow green mound. "Can you
tell me what this is?"

The old fellow stopped; on his face had come a look as
though he were thinking: "You've come to the right shop,
mister!"

" 'Tes a grave," he said.

"But why out here?"

The old man smiled. "That's a tale, as yu may say. An'
not the first time as I've a-told et—there's plenty folks
asks 'bout that bit o' turf. 'Maid's Grave' us calls et,
'ereabouts."

Ashurst held out his pouch. "Have a fill?"

The old man touched his hat again, and slowly filled an
old clay pipe. His eyes, looking upward out of a mass of
wrinkles and hair, were still quite bright.

"If yu don' mind, zurr, I'll zet down—my leg's 'urtin' a
bit to-day." And he sat down on the mound of turf.

"There's always a vlower on this grave. An' 'tain't so
very lonesome, neither; brave lot o' folks goes by now, in
they new motor cars an' things—not as 'twas in th' old
days. She've a-got company up 'ere. 'Twas a poor soul
killed 'erself."

"I see!" said Ashurst. "Cross-roads burial. I didn't
know that custom was kept up."

"Ah! but 'twas a main long time ago. Us 'ad a parson
as was very God-fearin' then. Let me see, I've 'ad my
pension six year come Michaelmas, an' I were just on
fifty when 't 'appened. There's none livin' knows more

about et than what I du. She belonged close 'ere; same farm as where I used to work along o' Mrs. Narracombe— 'tes Nick Narracombe's now; I dus a bit for 'im still, odd times."

Ashurst, who was leaning against the gate, lighting his pipe, left his curved hands before his face for long after the flame of the match had gone out.

"Yes?" he said, and to himself his voice sounded hoarse ınd queer.

"She was one in an 'underd, poor maid! I putts a vlower 'ere every time I passes. Pretty maid an' gude maid she was, though they wouldn't burry 'er up tu th' church, nor where she wanted to be burried neither." The old laborer paused, and put his hairy, twisted hand flat down on the turf beside the bluebells.

"Yes?" said Ashurst.

"In a manner of speakin'," the old man went on, "I think as 'twas a love-story—though there's no one never knu for zartin. Yu can't tell what's in a maid's 'ead—but that's wot I think about it." He drew his hand along the turf. "I was fond o' that maid—don' know as there was any one as wasn' fond of 'er. But she was tu lovin'-'earted —that's where 'twas, I think." He looked up. And Ashurst, whose lips were trembling in the cover of his beard, murmured again: "Yes?"

" 'Twas in the spring, 'bout now as't might be, or a little later—blossom time—an' we 'ad one o' they young college gentlemen stayin' at the farm—nice feller tu, with 'is 'ead in the air. I liked 'e very well, an' I never see nothin' between 'em, but to my thinkin' 'e turned the maid's fancy." The old man took the pipe out of his mouth, spat, and went on:

"Yu see, 'e went away sudden one day, an' never come back. They got 'is knapsack and bits o' things down there still. That's what stuck in my mind—'is never sendin' for 'em. 'Is name was Ashes, or somethin' like that."

"Yes?" said Ashurst once more.

The old man licked his lips.

"'Er never said nothin', but from that day 'er went kind of dazed lukin'; didn' seem rightly therr at all. I never knu a 'uman creature so changed in me life—never. There was another young feller at the farm—Joe Biddaford 'is name wer', that was praaperly sweet on 'er, tu; I guess 'e used to plague 'er wi' 'is attentions. She got to luke quite wild. I'd zee her sometimes of an avenin' when I was bringin' up the calves; ther' she'd stand in th' orchard, under the big apple-tree, lukin' straight before 'er. 'Well,' I used t' think, 'I dunno what 'tes that's the matter wi' yu, but yu'm lukin' pittiful, that yu be!'"

The old man relit his pipe, and sucked at it reflectively.

"Yes?" said Ashurst.

"I remembers one day I said to 'er: 'What's the matter, Megan?'—'er name was Megan David, she come from Wales same as 'er aunt, ol' Missis Narracombe. 'Yu'm frettin' about something,' I says. 'No, Jim,' she says, 'I'm not frettin'.' 'Yes, yu be!' I says. 'No,' she says, and tu tears cam' rollin' out. 'Yu'm cryin'—what's that, then?' I says. She putts 'er 'and over 'er 'eart: 'It 'urts me,' she says; 'but 'twill sune be better,' she says. 'But if anything shude 'appen to me, Jim, I wants to be buried under this 'ere apple-tree.' I laughed. 'What's goin' to 'appen to yu?' I says: 'don't 'ee be fulish.' 'No,' she says, 'I won't be fulish.' Well, I know what maids are, an' I never thought no more about et, till tu days arter that, 'bout six in the avenin' I was comin' up wi' the calves, when I see somethin' dark lyin' in the strame, close to that big apple-tree. I says to meself: 'Is that a pig—funny place for a pig to get to!' an' I goes up to et, an' I see what 'twas."

The old man stopped: his eyes, turned upward, had a bright, suffering look.

"'Twas the maid, in a little narrer pool ther' that's made by the stoppin' of a rock—where I see the young gentleman bathin' once or twice. 'Er was lyin' on 'er face in the watter. There was a plant o' goldie-cups growin' out o' the stone just above 'er 'ead. An' when I come to luke at 'er face, 'twas luvly, butiful, so calm's a baby's—wonderful butiful et was. When the doctor saw 'er, 'e said: ' 'Er culdn' never a-done it in that little bit o' watter if 'er 'adn't a-been in an extarsy.' Ah! an' judgin' from 'er face, that was just 'ow she was. Et made me cry praaper—butiful et was! 'Twas June then, but she'd a-found a little bit of apple blossom left over somewheres, and stuck et in 'er 'air. That's why I thinks 'er must a-been in an extarsy, to go to et gay, like that. Why! there wasn't more than a fute and 'arf o' watter. But I tell 'ee one thing—that meadder's 'arnted; I knu et, an' she knu et; an' no one'll persuade me as 'tesn't. I told 'em what she said to me 'bout bein' burried under th' apple-tree. But I think that turned 'em—made et luke tu much 's ef she'd 'ad it in 'er mind deliberate; an' so they burried 'er up 'ere. Parson we 'ad then was very particular, 'e was."

Again the old man drew his hand over the turf.

" 'Tes wonderful, et seems," he added slowly, "what maids 'll du for love. She 'ad a lovin' 'eart; I guess 'twas broken. But us never *knu* nothin'!"

He looked up as if for approval of his story, but Ashurst had walked past him as if he were not there.

Up on the top of the hill, beyond where he had spread the lunch, over, out of sight, he lay down on his face. So had his virtue been rewarded, and "the Cyprian," goddess of love, taken her revenge! And before his eyes, dim with tears, came Megan's face with the sprig of apple blossoms in her dark, wet hair. 'What did I do that was wrong?' he thought. 'What did I do?' But he could not answer. Spring, with its rush of passion, its flowers and song—the spring in his heart and Megan's! Was it just Love seeking a victim! The Greek was right, then—the words of the "Hippolytus" as true to-day!

> *"For mad is the heart of Love,*
>   *And gold the gleam of his wing;*
>   *And all to the spell thereof*
>   *Bend when he makes his spring.*
> *All life that is wild and young*
>   *In mountain and wave and stream,*
> *All that of earth is sprung,*
>   *Or breathes in the red sunbeam;*
> *Yea, and Mankind. O'er all a royal throne*
> *Cyprian, Cyprian, is thine alone!"*

The Greek was right! Megan! Poor little Megan—coming over the hill! Megan under the old apple-tree waiting and looking! Megan dead, with beauty printed on her! . . .

A voice said:

"Oh, there you are! Look."

Ashurst rose, took his wife's sketch, and stared at it in silence.

"Is the foreground right, Frank?"

"Yes."

"But there's something wanting, isn't there?"

Ashurst nodded. Wanting? The apple-tree, the singing, and the gold!

# THE PRUSSIAN OFFICER
## *by D. H. Lawrence*

### I

THEY had marched more than thirty kilometers since dawn, along the white, hot road where occasional thickets of trees threw a moment of shade, then out into the glare again. On either hand, the valley, wide and shallow, glittered with heat; dark green patches of rye pale young corn, fallow and meadow and black pine woods spread in a dull, hot diagram under a glistening sky. But right in front the mountains ranged across, pale blue and very still, snow gleaming gently out of the deep atmosphere. And towards the mountains, on and on, the regiment marched between the rye fields and the meadows, between the scraggy fruit trees set regularly on either side the high road. The burnished, dark green rye threw off a suffocating heat, the mountains drew gradually nearer and more distinct. While the feet of the soldiers grew hotter, sweat ran through their hair under their helmets, and their knapsacks could burn no more in contact with their shoulders, but seemed instead to give off a cold, prickly sensation.

He walked on and on in silence, staring at the mountains ahead, that rose sheer out of the land, and stood fold behind fold, half earth, half heaven, the heaven, the barrier with slits of soft snow, in the pale, bluish peaks.

He could now walk almost without pain. At the start, he had determined not to limp. It had made him sick to take the first steps, and during the first mile or so, he had compressed his breath, and the cold drops of

sweat had stood on his forehead. But he had walked it
off. What were they after all but bruises! He had looked
at them, as he was getting up: deep bruises on the backs
of his thighs. And since he had made his first step in the
morning, he had been conscious of them, till now he had
a tight, hot place in his chest, with suppressing the pain,
and holding himself in. There seemed no air when he
breathed. But he walked almost lightly.

The Captain's hand had trembled at taking his coffee
at dawn: his orderly saw it again. And he saw the fine
figure of the Captain wheeling on horseback at the farmhouse ahead, a handsome figure in pale blue uniform with
facings of scarlet, and the metal gleaming on the black
helmet and the sword-scabbard, and dark streaks of sweat
coming on the silky bay horse. The orderly felt he was
connected with that figure moving so suddenly on horseback: he followed it like a shadow, mute and inevitable
and damned by it. And the officer was always aware of
the tramp of the company behind, the march of his
orderly among the men.

The Captain was a tall man of about forty, gray at
the temples. He had a handsome, finely knit figure, and
was one of the best horsemen in the West. His orderly,
having to rub him down, admired the amazing riding
muscles of his loins.

For the rest, the orderly scarcely noticed the officer
any more than he noticed himself. It was rarely he saw
his master's face: he did not look at it. The Captain had
reddish-brown, stiff hair, that he wore short upon his
skull. His mustache was also cut short and bristly
over a full, brutal mouth. His face was rather rugged,
the cheeks thin. Perhaps the man was the more handsome for the deep lines in his face, the irritable tension
of his brow, which gave him the look of a man who fights
with life. His fair eyebrows stood bushy over light blue
eyes that were always flashing with cold fire.

He was a Prussian aristocrat, haughty and overbearing.
But his mother had been a Polish Countess. Having made
too many gambling debts when he was young, he had
ruined his prospects in the Army, and remained an in-
fantry captain. He had never married: his position did
not allow of it, and no woman had ever moved him to
it. His time he spent riding—occasionally he rode one of
his own horses at the races—and at the officers' club.
Now and then he took himself a mistress. But after such
an event, he returned to duty with his brow still more
tense, his eyes still more hostile and irritable. With the
men, however, he was merely impersonal, though a devil
when roused; so that, on the whole, they feared him,
but had no great aversion from him. They accepted him
as the inevitable.

To his orderly he was at first cold and just and indifferent: he did not fuss over trifles. So that his servant
knew practically nothing about him, except just what
orders he would give, and how he wanted them obeyed.
That was quite simple. Then the change gradually came.

The orderly was a youth of about twenty-two, of
medium height, and well built. He had strong, heavy
limbs, was swarthy, with a soft, black, young mustache.
There was something altogether warm and young about
him. He had firmly marked eyebrows over dark, expressionless eyes, that seemed never to have thought,
only to have received life direct through his senses, and
acted straight from instinct.

Gradually the officer had become aware of his servant's
young, vigorous, unconscious presence about him. He
could not get away from the sense of the youth's person,
while he was in attendance. It was like a warm flame upon
the older man's tense, rigid body, that had become almost
unliving, fixed. There was something so free and self-
contained about him, and something in the young fellow's
movement, that made the officer aware of him. And this

irritated the Prussian. He did not choose to be touched
into life by his servant. He might easily have changed
his man, but he did not. He now very rarely looked direct
at his orderly, but kept his face averted, as if to avoid
seeing him. And yet as the young soldier moved unthink-
ing about the apartment, the elder watched him, and
would notice the movement of his strong young shoulders
under the blue cloth, the bend of his neck. And it irritated
him. To see the soldier's young, brown, shapely peasant's
hand grasp the loaf or the wine-bottle sent a flash of hate
or of anger through the elder man's blood. It was not
that the youth was clumsy: it was rather the blind, in-
stinctive sureness of movement of an unhampered young
animal that irritated the officer to such a degree.

Once, when a bottle of wine had gone over, and the
red gushed out on to the tablecloth, the officer had started
up with an oath, and his eyes, bluey like fire, had held
those of the confused youth for a moment. It was a shock
for the young soldier. He felt something sink deeper,
deeper into his soul, where nothing had ever gone before.
It left him rather blank and wondering. Some of his
natural completeness in himself was gone, a little uneasiness took its place. And from that time an undis-
covered feeling had held between the two men.

Henceforward the orderly was afraid of really meeting
his master. His subconsciousness remembered those steely
blue eyes and the harsh brows, and did not intend to meet
them again. So he always stared past his master, and
avoided him. Also, in a little anxiety, he waited for the
three months to have gone, when his time would be up.
He began to feel a constraint in the Captain's presence,
and the soldier even more than the officer wanted to be
left alone, in his neutrality as servant.

He had served the Captain for more than a year, and
knew his duty. This he performed easily, as if it were
natural to him. The officer and his commands he took for

granted, as he took the sun and the rain, and he served
as a matter of course. It did not implicate him personally.

But now if he were going to be forced into a personal
interchange with his master he would be like a wild thing
caught; he felt he must get away.

But the influence of the young soldier's being had
penetrated through the officer's stiffened discipline, and
perturbed the man in him. He, however, was a gentleman, with long, fine hands and cultivated movements, and
was not going to allow such a thing as the stirring of his
innate self. He was a man of passionate temper, who had
always kept himself suppressed. Occasionally there had
been a duel, an outburst before the soldiers. He knew
himself to be always on the point of breaking out. But
he kept himself hard to the idea of the Service. Whereas
the young soldier seemed to live out his warm, full nature,
to give it off in his very movements, which had a certain
zest, such as wild animals have in free movement. And
this irritated the officer more and more.

In spite of himself, the Captain could not regain his
neutrality of feeling towards his orderly. Nor could he
leave the man alone. In spite of himself, he watched him,
gave him sharp orders, tried to take up as much of his
time as possible. Sometimes he flew into a rage with the
young soldier, and bullied him. Then the orderly shut
himself off, as it were out of earshot, and waited, with
sullen, flushed face, for the end of the noise. The words
never pierced to his intelligence. He made himself, pro-
tectively, impervious to the feelings of his master.

He had a scar on his left thumb, a deep seam going
across the knuckle. The officer had long suffered from it,
and wanted to do something to it. Still it was there, ugly
and brutal on the young, brown hand. At last the Captain's reserve gave way. One day, as the orderly was
smoothing out the tablecloth, the officer pinned down his
thumb with a pencil, asking:

"How did you come by that?"

The young man winced and drew back at attention. "A wood ax, Herr Hauptmann," he answered.

The officer waited for further explanation. None came. The orderly went about his duties. The elder man was sullenly angry. His servant avoided him. And the next day he had to use all his will power to avoid seeing the scarred thumb. He wanted to get hold of it and— A hot flame ran in his blood.

He knew his servant would soon be free, and would be glad. As yet, the soldier had held himself off from the elder man. The Captain grew madly irritable. He could not rest when the soldier was away, and when he was present, he glared at him with tormented eyes. He hated those fine, black brows over the unmeaning, dark eyes, he was infuriated by the free movement of the handsome limbs, which no military discipline could make stiff. And he became harsh and cruelly bullying, using contempt and satire. The young soldier only grew more mute and expressionless.

"What cattle were you bred by, that you can't keep straight eyes? Look me in the eyes when I speak to you."

And the soldier turned his dark eyes to the other's face, but there was no sight in them: he stared with the slightest possible cast, holding back his sight, perceiving the blue of his master's eyes, but receiving no look from them. And the elder man went pale, and his reddish eyebrows twitched. He gave his order, barrenly.

Once he flung a heavy military glove into the young soldier's face. Then he had the satisfaction of seeing the black eyes flare up into his own, like a blaze when straw is thrown on a fire. And he had laughed with a little tremor and a sneer.

But there were only two months more. The youth instinctively tried to keep himself intact: he tried to serve the officer as if the latter were an abstract authority and not a man. All his instinct was to avoid personal contact, even definite hate. But in spite of himself the hate grew, responsive to the officer's passion. However, he put it in the background. When he had left the Army he could dare acknowledge it. By nature he was active, and had many friends. He thought what amazing good fellows they were. But, without knowing it, he was alone. Now this solitariness was intensified. It would carry him through his term. But the officer seemed to be going irritably insane, and the youth was deeply frightened

The soldier had a sweetheart, a girl from the mountains, independent and primitive. The two walked together, rather silently. He went with her, not to talk, but to have his arm round her, and for the physical contact. This eased him, made it easier for him to ignore the Captain; for he could rest with her held fast against his chest. And she, in some unspoken fashion, was there for him. They loved each other.

The Captain perceived it, and was mad with irritation He kept the young man engaged all the evenings long, and took pleasure in the dark look that came on his face. Occasionally, the eyes of the two men met, those of the younger sullen and dark, doggedly unalterable, those of the elder sneering with restless contempt.

The officer tried hard not to admit the passion that had got hold of him. He would not know that his feeling for his orderly was anything but that of a man incensed by his stupid, perverse servant. So, keeping quite justified and conventional in his consciousness, he let the other thing run on. His nerves, however, were suffering. At last he slung the end of a belt in his servant's face. When he saw the youth start back, the pain-tears in his eyes and the blood on his mouth, he had felt at once a thrill of deep pleasure and of shame.

But this, he acknowledged to himself, was a thing he had never done before. The fellow was too exasperating.

His own nerves must be going to pieces. He went away for some days with a woman.

It was a mockery of pleasure. He simply did not want the woman. But he stayed on for his time. At the end of it, he came back in an agony of irritation, torment, and misery. He rode all the evening, then came straight in to supper. His orderly was out. The officer sat with his long, fine hands lying on the table, perfectly still, and all his blood seemed to be corroding.

At last his servant entered. He watched the strong, easy young figure, the fine eyebrows, the thick black hair. In a week's time the youth had got back his old well-being. The hands of the officer twitched and seemed to be full of mad flame. The young man stood at attention, unmoving, shut off.

The meal went in silence. But the orderly seemed eager. He made a clatter with the dishes.

"Are you in a hurry?" asked the officer, watching the intent, warm face of his servant. The other did not reply.

"Will you answer my question?" said the Captain.

"Yes, sir," replied the orderly, standing with his pile of deep Army plates. The Captain waited, looked at him, then asked again:

"Are you in a hurry?"

"Yes, sir," came the answer, that sent a flash through the listener.

"For what?"

"I was going out, sir."

"I want you this evening."

There was a moment's hesitation. The officer had a curious stiffness of countenance.

"Yes, sir," replied the servant, in his throat.

"I want you to-morrow evening also—in fact, you may consider your evenings occupied, unless I give you leave."

The mouth with the young mustache set close.

"Yes, sir," answered the orderly, loosening his lips for a moment.

He again turned to the door.

"And why have you a piece of pencil in your ear?"

The orderly hesitated, then continued on his way without answering. He set the plates in a pile outside the door, took the stump of pencil from his ear, and put it in his pocket. He had been copying a verse for his sweetheart's birthday card. He returned to finish clearing the table. The officer's eyes were dancing, he had a little, eager smile.

"Why have you a piece of pencil in your ear?" he asked.

The orderly took his hands full of dishes. His master was standing near the great green stove, a little smile on his face, his chin thrust forward. When the young soldier saw him his heart suddenly ran hot. He felt blind. Instead of answering, he turned dazedly to the door. As he was crouching to set down the dishes, he was pitched forward by a kick from behind. The pots went in a stream down the stairs, he clung to the pillar of the banisters. And as he was rising he was kicked heavily again, and again, so that he clung sickly to the post for some moments. His master had gone swiftly into the room and closed the door. The maid-servant downstairs looked up the staircase and made a mocking face at the crockery disaster.

The officer's heart was plunging. He poured himself a glass of wine, part of which he spilled on the floor, and gulped the remainder, leaning against the cool, green stove. He heard his man collecting the dishes from the stairs. Pale, as if intoxicated, he waited. The servant entered again. The Captain's heart gave a pang, as of pleasure, seeing the young fellow bewildered and uncertain on his feet, with pain.

"Schöner!" he said.

The soldier was a little slower in coming to attention.

"Yes, sir!"

The youth stood before him, with pathetic young mustache, and fine eyebrows very distinct on his forehead of dark marble.

"I asked you a question."

"Yes, sir."

The officer's tone bit like acid.

"Why had you a pencil in your ear?"

Again the servant's heart ran hot, and he could not breathe. With dark, strained eyes, he looked at the officer, as if fascinated. And he stood there sturdily planted, unconscious. The withering smile came into the Captain's eyes, and he lifted his foot.

"I—I forgot it—sir," panted the soldier, his dark eyes fixed on the other man's dancing blue ones.

"What was it doing there?"

He saw the young man's breast heaving as he made an effort for words.

"I had been writing."

"Writing what?"

Again the soldier looked him up and down. The officer could hear him panting. The smile came into the blue eyes. The soldier worked his dry throat, but could not speak. Suddenly the smile lit like a flame on the officer's face, and a kick came heavily against the orderly's thigh. The youth moved a pace sideways. His face went dead, with two black, staring eyes.

"Well?" said the officer.

The orderly's mouth had gone dry, and his tongue rubbed in it as on dry brown-paper. He worked his throat. The officer raised his foot. The servant went stiff.

"Some poetry, sir," came the crackling, unrecognizable sound of his voice.

"Poetry, what poetry?" asked the Captain with a sickly smile.

Again there was the working in the throat. The Captain's heart had suddenly gone down heavily, and he stood sick and tired.

"For my girl, sir," he heard the dry, inhuman sound.

"Oh!" he said, turning away. "Clear the table."

"Click!" went the soldier's throat; then again, "click!" and then the half-articulate:

"Yes, sir."

The young soldier was gone, looking old, and walking heavily.

The officer, left alone, held himself rigid, to prevent himself from thinking. His instinct warned him that he must not think. Deep inside him was the intense gratification of his passion, still working powerfully. Then there was a counter-action, a horrible breaking down of something inside him, a whole agony of reaction. He stood there for an hour motionless, a chaos of sensations, but rigid with a will to keep blank his consciousness, to prevent his mind grasping. And he held himself so until the worst of the stress had passed, when he began to drink, drank himself to an intoxication, till he slept obliterated. When he woke in the morning he was shaken to the base of his nature. But he had fought off the realization of what he had done. He had prevented his mind from taking it in, had suppressed it along with his instincts, and the conscious man had nothing to do with it. He felt only as after a bout of intoxication, weak, but the affair itself all dim and not to be recovered. Of the drunkenness of his passion he successfully refused remembrance. And when his orderly appeared with coffee, the officer assumed the same self he had had the morning before. He refused the event of the past night—denied it had ever been—and was successful in his denial. He had not done any such thing—not he himself. Whatever there might be lay at the door of a stupid, insubordinate servant.

The orderly had gone about in a stupor all the evening. He drank some beer because he was parched, but not much, the alcohol made his feeling come back, and he could not bear it. He was dulled, as if nine-tenths of the ordinary man in him were inert. He crawled about disfigured. Still, when he thought of the kicks, he went sick, and when he thought of the threat of more kicking, in the room afterwards, his heart went hot and faint, and he panted, remembered the one that had come. He had been forced to say, "For my girl." He was much too done even to want to cry. His mouth hung slightly open, like an idiot's. He felt vacant, and wasted. So, he wandered at his work, painfully, and very slowly and clumsily, fumbling blindly with the brushes, and finding it difficult, when he sat down, to summon the energy to move again. His limbs, his jaw, were slack and nerveless. But he was very tired. He got to bed at last, and slept inert, relaxed, in a sleep that was rather stupor than slumber, a dead night of stupefaction shot through with gleams of anguish.

In the morning were the maneuvers. But he woke even before the bugle sounded. The painful ache in his chest, the dryness of his throat, the awful steady feeling of misery made his eyes come awake and dreary at once. He knew, without thinking, what had happened. And he knew that the day had come again, when he must go on with his round. The last bit of darkness was being pushed out of the room. He would have to move his inert body and go on. He was so young, and had known so little trouble, that he was bewildered. He only wished it would stay night, so that he could lie still, covered up by the darkness. And yet nothing would prevent the day from coming, nothing would save him from having to get up and saddle the Captain's horse, and make the Captain's coffee. It was there, inevitable. And then, he thought, it was impossible. Yet they would not leave him free. He must go and take the coffee to the Captain. He was too stunned to understand it. He only knew it was inevitable—inevitable, however long he lay inert.

At last, after heaving at himself, for he seemed to be a mass of inertia, he got up. But he had to force every one of his movements from behind, with his will. He felt lost, and dazed, and helpless. Then he clutched hold of the bed, the pain was so keen. And looking at his thighs, he saw the darker bruises on his swarthy flesh and he knew that, if he pressed one of his fingers on one of the bruises, he should faint. But he did not want to faint—he did not want anybody to know. No one should ever know. It was between him and the Captain. There were only the two people in the world now—himself and the Captain.

Slowly, economically, he got dressed and forced himself to walk. Everything was obscure, except just what he had his hands on. But he managed to get through his work. The very pain revived his dull senses. The worst remained yet. He took the tray and went up to the Captain's room. The officer, pale and heavy, sat at the table. The orderly, as he saluted, felt himself put out of existence. He stood still for a moment submitting to his own nullification—then he gathered himself, seemed to regain himself, and then the Captain began to grow vague, unreal, and the younger soldier's heart beat up. He clung to this situation—that the Captain did not exist —so that he himself might live. But when he saw his officer's hand tremble as he took the coffee, he felt everything falling shattered. And he went away, feeling as if he himself were coming to pieces, disintegrated. And when the Captain was there on horseback, giving orders, while he himself stood, with rifle and knapsack, sick with pain, he felt as if he must shut his eyes—as if he must shut his eyes on everything. It was only the long agony of marching with a parched throat that filled him with one single, sleep-heavy intention: to save himself.

## II

He was getting used even to his parched throat. That
the snowy peaks were radiant among the sky, that the
whity-green glacier-river twisted through its pale shoals,
in the valley below, seemed almost supernatural. But he
was going mad with fever and thirst. He plodded on un-
complaining. He did not want to speak, not to anybody.
There were two gulls, like flakes of water and snow, over
the river. The scent of green rye soaked in sunshine
came like a sickness. And the march continued, monot-
onously, almost like a bad sleep.

At the next farmhouse, which stood low and broad
near the high road, tubs of water had been put out. The
soldiers clustered round to drink. They took off their
helmets, and the steam mounted from their wet hair.
The Captain sat on horseback, watching. He needed to
see his orderly. His helmet threw a dark shadow over his
light, fierce eyes, but his mustache and mouth and chin
were distinct in the sunshine. The orderly must move
under the presence of the figure of the horseman. It was
not that he was afraid, or cowed. It was as if he were
disemboweled, made empty, like an empty shell. He felt
himself as nothing, a shadow creeping under the sunshine.
And, thirsty as he was, he could scarcely drink, feeling
the Captain near him. He would not take off his helmet
to wipe his wet hair. He wanted to stay in shadow, not
to be forced into consciousness. Starting, he saw the
light heel of the officer prick the belly of the horse; the
Captain cantered away, and he himself could relapse into
vacancy.

Nothing, however, could give him back his living place
in the hot, bright morning. He felt like a gap among
it all. Whereas the Captain was prouder, overriding. A
hot flash went through the young servant's body. The

Captain was firmer and prouder with life, he himself was empty as a shadow. Again the flash went through him, dazing him out. But his heart ran a little firmer.

The company turned up the hill, to make a loop for the return. Below, from among the trees, the farm-bell clanged. He saw the laborers, mowing barefoot at the thick grass, leave off their work and go downhill, their scythes hanging over their shoulders, like long, bright claws curving down behind them. They seemed like dream-people, as if they had no relation to himself. He felt as in a blackish dream: as if all the other things were there and had form, but he himself was only a consciousness, a gap that could think and perceive.

The soldiers were tramping silently up the glaring hillside. Gradually his head began to revolve, slowly, rhythmically. Sometimes it was dark before his eyes, as if he saw this world through a smoked glass, frail shadows and unreal. It gave him a pain in his head to walk.

The air was too scented, it gave no breath. All the lush green-stuff seemed to be issuing its sap, till the air was deathly, sickly with the smell of greenness. There was the perfume of clover, like pure honey and bees. Then there grew a faint acrid tang—they were near the beeches; and then a queer clattering noise, and a suffocating, hideous smell; they were passing a flock of sheep, a shepherd in a black smock, holding his crook. Why should the sheep huddle together under this fierce sun? He felt that the shepherd would not see him, though he could see the shepherd.

At last there was the halt. They stacked rifles in a conical stack, put down their kit in a scattered circle around it, and dispersed a little, sitting on a small knoll high on the hillside. The chatter began. The soldiers were steaming with heat, but were lively. He sat still, seeing the blue mountains rising upon the land, twenty kilometers away. There was a blue fold in the ranges, then out of that, at the foot, the broad, pale bed of the river, stretches of whity-green water between pinkish-gray shoals among the dark pine woods. There it was, spread out a long way off. And it seemed to come downhill, the river. There was a raft being steered, a mile away. It was a strange country. Nearer, a red-roofed, broad farm with white base and square dots of windows crouched beside the wall of beech foliage on the wood's edge. There were long strips of rye and clover and pale green corn. And just at his feet, below the knoll, was a darkish bog, where globe flowers stood breathless still on their slim stalks. And some of the pale gold bubbles were burst, and a broken fragment hung in the air. He thought he was going to sleep.

Suddenly something moved into this colored mirage before his eyes. The Captain, a small, light-blue and scarlet figure, was trotting evenly between the strips of corn, along the level brow of the hill. And the man making flag-signals was coming on. Proud and sure moved the horseman's figure, the quick, bright thing, in which was concentrated all the light of this morning, which for the rest lay a fragile, shining shadow. Submissive, apathetic, the young soldier sat and stared. But as the horse slowed to a walk, coming up the last steep path, the great flash flared over the body and soul of the orderly. He sat waiting. The back of his head felt as if it were weighted with a heavy piece of fire. He did not want to eat. His hands trembled slightly as he moved them. Meanwhile the officer on horseback was approaching slowly and proudly. The tension grew in the orderly's soul. Then again, seeing the Captain ease himself on the saddle, the flash blazed through him.

The Captain looked at the patch of light blue and scarlet, and dark heads, scattered closely on the hillside. It pleased him. The command pleased him. And he was feeling proud. His orderly was among them in common subjection. The officer rose a little on his stirrups to look. The young soldier sat with averted, dumb face. The Captain relaxed on his seat. His slim-legged, beautiful horse, brown as a beech nut, walked proudly uphill. The Captain passed into the zone of the company's atmosphere: a hot smell of men, of sweat, of leather. He knew it very well. After a word with the lieutenant, he went a few paces higher, and sat there, a dominant figure, his sweat-marked horse swishing its tail, while he looked down on his men, on his orderly, a nonentity among the crowd.

The young soldier's heart was like fire in his chest, and he breathed with difficulty. The officer, looking downhill, saw three of the young soldiers, two pails of water between them, staggering across a sunny green field. A table had been set up under a tree, and there the slim lieutenant stood, importantly busy. Then the Captain summoned himself to an act of courage. He called his orderly.

The flame leapt into the young soldier's throat as he heard the command, and he rose blindly, stifled. He saluted, standing below the officer. He did not look up. But there was the flicker in the Captain's voice.

"Go to the inn and fetch me . . ." the officer gave his commands. "Quick!" he added.

At the last word, the heart of the servant leapt with a flash, and he felt the strength come over his body. But he turned in mechanical obedience, and set off at a heavy run downhill, looking almost like a bear, his trousers bagging over his military boots. And the officer watched this blind, plunging run all the way.

But it was only the outside of the orderly's body that was obeying so humbly and mechanically. Inside had gradually accumulated a core into which all the energy of that young life was compact and concentrated. He executed his commission, and plodded quickly back uphill. There was a pain in his head, as he walked, that made him twist his features unknowingly. But hard there in the center of his chest was himself, himself, firm, and not to be plucked to pieces.

The Captain had gone up into the wood. The orderly plodded through the hot, powerfully smelling zone of the company's atmosphere. He had a curious mass of energy inside him now. The Captain was less real than himself. He approached the green entrance to the wood. There, in the half-shade, he saw the horse standing, the sunshine and the flickering shadow of leaves dancing over his brown body. There was a clearing where timber had lately been felled. Here, in the gold-green shade beside the brilliant cup of sunshine, stood two figures, blue and pink, the bits of pink showing out plainly. The Captain was talking to his lieutenant.

The orderly stood on the edge of the bright clearing, where great trunks of trees, stripped and glistening, lay stretched like naked, brown-skinned bodies. Chips of wood littered the trampled floor, like splashed light, and the bases of the felled trees stood here and there, with their raw, level tops. Beyond was the brilliant, sunlit green of a beech.

"Then I will ride forward," the orderly heard his Captain say. The lieutenant saluted and strode away. He himself went forward. A hot flash passed through his belly, as he tramped towards his officer.

The Captain watched the rather heavy figure of the young soldier stumble forward, and his veins, too, ran hot. This was to be man to man between them. He yielded before the solid, stumbling figure with bent head. The orderly stooped and put the food on a level-sawn tree-base. The Captain watched the glistening, sun-inflamed, naked hands. He wanted to speak to the young soldier, but could not. The servant propped a bottle against his thigh, pressed open the cork, and poured out the beer into the mug. He kept his head bent. The Captain accepted the mug.

"Hot!" he said, as if amiably.

The flame sprang out of the orderly's heart, nearly suffocating him.

"Yes, sir," he replied, between shut teeth.

And he heard the sound of the Captain's drinking, and he clenched his fists, such a strong torment came into his wrists. Then came the faint clang of the closing of the pot-lid. He looked up. The Captain was watching him. He glanced swiftly away. Then he saw the officer stoop and take a piece of bread from the tree-base. Again the flash of flame went through the young soldier, seeing the stiff body stoop beneath him, and his hands jerked. He looked away. He could feel the officer was nervous. The bread fell as it was being broken. The officer ate the other piece. The two men stood tense and still, the master laboriously chewing his bread, the servant staring with averted face, his fist clenched.

Then the young soldier started. The officer had pressed open the lid of the mug again. The orderly watched the lid of the mug, and the white hand that clenched the handle, as if he were fascinated. It was raised. The youth followed it with his eyes. And then he saw the thin, strong throat of the elder man moving up and down as he drank, the strong jaw working. And the instinct which had been jerking at the young man's wrist suddenly jerked free. He jumped, feeling as if it were rent in two by a strong flame.

The spur of the officer caught in a tree-root, he went down backwards with a crash, the middle of his back thudding sickeningly against a sharp-edged tree-base, the pot flying away. And in a second the orderly, with serious, earnest young face, and underlip between his teeth, had got his knee in the officer's chest and was pressing the chin backward over the farther edge of the tree-stump, pressing, with all his heart behind in a passion of relief, the tension of his wrists exquisite with relief. And with the base of his palms he shoved at the chin, with all his might. And it was pleasant, too, to have that chin, that hard jaw already slightly rough with beard, in his hands. He did not relax one hair's breadth, but, all the force of all his blood exulting in his thrust, he shoved back the head of the other man, till there was a little "cluck" and a crunching sensation. Then he felt as if his head went to vapor. Heavy convulsions shook the body of the officer, frightening and horrifying the young soldier. Yet it pleased him, too, to repress them. It pleased him to keep his hands pressing back the chin, to feel the chest of the other man yield in expiration to the weight of his strong, young knees, to feel the hard twitchings of the prostrate body jerking his own whole frame. which was pressed down on it.

But it went still. He could look into the nostrils of the other man, the eyes he could scarcely see. How curiously the mouth was pushed out, exaggerating the full lips, and the mustache bristling up from them. Then, with a start, he noticed the nostrils gradually filled with blood. The red brimmed, hesitated, ran over and went in a thin trickle down the face to the eyes.

It shocked and distressed him. Slowly, he got up. The body twitched and sprawled there, inert. He stood and looked at it in silence. It was a pity *it* was broken. It represented more than the thing which had kicked and bullied him. He was afraid to look at the eyes. They were hideous now, only the whites showing, and the blood running to them. The face of the orderly was drawn with horror at the sight. Well, it was so. In his heart he was satisfied. He had hated the face of the Captain. It was extinguished now. There was a heavy relief in the orderly's soul. That was as it should be. But he could not bear to see the long, military body lying broken over the tree-base, the fine fingers crisped. He wanted to hide it away.

Quickly, busily, he gathered it up and pushed it under the felled tree-trunks, which rested their beautiful, smooth length either end on logs. The face was horrible with blood. He covered it with the helmet. Then he pushed the limbs straight and decent, and brushed the dead leaves off the fine cloth of the uniform. So, it lay quite still in the shadow under there. A little strip of sunshine ran along the breast, from a chink between the logs. The orderly sat by it for a few moments. Here his own life also ended.

Then, through his daze, he heard the lieutenant, in a loud voice, explaining to the men outside the wood, that they were to suppose the bridge on the river below was held by the enemy. Now they were to march to the attack in such and such a manner. The lieutenant had no gift of expression. The orderly, listening from habit, got muddled. And when the lieutenant began it all again he ceased to hear.

He knew he must go. He stood up. It surprised him that the leaves were glittering in the sun, and the chips of wood reflecting white from the ground. For him a change had come over the world. But for the rest it had not—all seemed the same. Only he had left it. And he could not go back. It was his duty to return with the beer-pot and the bottle. He could not. He had left all that. The lieutenant was still hoarsely explaining. He must go, or they would overtake him. And he could not bear contact with any one now.

He drew his fingers over his eyes, trying to find out where he was. Then he turned away He saw the horse standing in the path. He went up to it and mounted. It hurt him to sit in the saddle. The pain of keeping his seat occupied him as they cantered through the wood. He would not have minded anything, but he could not get away from the sense of being divided from the others. The path led out of the trees. On the edge of the wood he pulled up and stood watching. There in the spacious sunshine of the valley soldiers were moving in a little swarm. Every now and then, a man harrowing on a strip of fallow shouted to his oxen, at the turn. The village and the white-towered church was small in the sunshine. And he no longer belonged to it—he sat there, beyond, like a man outside in the dark. He had gone out from everyday life into the unknown, and he could not, he even did not want to go back.

Turning from the sun-blazing valley, he rode deep into the wood. Tree-trunks, like people standing gray and still, took no notice as he went. A doe, herself a moving bit of sunshine and shadow, went running through the flecked shade. There were bright green rents in the foliage. Then it was all pine wood, dark and cool. And he was sick with pain, he had an intolerable great pulse in his head, and he was sick. He had never been ill in his life. He felt lost, quite dazed with all this.

Trying to get down from the horse, he fell, astonished at the pain and his lack of balance. The horse shifted uneasily. He jerked its bridle and sent it cantering jerkily away. It was his last connection with the rest of things.

But he only wanted to lie down and not be disturbed. Stumbling through the trees, he came on a quiet place where beeches and pine trees grew on a slope. Im mediately he had lain down and closed his eyes, his consciousness went racing on without him. A big pulse of sickness beat in him as if it throbbed through the whole earth. He was burning with dry heat. But he was too busy, too tearingly active in the incoherent race of delirium to observe.

III

He came to with a start. His mouth was dry and hard, his heart beat heavily, but he had not the energy to get up. His heart beat heavily. Where was he?—the barracks

—at home? There was something knocking. And, making
an effort, he looked round—trees, and litter of greenery,
and reddish, bright, still pieces of sunshine on the floor.
He did not believe he was himself, he did not believe
what he saw. Something was knocking. He made a struggle towards consciousness, but relapsed. Then he struggled
again. And gradually his surroundings fell into relation-
ship with himself. He knew, and a great pang of fear
went through his heart. Somebody was knocking. He
could see the heavy, black rags of a fir tree overhead.
Then everything went black. Yet he did not believe he
had closed his eyes. He had not. Out of the blackness
sight slowly emerged again. And some one was knocking.
Quickly, he saw the blood-disfigured face of his Captain,
which he hated. And he held himself still with horror.
Yet, deep inside him, he knew that it was so, the Captain
should be dead. But the physical delirium got hold of him.
Some one was knocking. He lay perfectly still, as if dead,
with fear. And he went unconscious.

When he opened his eyes again, he started, seeing
something creeping swiftly up a tree-trunk. It was a little
bird. And the bird was whistling overhead. Tap-tap-tap—
it was the small, quick bird rapping the tree-trunk with
its beak, as if its head were a little round hammer. He
watched it curiously. It shifted sharply, in its creeping
fashion. Then, like a mouse, it slid down the bare trunk.
Its swift creeping sent a flash of revulsion through him.
He raised his head. It felt a great weight. Then, the
little bird ran out of the shadow across a still patch of
sunshine, its little head bobbing swiftly, its white legs
twinkling brightly for a moment. How neat it was in
its build, so compact, with pieces of white on its wings.
There were several of them. They were so pretty—but
they crept like swift, erratic mice, running here and there
among the beech-mast.

He lay down again exhausted, and his consciousness lapsed. He had a horror of the little creeping birds. All his blood seemed to be darting and creeping in his head. And yet he could not move.

He came to with a further ache of exhaustion. There was the pain in his head, and the horrible sickness, and his inability to move. He had never been ill in his life. He did not know where he was or what he was. Probably he had got sunstroke. Or what else?—he had silenced the Captain forever—some time ago—oh, a long time ago. There had been blood on his face, and his eyes had turned upwards. It was all right, somehow. It was peace. But now he had got beyond himself. He had never been here before. Was it life, or not life? He was by himself. They were in a big, bright place, those others, and he was outside. The town, all the country, a big bright place of light: and he was outside, here, in the darkened open beyond, where each thing existed alone. But they would all have to come out there sometime, those others. Little, and left behind him, they all were. There had been father· and mother and sweetheart. What did they all matter? This was the open land.

He sat up. Something scuffled. It was a little, brown squirrel running in lovely, undulating bounds over the floor, its red tail completing the undulation of its body— and then, as it sat up, furling and unfurling. He watched it, pleased. It ran on again, friskily, enjoying itself. It flew wildly at another squirrel, and they were chasing each other, and making little scolding, chattering noises. The soldier wanted to speak to them. But only a hoarse sound came out of his throat. The squirrels burst away— they flew up the trees. And then he saw the one peeping round at him, halfway up a tree-trunk. A start of fear went through him, though, in so far as he was conscious, he was amused. It still stayed, its little, keen face staring at him halfway up the tree-trunk, its little ears pricked up, its clawy little hands clinging to the bark, its white breast reared. He started from it in panic.

Struggling to his feet, he lurched away. He went on walking, walking, looking for something—for a drink. His brain felt hot and inflamed for want of water. He stumbled on. Then he did not know anything. He went unconscious as he walked. Yet he stumbled on, his mouth open.

When, to his dumb wonder, he opened his eyes on the world again, he no longer tried to remember what it was. There was thick, golden light behind golden-green glitterings, and tall gray-purple shafts, and darknesses further off, surrounding him, growing deeper. He was conscious of a sense of arrival. He was amid the reality, on the real, dark bottom. But there was the thirst burning in his brain. He felt lighter, not so heavy. He supposed it was newness. The air was muttering with thunder. He thought he was walking wonderfully swiftly and was coming straight to relief—or was it to water?

Suddenly he stood still with fear. There was a tremendous flare of gold, immense—just a few dark trunks like bars between him and it. All the young level wheat was burnished gold glaring on its silky green. A woman, full-skirted, a black cloth on her head for head-dress, was passing like a block of shadow through the glistening, green corn, into the full glare. There was a farm, too, pale blue in shadow, and the timber black. And there was a church spire, nearly fused away in the gold. The woman moved on, away from him. He had no language with which to speak to her. She was the bright, solid unreality. She would make a noise of words that would confuse him, and her eyes would look at him without seeing him. She was crossing there to the other side. He stood against a tree.

When at last he turned, looking down the long, bare grove whose flat bed was already filling dark, he saw the mountains in a wonder-light, not far away, and radiant. Behind the soft, gray ridge of the nearest range the further mountains stood golden and pale gray, the snow all radiant like pure, soft gold. So still, gleaming in the sky, fashioned pure out of the ore of the sky, they shone in their silence. He stood and looked at them, his face illuminated. And like the golden, lustrous gleaming of the snow he felt his own thirst bright in him. He stood and gazed, leaning against a tree. And then everything slid away into space.

During the night the lightning fluttered perpetually, making the whole sky white. He must have walked again. The world hung livid round him for moments, fields a level sheen of gray-green light, trees in dark bulk, and the range of clouds black across a white sky. Then the darkness fell like a shutter, and the night was whole. A faint flutter of a half-revealed world that could not quite leap out of the darkness!—Then there again stood a sweep of pallor for the land, dark shapes looming, a range of clouds hanging overhead. The world was a ghostly shadow, thrown for a moment upon the pure darkness, which returned ever whole and complete.

And the mere delirium of sickness and fever went on inside him—his brain opening and shutting like the night—then sometimes convulsions of terror from something with great eyes that stared round a tree—then the long agony of the march, and the sun decomposing his blood—then the pang of hate for the Captain, followed by a pang of tenderness and ease. But everything was distorted, born of an ache and resolving into an ache.

In the morning he came definitely awake. Then his brain flamed with the sole horror of thirstiness! The sun was on his face, the dew was steaming from his wet clothes. Like one possessed, he got up. There, straight in front of him, blue and cool and tender, the mountains ranged across the pale edge of the morning sky. He wanted them—he wanted them alone—he wanted to leave himself and be identified with them. They did not move, they were still and soft, with white, gentle markings of snow. He stood still, mad with suffering, his hands crisping and clutching. Then he was twisting in a paroxysm on the grass.

He lay still, in a kind of dream of anguish. His thirst seemed to have separated itself from him, and to stand apart, a single demand. Then the pain he felt was another single self. Then there was the clog of his body, another separate thing. He was divided among all kinds of separate beings. There was some strange, agonized connection between them, but they were drawing further apart. Then they would all split. The sun, drilling down on him, was drilling through the bond. Then they would all fall, fall through the everlasting lapse of space. Then again, his consciousness reasserted itself. He roused on to his elbow and stared at the gleaming mountains. There they ranked, all still and wonderful between earth and heaven. He stared till his eyes went black, and the mountains, as they stood in their beauty, so clean and cool, seemed to have it, that which was lost in him.

### IV

When the soldiers found him, three hours later, he was lying with his face over his arm, his black hair giving off heat under the sun. But he was still alive. Seeing the open, black mouth the young soldiers dropped him in horror.

He died in the hospital at night, without having seen again.

The doctors saw the bruises on his legs, behind, and were silent.

The bodies of the two men lay together, side by side, in the mortuary, the one white and slender, but laid rigidly at rest, the other locking as if every moment it must rouse into life again, so young and unused, from a slumber.

# MISS BRILL
## *by Katherine Mansfield*

ALTHOUGH it was so brilliantly fine—the blue sky
powdered with gold and great spots of light like white wine
splashed over the Jardins Publiques—Miss Brill was glad
that she had decided on her fur. The air was motionless,
but when you opened your mouth there was just a faint
chill, like a chill from a glass of iced water before you
sip, and now and again a leaf came drifting—from nowhere, from the sky. Miss Brill put up her hand and
touched her fur. Dear little thing! It was nice to feel it
again. She had taken it out of its box that afternoon,
shaken out the moth-powder, given it a good brush, and
rubbed the life back into the dim little eyes. "What has
been happening to me?" said the sad little eyes. Oh,
how sweet it was to see them snap at her again from the
red eiderdown! . . . But the nose, which was of some
black composition, wasn't at all firm. It must have had
a knock, somehow. Never mind—a little dab of black
sealing-wax when the time came—when it was absolutely
necessary. . . . Little rogue! Yes, she really felt like
that about it. Little rogue biting its tail just by her left
ear. She could have taken it off and laid it on her lap
and stroked it. She felt a tingling in her hands and arms,
but that came from walking, she supposed. And when
she breathed, something light and sad—no, not sad, exactly—something gentle seemed to move in her bosom.

There were a number of people out this afternoon, far
more than last Sunday. And the band sounded louder
and gayer. That was because the Season had begun. For
although the band played all the year round on Sundays,

out of season it was never the same. It was like some one
playing with only the family to listen; it didn't care how
it played if there weren't any strangers present. Wasn't
the conductor wearing a new coat, too? She was sure it
was new. He scraped with his foot and flapped his arms
like a rooster about to crow, and the bandsmen sitting
in the green rotunda blew out their cheeks and glared
at the music. Now there came a little "flutey" bit—very
pretty!—a little chain of bright drops. She was sure it
would be repeated. It was; she lifted her head and smiled.

Only two people shared her "special" seat: a fine old
man in a velvet coat, his hands clasped over a huge carved
walking-stick, and a big old woman, sitting upright, with
a roll of knitting on her embroidered apron. They did
not speak. This was disappointing, for Miss Brill always
looked forward to the conversation. She had become really
quite expert, she thought, at listening as though she didn't
listen, at sitting in other people's lives just for a minute
while they talked round her.

She glanced, sideways, at the old couple. Perhaps they
would go soon. Last Sunday, too, hadn't been as interesting as usual. An Englishman and his wife, he wearing
a dreadful Panama hat and she button boots. And she'd
gone on the whole time about how she ought to wear
spectacles; she knew she needed them; but that it was
no good getting any; they'd be sure to break and they'd
never keep on. And he'd been so patient. He'd suggested
everything—gold rims, the kind that curved round your
ears, little pads inside the bridge. No, nothing would
please her. "They'll always be sliding down my nose!"
Miss Brill had wanted to shake her.

The old people sat on the bench, still as statues. Never
mind, there was always the crowd to watch. To and fro,
in front of the flower-beds and the band rotunda, the
couples and groups paraded, stopped to talk, to greet,
to buy a handful of flowers from the old beggar who had

his tray fixed to the railings. Little children ran among
them, swooping and laughing; little boys with big white
silk bows under their chins, little girls, little French dolls,
dressed up in velvet and lace. And sometimes a tiny stag-
gerer came suddenly rocking into the open from under
the trees, stopped, stared, as suddenly sat down "flop,"
until its small high-stepping mother, like a young hen,
rushed scolding to its rescue. Other people sat on the
benches and green chairs, but they were nearly always
the same, Sunday after Sunday, and—Miss Brill had
often noticed—there was something funny about nearly
all of them. They were odd, silent, nearly all old, and
from the way they stared they looked as though they'd
just come from dark little rooms or even—even cup-
boards!

Behind the rotunda the slender trees with yellow leaves
down drooping, and through them just a line of sea, and
beyond the blue sky with gold-veined clouds.

Tum-tum-tum tiddle-um! tiddle-um! tum tiddlev-um
tum ta! blew the band.

Two young girls in red came by and two young soldiers
in blue met them, and they laughed and paired and went
off arm-in-arm. Two peasant women with funny straw hats
passed, gravely, leading beautiful smoke-colored donkeys.
A cold, pale nun hurried by. A beautiful woman came
along and dropped her bunch of violets, and a little boy ran
after to hand them to her, and she took them and threw
them away as if they'd been poisoned. Dear me! Miss Brill
didn't know whether to admire that or not! And now an
ermine toque and a gentleman in gray met just in front of
her. He was tall, stiff, dignified, and she was wearing the
ermine toque she'd bought when her hair was yellow. Now
everything, her hair, her face, even her eyes, was the same
color as the shabby ermine, and her hand, in its cleaned
glove, lifted to dab her lips, was a tiny yellowish paw. Oh,
she was so pleased to see him—delighted! She rather

thought they were going to meet that afternoon. She described where she'd been—everywhere, here, there, along by the sea. The day was so charming—didn't he agree? And wouldn't he, perhaps? . . . But he shook his head, lighted a cigarette, slowly breathed a great deep puff into her face, and, even while she was still talking and laughing, flicked the match away and walked on. The ermine toque was alone; she smiled more brightly than ever. But even the band seemed to know what she was feeling and played more softly, played tenderly, and the drum beat, 'The Brute! The Brute!" over and over. What would she do? What was going to happen now? But as Miss Brill wondered, the ermine toque turned, raised her hand as though she'd seen some one else, much nicer, just over there, and pattered away. And the band changed again and played more quickly, more gayly than ever, and the old couple on Miss Brill's seat got up and marched away, and such a funny old man with long whiskers hobbled along in time to the music and was nearly knocked over by four girls walking abreast.

Oh, how fascinating it was! How she enjoyed it! How she loved sitting here, watching it all! It was like a play. It was exactly like a play. Who could believe the sky at the back wasn't painted? But it wasn't till a little brown dog trotted on solemn and then slowly trotted off, like a little "theater" dog, a little dog that had been drugged, that Miss Brill discovered what it was that made it so exciting. They were all on the stage. They weren't only the audience, not only looking on; they were acting. Even she had a part and came every Sunday. No doubt somebody would have noticed if she hadn't been there; she was part of the performance after all. How strange she'd never thought of it like that before! And yet it explained why she made such a point of starting from home at just the same time each week—so as not to be late for the performance—and it also explained why she had quite a queer, shy feeling at telling her English pupils how she spent her Sunday afternoons. No wonder! Miss Brill nearly laughed out loud. She was on the stage. She thought of the old invalid gentleman to whom she read the newspaper four afternoons a week while he slept in the garden. She had got quite used to the frail head on the cotton pillow, the hollowed eyes, the open mouth and the high pinched nose. If he'd been dead she mightn't have noticed for weeks; she wouldn't have minded. But suddenly he knew he was having the paper read to him by an actress! "An actress!" The old head lifted; two points of light quivered in the old eyes. "An actress—are ye?" And Miss Brill smoothed the newspaper as though it were the manuscript of her part and said gently: "Yes, I have been an actress for a long time."

The band had been having a rest. Now they started again. And what they played was warm, sunny, yet there was just a faint chill—a something, what was it?—not sadness—no, not sadness—a something that made you want to sing. The tune lifted, lifted, the light shone; and it seemed to Miss Brill that in another moment all of them, all the whole company, would begin singing. The young ones, the laughing ones who were moving together, they would begin, and the men's voices, very resolute and brave, would join them. And then she too, she too, and the others on the benches—they would come in with a kind of accompaniment—something low, that scarcely rose or fell, something so beautiful—moving. . . . And Miss Brill's eyes filled with tears and she looked smiling at all the other members of the company. Yes, we understand, we understand, she thought—though what they understood she didn't know.

Just at that moment a boy and a girl came and sat down where the old couple had been. They were beautifully dressed; they were in love. The hero and heroine, of course, just arrived from his father's yacht. And still

soundlessly singing, still with that trembling smile, Miss
Brill prepared to listen.

"No, not now," said the girl. "Not here, I can't."

"But why? Because of that stupid old thing at the end
there?" asked the boy. "Why does she come here at all—
who wants her? Why doesn't she keep her silly old mug
at home?"

"It's her fu-fur which is so funny," giggled the girl.
"It's exactly like a fried whiting."

"Ah, be off with you!" said the boy in an angry whisper.
Then: "Tell me, ma petite chère—"

"No, not here," said the girl. "Not *yet*."

.         .         .         .         .         .         .

On her way home she usually bought a slice of honey-
cake at the baker's. It was her Sunday treat. Sometimes
there was an almond in her slice, sometimes not. It made a
great difference. If there was an almond it was like carrying home a tiny present—a surprise—something that might
very well not have been there. She hurried on the almond
Sundays and struck the match for the kettle in quite a
dashing way.

But to-day she passed the baker's by, climbed the stairs,
went into the little dark room—her room like a cupboard
—and sat down on the red eiderdown. She sat there for a
long time. The box that the fur came out of was on the
bed. She unclasped the necklet quickly; quickly, without
looking, laid it inside. But when she put the lid on she
thought she heard something crying.

# THE LETTER
*by W. Somerset Maugham*

OUTSIDE on the quay the sun beat fiercely. A stream of motors, lorries and busses, private cars and hirelings, sped up and down the crowded thoroughfare, and every chauffeur blew his horn; rickshaws threaded their nimble path amid the throng, and the panting coolies found breath to yell at one another; coolies, carrying heavy bales, sidled along with their quick jog-trot and shouted to the passer-by to make way; itinerant vendors proclaimed their wares. Singapore is the meeting-place of a hundred peoples; and men of all colors, black Tamils, yellow Chinks, brown Malays, Armenians, Jews and Bengalis, called to one another in raucous tones. But inside the office of Messrs. Ripley, Joyce and Naylor it was pleasantly cool; it was dark after the dusty glitter of the street and agreeably quiet after its unceasing din. Mr. Joyce sat in his private room, at the table, with an electric fan turned full on him. He was leaning back, his elbows on the arms of the chair, with the tips of the outstretched fingers of one hand resting neatly against the tips of the outstretched fingers of the other. His gaze rested on the battered volumes of the Law Reports which stood on a long shelf in front of him. On the top of a cupboard were square boxes of japanned tin, on which were painted the names of various clients.

There was a knock at the door.

"Come in."

A Chinese clerk, very neat in his white ducks, opened it.

"Mr. Crosbie is here, sir."

He spoke beautiful English, accenting each word with

precision, and Mr. Joyce had often wondered at the extent of his vocabulary. Ong Chi Seng was a Cantonese, and he had studied law at Gray's Inn. He was spending a year or two with Messrs. Ripley, Joyce and Naylor in order to prepare himself for practice on his own account. He was industrious, obliging, and of exemplary character.

"Show him in," said Mr. Joyce.

He rose to shake hands with his visitor and asked him to sit down. The light fell on him as he did so. The face of Mr. Joyce remained in shadow. He was by nature a silent man, and now he looked at Robert Crosbie for quite a minute without speaking. Crosbie was a big fellow, well over six feet high, with broad shoulders, and muscular. He was a rubber-planter, hard with the constant exercise of walking over the estate, and with the tennis which was his relaxation when the day's work was over. He was deeply sunburned. His hairy hands, his feet in clumsy boots, were enormous, and Mr. Joyce found himself thinking that a blow of that great fist would easily kill the fragile Tamil. But there was no fierceness in his blue eyes; they were confiding and gentle; and his face, with its big, undistinguished features, was open, frank and honest. But at this moment it bore a look of deep distress. It was drawn and haggard.

"You look as though you hadn't had much sleep the last night or two," said Mr. Joyce.

"I haven't."

Mr. Joyce noticed now the old felt hat, with its broad double brim, which Crosbie had placed on the table; and then his eyes traveled to the khaki shorts he wore showing his red hairy thighs, the tennis shirt open at the neck, without a tie, and the dirty khaki jacket with the ends of the sleeves turned up. He looked as though he had just come in from a long tramp among the rubber trees Mr. Joyce gave a slight frown.

"You must pull yourself together, you know. You must keep your head."

"Oh, I'm all right."

"Have you seen your wife to-day?"

"No, I'm to see her this afternoon. You know, it is a damned shame that they should have arrested her."

"I think they had to do that," Mr. Joyce answered in his level, soft tone.

"I should have thought they'd have let her out on bail."

"It's a very serious charge."

"It is damnable. She did what any decent woman would do in her place. Only, nine women out of ten wouldn't have the pluck. Leslie's the best woman in the world. She wouldn't hurt a fly. Why, hang it all, man, I've been married to her for twelve years, do you think I don't know her? God, if I'd got hold of the man I'd have wrung his neck, I'd have killed him without a moment's hesitation. So would you."

"My dear fellow, everybody's on your side. No one has a good word to say for Hammond. We're going to get her off. I don't suppose either the assessors or the judge will go into court without having already made up their minds to bring in a verdict of not guilty."

"The whole thing's a farce," said Crosbie violently. "She ought never to have been arrested in the first place, and then it's terrible, after all the poor girl's gone through, to subject her to the ordeal of a trial. There's not a soul I've met since I've been in Singapore, man or woman, who hasn't told me that Leslie was absolutely justified. I think it's awful to keep her in prison all these weeks."

"The law is the law. After all, she confesses that she killed the man. It is terrible, and I'm dreadfully sorry for both you and for her."

"I don't matter a hang," interrupted Crosbie.

"But the fact remains that murder has been committed, and in a civilized community a trial is inevitable."

"Is it murder to exterminate noxious vermin? She shot him as she would have shot a mad dog."

Mr. Joyce leaned back again in his chair and once more placed the tips of his ten fingers together. The little construction he formed looked like the skeleton of a roof. He was silent for a moment.

"I should be wanting in my duty as your legal adviser," he said at last, in an even voice, looking at his client with his cool, brown eyes, "if I did not tell you that there is one point which causes me just a little anxiety. If your wife had only shot Hammond once, the whole thing would be absolutely plain sailing. Unfortunately she fired six times."

"Her explanation is perfectly simple. In the circumstances any one would have done the same."

"I daresay," said Mr. Joyce, "and of course I think the explanation is very reasonable. But it's no good closing our eyes to the facts. It's always a good plan to put yourself in another man's place, and I can't deny that if I were prosecuting for the Crown that is the point on which I should center my inquiry."

"My dear fellow, that's perfectly idiotic."

Mr. Joyce shot a sharp glance at Robert Crosbie. The shadow of a smile hovered over his shapely lips. Crosbie was a good fellow, but he could hardly be described as intelligent.

"I daresay it's of no importance," answered the lawyer, "I just thought it was a point worth mentioning. You haven't got very long to wait now, and when it's all over I recommend you to go off somewhere with your wife on a trip, and forget all about it. Even though we are almost dead certain to get an acquittal, a trial of that sort is anxious work, and you'll both want a rest."

For the first time Crosbie smiled, and his smile strangely changed his face. You forgot the uncouthness and saw only the goodness of his soul.

"I think I shall want it more than Leslie. She's borne up wonderfully. By God, there's a plucky little woman for you."

"Yes, I've been very much struck by her self-control," said the lawyer. "I should never have guessed that she was capable of such determination."

His duties as her counsel had made it necessary for him to have a good many interviews with Mrs. Crosbie since her arrest. Though things had been made as easy as could be for her, the fact remained that she was in jail, awaiting her trial for murder, and it would not have been surprising if her nerves had failed her. She appeared to bear her ordeal with composure. She read a great deal, took such exercise as was possible, and by favor of the authorities worked at the pillow lace which had always formed the entertainment of her long hours of leisure. When Mr. Joyce saw her, she was neatly dressed in cool, fresh, simple frocks, her hair was carefully arranged, and her nails were manicured. Her manner was collected. She was able even to jest upon the little inconveniences of her position. There was something casual about the way in which she spoke of the tragedy, which suggested to Mr. Joyce that only her good breeding prevented her from finding something a trifle ludicrous in a situation which was eminently serious. It surprised him, for he had never thought that she had a sense of humor.

He had known her off and on for a good many years. When she paid visits to Singapore she generally came to dine with his wife and himself, and once or twice she had passed a week-end with them at their bungalow by the sea. His wife had spent a fortnight with her on the estate, and had met Geoffrey Hammond several times. The two couples had been on friendly, if not on intimate, terms, and it was on this account that Robert Crosbie had rushed over to Singapore immediately after the catastrophe and

begged Mr. Joyce to take charge personally of his unhappy
wife's defense.

The story she told him the first time he saw her, she
had never varied in the smallest detail. She told it as
coolly then, a few hours after the tragedy, as she told it
now. She told it connectedly, in a level, even voice, and her
only sign of confusion was when a slight color came into
her cheeks as she described one or two of its incidents.
She was the last woman to whom one would have expected such a thing to happen. She was in the early
thirties, a fragile creature, neither short nor tall, and
graceful rather than pretty. Her wrists and ankles were
very delicate, but she was extremely thin, and you could
see the bones of her hands through the white skin, and
the veins were large and blue. Her face was colorless,
slightly sallow, and her lips were pale. You did not notice
the color of her eyes. She had a great deal of light brown
hair, and it had a slight natural wave; it was the sort of
hair that with a little touching-up would have been very
pretty, but you could not imagine that Mrs. Crosbie would
think of resorting to any such device. She was a quiet,
pleasant, unassuming woman. Her manner was engaging,
and if she was not very popular it was because she suffered from a certain shyness. This was comprehensible
enough, for the planter's life is lonely, and in her own
house, with people she knew, she was in her quiet way
charming. Mrs. Joyce, after her fortnight's stay, had told
her husband that Leslie was a very agreeable hostess.
There was more in her, she said, than people thought;
and when you came to know her you were surprised how
much she had read and how entertaining she could be.

She was the last woman in the world to commit murder.

Mr. Joyce dismissed Robert Crosbie with such reas-
suring words as he could find and, once more alone in his
office, turned over the pages of the brief. But it was a
mechanical action, for all its details were familiar to him.

The case was the sensation of the day, and it was discussed in all the clubs, at all the dinner tables, up and down the Peninsula, from Singapore to Penang. The facts that Mrs. Crosbie gave were simple. Her husband had gone to Singapore on business, and she was alone for the night. She dined by herself, late, at a quarter to nine, and after dinner sat in the sitting-room working at her lace. It opened on the veranda. There was no one in the bungalow, for the servants had retired to their own quarters at the back of the compound. She was surprised to hear a step on the gravel path in the garden, a booted step, which suggested a white man rather than a native, for she had not heard a motor drive up, and she could not imagine who could be coming to see her at that time of night. Some one ascended the few stairs that led up to the bungalow, walked across the veranda, and appeared at the door of the room in which she sat. At the first moment she did not recognize the visitor. She sat by a shaded lamp, and he stood with his back to the darkness.

"May I come in?" he said.

She did not even recognize the voice.

"Who is it?" she asked.

She worked with spectacles, and she took them off as she spoke.

"Geoff. Hammond."

"Of course. Come in and have a drink."

She rose and shook hands with him cordially. She was a little surprised to see him, for though he was a neighbor neither she nor Robert had been lately on very intimate terms with him, and she had not seen him for some weeks. He was the manager of a rubber estate nearly eight miles from theirs, and she wondered why he had chosen this late hour to come and see them.

"Robert's away," she said. "He had to go to Singapore for the night."

Perhaps he thought his visit called for some explanation for he said:

"I'm sorry. I felt rather lonely to-night, so I thought I'd just come along and see how you were getting on."

"How on earth did you come? I never heard a car."

"I left it down the road. I thought you might both be in bed and asleep."

This was natural enough. The planter gets up at dawn in order to take the roll-call of the workers, and soon after dinner he is glad to go to bed. Hammond's car was in point of fact found next day a quarter of a mile from the bungalow.

Since Robert was away there was no whisky and soda in the room. Leslie did not call the boy, who was probably asleep, but fetched it herself. Her guest mixed himself a drink and filled his pipe.

Geoff. Hammond had a host of friends in the colony. He at this time in the late thirties, but he had come out as a lad. He had been one of the first to volunteer on the outbreak of war, and had done very well. A wound in the knee caused him to be invalided out of the army after two years, but he returned to the Federated Malay States with a D.S.O. and an M.C. He was one of the best billiard-players in the colony. He had been a beautiful dancer and a fine tennis player, but though able no longer to dance, and his tennis, with a stiff knee, was not so good as it had been, he had the gift of popularity and was universally liked. He was a tall, good-looking fellow, with attractive blue eyes and a fine head of black, curling hair. Old stagers said his only fault was that he was too fond of the girls, and after the catastrophe they shook their heads and vowed that they had always known this would get him into trouble.

He began now to talk to Leslie about the local affairs, the forthcoming races in Singapore, the price of rubber, and his chances of killing a tiger which had been lately seen in the neighborhood. She was anxious to finish by a certain date the piece of lace on which she was working, for she wanted to send it home for her mother's birthday, and so put on her spectacles again, and drew towards her chair the little table on which stood the pillow.

"I wish you wouldn't wear those great horn-spectacles," he said. "I don't know why a pretty woman should do her best to look plain."

She was a trifle taken aback at this remark. He had never used that tone with her before. She thought the the best thing was to make light of it.

"I have no pretensions to being a raving beauty, you know, and if you ask me point blank, I'm bound to tell you that I don't care two pins if you think me plain or not."

"I don't think you're plain. I think you're awfully pretty."

"Sweet of you," she answered, ironically. "But in that case I can only think you half-witted."

He chuckled. But he rose from his chair and sat down in another by her side.

"You're not going to have the face to deny that you have the prettiest hands in the world," he said.

He made a gesture as though to take one of them. She gave him a little tap.

"Don't be an idiot. Sit down where you were before and talk sensibly, or else I shall send you home."

He did not move.

"Don't you know that I'm awfully in love with you?" he said.

She remained quite cool.

"I don't. I don't believe it for a minute, and even if it were true I don't want you to say it."

She was the more surprised at what he was saying, since during the seven years she had known him he had never paid her any particular attention. When he came back from the war they had seen a good deal of one another, and once when he was ill Robert had gone over and brought him back to their bungalow in his car. He had stayed with them then for a fortnight. But their interests were dissimilar, and the acquaintance had never ripened into friendship. For the last two or three years they had seen little of him. Now and then he came over to play tennis, now and then they met him at some planter's who was giving a party, but it often happened that they did not set eyes on him for a month at a time.

Now he took another whisky and soda. Leslie wondered if he had been drinking before. There was something odd about him, and it made her a trifle uneasy. She watched him help himself with disapproval.

"I wouldn't drink any more if I were you," she said, good-humoredly still.

He emptied his glass and put it down.

"Do you think I'm talking to you like this because I'm drunk?" he asked abruptly.

"That is the most obvious explanation, isn't it?"

"Well, it's a lie. I've loved you ever since I first knew you. I've held my tongue as long as I could, and now it's got to come out. I love you, I love you, I love you."

She rose and carefully put aside the pillow.

"Good night," she said.

"I'm not going now."

At last she began to lose her temper.

"But, you poor fool, don't you know that I've never loved any one but Robert, and even if I didn't love Robert you're the last man I should care for."

"What do I care? Robert's away."

"If you don't go away this minute I shall call the boys, and have you thrown out."

"They're out of earshot."

She was very angry now. She made a movement as

though to go on to the veranda from which the house-boy
would certainly hear her, but he seized her arm.

"Let me go," she cried furiously.

"Not much. I've got you now."

She opened her mouth and called "Boy, boy," but with
a quick gesture he put his hand over it. Then before she
knew what he was about he had taken her in his arms and
was kissing her passionately. She struggled, turning her
lips away from his burning mouth.

"No, no, no," she cried. "Leave me alone. I won't."

She grew confused about what happened then. All that
had been said before she remembered accurately, but now
his words assailed her ears through a mist of horror and
fear. He seemed to plead for her love. He broke into
violent protestations of passion. And all the time he held
her in his tempestuous embrace. She was helpless, for he
was a strong, powerful man, and her arms were pinioned
to her sides; her struggles were unavailing, and she felt
herself grow weaker; she was afraid she would faint, and
his hot breath on her face made her feel desperately sick.
He kissed her mouth, her eyes, her cheeks, her hair. The
pressure of his arms was killing her. He lifted her off her
feet. She tried to kick him, but he only held her more
closely. He was carrying her now. He wasn't speaking
any more, but she knew that his face was pale and his eyes
hot with desire. He was taking her into the bedroom. He
was no longer a civilized man, but a savage. And as he ran
he stumbled against a table which was in the way. His
stiff knee made him a little awkward on his feet, and with
the burden of the woman in his arms he fell. In a moment
she had snatched herself away from him. She ran round
the sofa. He was up in a flash, and flung himself towards
her. There was a revolver on the desk. She was not a
nervous woman, but Robert was to be away for the night,
and she had meant to take it into her room when she went
to bed. That was why it happened to be there. She was

frantic with terror now. She did not know what she was
doing. She heard a report. She saw Hammond stagger.
He gave a cry. He said something, she didn't know what.
He lurched out of the room on to the veranda. She was
in a frenzy now, she was beside herself, she followed him
out, yes, that was it, she must have followed him out,
though she remembered nothing of it, she followed firing
automatically, shot after shot, till the six chambers were
empty. Hammond fell down on the floor of the veranda.
He crumpled up into a bloody heap.

When the boys, startled by the reports, rushed up, they
found her standing over Hammond with the revolver still
in her hand, and Hammond lifeless. She looked at them
for a moment without speaking. They stood in a frightened, huddled bunch. She let the revolver fall from her
hand, and without a word turned and went into the sitting-
room. They watched her go into her bedroom and turn the
key in the lock. They dared not touch the dead body, but
looked at it with terrified eyes, talking excitedly to one
another in undertones. Then the head-boy collected himself; he had been with them for many years, he was
Chinese and a level-headed fellow. Robert had gone into
Singapore on his motor-cycle, and the car stood in the
garage. He told the seis to get it out; they must go at
once to the Assistant District Officer and tell him what had
happened. He picked up the revolver and put it in his
pocket. The A.D.O., a man called Withers, lived on the
outskirts of the nearest town, which was about thirty-five
miles away. It took them an hour and a half to reach him.
Every one was asleep, and they had to rouse the boys.
Presently Withers came out and they told him their
errand. The head-boy showed him the revolver in proof of
what he said. The A.D.O. went into his room to dress,
sent for his car, and in a little while was following them
back along the deserted road. The dawn was just breaking
as he reached the Crosbies' bungalow. He ran up the steps

⌄f the veranda, and stopped short as he saw Hammond's
body lying where he fell. He touched the face. It was
quite cold.

"Where's mem?" he asked the house-boy.

The Chinese pointed to the bedroom. Withers went to
the door and knocked. There was no answer. He knocked
again.

"Mrs. Crosbie," he called.

"Who is it?"

"Withers."

There was another pause. Then the door was unlocked
and slowly opened. Leslie stood before him. She had not
been to bed, and wore the tea-gown in which she had
dined. She stood and looked silently at the A.D.O.

"Your house-boy fetched me," he said. "Hammond.
What have you done?"

"He tried to rape me, and I shot him."

"My God. I say, you'd better come out here. You must
tell me exactly what happened."

"Not now. I can't. You must give me time. Send for my
husband."

Withers was a young man, and he did not know exactly
what to do in an emergency which was so out of the run
of his duties. Leslie refused to say anything till at last
Robert arrived. Then she told the two men the story, from
which since then, though she had repeated it over and over
again, she had never in the slightest degree diverged.

The point to which Mr. Joyce recurred was the shooting.
As a lawyer he was bothered that Leslie had fired not
once, but six times, and the examination of the dead man
showed that four of the shots had been fired close to the
body. One might almost have thought that when the man
fell she stood over him and emptied the contents of the
revolver into him. She confessed that her memory, so
accurate for all that had preceded, failed her here. Her
mind was blank. It pointed to an uncontrollable fury; but

uncontrollable fury was the last thing you would have
expected from this quiet and demure woman. Mr. Joyce
had known her a good many years, and had always thought
her an unemotional person; during the weeks that had
passed since the tragedy her composure had been amazing.

Mr. Joyce shrugged his shoulders.

"The fact is, I suppose," he reflected, "that you can
never tell what hidden possibilities of savagery there are
in the most respectable of women."

There was a knock at the door.

"Come in."

The Chinese clerk entered and closed the door behind
him. He closed it gently, with deliberation, but decidedly,
and advanced to the table at which Mr. Joyce was sitting.

"May I trouble you, sir, for a few words private conversation?" he said.

The elaborate accuracy with which the clerk expressed
himself always faintly amused Mr. Joyce, and now he
smiled.

"It's no trouble, Chi Seng," he replied.

"The matter on which I desire to speak to you, sir, is
delicate and confidential."

"Fire away."

Mr. Joyce met his clerk's shrewd eyes. As usual Ong
Chi Seng was dressed in the height of local fashion. He
wore very shiny patent leather shoes and gay silk socks.
In his black tie was a pearl and ruby pin, and on the
fourth finger of his left hand a diamond ring. From the
pocket of his neat white coat protruded a gold fountain
pen and a gold pencil. He wore a gold wrist-watch, and on
the bridge of his nose invisible pince-nez. He gave a
little cough.

"The matter has to do with the case R. *v.* Crosbie, sir."

"Yes?"

"A circumstance has come to my knowledge, sir, which
seems to me to put a different complexion on it."

"What circumstance?"

"It has come to my knowledge, sir, that there is a letter in existence from the defendant to the unfortunate victim of the tragedy."

"I shouldn't be at all surprised. In the course of the last seven years I have no doubt that Mrs. Crosbie often had occasion to write to Mr. Hammond."

Mr. Joyce had a high opinion of his clerk's intelligence and his words were designed to conceal his thoughts.

"That is very probable, sir. Mrs. Crosbie must have communicated with the deceased frequently, to invite him to dine with her for example, or to propose a tennis game. That was my first thought when the matter was brought to my notice. This letter, however, was written on the day of the late Mr. Hammond's death."

Mr. Joyce did not flicker an eyelash. He continued to look at Ong Chi Seng with the smile of faint amusement with which he generally talked to him.

"Who has told you this?"

"The circumstances were brought to my knowledge, sir, by a friend of mine."

Mr. Joyce knew better than to insist.

"You will no doubt recall, sir, that Mrs. Crosbie has stated that until the fatal night she had had no communication with the deceased for several weeks."

"Have you got the letter?"

"No, sir."

"What are its contents?"

"My friend gave me a copy. Would you like to peruse it, sir?"

"I should."

Ong Chi Seng took from an inside pocket a bulky wallet. It was filled with papers, Singapore dollar notes and cigarette cards. From the confusion he presently extracted a half sheet of thin note-paper and placed it before Mr. Joyce. The letter read as follows:—

*R. will be away for the night. I absolutely must see you. I shall expect you at eleven. I am desperate, and if you don't come I won't answer for the consequences. Don't drive up.—L.*

It was written in the flowing hand which the Chinese were taught at the foreign schools. The writing, so lacking in character, was oddly incongruous with the ominous words.

"What makes you think that this note was written by Mrs. Crosbie?"

"I have every confidence in the veracity of my informant, sir," replied Ong Chi Seng. "And the matter can very easily be put to the proof. Mrs. Crosbie will, no doubt, be able to tell you at once whether she wrote such a letter or not."

Since the beginning of the conversation Mr. Joyce had not taken his eyes off the respectable countenance of his clerk. He wondered now if he discerned in it a faint expression of mockery.

"It is inconceivable that Mrs. Crosbie should have written such a letter," said Mr. Joyce.

"If that is your opinion, sir, the matter is of course ended. My friend spoke to me on the subject only because he thought, as I was in your office, you might like to know of the existence of this letter before a communication was made to the Deputy Public Prosecutor."

"Who has the original?" asked Mr. Joyce sharply.

Ong Chi Seng made no sign that he perceived in this question and its manner a change of attitude.

"You will remember, sir, no doubt, that after the death of Mr. Hammond it was discovered that he had had relations with a Chinese woman. The letter is at present in her possession."

That was one of the things that had turned public opinion most vehemently against Hammond. It came to be known that for several months he had had a Chinese woman living in his house.

For a moment neither of them spoke. Indeed everything had been said and each understood the other perfectly.

"I'm obliged to you, Chi Seng. I will give the matter my consideration."

"Very good, sir. Do you wish me to make a communication to that effect to my friend?"

"I daresay it would be as well if you kept in touch with him," Mr. Joyce answered with gravity.

"Yes, sir."

The clerk noiselessly left the room, shutting the door again with deliberation, and left Mr. Joyce to his reflections. He stared at the copy, in its neat, impersonal writing, of Leslie's letter. Vague suspicions troubled him. They were so disconcerting that he made an effort to put them out of his mind. There must be a simple explanation of the letter, and Leslie without doubt could give it at once, but, by heaven, an explanation was needed. He rose from his chair, put the letter in his pocket, and took his topee. When he went out Ong Chi Seng was busily writing at his desk.

"I'm going out for a few minutes, Chi Seng," he said.

"Mr. George Reed is coming by appointment at twelve o'clock, sir. Where shall I say you've gone?"

Mr. Joyce gave him a thin smile.

"You can say that you haven't the least idea."

But he knew perfectly well that Ong Chi Seng was aware that he was going to the jail. Though the crime had been committed in Belanda and the trial was to take place at Belanda Bharu, since there was in the jail no convenience for the detention of a white woman Mrs. Crosbie had been brought to Singapore.

When she was led into the room in which he waited she held out her thin, distinguished hand, and gave him a pleasant smile. She was as ever neatly and simply dressed.

and her abundant, pale hair was arranged with care.

"I wasn't expecting to see you this morning," she said, graciously.

She might have been in her own house, and Mr. Joyce almost expected to hear her call the boy and tell him to bring the visitor a gin pahit.

"How are you?" he asked.

"I'm in the best of health, thank you." A flicker of amusement flashed across her eyes. "This is a wonderful place for a rest cure."

The attendant withdrew and they were left alone.

"Do sit down," said Leslie.

He took a chair. He did not quite know how to begin. She was so cool that it seemed almost impossible to say to her the thing he had come to say. Though she was not pretty there was something agreeable in her appearance. She had elegance, but it was the elegance of good breeding in which there was nothing of the artifice of society. You had only to look at her to know what sort of people she had and what kind of surroundings she had lived in. Her fragility gave her a singular refinement. It was impossible to associate her with the vaguest idea of grossness.

"I'm looking forward to seeing Robert this afternoon," she said, in her good-humored, easy voice. (It was a pleasure to hear her speak, her voice and her accent were so distinctive of her class.) "Poor dear, it's been a great trial to his nerves. I'm thankful it'll all be over in a few days."

"It's only five days now."

"I know. Each morning when I awake I say to myself, 'one less.'" She smiled then. "Just as I used to do at school and the holidays were coming."

"By the way, am I right in thinking that you had no communication whatever with Hammond for several weeks before the catastrophe?"

"I'm quite positive of that. The last time we met was

at a tennis-party at the MacFarrens. I don't think I said more than two words to him. They have two courts, you know, and we didn't happen to be in the same sets."

"And you haven't written to him?"

"Oh, no."

"Are you quite sure of that?"

"Oh, quite," she answered, with a little smile. "There was nothing I should write to him for except to ask him to dine or to play tennis, and I hadn't done either for months."

"At one time you'd been on fairly intimate terms with him. How did it happen that you had stopped asking him to anything?"

Mrs. Crosbie shrugged her thin shoulders.

"One gets tired of people. We hadn't anything very much in common. Of course, when he was ill Robert and I did everything we could for him, but the last year or two he'd been quite well, and he was very popular. He had a good many calls on his time, and there didn't seem to be any need to shower invitations upon him."

"Are you quite certain that was all?"

Mrs. Crosbie hesitated for a moment.

"Well, I may just as well tell you. It had come to our ears that he was living with a Chinese woman, and Robert said he wouldn't have him in the house. I had seen her myself."

Mr. Joyce was sitting in a straight-backed armchair, resting his chin on his hand, and his eyes were fixed on Leslie. Was it his fancy that, as she made this remark, her black pupils were filled on a sudden, for the fraction of a second, with a dull red light? The effect was startling. Mr. Joyce shifted in his chair. He placed the tips of his ten fingers together. He spoke very slowly, choosing his words.

"I think I should tell you that there is in existence a letter in your handwriting to Geoff. Hammond."

He watched her closely. She made no movement, nor did her face change color, but she took a noticeable time to reply.

"In the past I've often sent him little notes to ask him to something or other, or to get me something when I knew he was going to Singapore."

"This letter asks him to come and see you because Robert was going to Singapore."

"That's impossible. I never did anything of the kind."

"You'd better read it for yourself."

He took it out of his pocket and handed it to her. She gave it a glance and with a smile of scorn handed it back to him.

"That's not my handwriting."

"I know, it's said to be an exact copy of the original."

She read the words now, and as she read a horrible change came over her. Her colorless face grew dreadful to look at. It turned green. The flesh seemed on a sudden to fall away and her skin was tightly stretched over the bones. Her lips receded, showing her teeth, so that she had the appearance of making a grimace. She stared at Mr. Joyce with eyes that started from their sockets. He was looking now at a gibbering death's head.

"What does it mean?" she whispered.

Her mouth was so dry that she could utter no more than a hoarse sound. It was no longer a human voice.

"That is for you to say," he answered.

"I didn't write it. I swear I didn't write it."

"Be very careful what you say. If the original is in your handwriting it would be useless to deny it."

"It would be a forgery."

"It would be difficult to prove that. It would be easy to prove that it was genuine."

A shiver passed through her lean body. But great beads of sweat stood on her forehead. She took a handkerchief from her bag and wiped the palms of her hands. She glanced at the letter again and gave Mr. Joyce a sidelong look.

"It's not dated. If I had written it and forgotten all about it, it might have been written years ago. If you'll give me time, I'll try and remember the circumstances."

"I noticed there was no date. If this letter were in the hands of the prosecution they would cross-examine the boys. They would soon find out whether some one took a letter to Hammond on the day of his death."

Mrs. Crosbie clasped her hands violently and swayed in her chair so that he thought she would faint.

"I swear to you that I didn't write that letter."

Mr. Joyce was silent for a little while. He took his eyes from her distraught face, and looked down on the floor. He was reflecting.

"In these circumstances we need not go into the matter further," he said slowly, at last breaking the silence. "If the possessor of this letter sees fit to place it in the hands of the prosecution you will be prepared."

His words suggested that he had nothing more to say to her, but he made no movement of departure. He waited. To himself he seemed to wait a very long time. He did not look at Leslie, but he was conscious that she sat very still. She made no sound. At last it was he who spoke.

"If you have nothing more to say to me I think I'll be getting back to my office."

"What would any one who read the letter be inclined to think that it meant?" she asked then.

"He'd know that you had told a deliberate lie," answered Mr. Joyce sharply.

"When?"

"You have stated definitely that you had had no communication with Hammond for at least three months."

"The whole thing has been a terrible shock to me. The events of that dreadful night have been a nightmare. It's not very strange if one detail has escaped my memory."

"It would be unfortunate when your memory has reproduced so exactly every particular of your interview with Hammond, that you should have forgotten so important a point as that he came to see you in the bungalow on the night of his death at your express desire."

"I hadn't forgotten. After what happened I was afraid to mention it. I thought you'd none of you believe my story if I admitted that he'd come at my invitation. I daresay it was stupid of me; but I lost my head, and after I'd said once that I'd had no communication with Hammond I was obliged to stick to it."

By now Leslie had recovered her admirable composure, and she met Mr. Joyce's appraising glance with candor. Her gentleness was very disarming.

"You will be required to explain, then, *why* you asked Hammond to come and see you when Robert was away for the night."

She turned her eyes full on the lawyer. He had been mistaken in thinking them insignificant, they were rather fine eyes, and unless he was mistaken they were bright now with tears. Her voice had a little break in it.

"It was a surprise I was preparing for Robert. His birthday is next month. I knew he wanted a new gun and you know I'm dreadfully stupid about sporting things. I wanted to talk to Geoff. about it. I thought I'd get him to order it for me."

"Perhaps the terms of the letter are not very clear to your recollection. Will you have another look at it?"

"No, I don't want to," she said quickly.

"Does it seem to you the sort of letter a woman would write to a somewhat distant acquaintance because she wanted to consult him about buying a gun?"

"I daresay it's rather extravagant and emotional. I do express myself like that, you know. I'm quite prepared to admit it's very silly." She smiled. "And after all, Geoff. Hammond wasn't quite a distant acquaintance. When he

was ill I'd nursed him like a mother. I asked him to come
when Robert was away, because Robert wouldn't have him
in the house."

Mr. Joyce was tired of sitting so long in the same
position. He rose and walked once or twice up and down
the room, choosing the words he proposed to say; then he
leaned over the back of the chair in which he had been
sitting. He spoke slowly in a tone of deep gravity.

"Mrs. Crosbie, I want to talk to you very, very seriously.
This case was comparatively plain sailing. There was only
one point which seemed to me to require explanation: as
far as I could judge, you had fired no less than four shots
into Hammond when he was lying on the ground. It was
hard to accept the possibility that a delicate, frightened,
and habitually self-controlled woman, of gentle nature and
refined instincts, should have surrendered to an absolutely
uncontrolled frenzy. But of course it was admissible. Although Geoffrey Hammond was much liked and on the
whole thought highly of, I was prepared to prove that he
was the sort of man who might be guilty of the crime
which in justification of your act you accused him of. The
fact, which was discovered after his death, that he had
been living with a Chinese woman gave us something
very definite to go upon. That robbed him of any sympathy which might have been felt for him. We made up
our minds to make use of the odium which such a connection cast upon him in the minds of all respectable
people. I told your husband this morning that I was certain
of an acquittal, and I wasn't just telling him that to give
him heart. I do not believe the assessors would have left
the court."

They looked into one another's eyes. Mrs. Crosbie was
strangely still. She was like a little bird paralyzed by the
fascination of a snake. He went on in the same quiet
tones.

"But this letter has thrown an entirely different com-

plexion on the case. I am your legal adviser, I shall represent you in Court. I take your story as you tell it me, and
I shall conduct your defense according to its terms. It
may be that I believe your statements, and it may be
that I doubt them. The duty of counsel is to persuade the
Court that the evidence placed before it is not such as to
justify it in bringing in a verdict of guilty, and any private
opinion he may have of the guilt or innocence of his client
is entirely beside the point."

He was astonished to see in Leslie's eyes the flicker of a
smile. Piqued, he went on somewhat dryly.

"You're not going to deny that Hammond came to your
house at your urgent, and I may even say, hysterical invitation?"

Mrs. Crosbie, hesitating for an instant, seemed to
consider.

"They can prove that the letter was taken to his bungalow by one of the house-boys. He rode over on his
bicycle."

"You mustn't expect other people to be stupider than
you. The letter will put them on the track of suspicions
which have entered nobody's head. I will not tell you what
I personally thought when I saw the copy. I do not wish
you to tell me anything but what is needed to save your
neck."

Mrs. Crosbie gave a shrill cry. She sprang to her feet,
white with terror.

"You don't think they'd hang me?"

"If they came to the conclusion that you hadn't killed
Hammond in self-defense, it would be the duty of the
assessors to bring in a verdict of guilty. The charge is
murder. It would be the duty of the judge to sentence
you to death."

"But what can they prove?" she gasped.

"I don't know what they can prove. You know. I don't
want to know. But if their suspicions are aroused, if they

begin to make inquiries, if the natives are questioned—
what is it that can be discovered?"

She crumpled up suddenly. She fell on the floor before
he could catch her. She had fainted. He looked round the
room for water, but there was none there, and he did not
want to be disturbed. He stretched her out on the floor,
and kneeling beside her waited for her to recover. When
she opened her eyes he was disconcerted by the ghastly
fear that he saw in them.

"Keep quite still," he said. "You'll be better in a
moment."

"You won't let them hang me," she whispered.

She began to cry, hysterically, while in undertones he
sought to quieten her.

"For goodness' sake pull yourself together," he said.

"Give me a minute."

Her courage was amazing. He could see the effort she
made to regain her self-control, and soon she was once
more calm.

"Let me get up now."

He gave her his hand and helped her to her feet, Taking
her arm, he led her to the chair. She sat down wearily.

"Don't talk to me for a minute or two," she said.

"Very well."

When at last she spoke it was to say something which
he did not expect. She gave a little sigh.

"I'm afraid I've made rather a mess of things," she
said.

He did not answer, and once more there was a silence.

"Isn't it possible to get hold of the letter?" she said
at last.

"I do not think anything would have been said to me
about it, if the person in whose possession it is was not
prepared to sell it."

"Who's got it?"

"The Chinese woman who was living in Hammond's house."

A spot of color flickered for an instant on Leslie's cheek-bones.

"Does she want an awful lot for it?"

"I imagine that she has a very shrewd idea of its value. I doubt if it would be possible to get hold of it except for a very large sum."

"Are you going to let me be hanged?"

"Do you think it's so simple as all that to secure possession of an unwelcome piece of evidence? It's no different from suborning a witness. You have no right to make any such suggestion to me."

"Then what is going to happen to me?"

"Justice must take its course."

She grew very pale. A little shudder passed through her body.

"I put myself in your hands. Of course I have no right to ask you to do anything that isn't proper."

Mr. Joyce had not bargained for the little break in her voice which her habitual self-restraint made quite intolerably moving. She looked at him with humble eyes, and he thought that if he rejected their appeal they would haunt him for the rest of his life. After all, nothing could bring poor Hammond back to life again. He wondered what really was the explanation of that letter. It was not fair to conclude from it that she had killed Hammond without provocation. He had lived in the East a long time and his sense of professional honor was not perhaps so acute as it had been twenty years before. He stared at the floor. He made up his mind to do something which he knew was unjustifiable, but it stuck in his throat and he felt dully resentful towards Leslie. It embarrassed him a little to speak.

"I don't know exactly what your husband's circumstances are?"

Flushing a rosy red, she shot a swift glance at him.

"He has a good many tin shares and a small share in two or three rubber estates. I suppose he could raise money."

"He would have to be told what it was for."

She was silent for a moment. She seemed to think.

"He's in love with me still. He would make any sacrifice to save me. Is there any need for him to see the letter?"

Mr. Joyce frowned a little, and, quick to notice, she went on.

"Robert is an old friend of yours. I'm not asking you to do anything for me, I'm asking you to save a rather simple, kind man who never did you any harm from all the pain that's possible."

Mr. Joyce did not reply. He rose to go and Mrs. Crosbie, with the grace that was natural to her, held out her hand. She was shaken by the scene, and her look was haggard, but she made a brave attempt to speed him with courtesy.

"It's so good of you to take all this trouble for me. I can't begin to tell you how grateful I am."

Mr. Joyce returned to his office. He sat in his own room, quite still, attempting to do no work, and pondered. His imagination brought him many strange ideas. He shuddered a little. At last there was the discreet knock on the door which he was expecting. Ong Chi Seng came in.

"I was just going out to have my tiffin, sir," he said.

"All right."

"I didn't know if there was anything you wanted before I went, sir."

"I don't think so. Did you make another appointment for Mr. Reed?"

"Yes, sir. He will come at three o'clock."

"Good."

Ong Chi Seng turned away, walked to the door, and put

his long slim fingers on the handle. Then, as though on an afterthought, he turned back.

"Is there anything you wish me to say to my friend, sir?"

Although Ong Chi Seng spoke English so admirably he had still a difficulty with the letter R, and he pronounced it "fliend."

"What friend?"

"About the letter Mrs. Crosbie wrote to Hammond leceased, sir."

"Oh! I'd forgotten about that. I mentioned it to Mrs. Crosbie and she denies having written anything of the sort. It's evidently a forgery."

Mr. Joyce took the copy from his pocket and handed it to Ong Chi Seng. Ong Chi Seng ignored the gesture.

"In that case, sir, I suppose there would be no objection if my fliend delivered the letter to the Deputy Public Prosecutor."

"None. But I don't quite see what good that would do your friend."

"My fliend, sir, thought it was his duty in the interests of justice."

"I am the last man in the world to interfere with any one who wishes to do his duty, Chi Seng."

The eyes of the lawyer and of the Chinese clerk met. Not the shadow of a smile hovered on the lips of either, but they understood each other perfectly.

"I quite understand, sir," said Ong Chi Seng, "but from my study of the case R. *v.* Crosbie I am of opinion that the production of such a letter would be damaging to our client."

"I have always had a very high opinion of your legal acumen, Chi Seng."

"It has occurred to me, sir, that if I could persuade my fliend to induce the Chinese woman who has the letter to deliver it into our hands it would save a great deal of trouble."

Mr. Joyce idly drew faces on his blotting-paper.

"I suppose your friend is a business man. In what circumstances do you think he would be induced to part with the letter?"

"He has not got the letter. The Chinese woman has the letter. He is only a relation of the Chinese woman. She is an ignorant woman; she did not know the value of that letter till my fliend told her."

"What value did he put on it?"

"Ten thousand dollars, sir."

"Good God! Where on earth do you suppose Mrs. Crosbie can get ten thousand dollars! I tell you the letter's a forgery."

He looked up at Ong Chi Seng as he spoke. The clerk was unmoved by the outburst. He stood at the side of the desk, civil, cool and observant.

"Mr. Crosbie owns an eighth share of the Betong Rubber Estate and a sixth share of the Selantan River Rubber Estate. I have a fliend who will lend him the money on the security of his property."

"You have a large circle of acquaintance, Chi Seng."

"Yes, sir."

"Well, you can tell them all to go to hell. I would never advise Mr. Crosbie to give a penny more than five thousand for a letter that can be very easily explained."

"The Chinese woman does not want to sell the letter, sir. My fliend took a long time to persuade her. It is useless to offer her less than the sum mentioned."

Mr. Joyce looked at Ong Chi Seng for at least three minutes. The clerk bore the searching scrutiny without embarrassment. He stood in a respectful attitude with downcast eyes. Mr. Joyce knew his man. Clever fellow, Chi Seng, he thought, I wonder how much he's going to get out of it.

"Ten thousand dollars is a very large sum."

"Mr. Crosbie will certainly pay it rather than see his wife hanged, sir."

Again Mr. Joyce paused. What more did Chi Seng know than he had said? He must be pretty sure of his ground if he was obviously so unwilling to bargain. That sum had been fixed because whoever it was that was managing the affair knew it was the largest amount that Robert Crosbie could raise.

"Where is the Chinese woman now?" asked Mr. Joyce.

"She is staying at the house of my fliend, sir."

"Will she come here?"

"I think it more better if you go to her, sir. I can take you to the house to-night and she will give you the letter. She is a very ignorant woman, sir, and she does not understand checks."

"I wasn't thinking of giving her a check. I will bring banknotes with me."

"It would only be waste of valuable time to bring less than ten thousand dollars, sir."

"I quite understand."

"I will go and tell my fliend after I have had my tiffin, sir."

"Very good. You'd better meet me outside the club at ten o'clock to-night."

"With pleasure, sir," said Ong Chi Seng.

He gave Mr. Joyce a little bow and left the room. Mr. Joyce went out to have luncheon, too. He went to the club and here, as he had expected, he saw Robert Crosbie. He was sitting at a crowded table, and as he passed him, looking for a place, Mr. Joyce touched him on the shoulder.

"I'd like a word or two with you before you go," he said.

"Right you are. Let me know when you're ready."

Mr. Joyce had made up his mind how to tackle him.

He played a rubber of bridge after luncheon in order to allow time for the club to empty itself. He did not want on this particular matter to see Crosbie in his office. Presently Crosbie came into the card-room and looked on till the game was finished. The other players went on their various affairs, and the two were left alone.

"A rather unfortunate thing has happened, old man," said Mr. Joyce, in a tone which he sought to render as casual as possible. "It appears that your wife sent a letter to Hammond asking him to come to the bungalow on the night he was killed."

"But that's impossible," cried Crosbie. "She's always stated that she had had no communication with Hammond. I know from my own knowledge that she hadn't set eyes on him for a couple of months."

"The fact remains that the letter exists. It's in the possession of the Chinese woman Hammond was living with. Your wife meant to give you a present on your birthday, and she wanted Hammond to help her to get it. In the emotional excitement that she suffered from after the tragedy, she forgot all about it, and having once denied having any communication with Hammond she was afraid to say that she had made a mistake. It was, of course, very unfortunate, but I daresay it was not unnatural."

Crosbie did not speak. His large, red face bore an expression of complete bewilderment, and Mr. Joyce was at once relieved and exasperated by his lack of comprehension. He was a stupid man, and Mr. Joyce had no patience with stupidity. But his distress since the catastrophe had touched a soft spot in the lawyer's heart; and Mrs. Crosbie had struck the right note when she asked him to help her, not for her sake, but for her husband's.

"I need not tell you that it would be very awkward if this letter found its way into the hands of the prosecution. Your wife has lied, and she would be asked to explain the lie. It alters things a little if Hammond did not intrude, an unwanted guest, but came to your house by invitation. It would be easy to arouse in the assessors a certain indecision of mind."

Mr. Joyce hesitated. He was face to face now with his decision. If it had been a time for humor, he could have smiled at the reflection that he was taking so grave a step, and that the man for whom he was taking it had not the smallest conception of its gravity. If he gave the matter a thought, he probably imagined that what Mr. Joyce was doing was what any lawyer did in the ordinary run of business.

"My dear Robert, you are not only my client, but my friend. I think we must get hold of that letter. It'll cost a good deal of money. Except for that I should have preferred to say nothing to you about it."

"How much?"

"Ten thousand dollars."

"That's a devil of a lot. With the slump and one thing and another it'll take just about all I've got."

"Can you get it at once?"

"I suppose so. Old Charlie Meadows will let me have it on my tin shares and on those two estates I'm interested in."

"Then will you?"

"Is it absolutely necessary?"

"If you want your wife to be acquitted."

Crosbie grew very red. His mouth sagged strangely.

"But . . ." he could not find words, his face now was purple. "But I don't understand. She can explain. You don't mean to say they'd find her guilty? They couldn't hang her for putting a noxious vermin out of the way."

"Of course they wouldn't hang her. They might only find her guilty of manslaughter. She'd probably get off with two or three years."

Crosbie started to his feet and his red face was distraught with horror.

"Three years."

Then something seemed to dawn in that slow intelligence of his. His mind was darkness across which shot
suddenly a flash of lightning, and though the succeeding
darkness was as profound, there remained the memory of
something not seen but perhaps just descried. Mr. Joyce
saw that Crosbie's big red hands, coarse and hard with all
the odd jobs he had set them to, trembled.

"What was the present she wanted to make me?"

"She says she wanted to give you a new gun."

Once more that great red face flushed a deeper red.

"When have you got to have the money ready?"

There was something odd in his voice now. It sounded
as though he spoke with invisible hands clutching at his
throat.

"At ten o'clock to-night. I thought you could bring it
to my office at about six."

"Is the woman coming to you?"

"No, I'm going to her."

"I'll bring the money. I'll come with you."

Mr. Joyce looked at him sharply.

"Do you think there's any need for you to do that? I
think it would be better if you left me to deal with this
matter by myself."

"It's my money, isn't it? I'm going to come."

Mr. Joyce shrugged his shoulders. They rose and shook
hands. Mr. Joyce looked at him curiously.

At ten o'clock they met in the empty club.

"Everything all right?" asked Mr. Joyce.

"Yes. I've got the money in my pocket."

"Let's go then."

They walked down the steps. Mr. Joyce's car was waiting for them in the square, silent at that hour, and as they
came to it Ong Chi Seng stepped out of the shadow of a
house. He took his seat beside the driver and gave him
a direction. They drove past the Hotel de l'Europe and

turned up by the Sailor's Home to get into Victoria Street.
Here the Chinese shops were still open, idlers lounged
about, and in the roadway rickshaws and motor-cars and
gharries gave a busy air to the scene. Suddenly their car
stopped and Chi Seng turned round.

"I think it more better if we walk here, sir," he said.

They got out and he went on. They followed a step or
two behind. Then he asked them to stop.

"You wait here, sir. I go in and speak to my fliend."

He went into a shop, open to the street, where three or
four Chinese were standing behind the counter. It was one
of those strange shops where nothing was on view, and you
wondered what it was they sold there. They saw him
address a stout man in a duck suit with a large gold chain
across his breast, and the man shot a quick glance out
into the night. He gave Chi Seng a key and Chi Seng
came out. He beckoned to the two men waiting and slid
into a doorway at the side of the shop. They followed him
and found themselves at the foot of a flight of stairs.

"If you wait a minute I will light a match," he said,
always resourceful. "You come upstairs, please."

He held a Japanese match in front of them, but it
scarcely dispelled the darkness and they groped their way
up behind him. On the first floor he unlocked a door and
going in lit a gas-jet.

"Come in, please," he said.

It was a small square room, with one window, and the
only furniture consisted of two low Chinese beds covered
with matting. In one corner was a large chest, with an
elaborate lock, and on this stood a shabby tray with an
opium pipe on it and a lamp. There was in the room the
faint, acrid scent of the drug. They sat down and Ong
Chi Seng offered them cigarettes. In a moment the door
was opened by the fat Chinaman whom they had seen
behind the counter. He bade them good evening in very

good English, and sat down by the side of his fellow-
countryman.

"The Chinese woman is just coming," said Chi Seng.

A boy from the shop brought in a tray with a teapot
and cups and the Chinaman offered them a cup of tea.
Crosbie refused. The Chinese talked to one another in
undertones, but Crosbie and Mr. Joyce were silent. At
last there was the sound of a voice outside; some one was
calling in a low tone; and the Chinaman went to the door.
He opened it, spoke a few words, and ushered a woman
in. Mr. Joyce looked at her. He had heard much about
her since Hammond's death, but he had never seen her.
She was a stoutish person, not very young, with a broad
phlegmatic face, she was powdered and rouged and her
eyebrows were a thin black line, but she gave you the
impression of a woman of character. She wore a pale blue
jacket and a white skirt, her costume was not quite
European nor quite Chinese, but on her feet were little
Chinese silk slippers. She wore heavy gold chains round
her neck, gold bangles on her wrists, gold ear-rings and
elaborate gold pins in her black hair. She walked in slowly,
with the air of a woman sure of herself, but with a certain
heaviness of tread, and sat down on the bed beside Ong
Chi Seng. He said something to her and nodding she gave
an incurious glance at the two white men.

"Has she got the letter?" asked Mr. Joyce.

"Yes, sir."

Crosbie said nothing, but produced a roll of five hun-
dred-dollar notes. He counted out twenty and handed them
to Chi Seng.

"Will you see if that is correct?"

The clerk counted them and gave them to the fat
Chinaman.

"Quite correct, sir."

The Chinaman counted them once more and put them in
his pocket. He spoke again to the woman and she drew

from her bosom a letter. She gave it to Chi Seng who cast his eyes over it.

"This is the right document, sir," he said, and was about to give it to Mr. Joyce when Crosbie took it from him.

"Let me look at it," he said.

Mr. Joyce watched him read and then held out his hand for it.

"You'd better let me have it."

Crosbie folded it up deliberately and put it in his pocket.

"No, I'm going to keep it myself. It's cost me enough money."

Mr. Joyce made no rejoinder. The three Chinese watched the little passage, but what they thought about it, or whether they thought, it was impossible to tell from their impassive countenances. Mr. Joyce rose to his feet.

"Do you want me any more to-night, sir?" said Ong Chi Seng.

"No." He knew that the clerk wished to stay behind in order to get his agreed share of the money, and he turned to Crosbie. "Are you ready?"

Crosbie did not answer, but stood up. The Chinaman went to the door and opened it for them. Chi Seng found a bit of candle and lit it in order to light them down, and the two Chinese accompanied them to the street. They left the woman sitting quietly on the bed smoking a cigarette. When they reached the street the Chinese left them and went once more upstairs.

"What are you going to do with that letter?" asked Mr. Joyce.

"Keep it."

They walked to where the car was waiting for them and here Mr. Joyce offered his friend a lift. Crosbie shook his head.

"I'm going to walk." He hesitated a little and shuffled his feet. "I went to Singapore on the night of Hammond's death partly to buy a new gun that a man I knew wanted to dispose of. Good night."

He disappeared quickly into the darkness.

Mr. Joyce was quite right about the trial. The assessors went into court fully determined to acquit Mrs. Crosbie. She gave evidence on her own behalf. She told her story simply and with straightforwardness. The D.P.P. was a kindly man and it was plain that he took no great pleasure in his task. He asked the necessary questions in a deprecating manner. His speech for the prosecution might really have been a speech for the defense, and the assessors took less than five minutes to consider their popular verdict. It was impossible to prevent the great outburst of applause with which it was received by the crowd that packed the court house. The judge congratulated Mrs. Crosbie and she was a free woman.

No one had expressed a more violent disapprobation of Hammond's behavior than Mrs. Joyce; she was a woman loyal to her friends and she had insisted on the Crosbies staying with her after the trial, for she in common with every one else had no doubt of the result, till they could make arrangements to go away. It was out of the question for poor, dear, brave Leslie to return to the bungalow at which the horrible catastrophe had taken place. The trial was over by half-past twelve and when they reached the Joyces' house a grand luncheon was awaiting them. Cocktails were ready, Mrs. Joyce's million-dollar cocktail was celebrated through all the Malay States, and Mrs. Joyce drank Leslie's health. She was a talkative, vivacious woman, and now she was in the highest spirits. It was fortunate, for the rest of them were silent. She did not wonder, her husband never had much to say, and the other two were naturally exhausted from the long strain to which they had been subjected. During luncheon she carried on a bright and spirited monologue. Then coffee was served.

"Now, children," she said in her gay, bustling fashion "you must have a rest and after tea I shall take you both for a drive to the sea."

Mr. Joyce, who lunched at home only by exception, had of course to go back to his office.

"I'm afraid I can't do that, Mrs. Joyce," said Crosbie. "I've got to get back to the estate at once."

"Not to-day?" she cried.

"Yes, now. I've neglected it for too long and I have urgent business. But I shall be very grateful if you will keep Leslie until we have decided what to do."

Mrs. Joyce was about to expostulate, but her husband prevented her.

"If he must go, he must, and there's an end of it."

There was something in the lawyer's tone which made her look at him quickly. She held her tongue and there was a moment's silence. Then Crosbie spoke again.

"If you'll forgive me, I'll start at once so that I can get there before dark." He rose from the table. "Will you come and see me off, Leslie!"

"Of course."

They went out of the dining-room together.

"I think that's rather inconsiderate of him," said Mrs. Joyce. "He must know that Leslie wants to be with him just now."

"I'm sure he wouldn't go if it wasn't absolutely necessary."

"Well, I'll just see that Leslie's room is ready for her. She wants a complete rest, of course, and then amusement."

Mrs. Joyce left the room and Joyce sat down again. In a short time he heard Crosbie start the engine of his motor-cycle and then noisily scrunch over the gravel of the garden path. He got up and went into the drawing-room. Mrs. Crosbie was standing in the middle of it, looking into space, and in her hand was an open letter. He recognized it. She gave him a glance as he came in and he saw that she was deathly pale.

"He knows," she whispered.

Mr. Joyce went up to her and took the letter from her hand. He lit a match and set the paper afire. She watched it burn. When he could hold it no longer he dropped it on the tiled floor and they both looked at the paper curl and blacken. Then he trod it into ashes with his foot.

"What does he know?"

She gave him a long, long stare and into her eyes came a strange look. Was it contempt or despair? Mr. Joyce could not tell.

"He knows that Geoff. was my lover."

Mr. Joyce made no movement and uttered no sound.

"He'd been my lover for years. He became my lover almost immediately after he came back from the war. We knew how careful we must be. When we became lovers I pretended I was tired of him, and he seldom came to the house when Robert was there. I used to drive out to a place we knew and he met me, two or three times a week, and when Robert went to Singapore he used to come to the bungalow late, when the boys had gone for the night. We saw one another constantly, all the time, and not a soul had the smallest suspicion of it. And then lately, a year ago, he began to change. I didn't know what was the matter. I couldn't believe that he didn't care for me any more. He always denied it. I was frantic. I made him scenes. Sometimes I thought he hated me. Oh, if you knew what agonies I endured. I passed through hell. I knew he didn't want me any more and I wouldn't let him go. Misery! Misery! I loved him. I'd given him everything. He was all my life. And then I heard he was living with a Chinese woman. I couldn't believe it. I wouldn't believe it. At last I saw her, I saw her with my own eyes, walking in the village, with her gold bracelets and her necklaces, an old, fat, Chinese woman. She was older than

I was. Horrible! They all knew in the kampong that she
was his mistress. And when I passed her, she looked at
me and I knew that she knew I was his mistress too. I
sent for him. I told him I must see him. You've read the
letter. I was mad to write it. I didn't know what I was
doing. I didn't care. I hadn't seen him for ten days. It was
a lifetime. And when last we'd parted he took me in his
arms and kissed me, and told me not to worry. And he
went straight from my arms to hers."

She had been speaking in a low voice, vehemently, and
now she stopped and wrung her hands.

"That damned letter. We'd always been so careful. He
always tore up any word I wrote to him the moment he'd
read it. How was I to know he'd leave that one? He came,
and I told him I knew about the Chinawoman. He denied
it. He said it was only scandal. I was beside myself. I
don't know what I said to him. Oh, I hated him then. I
tore him limb from limb. I said everything I could to
wound him. I insulted him. I could have spat in his face.
And at last he turned on me. He told me he was sick and
tired of me and never wanted to see me again. He said I
bored him to death. And then he acknowledged that it was
true about the Chinawoman. He said he'd known her for
years, before the war, and she was the only woman who
really meant anything to him, and the rest was just
pastime. And he said he was glad I knew, and now at last
I'd leave him alone. And then I don't know what happened, I was beside myself, I saw red. I seized the revolver and I fired. He gave a cry and I saw I'd hit him.
He staggered and rushed for the veranda. I ran after
him and fired again. He fell, and then I stood over him
and I fired and fired till the revolver went click, click, and
I knew there were no more cartridges."

At last she stopped, panting. Her face was no longer
human, it was distorted with cruelty, and rage and pain.
You would never have thought that this quiet, refined

woman was capable of such fiendish passion. Mr. Joyce took a step backwards. He was absolutely aghast at the sight of her. It was not a face, it was a gibbering, hideous mask. Then they heard a voice calling from another room, a loud, friendly, cheerful voice. It was Mrs. Joyce.

"Come along, Leslie darling, your room's ready. You must be dropping with sleep."

Mrs. Crosbie's features gradually composed themselves. Those passions, so clearly delineated, were smoothed away as with your hand you would smooth a crumpled paper, and in a minute the face was cool and calm and unlined She was a trifle pale, but her lips broke into a pleasant, affable smile. She was once more the well-bred and even distinguished woman.

"I'm coming, Dorothy dear. I'm sorry to give you so much trouble."

# Seven American Stories

# THE SNOWS OF KILIMANJARO
## *by Ernest Hemingway*

*Kilimanjaro is a snow covered mountain 19,170 feet high, and is said to be the highest mountain in Africa. Its western summit is called the Masai "Ngàje Ngài," the House of God. Close to the western summit there is the dried and frozen carcass of a leopard. No one has explained what the leopard was seeking at that altitude.*

"THE marvelous thing is that it's painless," he said. "That's how you know when it starts."

"Is it really?"

"Absolutely. I'm awfully sorry about the odor though. That must bother you."

"Don't! Please don't."

"Look at them," he said. "Now is it sight or is it scent that brings them like that?"

The cot the man lay on was in the wide shade of a mimosa tree and as he looked out past the shade onto the glare of the plain there were three of the big birds squatted obscenely, while in the sky a dozen more sailed, making quick-moving shadows as they passed.

"They've been there since the day the truck broke down," he said. "Today's the first time any have lit on the ground. I watched the way they sailed very carefully at first in case I ever wanted to use them in a story. That's funny now."

"I wish you wouldn't," she said.

"I'm only talking," he said. "It's much easier if I talk. But I don't want to bother you."

"You know it doesn't bother me," she said. "It's that I've gotten so very nervous not being able to do anything. I think we might make it as easy as we can until the plane comes."

"Or until the plane doesn't come."

"Please tell me what I can do. There must be something I can do."

"You can take the leg off and that might stop it, though I doubt it. Or you can shoot me. You're a good shot now. I taught you to shoot, didn't I?"

"Please don't talk that way. Couldn't I read to you?"

"Read what?"

"Anything in the book bag that we haven't read."

"I can't listen to it," he said. "Talking is the easiest. We quarrel and that makes the time pass."

"I don't quarrel. I never want to quarrel. Let's not quarrel any more. No matter how nervous we get. Maybe they will be back with another truck today. Maybe the plane will come."

"I don't want to move," the man said. "There is no sense in moving now except to make it easier for you."

"That's cowardly."

"Can't you let a man die as comfortably as he can without calling him names? What's the use of slanging me?"

"You're not going to die."

"Don't be silly. I'm dying now. Ask those bastards." He looked over to where the huge, filthy birds sat, their naked heads sunk in the hunched feathers. A fourth planed down, to run quick-legged and then waddle slowly toward the others.

"They are around every camp. You never notice them. You can't die if you don't give up."

"Where did you read that? You're such a bloody fool."

"You might think about some one else."

"For Christ's sake," he said, "that's been my trade."

He lay then and was quiet for a while and looked across the heat shimmer of the plain to the edge of the bush. There were a few Tommies that showed minute and white against the yellow and, far off, he saw a herd of zebra, white against the green of the bush. This was a pleasant camp under big trees against a hill, with good water, and close by, a nearly dry water hole where sand grouse flighted in the mornings.

"Wouldn't you like me to read?" she asked. She was sitting on a canvas chair beside his cot. "There's a breeze coming up."

"No thanks."

"Maybe the truck will come."

"I don't give a damn about the truck."

"I do."

"You give a damn about so many things that I don't."

"Not so many, Harry."

"What about a drink?"

"It's supposed to be bad for you. It said in Black's to avoid all alcohol. You shouldn't drink."

"Molo!" he shouted.

"Yes Bwana."

"Bring whiskey-soda."

"Yes Bwana."

"You shouldn't," she said.   That's what I mean by giving up. It says it's bad for you. I know it's bad for you."

"No," he said. "It's good for me."

So now it was all over, he thought. So now he would never have a chance to finish it. So this was the way it ended in a bickering over a drink. Since the gangrene started in his right leg he had no pain and with the pain the horror had gone and all he felt now was a great tiredness and anger that this was the end of it. For this, that now was coming, he had very little curiosity. For years it had obsessed him; but now it meant nothing in itself. It was strange how easy being tired enough made it.

Now he would never write the things that he had saved to write until he knew enough to write them well. Well, he would not have to fail at trying to write them either. Maybe you could never write them, and that was why you put them off and delayed the starting. Well he would never know, now.

"I wish we'd never come," the woman said. She was looking at him holding the glass and biting her lip. "You never would have gotten anything like this in Paris. You always said you loved Paris. We could have stayed in Paris or gone anywhere. I'd have gone anywhere. I said I'd go anywhere you wanted. If you wanted to shoot we could have gone shooting in Hungary and been comfortable."

"Your bloody money," he said.

"That's not fair," she said. "It was always yours as much as mine. I left everything and I went wherever you wanted to go and I've done what you wanted to do. But I wish we'd never come here."

"You said you loved it."

"I did when you were all right. But now I hate it. I don't see why that had to happen to your leg. What have we done to have that happen to us?"

"I suppose what I did was to forget to put iodine on it when I first scratched it. Then I didn't pay any attention to it because I never infect. Then, later, when it got bad, it was probably using that weak carbolic solution when the other antiseptics ran out that paralyzed the minute blood vessels and started the gangrene." He looked at her. "What else?"

"I don't mean that."

"If we would have hired a good mechanic instead of a half-baked kikuyu driver, he would have checked the oil and never burned out that bearing in the truck."

"I don't mean that."

"If you hadn't left your own people, your God-damned Old Westbury, Saratoga, Palm Beach people to take me on——"

"Why, I loved you. That's not fair. I love you now. I'll always love you. Don't you love me?"

"No," said the man. "I don't think so. I never have."

"Harry, what are you saying? You're out of your head."

"No. I haven't any head to go out of."

"Don't drink that," she said. "Darling, please don't drink that. We have to do everything we can."

"You do it," he said. "I'm tired."

*Now in his mind he saw a railway station at Karagatch and he was standing with his pack and that was the headlight of the Simplon-Orient cutting the dark now and he was leaving Thrace then after the retreat. That was one of the things he had saved to write, with, in the morning at breakfast, looking out the window and seeing snow on the mountains in Bulgaria and Nansen's Secretary asking the old man if it were snow and the old man looking at it and saying, No, that's not snow. It's too early for snow. And the Secretary repeating to the other girls, No, you see. It's not snow and them all saying, It's not snow we were mistaken. But it was the snow all right and he sent them on into it when he evolved exchange of populations. And it was snow they tramped along in until they died that winter.*

*It was snow too that fell all Christmas week that year up in the Gauertal, that year they lived in the woodcutter's house with the big square porcelain stove that filled half the room, and they slept on mattresses filled with beech leaves, the time the deserter came with his feet bloody in the snow. He said the police were right behind him and they gave him woolen socks and held the gendarmes talking until the tracks had drifted over.*

*In Schrunz, on Christmas day, the snow was so bright it hurt your eyes when you looked out from the weinstube and saw every one coming home from church. That was where they walked up the sleigh-smoothed urine-yellowed road along the river with the steep pine hills, skis heavy on the shoulder, and where they ran that great run down the glacier above the Madlener-haus, the snow as smooth to see as cake frosting and as light as powder and he remembered the noiseless rush the speed made as you dropped down like a bird.*

*They were snow-bound a week in the Madlener-haus that time in the blizzard playing cards in the smoke by the lantern light and the stakes were higher all the time as Herr Lent lost more. Finally he lost it all. Everything, the skischule money and all the season's profit and then his capital. He could see him with his long nose, picking up the cards and then opening, "Sans Voir." There was always gambling then. When there was no snow you gambled and when there was too much you gambled. He thought of all the time in his life he had spent gambling.*

*But he had never written a line of that, nor of that cold, bright Christmas day with the mountains showing across the plain that Barker had flown across the lines to bomb the Austrian officers' leave train, machine-gunning them as they scattered and ran. He remembered Barker afterwards coming into the mess and starting to tell about it. And how quiet it got and then somebody saying, "You bloody murderous bastard."*

*Those were the same Austrians they killed then that he skied with later. No not the same. Hans, that he skied with all that year, had been in the Kaiser-Jägers and when they went hunting hares together up the little valley above the saw-mill they had talked of the fighting on Pasubio and of the attack on Pertica and Asalone and he had never written a word of that. Nor of Monte Corno, nor the Siete Commun, nor of Arsiedo.*

*How many winters had he lived in the Voralberg and the Arlberg? It was four and then he remembered the man who had the fox to sell when they had walked into Bludenz that time to buy presents, and the cherry-pit taste of good kirsch, the fast-slipping rush of running powder-snow on crust, singing "Hi! Ho! said Rolly!" as you ran down the last stretch to the steep drop, taking it straight, then running the orchard in three turns and out across the ditch and onto the icy road behind the inn. Knocking your bindings loose, kicking the skis free and leaning them up against the wooden*

*wall of the inn, the lamplight coming from the window,*
*where inside, in the smoky, new-wine-smelling warmth, they*
*were playing the accordion.*

"Where did we stay in Paris?" asked the woman who was
sitting by him in a canvas chair, now, in Africa.

"At the Crillon. You know that."

"Why do I know that?"

"That's where we always stayed."

"No. Not always."

"There and at the Pavillion Henri-Quatre in St. Germain.
You said you loved it there."

"Love is a dunghill," said Harry. "And I'm the cock that
gets on it to crow."

"If you have to go away," she said, "is it absolutely necessary to kill off everything you leave behind? I mean do
you have to take away everything? Do you have to kill
your horse, and your wife and burn your saddle and your
armour?"

"Yes," he said. "Your damned money was my armour.
My Swift and my Armour."

"Don't."

"All right. I'll stop that. I don't want to hurt you."

"It's a little bit late now."

"All right then. I'll go on hurting you. It's more amusing.
The only thing I ever really like to do with you I can't do
now."

"No, that's not true. You liked to do many things and
everything you wanted to do I did."

"Oh, for Christ sake stop bragging, will you?"

He looked at her and saw her crying.

"Listen," he said. "Do you think that it is fun to do this?
I don't know why I'm doing it. It's trying to kill to keep
yourself alive, I imagine. I was all right when we started
talking. I didn't mean to start this, and now I'm crazy as a
coot and being as cruel to you as I can be. Don't pay any

attention, darling, to what I say. I love you, really. You know I love you. I've never loved any one else the way I love you."

He slipped into the familiar lie he made his bread and butter by.

"You're sweet to me."

"You bitch," he said. "You rich bitch. That's poetry. I'm full of poetry now. Rot and poetry. Rotten poetry."

"Stop it. Harry, why do you have to turn into a devil now?"

"I don't like to leave anything," the man said. "I don't like to leave things behind."

* * *

It was evening now and he had been asleep. The sun was gone behind the hill and there was a shadow all across the plain and the small animals were feeding close to camp; quick dropping heads and switching tails, he watched them keeping well out away from the bush now. The birds no longer waited on the ground. They were all perched heavily in a tree. There were many more of them. His personal boy was sitting by the bed.

"Memsahib's gone to shoot," the boy said. "Does Bwana want?"

"Nothing."

She had gone to kill a piece of meat and, knowing how he liked to watch the game, she had gone well away so she would not disturb this little pocket of the plain that he could see. She was always thoughtful, he thought. On anything she knew about, or had read, or that she had ever heard.

It was not her fault that when he went to her he was already over. How could a woman know that you meant nothing that you said; that you spoke only from habit and to be comfortable? After he no longer meant what he said, his lies were more successful with women than when he had told them the truth.

It was not so much that he lied as that there was no truth to tell. He had had his life and it was over and then he went on living it again with different people and more money, with the best of the same places, and some new ones.

You kept from thinking and it was all marvellous. You were equipped with good insides so that you did not go to pieces that way, the way most of them had, and you made an attitude that you cared nothing for the work you used to do, now that you could no longer do it. But, in yourself, you said that you would write about these people; about the very rich; that you were really not of them but a spy in their country; that you would leave it and write of it and for once it would be written by some one who knew what he was writing of. But he would never do it, because each day of not writing, of comfort, of being that which he despised, dulled his ability and softened his will to work so that, finally, he did no work at all. The people he knew now were all much more comfortable when he did not work. Africa was where he had been happiest in the good time of his life, so he had come out here to start again. They had made this safari with the minimum of comfort. There was no hardship; but there was no luxury and he had thought that he could get back into training that way. That in some way he could work the fat off his soul the way a fighter went into the mountains to work and train in order to burn it out of his body.

She had liked it. She said she loved it. She loved anything that was exciting, that involved a change of scene, where there were new people and where things were pleasant. And he had felt the illusion of returning strength of will to work. Now if this was how it ended, and he knew it was, he must not turn like some snake biting itself because its back was broken. It wasn't this woman's fault. If it had not been she it would have been another. If he lived by a lie he should try to die by it. He heard a shot beyond the hill.

She shot very well, this good, this rich bitch, this kindly

caretaker and destroyer of his talent. Nonsense. He had destroyed his talent himself. Why should he blame this woman because she kept him well? He had destroyed his talent by not using it, by betrayals of himself and what he believed in, by drinking so much that he blunted the edge of his perceptions, by laziness, by sloth, and by snobbery, by pride and by prejudice, by hook and by crook. What was this? A catalogue of old books? What was his talent anyway? It was a talent all right but instead of using it, he had traded on it. It was never what he had done, but always what he could do. And he had chosen to make his living with something else instead of a pen or a pencil. It was strange, too, wasn't it, that when he fell in love with another woman, that woman should always have more money than the last one? But when he no longer was in love, when he was only lying, as to this woman, now, who had the most money of all, who had all the money there was, who had had a husband and children, who had taken lovers and been dissatisfied with them, and who loved him dearly as a writer, as a man, as a companion and as a proud possession; it was strange that when he did not love her at all and was lying, that he should be able to give her more for her money than when he had really loved.

We must all be cut out for what we do, he thought. However you make your living is where your talent lies. He had sold vitality, in one form or another, all his life and when your affections are not too involved you give much better value for the money. He had found that out but he would never write that, now, either. No, he would not write that, although it was well worth writing.

Now she came in sight, walking across the open toward the camp. She was wearing jodhpurs and carrying her rifle. The two boys had a Tommie slung and they were coming along behind her. She was still a good-looking woman, he thought, and she had a pleasant body. She had a great talent and appreciation for the bed, she was not pretty, but he liked her face, she read enormously, liked to ride and shoot and, certainly, she drank too much. Her husband had died when she was still a comparatively young woman and for a while she had devoted herself to her two just-grown children, who did not need her and were embarrassed at having her about, to her stable of horses, to books, and to bottles. She liked to read in the evening before dinner and she drank Scotch and soda while she read. By dinner she was fairly drunk and after a bottle of wine at dinner she was usually drunk enough to sleep.

That was before the lovers. After she had the lovers she did not drink so much because she did not have to be drunk to sleep. But the lovers bored her. She had been married to a man who had never bored her and these people bored her very much.

Then one of her two children was killed in a plane crash and after that was over she did not want the lovers, and drink being no anæsthetic she had to make another life. Suddenly, she had been acutely frightened of being alone. But she wanted some one that she respected with her.

It had begun very simply. She liked what he wrote and she had always envied the life he led. She thought he did exactly what he wanted to. The steps by which she had acquired him and the way in which she had finally fallen in love with him were all part of a regular progression in which she had built herself a new life and he had traded away what remained of his old life.

He had traded it for security, for comfort too, there was no denying that, and for what else? He did not know. She would have bought him anything he wanted. He knew that. She was a damned nice woman too. He would as soon be in bed with her as any one; rather with her, because she was richer, because she was very pleasant and appreciative and because she never made scenes. And now this life that she had built again was coming to a term because he had not used iodine two weeks ago when a thorn had scratched his

knee as they moved forward trying to photograph a herd
of waterbuck standing, their heads up, peering while their
nostrils searched the air, their ears spread wide to hear the
first noise that would send them rushing into the bush.
They had bolted, too, before he got the picture.

Here she came now.

He turned his head on the cot to look toward her. "Hello,"
he said.

"I shot a Tommy ram," she told him. "He'll make you
good broth and I'll have them mash some potatoes with the
Klim. How do you feel?"

"Much better."

"Isn't that lovely? You know I thought perhaps you
would. You were sleeping when I left."

"I had a good sleep. Did you walk far?"

"No. Just around behind the hill. I made quite a good
shot on the Tommy."

"You shoot marvellously, you know."

"I love it. I've loved Africa. Really. If *you're* all right
it's the most fun that I've ever had. You don't know the
fun it's been to shoot with you. I've loved the country."

"I love it too."

"Darling, you don't know how marvellous it is to see you
feeling better. I couldn't stand it when you felt that way.
You won't talk to me like that again, will you? Promise me?"

"No," he said. "I don't remember what I said."

"You don't have to destroy me. Do you? I'm only a
middle-aged woman who loves you and wants to do what
you want to do. I've been destroyed two or three times
already. You wouldn't want to destroy me again, would
you?"

"I'd like to destroy you a few times in bed," he said.

"Yes. That's the good destruction. That's the way we're
made to be destroyed. The plane will be here tomorrow."

"How do you know?"

"I'm sure. It's bound to come. The boys have the wood all

ready and the grass to make the smudge. I went down and looked at it again today. There's plenty of room to land and we have the smudges ready at both ends."

"What makes you think it will come tomorrow?"

"I'm sure it will. It's overdue now. Then, in town, they will fix up your leg and then we will have some good destruction. Not that dreadful talking kind."

"Should we have a drink? The sun is down."

"Do you think you should?"

"I'm having one."

"We'll have one together. *Molo, letti dui whiskey-soda!*" she called.

"You'd better put on your mosquito boots," he told her.

"I'll wait till I bathe . . ."

While it grew dark they drank and just before it was dark and there was no longer enough light to shoot, a hyena crossed the open on his way around the hill.

"That bastard crosses there every night," the man said. "Every night for two weeks."

"He's the one makes the noise at night. I don't mind it. They're a filthy animal though."

Drinking together, with no pain now except the discomfort of lying in the one position, the boys lighting a fire, its shadow jumping on the tents, he could feel the return of acquiescence in this life of pleasant surrender. She *was* very good to him. He had been cruel and unjust in the afternoon. She was a fine woman, marvellous really. And just then it occurred to him that he was going to die.

It came with a rush; not as a rush of water nor of wind; but of a sudden evil-smelling emptiness and the odd thing was that the hyena slipped lightly along the edge of it.

"What is it, Harry?" she asked him.

"Nothing," he said. "You had better move over to the other side. To windward."

"Did Molo change the dressing?"

"Yes. I'm just using the boric now."

"How do you feel?"

"A little wobbly."

"I'm going in to bathe," she said. "I'll be right out. I'll eat with you and then we'll put the cot in."

So, he said to himself, we did well to stop the quarrelling. He had never quarrelled much with this woman, while with the women that he loved he had quarrelled so much they had finally, always, with the corrosion of the quarrelling, killed what they had together. He had loved too much, demanded too much, and he wore it all out.

*He thought about alone in Constantinople that time, having quarrelled in Paris before he had gone out. He had whored the whole time and then, when that was over, and he had failed to kill his loneliness, but only made it worse, he had written her, the first one, the one who left him, a letter telling her how he had never been able to kill it. . . . How when he thought he saw her outside the Regence one time it made him go all faint and sick inside, and that he would follow a woman who looked like her in some way, along the Boulevard, afraid to see it was not she, afraid to lose the feeling it gave him. How every one he had slept with had only made him miss her more. How what she had done could never matter since he knew he could not cure himself of loving her. He wrote this letter at the Club, cold sober, and mailed it to New York asking her to write him at the office in Paris. That seemed safe. And that night missing her so much it made him feel hollow sick inside, he wandered up past Taxim's, picked a girl up and took her out to supper. He had gone to a place to dance with her afterward, she danced badly, and left her for a hot Armenian slut, that swung her belly against him so it almost scalded. He took her away from a British gunner subaltern after a row. The gunner asked him outside and they fought in the street on the cobbles in the dark. He'd hit him twice, hard, on the side of the jaw and when he didn't go down he knew he was in for a fight. The gunner hit him in the body, then beside his eye. He swung with his left again and landed and the gunner fell on him and grabbed his coat and tore the sleeve off and he clubbed him twice behind the ear and then smashed him with his right as he pushed him away. When the gunner went down his head hit first and he ran with the girl because they heard the M. P.'s coming. They got into a taxi and drove out to Rimmily Hissa along the Bosphorus, and around, and back in the cool night and went to bed and she felt as over-ripe as she looked but smooth, rose-petal, syrupy, smooth-bellied, big-breasted and needed no pillow under her buttocks, and he left her before she was awake looking blousy enough in the first daylight and turned up at the Peru Palace with a black eye, carrying his coat because one sleeve was missing.*

*That same night he left for Anatolia and he remembered, later on that trip, riding all day through fields of the poppies that they raised for opium and how strange it made you feel, finally, and all the distances seemed wrong, to where they had made the attack with the newly arrived Constantine officers, that did not know a God-damned thing, and the artillery had fired into the troops and the British observer had cried like a child.*

*That was the day he'd first seen dead men wearing white ballet skirts and upturned shoes with pompons on them. The Turks had come steadily and lumpily and he had seen the skirted men running and the officers shooting into them and running then themselves and he and the British observer had run too until his lungs ached and his mouth was full of the taste of pennies and they stopped behind some rocks and there were the Turks coming as lumpily as ever. Later he had seen the things that he could never think of and later still he had seen much worse. So when he got back to Paris that time he could not talk about it or stand to have it mentioned. And there in the café as he passed was that American poet with a pile of saucers in front of him and*

*a stupid look on his potato face talking about the Dada
movement with a Roumanian who said his name was Tristan
Tzara, who always wore a monocle and had a headache,
and, back at the apartment with his wife that now he loved
again, the quarrel all over, the madness all over, glad to be
home, the office sent his mail up to the flat. So then the letter in answer to the one he'd written came in on a platter
one morning and when he saw the handwriting he went
cold all over and tried to slip the letter underneath another.
But his wife said, "Who is that letter from, dear?" and that
was the end of the beginning of that.*

*He remembered the good times with them all, and the
quarrels. They always picked the finest places to have the
quarrels. And why had they always quarrelled when he was
feeling best? He had never written any of that because, at
first, he never wanted to hurt any one and then it seemed as
though there was enough to write without it. But he had
always thought that he would write it finally. There was
so much to write. He had seen the world change; not just
the events; although he had seen many of them and had
watched the people, but he had seen the subtler change and
he could remember how the people were at different times.
He had been in it and he had watched it and it was his duty
to write of it; but now he never would.*

"How do you feel?" she said. She had come out from the
tent now after her bath.

"All right."

"Could you eat now?" He saw Molo behind her with the
folding table and the other boy with the dishes.

"I want to write," he said.

"You ought to take some broth to keep your strength up."

"I'm going to die tonight," he said. "I don't need my
strength up."

"Don't be melodramatic, Harry, please," she said.

"Why don't you use your nose? I'm rotted half way up

my thigh now. What the hell should I fool with broth for? Molo bring whiskey-soda."

"Please take the broth," she said gently.

"All right."

The broth was too hot. He had to hold it in the cup until it cooled enough to take it and then he just got it down without gagging.

"You're a fine woman," he said. "Don't pay any attention to me."

She looked at him with her well-known, well-loved face from *Spur* and *Town and Country,* only a little the worse for drink, only a little the worse for bed, but *Town and Country* never showed those good breasts and those useful thighs and those lightly small-of-back-caressing hands, and as he looked and saw her well-known pleasant smile, he felt death come again. This time there was no rush. It was a puff, as of a wind that makes a candle flicker and the flame go tall.

"They can bring my net out later and hang it from the tree and build the fire up. I'm not going in the tent tonight. It's not worth moving. It's a clear night. There won't be any rain."

So this was how you died, in whispers that you did not hear. Well, there would be no more quarrelling. He could promise that. The one experience that he had never had he was not going to spoil now. He probably would. You spoiled everything. But perhaps he wouldn't.

"You can't take dictation, can you?"

"I never learned," she told him.

"That's all right."

There wasn't time, of course, although it seemed as though it telescoped so that you might put it all into one paragraph if you could get it right.

*There was a log house, chinked white with mortar, on a hill above the lake. There was a bell on a pole by the door*

*to call the people in to meals. Behind the house were fields
and behind the fields was the timber. A line of lombardy
poplars ran from the house to the dock. Other poplars ran
along the point. A road went up to the hills along the edge
of the timber and along that road he picked blackberries.
Then that log house was burned down and all the guns that
had been on deer foot racks above the open fireplace were
burned and afterwards their barrels, with the lead melted
in the magazines, and the stocks burned away, lay out on
the heap of ashes that were used to make lye for the big
iron soap kettles, and you asked Grandfather if you could
have them to play with, and he said, no. You see they were
his guns still and he never bought any others. Nor did he
hunt any more. The house was rebuilt in the same place out
of lumber now and painted white and from its porch you
saw the poplars and the lake beyond, but there were never
any more guns The barrels of the guns that had hung on
the deer feet on the wall of the log house lay out there on
the heap of ashes and no one ever touched them.*

*In the Black Forest, after the war, we rented a trout
stream and there were two ways to walk to it. One was
down the valley from Triberg and around the valley road in
the shade of the trees that bordered the white road, and then
up a side road that went up through the hills past many small
farms, with the big Schwarzwald houses, until that road
crossed the stream. That was where our fishing began.*

*The other way was to climb steeply up to the edge of the
woods and then go across the top of the hills through the
pine woods, and then out to the edge of a meadow and down
across this meadow to the bridge. There were birches along
the stream and it was not big, but narrow, clear and fast,
with pools where it had cut under the roots of the birches.
At the Hotel in Triberg the proprietor had a fine season. It
was very pleasant and we were all great friends. The next
year came the inflation and the money he had made the year*

*before was not enough to buy supplies to open the hotel and
he hanged himself.*

You could dictate that, but you could not dictate the Place
Contrescarpe where the flower sellers dyed their flowers in
the street and the dye ran over the paving where the autobus
started and the old men and the women, always drunk on
wine and bad marc; and the children with their noses running in the cold; the smell of dirty sweat and poverty and
drunkenness at the Café des Amateurs and the whores at
the Bal Musette they lived above. The Concierge who entertained the trooper of the Garde Republicaine in her loge,
his horse-hair-plumed helmet on a chair. The locataire across
the hall whose husband was a bicycle racer and her joy that
morning at the Crèmerie when she had opened L'Auto and
seen where he placed third in Paris-Tours, his first big
race. She had blushed and laughed and then gone upstairs
crying with the yellow sporting paper in her hand. The
husband of the woman who ran the Bal Musette drove a
taxi and when he, Harry, had to take an early plane the
husband knocked upon the door to wake him and they each
drank a glass of white wine at the zinc of the bar before
they started. He knew his neighbors in that quarter then
because they all were poor.

Around that Place there were two kinds; the drunkards
and the sportifs. The drunkards killed their poverty that
way; the sportifs took it out in exercise. They were the
descendants of the Communards and it was no struggle for
them to know their politics. They knew who had shot their
fathers, their relatives, their brothers, and their friends
when the Versailles troops came in and took the town after
the Commune and executed any one they could catch witn
calloused hands, or who wore a cap, or carried any other
sign he was a working man. And in that poverty, and in that
quarter across the street from a Boucherie Chevaline and a
wine co-operative he had written the start of all he was to
do. There never was another part of Paris that he loved

*like that, the sprawling trees, the old white plastered houses
painted brown below, the long green of the autobus in that
round square, the purple flower dye upon the paving, the
sudden drop down the hill of the rue Cardinal Lemoine to
the River, and the other way the narrow crowded world of
the rue Mouffetard. The street that ran up toward the
Panthéon and the other that he always took with the bicycle,
the only asphalted street in all that quarter, smooth under
the tires, with the high narrow houses and the cheap tall
hotel where Paul Verlaine had died. There were only two
rooms in the apartments where they lived and he had a
room on the top floor of that hotel that cost him sixty francs
a month where he did his writing, and from it he could see
the roofs and chimney pots and all the hills of Paris.*

*From the apartment you could only see the wood and coal
man's place. He sold wine too, bad wine. The golden horse's
head outside the Boucherie Chevaline where the carcasses
hung yellow gold and red in the open window, and the green
painted co-operative where they bought their wine; good
wine and cheap. The rest was plaster walls and the windows
of the neighbors. The neighbors who, at night, when some
one lay drunk in the street, moaning and groaning in that
typical French ivresse that you were propaganded to believe
did not exist, would open their windows and then the murmur of talk.*

*"Where is the policeman? When you don't want him the
bugger is always there. He's sleeping with some concierge.
Get the Agent." Till some one threw a bucket of water from
a window and the moaning stopped. "What's that? Water.
Ah, that's intelligent." And the windows shutting. Marie,
his femme de ménage, protesting against the eight-hour day
saying, "If a husband works until six he gets only a little
drunk on the way home and does not waste too much. If he
works only until five he is drunk every night and one has
no money. It is the wife of the working man who suffers
from this shortening of hours."*

"Wouldn't you like some more broth?" the woman asked him now.

"No, thank you very much. It is awfully good."

"Try just a little."

"I would like a whiskey-soda."

"It's not good for you."

"No. It's bad for me. Cole Porter wrote the words and the music. This knowledge that you're going mad for me."

"You know I like you to drink."

"Oh yes. Only it's bad for me."

When she goes, he thought. I'll have all I want. Not all I want but all there is. Ayee he was tired. Too tired. He was going to sleep a little while. He lay still and death was not there. It must have gone around another street. It went in pairs, on bicycles, and moved absolutely silently on the pavements.

*No, he had never written about Paris. Not the Paris that he cared about. But what about the rest that he had never written?*

*What about the ranch and the silvered gray of the sage brush, the quick, clear water in the irrigation ditches, and the heavy green of the alfalfa. The trail went up into the hills and the cattle in the summer were shy as deer. The bawling and the steady noise and slow moving mass raising a dust as you brought them down in the fall. And behind the mountains, the clear sharpness of the peak in the evening light and, riding down along the trail in the moonlight, bright across the valley. Now he remembered coming down through the timber in the dark holding the horse's tail when you could not see and all the stories that he meant to write.*

*About the half-wit chore boy who was left at the ranch that time and told not to let any one get any hay, and that old bastard from the Forks who had beaten the boy when he had worked for him stopping to get some feed. The boy refusing and the old man saying he would beat him again.*

*The boy got the rifle from the kitchen and shot him when
he tried to come into the barn and when they came back to
the ranch he'd been dead a week, frozen in the corral, and
the dogs had eaten part of him. But what was left you
packed on a sled wrapped in a blanket and roped on and you
got the boy to help you haul it, and the two of you took it
out over the road on skis, and sixty miles down to town
to turn the boy over. He having no idea that he would be
arrested. Thinking he had done his duty and that you were
his friend and he would be rewarded. He'd helped to haul
the old man in so everybody could know how bad the old
man had been and how he'd tried to steal some feed that
didn't belong to him, and when the sheriff put the handcuffs
on the boy he couldn't believe it. Then he'd started to cry.
That was one story he had saved to write. He knew at
least twenty good stories from out there and he had never
written one. Why?*

"You tell them why," he said.

"Why what, dear?"

"Why nothing."

She didn't drink so much, now, since she had him. But if
he lived he would never write about her, he knew that now.
Nor about any of them. The rich were dull and they drank
too much, or they played too much backgammon. They were
dull and they were repetitious. He remembered poor Julian
and his romantic awe of them and how he had started a story
once that began, "The very rich are different from you and
me." And how some one had said to Julian, Yes, they have
more money. But that was not humorous to Julian. He
thought they were a special glamourous race and when he
found they weren't it wrecked him just as much as any
other thing that wrecked him.

He had been contemptuous of those who wrecked. You
did not have to like it because you understood it. He could

beat anything, he thought, because no thing could hurt him if he did not care.

All right. Now he would not care for death. One thing he had always dreaded was the pain. He could stand pain as well as any man, until it went on too long, and wore him out, but here he had something that had hurt frightfully and just when he had felt it breaking him, the pain had stopped.

*He remembered long ago when Williamson, the bombing officer, had been hit by a stick bomb some one in a German patrol had thrown as he was coming in through the wire that night and, screaming, had begged every one to kill him. He was a fat man, very brave, and a good officer, although addicted to fantastic shows. But that night he was caught in the wire, with a flare lighting him up and his bowels spilled out into the wire, so when they brought him in, alive, they had to cut him loose. Shoot me, Harry. For Christ sake shoot me. They had had an argument one time about our Lord never sending you anything you could not bear and some one's theory had been that meant that at a certain time the pain passed you out automatically. But he had always remembered Williamson, that night. Nothing passed out Williamson until he gave him all his morphine tablets that he had always saved to use himself and then they did not work right away.*

Still this now, that he had, was very easy; and if it was no worse as it went on there was nothing to worry about. Except that he would rather be in better company.

He thought a little about the company that he would like to have.

No, he thought, when everything you do, you do too long, and do too late, you can't expect to find the people still there. The people all are gone. The party's over and you are with your hostess now.

I'm getting as bored with dying as with everything else, he thought.

"It's a bore," he said out loud.

"What is, my dear?"

"Anything you do too bloody long."

He looked at her face between him and the fire. She was leaning back in the chair and the firelight shone on her pleasantly lined face and he could see that she was sleepy. He heard the hyena make a noise just outside the range of the fire.

"I've been writing," he said. "But I got tired."

"Do you think you will be able to sleep?"

"Pretty sure. Why don't you turn in?"

"I like to sit here with you."

"Do you feel anything strange?" he asked her.

"No. Just a little sleepy."

"I do," he said.

He had just felt death come by again.

"You know the only thing I've never lost is curiosity," he said to her.

"You've never lost anything. You're the most complete man I've ever known."

"Christ," he said. "How little a woman knows. What is that? Your intuition?"

Because, just then, death had come and rested its head on the foot of the cot and he could smell its breath.

"Never believe any of that about a scythe and a skull," he told her. "It can be two bicycle policemen as easily, or be a bird. Or it can have a wide snout like a hyena."

It had moved up on him now, but it had no shape any more. It simply occupied space.

"Tell it to go away."

It did not go away but moved a little closer.

"You've got a hell of a breath," he told it. "You stinking bastard."

It moved up closer to him still and now he could not speak

to it, and when it saw he could not speak it came a little closer, and now he tried to send it away without speaking, but it moved in on him so its weight was all upon his chest, and while it crouched there and he could not move, or speak, he heard the woman say, "Bwana is asleep now. Take the cot up very gently and carry it into the tent."

He could not speak to tell her to make it go away and it crouched now, heavier, so he could not breathe. And then, while they lifted the cot, suddenly it was all right and the weight went from his chest.

It was morning and had been morning for some time and he heard the plane. It showed very tiny and then made a wide circle and the boys ran out and lit the fires, using kerosene, and piled on grass so there were two big smudges at each end of the level place and the morning breeze blew them toward the camp and the plane circled twice more, low this time, and then glided down and levelled off and landed smoothly and, coming walking toward him, was old Compton in slacks, a tweed jacket and a brown felt hat.

"What's the matter, old cock?" Compton said.

"Bad leg," he told him. "Will you have some breakfast?"

"Thanks. I'll just have some tea. It's the Puss Moth you know. I won't be able to take the Memsahib. There's only room for one. Your lorry is on the way."

Helen had taken Compton aside and was speaking to him. Compton came back more cheery than ever.

"We'll get you right in," he said. "I'll be back for the Mem. Now I'm afraid I'll have to stop at Arusha to refuel. We'd better get going."

"What about the tea?"

"I don't really care about it you know."

The boys had picked up the cot and carried it around the green tents and down along the rock and out onto the plain and along past the smudges that were burning brightly now, the grass all consumed, and the wind fanning the fire, to

the little plane. It was difficult getting him in, but once in
he lay back in the leather seat, and the leg was stuck straight
out to one side of the seat where Compton sat. Compton
started the motor and got in. He waved to Helen and to the
boys and, as the clatter moved into the old familiar roar,
they swung around with Compie watching· for wart-hog
holes and roared, bumping, along the stretch between the
fires and with the last bump rose and he saw them all standing below, waving, and the camp beside the hill, flattening
now, and the plain spreading, clumps of trees, and the bush
flattening, while the game trails ran now smoothly to the
dry waterholes, and there was a new water that he had never
known of. The zebra, small rounded backs now, and the
wildebeeste, big-headed dots seeming to climb as they moved
in long fingers across the plain, now scattering as the
shadow came toward them, they were tiny now, and the
movement had no gallop, and the plain as far as you could
see, gray-yellow now and ahead old Compie's tweed back
and the brown felt hat. Then they were over the first hills
and the wildebeeste were trailing up them, and then they
were over mountains with sudden depths of green-rising
forest and the solid bamboo slopes, and then the heavy forest
again, sculptured into peaks and hollows until they crossed,
and hills sloped down and then another plain, hot now, and
purple brown, bumpy with heat and Compie looking back to
see how he was riding. Then there were other mountains
dark ahead.

And then instead of going on to Arusha they turned left,
he evidently figured that they had the gas, and looking down
he saw a pink sifting cloud, moving over the ground, and
in the air, like the first snow in a blizzard, that comes from
nowhere, and he knew the locusts were coming up from the
South. Then they began to climb and they were going to the
East it seemed, and then it darkened and they were in a
storm, the rain so thick it seemed like flying through a
waterfall, and then they were out and Compie turned his

head and grinned and pointed and there, ahead, all he could see, as wide as all the world, great, high, and unbelievably white in the sun, was the square top of Kilimanjaro. And then he knew that there was where he was going.

Just then the hyena stopped whimpering in the night and started to make a strange, human, almost crying sound. The woman heard it and stirred uneasily. She did not wake. In her dream she was at the house on Long Island and it was the night before her daughter's début. Somehow her father was there and he had been very rude. Then the noise the hyena made was so loud she woke and for a moment she did not know where she was and she was very afraid. Then she took the flashlight and shone it on the other cot that they had carried in after Harry had gone to sleep. She could see his bulk under the mosquito bar but somehow he had gotten his leg out and it hung down alongside the cot. The dressings had all come down and she could not look at it.

"Molo," she called, "Molo! Molo!"

Then she said, "Harry, Harry!" Then her voice rising, "Harry! Please! Oh Harry!"

There was no answer and she could not hear him breathing.

Outside the tent the hyena made the same strange noise that had awakened her. But she did not hear him for the beating of her heart.

# PAUL'S CASE
## by Willa Cather

IT was Paul's afternoon to appear before the faculty of
the Pittsburgh High School to account for his various mis-
demeanors. He had been suspended a week ago, and his
father had called at the Principal's office and confessed
his perplexity about his son. Paul entered the faculty-room
suave and smiling. His clothes were a trifle outgrown,
and the tan velvet on the collar of his open overcoat was
frayed and worn; but for all that there was something
of the dandy about him, and he wore an opal pin in his
neatly knotted black four-in-hand, and a red carnation in
his buttonhole. This latter adornment the faculty somehow felt was not properly significant of the contrite spirit
befitting a boy under the ban of suspension.

Paul was tall for his age and very thin, with high,
cramped shoulders and a narrow chest. His eyes were
remarkable for a certain hysterical brilliancy, and he continually used them in a conscious, theatrical sort of way,
peculiarly offensive in a boy. The pupils were abnormally
large, as though he were addicted to belladonna, but there
was a glassy glitter about them which that drug does not
produce.

When questioned by the Principal as to why he was
there, Paul stated, politely enough, that he wanted to
come back to school. This was a lie, but Paul was quite
accustomed to lying; found it, indeed, indispensable for
overcoming friction. His teachers were asked to state their
respective charges against him, which they did with such
a rancor and aggrievedness as evinced that this was not a
usual case. Disorder and impertinence were among the

offenses named, yet each of his instructors felt that it was scarcely possible to put into words the real cause of the trouble, which lay in a sort of hysterically defiant manner of the boy's; in the contempt which they all knew he felt for them, and which he seemingly made not the least effort to conceal. Once, when he had been making a synopsis of a paragraph at the blackboard, his English teacher had stepped to his side and attempted to guide his hand. Paul had started back with a shudder and thrust his hands violently behind him. The astonished woman could scarcely have been more hurt and embarrassed had he struck at her. The insult was so involuntary and definitely personal as to be unforgettable. In one way and another, he had made all his teachers, men and women alike, conscious of the same feeling of physical aversion. In one class he habitually sat with his hand shading his eyes; in another he aways looked out of the window during the recitation; in another he made a running commentary on the lecture, with humorous intent.

His teachers felt this afternoon that his whole attitude was symbolized by his shrug and his flippantly red carnation flower, and they fell upon him without mercy, his English teacher leading the pack. He stood through it smiling, his pale lips parted over his white teeth. (His lips were continually twitching, and he had a habit of raising his eyebrows that was contemptuous and irritating to the last degree.) Older boys than Paul had broken down and shed tears under that ordeal, but his set smile did not once desert him, and his only sign of discomfort was the nervous trembling of the fingers that toyed with the buttons of his overcoat, and an occasional jerking of the other hand which held his hat. Paul was always smiling, always glancing about him, seeming to feel that people might be watching him and trying to detect something. This conscious expression, since it was so far as

possible from boyish mirthfulness, was usually attributed
to insolence or "smartness."

As the inquistion proceeded, one of his instructors repeated an impertinent remark of the boy's, and the Principal asked him whether he thought that a courteous speech
to make to a woman. Paul shrugged his shoulders slightly
and his eyebrows twitched.

"I don't know," he replied. "I didn't mean to be polite
or impolite, either. I guess it's a sort of way I have, of
saying things regardless."

The Principal asked him whether he didn't think that a
way it would be well to get rid of. Paul grinned and said
he guessed so. When he was told that he could go, he
bowed gracefully and went out. His bow was like a repe-
tition of the scandalous red carnation.

His teachers were in despair, and his drawing master
voiced the feeling of them all when he declared there was
something about the boy which none of them understood.
He added: "I don't really believe that smile of his comes
altogether from insolence; there's something sort of
haunted about it. The boy is not strong, for one thing.
There is something wrong about the fellow."

The drawing master had come to realize that, in looking
at Paul, one saw only his white teeth and the forced anima-
tion of his eyes. One warm afternoon the boy had gone to
sleep at his drawing-board, and his master had noted with
amazement what a white, blue-veined face it was; drawn
and wrinkled like an old man's about the eyes, the lips
twitching even in his sleep.

His teachers left the building dissatisfied and unhappy;
humiliated to have felt so vindictive towards a mere boy, to
have uttered this feeling in cutting terms, and to have set
each other on, as it were, in the gruesome game of intem-
perate reproach. One of them rememberd having seen a
miserable street cat set at bay by a ring of tormentors.

As for Paul, he ran down the hill whistling the Soldiers'

Chorus from *Faust,* looking wildly behind him now and then to see whether some of his teachers were not there to witness his light-heartedness. As it was now late in the afternoon and Paul was on duty that evening as usher at Carnegie Hall, he decided that he would not go home to supper.

When he reached the concert hall the doors were not yet open. It was chilly outside, and he decided to go up into the picture gallery—always deserted at this hour—where there were some of Raffelli's gay studies of Paris streets and an airy blue Venetian scene or two that always exhilarated him. He was delighted to find no one in the gallery but the old guard, who sat in the corner, a newspaper on his knee, a black patch over one eye and the other closed. Paul possessed himself of the place and walked confidently up and down, whistling under his breath. After a while he sat down before a blue Rico and lost himself. When he bethought him to look at his watch, it was after seven o'clock, and he rose with a start and ran downstairs, making a face at Augustus Cæsar, peering out from the east-room, and an evil gesture at the Venus of Milo as he passed her on the stairway.

When Paul reached the ushers' dressing-room half-a-dozen boys were there already, and he began excitedly to tumble into his uniform. It was one of the few that at all approached fitting, and Paul thought it very becoming—though he knew the tight, straight coat accenuated his narrow chest, about which he was exceedingly sensitive. He was always excited while he dressed, twanging all over to the tuning of the strings and the preliminary flourishes of the horns in the music-room; but to-night he seemed quite beside himself, and he teased and plagued the boys until, telling him that he was crazy, they put him down on the floor and sat on him.

Somewhat calmed by his suppression, Paul dashed out to the front of the house to seat the early comers. He was

a model usher. Gracious and smiling he ran up and down
the aisles. Nothing was too much trouble for him; he carried messages ⸗ ¹ brought programs as though it were
his greatest pleasure in life, and all the people in his section
thought him a charming boy, feeling that he remembered
and admired them. As the house filled, he grew more and
more vivacious and animated, and the color came to his
cheeks and lips. It was very much as though this were a
great reception and Paul were the host. Just as the mu-
sicians came out to take their place, his English teacher
arrived with checks for the seats which a prominent manufacturer had taken for the season. She betrayed some
embarrassment when she handed Paul the tickets, and a
*hauteur* which subsequently made her feel very foolish.
Paul was startled for a moment, and had the feeling of
wanting to put her out; what business had she here among
all these fine people and gay colors? He looked her over
and decided that she was not appropriately dressed and
must be a fool to sit downstairs in such togs. The tickets
had probably been sent her out of kindness, he reflected,
as he put down a seat for her, and she had about as much
right to sit there as he had.

When the symphony began Paul sank into one of the
rear seats with a long sigh of relief, and lost himself as he
had done before the Rico. It was not that symphonies, as
such, meant anything in particular to Paul, but the first
sigh of the instruments seemed to free some hilarious
spirit within him; something that struggled there like the
Genius in the bottle found by the Arab fisherman. He felt
a sudden zest of life; the lights danced before his eyes and
the concert hall blazed into unimaginable splendor. When
the soprano soloist came on, Paul forgot even the nastiness
of his teacher's being there, and gave himself up to the
peculiar intoxication such personages always had for him.
The soloist chanced to be a German woman, by no means
in her first youth, and the mother of many children; but

she wore a satin gown and a tiara, and she had that
indefinable air of achievement, that world-shine upon her,
which always blinded Paul to any possible defects.

After a concert was over, Paul was often irritable and
wretched until he got to sleep,—and to-night he was even
more than usually restless. He had the feeling of not being
able to let down; of its being impossible to give up this
delicious excitement which was the only thing that could
be called living at all. During the last number he withdrew
and, after hastily changing his clothes in the dressing-
room, slipped out to the side door where the singer's
carriage stood. Here he began pacing rapidly up and down
the walk, waiting to see her come out.

Over yonder the Schenley, in its vacant stretch, loomed
big and square through the fine rain, the windows of its
twelve stories glowing like those of a lighted cardboard
house under a Christmas tree. All the actors and singers of
any importance stayed there when they were in the city,
and a number of the big manufacturers of the place lived
there in the winter. Paul had often hung about the hotel,
watching the people go in and out, longing to enter and
leave schoolmasters and dull care behind him forever.

At last the singer came out, accompanied by the conductor, who helped her into her carriage and closed the
door with a cordial *auf wiedersehen,*—which set Paul to
wondering whether she were not an old sweetheart of his.
Paul followed the carriage over to the hotel, walking so
rapidly as not to be far from the entrance when the
singer alighted and disappeared behind the swinging glass
doors which were opened by a negro in a tall hat and a
long coat. In the moment that the door was ajar, it
seemed to Paul that he, too, entered. He seemed to feel
himself go after her up the steps, into the warm, lighted
building, into an exotic, a tropical world of shiny, glistening surfaces and basking ease. He reflected upon the
mysterious dishes that were brought into the dining-room,

the green bottles in buckets of ice, as he had seen them in the supper party pictures of the Sunday supplement. A quick gust of wind brought the rain down with sudden vehemence, and Paul was startled to find that he was still outside in the slush of the gravel driveway; that his boots were letting in the water and his scanty overcoat was clinging wet about him; that the lights in front of the concert hall were out, and that the rain was driving in sheets between him and the orange glow of the windows above him. There it was, what he wanted—tangibly before him, like the fairy world of a Christmas pantomime; as the rain beat in his face, Paul wondered whether he were destined always to shiver in the black night outside, looking up at it.

He turned and walked reluctantly towards the car tracks. The end had to come sometime; his father in his night-clothes at the top of the stairs, explanations that did not explain, hastily improvised fictions that were forever tripping him up, his upstairs room and its horrible yellow wall-paper, the creaking bureau with the greasy plush collar-box, and over his painted wooden bed the pictures of George Washington and John Calvin, and the framed motto, "Feed my Lambs," which had been worked in red worsted by his mother, whom Paul could not remember.

Half an hour later, Paul alighted from the Negley Avenue car and went slowly down one of the side streets off the main thoroughfare. It was a highly respectable street, where all the houses were exactly alike, and where business men of moderate means begot and reared large families of children, all of whom went to Sabbath-school and learned the shorter catechism, and were interested in arithmetic; all of whom were as exactly alike as their homes, and of a piece with the monotony in which they lived. Paul never went up Cordelia Street without a shudder of loathing. His home was next the house of the Cumberland minister. He approached it to-night with the nerveless sense of defeat, the hopeless feeling of sinking back forever into ugliness and commonness that he had always had when he came home. The moment he turned into Cordelia Street he felt the waters close above his head. After each of these orgies of living, he experienced all the physical depression which follows a debauch; the loathing of respectable beds, of common food, of a house permeated by kitchen odors; a shuddering repulsion for the flavorless, colorless mass of everyday existence; a morbid desire for cool things and soft lights and fresh flowers.

The nearer he approached the house, the more absolutely unequal Paul felt to the sight of it all; his ugly sleeping chamber; the cold bathroom with the grimy zinc tub, the cracked mirror, the dripping spiggots; his father, at the top of the stairs, his hairy legs sticking out from his nightshirt, his feet thrust into carpet slippers. He was so much later than usual that there would certainly be inquiries and reproaches. Paul stopped short before the door. He felt that he could not be accosted by his father to-night; that he could not toss again on that miserable bed. He would not go in. He would tell his father that he had no car-fare, and it was raining so hard that he had gone home with one of the boys and stayed all night.

Meanwhile, he was wet and cold. He went around to the back of the house and tried one of the basement windows, found it open, raised it cautiously, and scrambled down the cellar wall to the floor. There he stood, holding his breath, terrified by the noise he had made; but the floor above him was silent, and there was no creak on the stairs. He found a soap-box, and carried it over to the soft ring of light that streamed from the furnace door, and sat down. He was terribly afraid of rats, so he did not try to sleep, but sat looking distrustfully at the dark, still terrified lest he might have awakened his father. In such reactions, after one of the experiences which made days and nights out of the dreary blanks of the calendar, when his senses were deadened, Paul's head was always singularly clear. Suppose his father had heard him getting in at the window and had come down and shot him for a burglar? Then, again, suppose his father had come down, pistol in hand, and he had cried out in time to save himself, and his father had been horrified to think how nearly he had killed him? Then, again, suppose a day should come when his father would remember that night, and wish there had been no warning cry to stay his hand? With this last supposition Paul entertained himself until daybreak.

The following Sunday was fine; the sodden November chill was broken by the last flash of autumnal summer. In the morning Paul had to go to church and Sabbath-school, as always. On seasonable Sunday afternoons the burghers of Cordelia Street usually sat out on their front "stoops," and talked to their neighbors on the next stoop, or called to those across the street in neighborly fashion. The men sat placidly on gay cushions upon the steps that led down to the sidewalk, while the women, in their Sunday "waists," sat in rockers on the cramped porches, pretending to be greatly at their ease. The children played in the streets; there were so many of them that the place resembled the recreation grounds of a kindergarten. The men on the steps—all in their shirt sleeves, their vests unbuttoned—sat with their legs well apart, their stomachs comfortably protruding, and talked of the prices of things, or told anecdotes of the sagacity of their various chiefs and overlords. They occasionally looked over the multitude of squabbling children, listened affectionately to their high-pitched, nasal voices, smiling to see their own proclivities reproduced in their offspring, and interspersed their legends of the iron kings with remarks about their sons' progress at school, their grades in arithmetic, and the amounts they had saved in their toy banks.

On this last Sunday of November, Paul sat all the after

noon on the lowest step of his "stoop," staring into the street, while his sisters, in their rockers, were talking to the minister's daughters next door about how many shirt-waists they had made in the last week, and how many waffles some one had eaten at the last church supper. When the weather was warm, and his father was in a particularly jovial frame of mind, the girls made lemonade, which was always brought out in a red-glass pitcher, orna-mented with forget-me-nots in blue enamel. This the girls thought very fine, and the neighbors joked about the suspicious color of the pitcher.

To-day Paul's father, on the top step, was talking to a young man who shifted a restless baby from knee to knee. He happened to be the young man who was daily held up to Paul as a model, and after whom it was his father's dearest hope that he would pattern. This young man was of a ruddy complexion, with a compressed, red mouth, and faded, near-sighted eyes, over which he wore thick spectacles, with gold bows that curved about his ears. He was clerk to one of the magnates of a great steel corpora-tion, and was looked upon in Cordelia Street as a young man with a future. There was a story that, some five years ago—he was now barely twenty-six—he had been a trifle "dissipated," but in order to curb his appetites and save the loss of time and strength that a sowing of wild oats might have entailed, he had taken his chief's advice, oft reiterated to his employees, and at twenty-one had married the first woman whom he could persuade to share his for-tunes. She happened to be an angular school mistress, much older than he, who also wore thick glasses, and who had now borne him four children, all near-sighted, like herself.

The young man was relating how his chief, now cruising in the Mediterranean, kept in touch with all the details of the business, arranging his office hours on his yacht just as though he were at home, and "knocking off work enough to keep two stenographers busy." His father told, in turn, the plan his corporation was considering, of putting in an electric railway plant at Cairo. Paul snapped his teeth; he had an awful apprehension that they might spoil it all before he got there. Yet he rather liked to hear these legends of the iron kings, that were told and retold on Sundays and holidays; these stories of palaces in Venice, yachts on the Mediterranean, and high play at Monte Carlo appealed to his fancy, and he was interested in the triumphs of cash boys who had become famous, though he had no mind for the cash-boy stage.

After supper was over, and he had helped to dry the dishes, Paul nervously asked his father whether he could go to George's to get some help in his geometry, and still more nervously asked for car-fare. This latter request he had to repeat, as his father, on principle, did not like to hear requests for money whether much or little. He asked Paul whether he could not go to some boy who lived nearer, and told him that he ought not to leave his school work until Sunday; but he gave him the dime. He was not a poor man, but he had a worthy ambition to come up in the world. His only reason for allowing Paul to usher was that he thought a boy ought to be earning a little.

Paul bounded upstairs, scrubbed the greasy odor of the dish-water from his hands with the ill-smelling soap he hated, and then shook over his fingers a few drops of violet water from the bottle he kept hidden in his drawer. He left the house with his geometry conspicuously under his arm, and the moment he got out of Cordelia Street and boarded a downtown car, he shook off the lethargy of two deadening days, and began to live again.

The leading juvenile of the permanent stock company which played at one of the downtown theaters was an acquaintance of Paul's, and the boy had been invited to drop in at the Sunday-night rehearsals whenever he could

For more than a year Paul had spent every available moment loitering about Charley Edwards's dressing-room. He had won a place among Edwards's following not only because the young actor, who could not afford to employ a dresser, often found him useful, but because he recognized in Paul something akin to what churchmen term "vocation."

It was at the theater and at Carnegie Hall that Paul really lived; the rest was but a sleep and a forgetting. This was Paul's fairy tale, and it had for him all the allurement of a secret love. The moment he inhaled the gassy, painty, dusty odor behind the scenes, he breathed like a prisoner set free, and felt within him the possibility of doing or saying splendid, brilliant things. The moment the cracked orchestra beat out the overture from *Martha,* or jerked at the serenade from *Rigoletto,* all stupid and ugly things slid from him, and his senses were deliciously, yet delicately fired.

Perhaps it was because, in Paul's world, the natural nearly always wore the guise of ugliness, that a certain element of artificiality seemed to him necessary in beauty. Perhaps it was because his experience of life elsewhere was so full of Sabbath-school picnics, petty economies, wholesome advice as to how to succeed in life, and the unescapable odors of cooking, that he found this existence so alluring, these smartly clad men and women so attractive, that he was so moved by these starry apple orchards that bloomed perennially under the lime-light.

It would be difficult to put it strongly enough how convincingly the stage entrance of that theater was for Paul the actual portal of Romance. Certainly none of the company ever suspected it, least of all Charley Edwards. It was very like the old stories that used to float about London of fabulously rich Jews, who had subterranean halls, with palms, and fountains, and soft lamps and richly appareled women who never saw the disenchanting light of London day. So, in the midst of that smoke-palled city enamored of figures and grimy toil, Paul had his secret temple, his wishing-carpet, his bit of blue-and-white Mediterranean shore bathed in perpetual sunshine.

Several of Paul's teachers had a theory that his imagination had been perverted by garish fiction; but the truth was, he scarcely ever read at all. The books at home were not such as would either tempt or corrupt a youthful mind, and as for reading the novels that some of his friends urged upon him—well, he got what he wanted much more quickly from music; any sort of music, from an orchestra to a barrel organ. He needed only the spark, the indescribable thrill that made his imagination master of his senses, and he could make plots and pictures enough of his own. It was equally true that he was not stage-struck—not, at any rate, in the usual acceptance of that expression. He had no desire to become an actor, any more than he had to become a musician. He felt no necessity to do any of these things; what he wanted was to see, to be in the atmosphere, float on the wave of it, to be carried out, blue league after blue league, away from everything.

After a night behind the scenes, Paul found the school-room more than ever repulsive; the bare floors and naked walls; the prosy men who never wore frock coats, or violets in their buttonholes; the women with their dull gowns, shrill voices, and pitiful seriousness about prepositions that govern the dative. He could not bear to have the other pupils think, for a moment, that he took these people seriously; he must convey to them that he considered it all trivial, and was there only by way of a joke, anyway. He had autograph pictures of all the members of the stock company which he showed his classmates, telling them the most incredible stories of his familiarity with these people, of his acquaintance with the soloists who came to Carnegie Hall, his suppers with them and the flowers he sent them. When these stories lost their effect, and his audience grew listless, he would bid all the boys good-by, announcing that he was going to travel for a while; going to Naples, to California, to Egypt. Then, next Monday, he would slip back, conscious and nervously smiling; his sister was ill, and he would have to defer his voyage until spring.

Matters went steadily worse with Paul at school. In the itch to let his instructors know how heartily he despised them, and how thoroughly he was appreciated elsewhere, he mentioned once or twice that he had no time to fool with theorems; adding—with a twitch of the eyebrows and a touch of that nervous bravado which so perplexed them—that he was helping the people down at the stock company; they were old friends of his.

The upshot of the matter was that the Principal went to Paul's father, and Paul was taken out of school and put to work. The manager at Carnegie Hall was told to get another usher in his stead; the doorkeeper at the theater was warned not to admit him to the house; and Charley Edwards remorsefully promised the boy's father not to see him again.

The members of the stock company were vastly amused when some of Paul's stories reached them—especially the women. They were hard-working women, most of them supporting indolent husbands or brothers, and they laughed rather bitterly at having stirred the boy to such fervid and florid inventions. They agreed with the faculty and with his father that Paul's was a bad case.

The east-bound train was plowing through a January snowstorm; the dull dawn was beginning to show gray when the engine whistled a mile out of Newark. Paul started up from the seat where he had lain curled in uneasy slumber, rubbed the breath-misted window glass with his hand, and peered out. The snow was whirling in curling eddies above the white bottom lands, and the drifts lay already deep in the fields and along the fences, while here and there the long dead grass and dried weed stalks protruded black above it. Lights shone from the scattered houses, and a gang of laborers who stood beside the track waved their lanterns.

Paul had slept very little, and he felt grimy and uncomfortable. He had made the all-night journey in a day coach because he was afraid if he took a Pullman he might be seen by some Pittsburgh business man who had noticed him in Denny & Carson's office. When the whistle woke him, he clutched quickly at his breast pocket, glancing about him with an uncertain smile. But the little, clay bespattered Italians were still sleeping, the slatternly women across the aisle were in open-mouthed oblivion, and even the crumby, crying babies were for the nonce stilled. Paul settled back to struggle with his impatience as best he could.

When he arrived at the Jersey City station, he hurried through his breakfast, manifestly ill at ease and keeping a sharp eye about him. After he reached the Twenty-third Street station, he consulted a cabman, and had himself driven to a men's furnishing establishment which was just opening for the day. He spent upward of two hours there, buying with endless reconsidering and great care. His new street suit he put on in the fitting-room; the frock coat and dress clothes he had bundled into the cab with his new shirts. Then he drove to a hatter's and a shoe house. His next errand was at Tiffany's, where he selected silver mounted brushes and a scarf-pin. He would not wait to have his silver marked, he said. Lastly, he stopped at a trunk shop on Broadway, and had his purchases packed into various traveling bags.

It was a little after one o'clock when he drove up to the Waldorf, and, after settling with the cabman, went into the office. He registered from Washington; said his mother and father had been abroad, and that he had come down to await the arrival of their steamer. He told his story plausibly and had no trouble, since he offered to pay for them in advance, in engaging his rooms; a sleeping-room, sitting-room and bath.

Not once, but a hundred times Paul had planned this entry into New York. He had gone over every detail of it with Charley Edwards, and in his scrapbook at home there were pages of description about New York hotels, cut from the Sunday papers.

When he was shown to his sitting-room on the eighth floor, he saw at a glance that everything was as it should be; there was but one detail in his mental picture that the place did not realize, so he rang for the bell boy and sent him down for flowers. He moved about nervously until the boy returned, putting away his new linen and fingering it delightedly as he did so. When the flowers came, he put them hastily into water, and then tumbled into a hot bath. Presently he came out of his white bathroom, resplendent in his new silk underwear, and playing with the tassels of his red robe. The snow was whirling so fiercely outside his windows that he could scarcely see across the street; but within, the air was deliciously soft and fragrant. He put the violets and jonquils on the tabouret beside the couch, and threw himself down with a long sigh, covering himself with a Roman blanket. He was thoroughly tired; he had been in such haste, he had stood up to such a strain, covered so much ground in the last twenty-four hours, that he wanted to think how it had all come about. Lulled by the sound of the wind, the warm air, and the cool fragrance of the flowers, he sank into deep, drowsy retrospection.

It had been wonderfully simple; when they had shut him out of the theater and concert hall, when they had taken away his bone, the whole thing was virtually determined. The rest was a mere matter of opportunity. The only thing that at all surprised him was his own courage—

for he realized well enough that he had always been tormented by fear, a sort of apprehensive dread that, of late
years, as the meshes of the lies he had told closed about
him, had been pulling the muscles of his body tighter and
tighter. Until now, he could not remember a time when he
had not been dreading something. Even when he was a
little boy, it was always there—behind him, or before, or
on either side. There had always been the shadowed corner,
the dark place into which he dared not look, but from
which something seemed always to be watching him—and
Paul had done things that were not pretty to watch, he
knew.

But now he had a curious sense of relief, as though he
had at last thrown down the gauntlet to the thing in the
corner.

Yet it was but a day since he had been sulking in the
traces; but yesterday afternoon that he had been sent to
the bank with Denny & Carson's deposit as usual—but
this time he was instructed to leave the book to be balanced.
There was above two thousand dollars in checks, and
nearly a thousand in the bank notes which he had taken
from the book and quietly transferred to his pocket. At
the bank he had made out a new deposit slip. His nerves
had been steady enough to permit of his returning to the
office, where he had finished his work and asked for a full
day's holiday to-morrow, Saturday, giving a perfectly
reasonable pretext. The bank book, he knew, would not be
returned before Monday or Tuesday, and his father would
be out of town for the next week. From the time he slipped
the bank notes into his pocket until he boarded the night
train for New York, he had not known a moment's hesitation.

How astonishingly easy it had all been; here he was, the
thing done; and this time there would be no awakening, no
figure at the top of the stairs. He watched the snow flakes
whirling by his window until he fell asleep.

When he awoke, it was four o'clock in the afternoon.
He bounded up with a start; one of his precious days gone
already! He spent nearly an hour in dressing, watching
every stage of his toilet carefully in the mirror. Everything
was quite perfect; he was exactly the kind of boy he had
always wanted to be.

When he went downstairs, Paul took a carriage and
drove up Fifth Avenue toward the Park. The snow had
somewhat abated; carriages and tradesmen's wagons were
hurrying soundlessly to and fro in the winter twilight;
boys in woolen mufflers were shoveling off the doorsteps;
the avenue stages made fine spots of color against the white
street. Here and there on the corners whole flower gardens
blooming behind glass windows, against which the snow
flakes stuck and melted; violets, roses, carnations, lilies of
the valley—somehow vastly more lovely and alluring that
they blossomed thus unnaturally in the snow. The Park
itself was a wonderful stage winter-piece.

When he returned, the pause of the twilight had ceased,
and the tune of the streets had changed. The snow was
falling faster, lights streamed from the hotels that reared
their many stories fearlessly up into the storm, defying the
raging Atlantic winds. A long, black stream of carriages
poured down the avenue, intersected here and there by
other streams, tending horizontally. There were a score of
cabs about the entrance of his hotel, and his driver had to
wait. Boys in livery were running in and out of the awning
stretched across the sidewalk, up and down the red velvet
carpet laid from the door to the street. Above, about,
within it all, was the rumble and roar, the hurry and toss
of thousands of human beings as hot for pleasure as himself, and on every side of him towered the glaring affirmation of the omnipotence of wealth.

The boy set his teeth and drew his shoulders together in
a spasm of realization; the plot of all dramas, the text of
all romances, the nerve-stuff of all sensations was whirling

about him like the snow flakes. He burnt like a faggot in a tempest.

When Paul came down to dinner, the music of the orchestra floated up the elevator shaft to greet him. As he stepped into the thronged corridor, he sank back into one of the chairs against the wall to get his breath. The lights, the chatter, the perfumes, the bewildering medley of color —he had, for a moment, the feeling of not being able to stand it. But only for a moment; these were his own people, he told himself. He went slowly about the corridors, through the writing-rooms, smoking-rooms, reception-rooms, as though he were exploring the chambers of an enchanted palace, built and peopled for him alone.

When he reached the dining-room he sat down at a table near a window. The flowers, the white linen, the many-colored wine glasses, the gay toilets of the women, the low popping of corks, the undulating repetitions of the *Blue Danube* from the orchestra, all flooded Paul's dream with bewildering radiance. When the roseate tinge of his champagne was added—that cold, precious, bubbling stuff that creamed and foamed in his glass—Paul wondered that there were honest men in the world at all. This was what all the world was fighting for, he reflected; this was what all the struggle was about. He doubted the reality of his past. Had he ever known a place called Cordelia Street, a place where fagged looking business men boarded the early car? Mere rivets in a machine they seemed to Paul,— sickening men, with combings of children's hair always hanging to their coats, and the smell of cooking in their clothes. Cordelia Street— Ah, that belonged to another time and country! Had he not always been thus, had he not sat here night after night, from as far back as he could remember, looking pensively over just such shimmering textures, and slowly twirling the stem of a glass like this one between his thumb and middle finger? He rather thought he had.

He was not in the least abashed or lonely. He had no especial desire to meet or to know any of these people; all he demanded was the right to look on and conjecture, to watch the pageant. The mere stage properties were all he contended for. Nor was he lonely later in the evening, in his loge at the Opera. He was entirely rid of his nervous misgivings, of his forced aggressiveness, of the imperative desire to show himself different from his surroundings. He felt now that his surroundings explained him. Nobody questioned the purple; he had only to wear it passively. He had only to glance down at his dress coat to reassure himself that here it would be impossible for any one to humiliate him.

He found it hard to leave his beautiful sitting-room to go to bed that night, and sat long watching the raging storm from his turret window. When he went to sleep, it was with the lights turned on in his bedroom; partly because of his old timidity, and partly so that, if he should wake in the night, there would be no wretched moment of doubt, no horrible suspicion of yellow wall-paper, or of Washington and Calvin above his bed.

On Sunday morning the city was practically snow-bound. Paul breakfasted late, and in the afternoon he fell in with a wild San Francisco boy, a freshman at Yale, who said he had run down for a "little flyer" over Sunday. The young man offered to show Paul the night side of the town, and the two boys went off together after dinner, not returning to the hotel until seven o'clock the next morning. They had started out in the confiding warmth of a champagne friendship, but their parting in the elevator was singularly cool. The freshman pulled himself together to make his train, and Paul went to bed. He awoke at two o'clock in the afternoon, very thirsty and dizzy, and rang for ice-water, coffee, and the Pittsburgh papers.

On the part of the hotel management, Paul excited no suspicion. There was this to be said for him, that he wore

his spoils with dignity and in no way made himself conspicuous. His chief greediness lay in his ears and eyes, and
his excesses were not offensive ones. His dearest pleasures
were the gray winter twilights in his sitting-room; his quiet
enjoyment of his flowers, his clothes, his wide divan, his
cigarette and his sense of power. He could not remember a
time when he had felt so at peace with himself. The mere
release from the necessity of petty lying, lying every day
and every day, restored his self-respect. He had never lied
for pleasure, even at school; but to make himself noticed
and admired, to assert his difference from other Cordelia
Street boys; and he felt a good deal more manly, more
honest, even, now that he had no need for boastful pretensions, now that he could, as his actor friends used to
say, "dress the part." It was characteristic that remorse
did not occur to him. His golden days went by without a
shadow, and he made each as perfect as he could.

On the eighth day after his arrival in New York, he
found the whole affair exploited in the Pittsburgh papers,
exploited with a wealth of detail which indicated that local
news of a sensational nature was at a low ebb. The firm of
Denny & Carson announced that the boy's father had
refunded the full amount of his theft, and that they had
no intention of prosecuting. The Cumberland minister had
been interviewed, and expressed his hope of yet reclaiming
the motherless lad, and Paul's Sabbath-school teacher declared that she would spare no effort to that end. The
rumor had reached Pittsburgh that the boy had been seen
in a New York hotel, and his father had gone East to find
him and bring him home.

Paul had just come in to dress for dinner; he sank into
a chair, weak in the knees, and clasped his head in his
hands. It was to be worse than jail, even; the tepid waters
of Cordelia Street were to close over him finally and forever. The gray monotony stretched before him in hopeless,
unrelieved years; Sabbath-school, Young People's Meet-

ing, the yellow-papered room, the damp dish-towels; it all rushed back upon him with sickening vividness. He had the old feeling that the orchestra had suddenly stopped, the sinking sensation that the play was over. The sweat broke out on his face, and he sprang to his feet, looked about him with his white, conscious smile, and winked at himself in the mirror. With something of the childish belief in miracles with which he had so often gone to class, all his lessons unlearned, Paul dressed and dashed whistling down the corridor to the elevator.

He had no sooner entered the dining-room and caught the measure of the music, than his remembrance was lightened by his old elastic power of claiming the moment, mounting with it, and finding it all sufficient. The glare and glitter about him, the mere scenic accessories had again, and for the last time, their old potency. He would show himself that he was game, he would finish the thing splendidly. He doubted, more than ever, the existence of Cordelia Street, and for the first time he drank his wine recklessly. Was he not, after all, one of these fortunate beings? Was he not still himself, and in his own place? He drummed a nervous accompaniment to the music and looked about him, telling himself over and over that it had paid.

He reflected drowsily, to the swell of the violin and the chill sweetness of his wine, that he might have done it more wisely. He might have caught an outbound steamer and been well out of their clutches before now. But the other side of the world had seemed too far away and too uncertain then; he could not have waited for it; his need had been too sharp. If he had to choose over again, he would do the same thing to-morrow. He looked affectionately about the dining-room, now gilded with a soft mist. Ah, it had paid indeed!

Paul was awakened next morning by a painful throbbing in his head and feet. He had thrown himself across the bed without undressing, and had slept with his shoes on. His limbs and hands were lead heavy, and his tongue and throat were parched. There came upon him one of those fateful attacks of clear-headedness that never occurred except when he was physically exhausted and his nerves hung loose. He lay still and closed his eyes and let the tide of realities wash over him.

His father was in New York; "stopping at some joint or other," he told himself. The memory of successive summers on the front stoop fell upon him like a weight of black water. He had not a hundred dollars left; and he knew now, more than ever, that money was everything, the wall that stood between all he loathed and all he wanted. The thing was winding itself up; he had thought of that on his first glorious day in New York, and had even provided a way to snap the thread. It lay on his dressing-table now; he had got it out last night when he came blindly up from dinner,—but the shiny metal hurt his eyes, and he disliked the look of it, anyway.

He rose and moved about with a painful effort, succumbing now and again to attacks of nausea. It was the old depression exaggerated; all the world had become Cordelia Street. Yet somehow he was not afraid of anything, was absolutely calm; perhaps because he had looked into the dark corner at last, and knew. It was bad enough, what he saw there; but somehow not so bad as his long fear of it had been. He saw everything clearly now. He had a feeling that he had made the best of it, that he had lived the sort of life he was meant to live, and for half an hour he sat staring at the revolver. But he told himself that was not the way, so he went downstairs and took a cab to the ferry.

When Paul arrived at Newark, he got off the train and took another cab, directing the driver to follow the Pennsylvania tracks out of the town. The snow lay heavy on the roadways and had drifted deep in the open fields. Only

here and there the dead grass or dried weed stalks projected, singularly black, above it. Once well into the
country, Paul dismissed the carriage and walked, flounder-
ing along the tracks, his mind a medley of irrelevant things.
He seemed to hold in his brain an actual picture of everything he had seen that morning. He remembered every
feature of both his drivers, the toothless old woman from
whom he had bought the red flowers in his coat, the agent
from whom he had got his ticket, and all of his fellow-
passengers on the ferry. His mind, unable to cope with
vital matters near at hand, worked feverishly and deftly
at sorting and grouping these images. They made for him
a part of the ugliness of the world, of the ache in his
head, and the bitter burning on his tongue. He stooped
and put a handful of snow into his mouth as he walked,
but that, too, seemed hot. When he reached a little hillside,
where the tracks ran through a cut some twenty feet below
him, he stopped and sat down.

The carnations in his coat were drooping with the cold,
he noticed; all their red glory over. It occurred to him that
all the flowers he had seen in the show windows that first
night must have gone the same way, long before this. It
was only one splendid breath they had, in spite of their
brave mockery at the winter outside the glass. It was a
losing game in the end, it seemed, this revolt against the
homilies by which the world is run. Paul took one of the
blossoms carefully from his coat and scooped a little hole
in the snow, where he covered it up. Then he dozed a
while, from his weak condition, seeming insensible to the
cold.

The sound of an approaching train woke him, and he
started to his feet, remembering only his resolution, and
afraid lest he should be too late. He stood watching the
approaching locomotive, his teeth chattering, his lips drawn
away from them in a frightened smile; once or twice he
glanced nervously sidewise, as though he were being

watched. When the right moment came, he jumped. As he fell, the folly of his haste occurred to him with merciless clearness, the vastness of what he had left undone. There flashed through his brain, clearer than ever before, the blue of Adriatic water, the yellow of Algerian sands.

He felt something strike his chest,—his body was being thrown swiftly through the air, on and on, immeasurably far and fast, while his limbs gently relaxed. Then, because the picture-making mechanism was crushed, the disturbing visions flashed into black, and Paul dropped back into the immense design of things.

# I'M A FOOL
## by Sherwood Anderson

It was a hard jolt for me, one of the most bitterest I ever had to face. And it all came about through my own foolishness, too. Even yet sometimes, when I think of it, I want to cry or swear or kick myself. Perhaps, even now, after all this time, there will be a kind of satisfaction in making myself look cheap by telling of it.

It began at three o'clock one October afternoon as I sat in the grand stand at the fall trotting and pacing meet at Sandusky, Ohio.

To tell the truth, I felt a little foolish that I should be sitting in the grand stand at all. During the summer before I had left my home town with Harry Whitehead and, with a nigger named Burt, had taken a job as swipe with one of the two horses Harry was campaigning through the fall race meets that year. Mother cried and my sister Mildred, who wanted to get a job as a school teacher in our town that fall, stormed and scolded about the house all during the week before I left. They both thought it something disgraceful that one of our family should take a place as a swipe with race horses. I've an idea Mildred thought my taking the place would stand in the way of her getting the job she'd been working so long for.

But after all I had to work, and there was no other work to be got. A big lumbering fellow of nineteen couldn't just hang around the house and I had got too big to mow people's lawns and sell newspapers. Little chaps who could get next to people's sympathies by their sizes were always getting jobs away from me. There was one fellow who kept saying to every one who wanted a lawn mowed or a cistern cleaned, that he was saving money to work his way through college, and I used to lay awake nights thinking up ways to injure him without being found out. I kept thinking of wagons running over him and bricks falling on his head as he walked along the street. But never mind him.

I got the place with Harry and I liked Burt fine. We got along splendid together. He was a big nigger with a lazy sprawling body and soft, kind eyes, and when it came to a fight he could hit like Jack Johnson. He had Bucephalus, a big black pacing stallion that could do 2.09 or 2.10, if he had to, and I had a little gelding named Doctor Fritz that never lost a race all fall when Harry wanted him to win.

We set out from home late in July in a box car with the two horses and after that, until late November, we kept moving along to the race meets and the fairs. It was a peachy time for me, I'll say that. Sometimes now I think that boys who are raised regular in houses, and never have a fine nigger like Burt for best friend, and go to high schools and college, and never steal anything, or get drunk a little, or learn to swear from fellows who know how, or come walking up in front of a grand stand in their shirt sleeves and with dirty horsey pants on when the races are going on and the grand stand is full of people all dressed up—What's the use of talking about it? Such fellows don't know nothing at all. They've never had no opportunity.

But I did. Burt taught me how to rub down a horse and put the bandages on after a race and steam a horse out and a lot of valuable things for any man to know. He could wrap a bandage on a horse's leg so smooth that if it had been the same color you would think it was his skin, and I guess he'd have been a big driver, too, and got to the top like Murphy and Walter Cox and the others if he hadn't been black.

Gee whizz, it was fun. You got to a county seat town, maybe say on a Saturday or Sunday, and the fair began the next Tuesday and lasted until Friday afternoon. Doctor Fritz would be, say in the 2.25 trot on Tuesday afternoon and on Thursday afternoon Bucephalus would knock 'em cold in the "free-for-all" pace. It left you a lot of time to hang around and listen to horse talk, and see Burt knock some yap cold that got too gay, and you'd find out about horses and men and pick up a lot of stuff you could use all the rest of your life, if you had some sense and salted down what you heard and felt and saw.

And then at the end of the week when the race meet was over, and Harry had run home to tend to his livery stable business, you and Burt hitched the two horses to carts and drove slow and steady across country, to the place for the next meeting, so as to not overheat the horses, etc., etc., you know.

Gee whizz, Gosh amighty, the nice hickorynut and beechnut and oaks and other kinds of trees along the roads, all brown and red, and the good smells, and Burt singing a song that was called "Deep River," and the country girls at the windows of houses and everything. You can stick your colleges up your nose for all me. I guess I know where I got my education.

Why, one of those little burgs of towns you come to on the way, say now on a Saturday afternoon, and Burt says, "Let's lay up here." And you did.

And you took the horses to a livery stable and fed them, and you got your good clothes out of a box and put them on.

And the town was full of farmers gaping, because they could see you were race horse people, and the kids maybe never see a nigger before and was afraid and run away when the two of us walked down their main street.

And that was before prohibition and all that foolishness, and so you went into a saloon, the two of you, and all the yaps come and stood around, and there was always some one pretended he was horsey and knew things and spoke up and began asking questions, and all you did was to lie and lie all you could about what horses you had, and I said I owned them, and then some fellow said "Will you have a drink of whisky?" and Burt knocked his eye out the way he could say, off-hand like, "Oh, well, all right, I'm agreeable to a little nip. I'll split a quart with you." Gee whizz.

But that isn't what I want to tell my story about. We got home late in November and I promised mother I'd quit the race horses for good. There's a lot of things you've got to promise a mother because she don't know any better.

And so, there not being any work in our town any more than when I left there to go to the races, I went off to Sandusky and got a pretty good place taking care of horses for a man who owned a teaming and delivery and storage and coal and real estate business there. It was a pretty good place with good eats, and a day off each week, and sleeping on a cot in a big barn, and mostly just shoveling in hay and oats to a lot of big good-enough skates of horses, that couldn't have trotted a race with a toad. I wasn't dissatisfied and I could send money home.

And then, as I started to tell you, the fall races come to Sandusky and I got the day off and I went. I left the job at noon and had on my good clothes and my new brown derby hat, I'd just bought the Saturday before, and a stand-up collar.

First of all I went downtown and walked about with the dudes. I've always thought to myself, "put up a good front" and so I did it. I had forty dollars in my pocket and so I went into the West House, a big hotel, and walked up to the cigar stand. "Give me three twenty-five

cent cigars," I said. There was a lot of horsemen and
strangers and dressed-up people from other towns standing
around in the lobby and in the bar, and I mingled amongst
them. In the bar there was a fellow with a cane and a
Windsor tie on, that it made me sick to look at him. I
like a man to be a man and dress up, but not to go put
on that kind of airs. So I pushed him aside, kind of rough,
and had me a drink of whisky. And then he looked at
me, as though he thought maybe he'd get gay, but he
changed his mind and didn't say anything. And then I
had another drink of whisky, just to show him something,
and went out and had a hack out to the races, all to myself,
and when I got there I bought myself the best seat I could
get up in the grand stand, but didn't go in for any of
those boxes. That's putting on too many airs.

And so there I was, sitting up in the grand stand as gay
as you please and looking down on the swipes coming
out with their horses, and with their dirty horsey pants
on and the horse blankets swung over their shoulders, same
as I had been doing all the year before. I liked one thing
about the same as the other, sitting up there and feeling
grand and being down there and looking up at the yaps
and feeling grander and more important, too. One thing's
about as good as another, if you take it just right. I've
often said that.

Well, right in front of me, in the grand stand that day,
there was a fellow with a couple of girls and they was
about my age. The young fellow was a nice guy all right.
He was the kind maybe that goes to college and then
comes to be a lawyer or maybe a newspaper editor or
something like that, but he wasn't stuck on himself. There
are some of that kind are all right and he was one of
the ones.

He had his sister with him and another girl and the
sister looked around over his shoulder, accidental at first,

not intending to start anything—she wasn't that kind—
and her eyes and mine happened to meet.

You know how it is. Gee, she was a peach! She had
on a soft dress, kind of a blue stuff and it looked carelessly
made, but was well sewed and made and everything. I
knew that much. I blushed when she looked right at me
and so did she. She was the nicest girl I've ever seen in
my life. She wasn't stuck on herself and she could talk
proper grammar without being like a school teacher or
something like that. What I mean is, she was O. K. I think
maybe her father was well-to-do, but not rich to make her
chesty because she was his daughter, as some are. Maybe
he owned a drug store or a drygoods store in their home
town, or something like that. She never told me and I
never asked.

My own people are all O. K. too, when you come to
that. My grandfather was Welsh and over in the old
country, in Wales he was— But never mind that.

The first heat of the first race come off and the young
fellow setting there with the two girls left them and went
down to make a bet. I knew what he was up to, but he
didn't talk big and noisy and let every one around know
he was a sport, as some do. He wasn't that kind. Well, he
came back and I heard him tell the two girls what horse
he'd bet on, and when the heat was trotted they all half
got to their feet and acted in the excited, sweaty way
people do when they've got money down on a race, and the
horse they bet on is up there pretty close at the end, and
they think maybe he'll come on with a rush, but he never
does because he hasn't got the old juice in him, come right
down to it.

And then, pretty soon, the horses came out for the 2.18
pace and there was a horse in it I knew. He was a horse
Bob French had in his string but Bob didn't own him. He

was a horse owned by a Mr. Mathers down at Marietta, Ohio.

This Mr. Mathers had a lot of money and owned some coal mines or something, and he had a swell place out in the country, and he was stuck on race horses, but was a Presbyterian or something, and I think more than likely his wife was one, too, maybe a stiffer one than himself. So he never raced his horses hisself, and the story round the Ohio race tracks was that when one of his horses got ready to go to the races he turned him over to Bob French and pretended to his wife he was sold.

So Bob had the horses and he did pretty much as he pleased and you can't blame Bob, at least, I never did. Sometimes he was out to win and sometimes he wasn't. I never cared much about that when I was swiping a horse. What I did want to know was that my horse had the speed and could go out in front, if you wanted him to.

And, as I'm telling you, there was Bob in this race with one of Mr. Mathers' horses, was named "About Ben Ahem" or something like that, and was fast as a streak. He was a gelding and had a mark of 2.21, but could step in .08 or .09.

Because when Burt and I were out, as I've told you, the year before, there was a nigger, Burt knew, worked for Mr. Mathers and we went out there one day when we didn't have no race on at the Marietta Fair and our boss Harry was gone home.

And so every one was gone to the fair but just this one nigger and he took us all through Mr. Mathers' swell house and he and Burt tapped a bottle of wine Mr. Mathers had hid in his bedroom, back in a closet, without his wife knowing, and he showed us this Ahem horse. Burt was always stuck on being a driver but didn't have much chance to get to the top, being a nigger, and he and

the other nigger gulped that whole bottle of wine and
Burt got a little lit up.

So the nigger let Burt take this About Ben Ahem and
step him a mile in a track Mr. Mathers had all to himself,
right there on the farm. And Mr. Mathers had one child,
a daughter, kinda sick and not very good looking, and she
came home and we had to hustle and get About Ben Ahem
stuck back in the barn.

I'm only telling you to get everything straight. At Sandusky, that afternoon I was at the fair, this young fellow
with the two girls was fussed, being with the girls and
losing his bet. You know how a fellow is that way. One
of them was his girl and the other his sister. I had figured
that out.

"Gee whizz," I says to myself, "I'm going to give him
the dope."

He was mighty nice when I touched him on the shoulder. He and the girls were nice to me right from the start
and clear to the end. I'm not blaming them.

And so he leaned back and I give him the dope on
About Ben Ahem. "Don't bet a cent on this first heat
because he'll go like an oxen hitched to a plow, but when
the first heat is over go right down and lay on your pile."
That's what I told him.

Well, I never saw a fellow treat any one sweller. There
was a fat man sitting beside the little girl, that had looked
at me twice by this time, and I at her, and both blushing,
and what did he do but have the nerve to turn and ask
the fat man to get up and change places with me so I
could set with his crowd.

Gee whizz, craps amighty. There I was. What a chump
I was to go and get gay up there in the West House
bar, and just because that dude was standing there with
a cane and that kind of a necktie on, to go and get all
balled up and drink that whisky, just to show off.

Of course she would know, me setting right beside her and letting her smell of my breath. I could have kicked myself right down out of that grand stand and all around that race track and made a faster record than most of the skates of horses they had there that year.

Because that girl wasn't any mutt of a girl. What wouldn't I have give right then for a stick of chewing gum to chew, or a lozenger, or some licorice, or most anything. I was glad I had those twenty-five cent cigars in my pocket and right away I give that fellow one and lit one myself. Then that fat man got up and we changed places and there I was, plunked right down beside her.

They introduced themselves and the fellow's best girl, he had with him, was named Miss Elinor Woodbury, and her father was a manufacturer of barrels from a place called Tiffin, Ohio. And the fellow himself was named Wilbur Wessen and his sister was Miss Lucy Wessen.

I suppose it was their having such swell names got me off my trolley. A fellow, just because he has been a swipe with a race horse, and works taking care of horses for a man in the teaming, delivery, and storage business, isn't any better or worse than any one else. I've often thought that, and said it too.

But you know how a fellow is. There's something in that kind of nice clothes, and the kind of nice eyes she had, and the way she had looked at me, awhile before, over her brother's shoulder, and me looking back at her, and both of us blushing.

I couldn't show her up for a boob, could I?

I made a fool of myself, that's what I did. I said my name was Walter Mathers from Marietta, Ohio, and then I told all three of them the smashingest lie you ever heard. What I said was that my father owned the horse About Ben Ahem and that he had let him out to this Bob French for racing purposes, because our family was proud and had never gone into racing that way, in our own name, I

mean. Then I had got started and they were all leaning
over and listening, and Miss Lucy Wessen's eyes were
shining, and I went the whole hog.

I told about our place down at Marietta, and about the
big stables and the grand brick house we had on a hill, up
above the Ohio River, but I knew enough not to do it in
no bragging way. What I did was to start things and then
let them drag the rest out of me. I acted just as reluctant
to tell as I could. Our family hasn't got any barrel factory,
and, since I've known us, we've always been pretty poor,
but not asking anything of any one at that, and my grandfather, over in Wales—but never mind that.

We set there talking like we had known each other for
years and years, and I went and told them that my father
had been expecting maybe this Bob French wasn't on the
square, and had sent me up to Sandusky on the sly to find
out what I could.

And I bluffed it through I had found out all about the
2.18 pace, in which About Ben Ahem was to start.

I said he would lose the first heat by pacing like a lame
cow and then he would come back and skin 'em alive after
that. And to back up what I said I took thirty dollars out
of my pocket and handed it to Mr. Wilbur Wessen and
asked him, would he mind, after the first heat, to go down
and place it on About Ben Ahem for whatever odds he
could get. What I said was that I didn't want Bob French
to see me and none of the swipes.

Sure enough the first heat come off and About Ben
Ahem went off his stride, up the back stretch, and looked
like a wooden horse or a sick one, and come in to be last.
Then this Wilbur Wessen went down to the betting place
under the grand stand and there I was with the two girls,
and when that Miss Woodbury was looking the other way
once, Lucy Wessen kinda, with her shoulder you know,
kinda touched me. Not just tucking down, I don't mean.

You know how a woman can do. They get close, but not getting gay either. You know what they do. Gee whizz.

And then they give me a jolt. What they had done, when I didn't know, was to get together, and they had decided Wilbur Wessen would bet fifty dollars, and the two girls had gone and put in ten dollars each, of their own money, too. I was sick then, but I was sicker later.

About the gelding, About Ben Ahem, and their winning their money, I wasn't worried a lot about that. It come out O. K. Ahem stepped the next three heats like a bushel of spoiled eggs going to market before they could be found out, and Wilbur Wessen had got nine to two for the money. There was something else eating at me.

Because Wilbur came back, after he had bet the money, and after that he spent most of his time talking to that Miss Woodbury, and Lucy Wessen and I was left alone together like on a desert island. Gee, if I'd only been on the square or if there had been any way of getting myself on the square. There ain't any Walter Mathers, like I said to her and them, and there hasn't ever been one, but if there was, I bet I'd go to Marietta, Ohio, and shoot him to-morrow.

There I was, big boob that I am. Pretty soon the race was over, and Wilbur had gone down and collected our money, and we had a hack down-town, and he stood us a swell supper at the West House, and a bottle of champagne beside.

And I was with that girl and she wasn't saying much, and I wasn't saying much either. One thing I know. She wasn't stuck on me because of the lie about my father being rich and all that. There's a way you know. . . . Craps amighty. There's a kind of girl, you see just once in your life, and if you don't get busy and make hay, then you're gone for good and all, and might as well go jump off a bridge. They give you a look from inside of them somewhere, and it ain't no vamping, and what it means is you want that girl to be your wife, and you want nice things around her like flowers and swell clothes, and you want her to have the kids you're going to have, and you want good music played and no rag time. Gee whizz.

There's a place over near Sandusky, across a kind of bay, and it's called Cedar Point. And after we had supper we went over to it in a launch, all by ourselves. Wilbur and Miss Lucy and that Miss Woodbury had to catch a ten o'clock train back to Tiffin, Ohio, because, when you're out with girls like that you can't get careless and miss any trains and stay out all night, like you can with some kinds of Janes.

And Wilbur blowed himself to the launch and it cost him fifteen cold punks, but I wouldn't never have knew if I hadn't listened. He wasn't no tin horn kind of a sport.

Over at the Cedar Point place, we didn't stay around where there was a gang of common kind of cattle at all.

There was big dance halls and dining places for yaps, and there was a beach you could walk along and get where it was dark, and we went there.

She didn't talk hardly at all and neither did I, and I was thinking how glad I was my mother was all right, and always made us kids learn to eat with a fork at table, and not swill soup, and not be noisy and rough like a gang you see around a race track that way.

Then Wilbur and his girl went away up the beach and Lucy and I sat down in a dark place, where there was some roots of old trees, the water had washed up, and after that the time, till we had to go back in the launch and they had to catch their trains, wasn't nothing at all. It went like winking your eye.

Here's how it was. The place we were setting in was dark, like I said, and there was the roots from that old stump sticking up like arms, and there was a watery smell, and the night was like—as if you could put your hand out and feel it—so warm and soft and dark and sweet like an orange.

I most cried and I most swore and I most jumped up and danced, I was so mad and happy and sad.

When Wilbur come back from being alone with his girl, and she saw him coming, Lucy she says, "We got to go to the train now," and she was most crying too, but she never knew nothing I knew, and she couldn't be so all busted up. And then, before Wilbur and Miss Woodbury got up to where we was, she put her face up and kissed me quick and put her head up against me and she was all quivering and— Gee whizz.

Sometimes I hope I have cancer and die. I guess you know what I mean. We went in the launch across the bay to the train like that, and it was dark, too. She whispered and said it was like she and I could get out of the boat and walk on the water, and it sounded foolish, but I knew what she meant.

And then quick we were right at the depot, and there was a big gang of yaps, the kind that goes to the fairs and crowded and milling around like cattle, and how could I tell her? "It won't be long because you'll write and I'll write to you." That's all she said.

I got a chance like a hay barn afire. A swell chance I got.

And maybe she would write me, down at Marietta that way, and the letter would come back, and stamped on the front of it by the U.S.A. "there ain't any such guy," or something like that, whatever they stamp on a letter that way.

And me trying to pass myself off for a big bug and a swell—to her, as decent a little body as God ever made. Craps amighty—a swell chance I got!

And then the train come in, and she got on it, and Wilbur Wessen he come and shook hands with me, and that Miss Woodbury was nice too and bowed to me, and I at her, and the train went and I busted out and cried like a kid.

Gee, I could have run after that train and made Dan Patch look like a freight train after a wreck but, socks amighty, what was the use? Did you ever see such a fool?

I'll bet you what—if I had an arm broke right now or a train had run over my foot—I wouldn't go to no doctor at all. I'd go set down and let her hurt and hurt—that's what I'd do.

I'll bet you what—if I hadn't a drunk that booze I'd a never been such a boob as to go tell such a lie—that couldn't never be made straight to a lady like her.

I wish I had that fellow right here that had on a Windsor tie and carried a cane. I'd smash him for fair. Gosh darn his eyes. He's a big fool—that's what he is.

And if I'm not another you just go find me one and I'll quit working and be a bum and give him my job. I don't care nothing for working, and earning money, and saving it for no such boob as myself.

# HAIRCUT
## by Ring Lardner

I GOT another barber that comes over from Carterville and helps me out Saturdays, but the rest of the time I can get along all right alone. You can see for yourself that this ain't no New York City and besides that, the most of the boys works all day and don't have no leisure to drop in here and get themselves prettied up.

You're a newcomer, ain't you? I thought I hadn't seen you round before. I hope you like it good enough to stay. As I say, we ain't no New York City or Chicago, but we have pretty good times. Not as good, though, since Jim Kendall got killed. When he was alive, him and Hod Meyers used to keep this town in an uproar. I bet they was more laughin' done here than any town its size in America.

Jim was comical, and Hod was pretty near a match for him. Since Jim's gone, Hod tries to hold his end up just the same as ever, but it's tough goin' when you ain't got nobody to kind of work with.

They used to be plenty fun in here Saturdays. This place is jam-packed Saturdays, from four o'clock on. Jim and Hod would show up right after their supper, round six o'clock. Jim would set himself down in that big chair, nearest the blue spittoon. Whoever had been settin' in that chair, why they'd get up when Jim come in and give it to him.

You'd of thought it was a reserved seat like they have sometimes in a theayter. Hod would generally always stand or walk up and down, or some Saturdays, of course, he'd be settin' in this chair part of the time, gettin' a haircut.

Well, Jim would set there a w'ile without openin' his mouth only to spit, and then finally he'd say to me, "Whitey,"

—my right name, that is, my right first name, is Dick, but everybody round here calls me Whitey—Jim would say, "Whitey, your nose looks like a rosebud tonight. You must of been drinkin' some of your aw de cologne."

So I'd say, "No, Jim, but you look like you'd been drinkin' somethin' of that kind or somethin' worse."

Jim would have to laugh at that, but then he'd speak up and say, "No, I ain't had nothin' to drink, but that ain't sayin' I wouldn't like somethin'. I wouldn't even mind if it was wood alcohol."

Then Hod Meyers would say, "Neither would your wife." That would set everybody to laughin' because Jim and his wife wasn't on very good terms. She'd of divorced him only they wasn't no chance to get alimony and she didn't have no way to take care of herself and the kids. She couldn't never understand Jim. He *was* kind of rough, but a good fella at heart.

Him and Hod had all kinds of sport with Milt Sheppard. I don't suppose you've seen Milt. Well, he's got an Adam's apple that looks more like a mushmelon. So I'd be shavin' Milt and when I'd start to shave down here on his neck, Hod would holler, "Hey, Whitey, wait a minute! Before you cut into it, let's make up a pool and see who can guess closest to the number of seeds."

And Jim would say, "If Milt hadn't of been so hoggish, he'd of ordered a half a cantaloupe instead of a whole one and it might not of stuck in his throat."

All the boys would roar at this and Milt himself would force a smile, though the joke was on him. Jim certainly was a card!

There's his shavin' mug, settin' on the shelf, right next to Charley Vail's. "Charles M. Vail." That's the druggist. He comes in regular for his shave, three times a week. And Jim's is the cup next to Charley's. "James H. Kendall." Jim won't need no shavin' mug no more, but I'll leave it there just the same for old time's sake. Jim certainly was a character!

Years ago, Jim used to travel for a canned goods concern over in Carterville. They sold canned goods. Jim had the whole northern half of the State and was on the road five days out of every week. He'd drop in here Saturdays and tell his experiences for that week. It was rich.

I guess he paid more attention to playin' jokes than makin' sales. Finally the concern let him out and he come right home here and told everybody he'd been fired instead of sayin' he'd resigned like most fellas would of.

It was a Saturday and the shop was full and Jim got up out of that chair and says, "Gentlemen, I got an important announcement to make. I been fired from my job."

Well, they asked him if he was in earnest and he said he was and nobody could think of nothin' to say till Jim finally broke the ice himself. He says, "I been sellin' canned goods and now I'm canned goods myself."

You see, the concern he'd been workin' for was a factory that made canned goods. Over in Carterville. And now Jim said he was canned himself. He was certainly a card!

Jim had a great trick that he used to play w'ile he was travelin'. For instance, he'd be ridin' on a train and they'd come to some little town like, well, like, we'll say, like Benton. Jim would look out the train window and read the signs on the stores.

For instance, they'd be a sign, "Henry Smith, Dry Goods." Well, Jim would write down the name and the name of the town and when he got to wherever he was goin' he'd mail back a postal card to Henry Smith at Benton and not sign no name to it, but he'd write on the card, well, somethin' like "Ask your wife about that book agent that spent the afternoon last week," or "Ask your Missus who kept her from gettin' lonesome the last time you was in Carterville." And he'd sign the card, "A Friend."

Of course, he never knew what really come of none of

these jokes, but he could picture what *probably* happened and that was enough.

Jim didn't work very steady after he lost his position with the Carterville people. What he did earn, doin' odd jobs round town, why he spent pretty near all of it on gin and his family might of starved if the stores hadn't of carried them along. Jim's wife tried her hand at dressmakin', but they ain't nobody goin' to get rich makin' dresses in this town.

As I say, she'd of divorced Jim, only she seen that she couldn't support herself and the kids and she was always hopin' that some day Jim would cut out his habits and give her more than two or three dollars a week.

They was a time when she would go to whoever he was workin' for and ask them to give her his wages, but after she done this once or twice, he beat her to it by borrowin' most of his pay in advance. He told it all round town, how he had outfoxed his Missus. He certainly was a caution!

But he wasn't satisfied with just outwittin' her. He was sore the way she had acted, tryin' to grab off his pay. And he made up his mind he'd get even. Well, he waited till Evans's Circus was advertised to come to town. Then he told his wife and two kiddies that he was goin' to take them to the circus. The day of the circus, he told them he would get the tickets and meet them outside the entrance to the tent.

Well, he didn't have no intentions of bein' there or buyin' tickets or nothin'. He got full of gin and laid round Wright's poolroom all day. His wife and the kids waited and waited and of course he didn't show up. His wife didn't have a dime with her, or nowhere else, I guess. So she finally had to tell the kids it was all off and they cried like they wasn't never goin' to stop.

Well, it seems, w'ile they was cryin', Doc Stair came along and he asked what was the matter, but Mrs. Kendall was stubborn and wouldn't tell him, but the kids told him

and he insisted on takin' them and their mother in the show.
Jim found this out afterwards and it was one reason why
he had it in for Doc Stair.

Doc Stair come here about a year and a half ago. He's
a mighty handsome young fella and his clothes always look
like he has them made to order. He goes to Detroit two or
three times a year and w'ile he's there he must have a tailor
take his measure and then make him a suit to order. They
cost pretty near twice as much, but they fit a whole lot better
than if you just bought them in a store.

For a w'ile everybody was wonderin' why a young doctor
like Doc Stair should come to a town like this where we
already got old Doc Gamble and Doc Foote that's both been
here for years and all the practice in town was always
divided between the two of them.

Then they was a story got round that Doc Stair's gal
had throwed him over, a gal up in the Northern Peninsula
somewheres, and the reason he come here was to hide himself away and forget it. He said himself that he thought
they wasn't nothin' like general practice in a place like ours
to fit a man to be a good all round doctor. And that's why
he'd came.

Anyways, it wasn't long before he was makin' enough
to live on, though they tell me that he never dunned nobody
for what they owed him, and the folks here certainly has
got the owin' habit, even in my business. If I had all that
was comin' to me for just shaves alone, I could go to Carterville and put up at the Mercer for a week and see a different
picture every night. For instance, they's old George Purdy
—but I guess I shouldn't ought to be gossipin'.

Well, last year, our coroner died, died of the flu. Ken
Beatty, that was his name. He was the coroner. So they had
to choose another man to be coroner in his place and they
picked Doc Stair. He laughed at first and said he didn't
want it, but they made him take it. It ain't no job that anybody would fight for and what a man makes out of it in a

year would just about buy seeds for their garden. Doc's the kind, though, that can't say no to nothin' if you keep at him long enough.

But I was goin' to tell you about a poor boy we got here in town—Paul Dickson. He fell out of a tree when he was about ten years old. Lit on his head and it done somethin' to him and he ain't never been right. No harm in him, but just silly. Jim Kendall used to call him cuckoo; that's a name Jim had for anybody that was off their head, only he called people's head their bean. That was another of his gags, callin' head bean and callin' crazy people cuckoo. Only poor Paul ain't crazy, but just silly.

You can imagine that Jim used to have all kinds of fun with Paul. He'd send him to the White Front Garage for a left-handed monkey wrench. Of course they ain't no such a thing as a left-handed monkey wrench.

And once we had a kind of a fair here and they was a baseball game between the fats and the leans and before the game started Jim called Paul over and sent him way down to Schrader's hardware store to get a key for the pitcher's box.

They wasn't nothin' in the way of gags that Jim couldn't think up, when he put his mind to it.

Poor Paul was always kind of suspicious of people, maybe on account of how Jim had kept foolin' him. Paul wouldn't have much to do with anybody only his own mother and Doc Stair and a girl here in town named Julie Gregg. That is, she ain't a girl no more, but pretty near thirty or over.

When Doc first come to town, Paul seemed to feel like here was a real friend and he hung round Doc's office most of the w'ile; the only time he wasn't there was when he'd go home to eat or sleep or when he seen Julie Gregg doin' her shoppin'.

When he looked out Doc's window and seen her, he'd run downstairs and join her and tag along with her to the different stores. The poor boy was crazy about Julie and she always treated him mighty nice and made him feel like he was welcome, though of course it wasn't nothin' but pity on her side.

Doc done all he could to improve Paul's mind and he told me once that he really thought the boy was gettin' better, that they was times when he was as bright and sensible as anybody else.

But I was goin' to tell you about Julie Gregg. Old Man Gregg was in the lumber business, but got to drinkin' and lost the most of his money and when he died, he didn't leave nothin' but the house and just enough insurance for the girl to skimp along on.

Her mother was a kind of a half invalid and didn't hardly ever leave the house. Julie wanted to sell the place and move somewheres else after the old man died, but the mother said she was born here and would die here. It was tough on Julie, as the young people round this town—well, she's too good for them.

She's been away to school and Chicago and New York and different places and they ain't no subject she can't talk on, where you take the rest of the young folks here and you mention anything to them outside of Gloria Swanson or Tommy Meighan and they think you're delirious. Did you see Gloria in Wages of Virtue? You missed somethin'!

Well, Doc Stair hadn't been here more than a week when he come in one day to get shaved and I recognized who he was as he had been pointed out to me, so I told him about my old lady. She's been ailin' for a couple years and either Doc Gamble or Doc Foote, neither one, seemed to be helpin' her. So he said he would come out and see her, but if she was able to get out herself, it would be better to bring her to his office where he could make a completer examination.

So I took her to his office and w'ile I was waitin' for her in the reception room, in come Julie Gregg. When somebody comes in Doc Stair's office, they's a bell that rings in his inside office so as he can tell they's somebody to see him.

So he left my old lady inside and come out to the front office and that's the first time him and Julie met and I guess it was what they call love at first sight. But it wasn't fifty-fifty. This young fella was the slickest lookin' fella she'd ever seen in this town and she went wild over him. To him she was just a young lady that wanted to see the doctor.

She'd came on about the same business I had. Her mother had been doctorin' for years with Doc Gamble and Doc Foote and without no results. So she'd heard they was a new doc in town and decided to give him a try. He promised to call and see her mother that same day.

I said a minute ago that it was love at first sight on her part. I'm not only judgin' by how she acted afterwards but how she looked at him that first day in his office. I ain't no mind reader, but it was wrote all over her face that she was gone.

Now Jim Kendall, besides bein' a jokesmith and a pretty good drinker, well, Jim was quite a lady-killer. I guess he run pretty wild durin' the time he was on the road for them Carterville people, and besides that, he'd had a couple little affairs of the heart right here in town. As I say, his wife could of divorced him, only she couldn't.

But Jim was like the majority of men, and women, too, I guess. He wanted what he couldn't get. He wanted Julie Gregg and worked his head off tryin' to land her. Only he'd of said bean instead of head.

Well, Jim's habits and his jokes didn't appeal to Julie and of course he was a married man, so he didn't have no more chance than, well, than a rabbit. That's an expression of Jim's himself. When somebody didn't have no chance to get elected or somethin', Jim would always say they didn't have no more chance than a rabbit.

He didn't make no bones about how he felt. Right in here, more than once, in front of the whole crowd, he said he was stuck on Julie and anybody that could get her for him was welcome to his house and his wife and kids included. But she wouldn't have nothin' to do with him; wouldn't even speak to him on the street. He finally seen he wasn't gettin' nowheres with his usual line so he decided to try the rough stuff. He went right up to her house one evenin' and when she opened the door he forced his way in and grabbed her. But she broke loose and before he could stop her, she run in the next room and locked the door and phoned to Joe Barnes. Joe's the marshal. Jim could hear who she was phonin' to and he beat it before Joe got there.

Joe was an old friend of Julie's pa. Joe went to Jim the next day and told him what would happen if he ever done it again.

I don't know how the news of this little affair leaked out. Chances is that Joe Barnes told his wife and she told somebody else's wife and they told their husband. Anyways, it did leak out and Hod Meyers had the nerve to kid Jim about it, right here in this shop. Jim didn't deny nothin' and kind of laughed it off and said for us all to wait; that lots of people had tried to make a monkey out of him, but he always got even.

Meanw'ile everybody in town was wise to Julie's bein' wild mad over the Doc. I don't suppose she had any idear how her face changed when him and her was together; of course she couldn't of, or she'd of kept away from him. And she didn't know that we was all noticin' how many times she made excuses to go up to his office or pass it on the other side of the street and look up in his window to see if he was there. I felt sorry for her and so did most other people.

Hod Meyers kept rubbin' it into Jim about how the Doc had cut him out. Jim didn't pay no attention to the kiddin' and you could see he was plannin' one of his jokes.

One trick Jim had was the knack of changin' his voice. He could make you think he was a girl talkin' and he could

mimic any man's voice. To show you how good he was along
this line, I'll tell you the joke he played on me once.

You know, in most towns of any size, when a man is dead
and needs a shave, why the barber that shaves him soaks him
five dollars for the job; that is, he don't soak *him,* but whoever ordered the shave. I just charge three dollars because
personally I don't mind much shavin' a dead person. They
lay a whole lot stiller than live customers. The only thing
is that you don't feel like talkin' to them and you get kind
of lonesome.

Well, about the coldest day we ever had here, two years
ago last winter, the phone rung at the house w'ile I was
home to dinner and I answered the phone and it was a
woman's voice and she said she was Mrs. John Scott and
her husband was dead and would I come out and shave him.

Old John had always been a good customer of mine. But
they live seven miles out in the country, on the Streeter
road. Still I didn't see how I could say no.

So I said I would be there, but would have to come in
a jitney and it might cost three or four dollars besides the
price of the shave. So she, or the voice, it said that was all
right, so I got Frank Abbott to drive me out to the place
and when I got there, who should open the door but old
John himself! He wasn't no more dead than, well, than a
rabbit.

It didn't take no private detective to figure out who had
played me this little joke. Nobody could of thought it up
but Jim Kendall. He certainly was a card!

I tell you this incident just to show you how he could
disguise his voice and make you believe it was somebody
else talkin'. I'd of swore it was Mrs. Scott had called me.
Anyways, some woman.

Well, Jim waited till he had Doc Stair's voice down pat;
then he went after revenge.

He called Julie up on a night when he knew Doc was over
in Carterville. She never questioned but what it was Doc's

voice. Jim said he must see her that night; he couldn't wait
no longer to tell her somethin'. She was all excited and told
him to come to the house. But he said he was expectin' an
important long distance call and wouldn't she please forget
her manners for once and come to his office. He said they
couldn't nothin' hurt her and nobody would see her and
he just *must* talk to her a little w'ile. Well, poor Julie fell
for it.

Doc always keeps a night light in his office, so it looked
to Julie like they was somebody there.

Meanw'ile Jim Kendall had went to Wright's poolroom,
where they was a whole gang amusin' themselves. The most
of them had drank plenty of gin, and they was a rough
bunch even when sober. They was always strong for Jim's
jokes and when he told them to come with him and see some
fun they give up their card games and pool games and followed along.

Doc's office is on the second floor. Right outside his door
they's a flight of stairs leadin' to the floor above. Jim and
his gang hid in the dark behind these stairs.

Well, Julie come up to Doc's door and rung the bell and
they was nothin' doin'. She rung it again and she rung it
seven or eight times. Then she tried the door and found it
locked. Then Jim made some kind of a noise and she heard
it and waited a minute, and then she says, "Is that you,
Ralph?" Ralph is Doc's first name.

They was no answer and it must of came to her all of
a sudden that she'd been bunked. She pretty near fell downstairs and the whole gang after her. They chased her all
the way home, hollerin', "Is that you, Ralph?" and "Oh,
Ralphie, dear, is that you?" Jim says he couldn't holler it
himself, as he was laughin' too hard.

Poor Julie! She didn't show up here on Main Street for
a long, long time afterward.

And of course Jim and his gang told everybody in town,
everybody but Doc Stair. They was scared to tell him, and

he might of never knowed only for Paul Dickson. The poor
cuckoo, as Jim called him, he was here in the shop one night
when Jim was still gloatin' yet over what he'd done to Julie.
And Paul took in as much of it as he could understand and
he run to Doc with the story.

It's a cinch Doc went up in the air and swore he'd make
Jim suffer. But it was a kind of a delicate thing, because if
it got out that he had beat Jim up, Julie was bound to hear
of it and then she'd know that Doc knew and of course
knowin' that he knew would make it worse for her than ever.
He was goin' to do somethin', but it took a lot of figurin'.

Well, it was a couple days later when Jim was here in
the shop again, and so was the cuckoo. Jim was goin' duck-
shootin' the next day and had came in lookin' for Hod
Meyers to go with him. I happened to know that Hod had
went over to Carterville and wouldn't be home till the end
of the week. So Jim said he hated to go alone and he guessed
he would call it off. Then poor Paul spoke up and said if
Jim would take him he would go along. Jim thought a w'ile
and then he said, well, he guessed a half-wit was better
than nothin'.

I suppose he was plottin' to get Paul out in the boat and
play some joke on him, like pushin' him in the water. Anyways, he said Paul could go. He asked him had he ever
shot a duck and Paul said no, he'd never even had a gun in
his hands. So Jim said he could set in the boat and watch
him and if he behaved himself, he might lend him his gun
for a couple of shots. They made a date to meet in the
mornin' and that's the last I seen of Jim alive.

Next mornin', I hadn't been open more than ten minutes
when Doc Stair come in. He looked kind of nervous. He
asked me had I seen Paul Dickson. I said no, but I knew
where he was, out duck-shootin' with Jim Kendall. So Doc
says that's what he had heard, and he couldn't understand
it because Paul had told him he wouldn't never have no
more to do with Jim as long as he lived.

He said Paul had told him about the joke Jim had played on Julie. He said Paul had asked him what he thought of the joke and the Doc had told him that anybody that would do a thing like that ought not to be let live.

I said it had been a kind of a raw thing, but Jim just couldn't resist no kind of a joke, no matter how raw. I said I thought he was all right at heart, but just bubblin' over with mischief. Doc turned and walked out.

At noon he got a phone call from old John Scott. The lake where Jim and Paul had went shootin' is on John's place. Paul had came runnin' up to the house a few minutes before and said they'd been an accident. Jim had shot a few ducks and then give the gun to Paul and told him to try his luck. Paul hadn't never handled a gun and he was nervous. He was shakin' so hard that he couldn't control the gun. He let fire and Jim sunk back in the boat, dead.

Doc Stair, bein' the coroner, jumped in Frank Abbott's flivver and rushed out to Scott's farm. Paul and old John was down on the shore of the lake. Paul had rowed the boat to shore, but they'd left the body in it, waitin' for Doc to come.

Doc examined the body and said they might as well fetch it back to town. They was no use leavin' it there or callin' a jury, as it was a plain case of accidental shootin'.

Personally I wouldn't never leave a person shoot a gun in the same boat I was in unless I was sure they knew somethin' about guns. Jim was a sucker to leave a new beginner have his gun, let alone a half-wit. It probably served Jim right, what he got. But still we miss him round here. He certainly was a card!

Comb it wet or dry?

# TURN ABOUT
## by William Faulkner

THE American—the older one—wore no pink Bed-fords. His breeches were of plain whipcord, like the tunic. And the tunic had no long London-cut skirts, so that below the Sam Browne the tail of it stuck straight out like the tunic of a military policeman beneath his holster belt. And he wore simple puttees and the easy shoes of a man of middle age, instead of Savile Row boots, and the shoes and the puttees did not match in shade, and the ordnance belt did not match either of them, and the pilot's wings on his breast were just wings. But the ribbon beneath them was a good ribbon, and the insigne on his shoulders were the twin bars of a captain. He was not tall. His face was thin, a little aquiline; the eyes intelligent and a little tired. He was past twenty-five; looking at him, one thought, not Phi Beta Kappa exactly, but Skull and Bones perhaps, or possibly a Rhodes scholarship.

One of the men who faced him probably could not see him at all. He was being held on his feet by an American military policeman. He was quite drunk, and in contrast with the heavy-jawed policeman who held him erect on his long, slim, boneless legs, he looked like a masquerading girl. He was possibly eighteen, tall, with a pink-and-white face and blue eyes, and a mouth like a girl's mouth. He wore a pea-coat, buttoned awry and stained with recent mud, and upon his blond head, at that unmistakable and rakish swagger which no other people can ever approach or imitate, the cap of a Royal Naval Officer.

"What's this, corporal?" the American captain said. "What's the trouble? He's an Englishman. You'd better let their M. P.'s take care of him."

"I know he is," the policeman said. He spoke heavily, breathing heavily, in the voice of a man under physical strain; for all his girlish delicacy of limb, the English boy was heavier—or more helpless—than he looked. "Stand up!" the policeman said. "They're officers!"

The English boy made an effort then. He pulled himself together, focusing his eyes. He swayed, throwing one arm about the policeman's neck, and with the other hand he saluted, his hand flicking, fingers curled a little, to his right ear, already swaying again and catching himself again. "Cheer-o, sir," he said. "Name's not Beatty, I hope."

"No," the captain said.

"Ah," the English boy said. "Hoped not. My mistake. No offense, what?"

"No offense," the captain said quietly. But he was looking at the policeman. The second American spoke. He was a lieutenant, also a pilot. But he was not twenty-five and he wore the pink breeches, the London boots, and his tunic might have been a British tunic save for the collar.

"It's one of those navy eggs," he said. "They pick them out of the gutters here all night long. You don't come to town often enough."

"Oh," the captain said. "I've heard about them. I remember now." He also remarked now that, though the street was a busy one—it was just outside a popular café—and there were many passers, soldier, civilian, women, yet none of them so much as paused, as though it were a familiar sight. He was looking at the policeman. "Can't you take him to his ship?"

"I thought of that before the captain did," the policeman said. "He says he can't go aboard his ship after dark because he puts the ship away at sundown."

"Puts it away?"

"Stand up, sailor!" the policeman said savagely, jerking at his lax burden. "Maybe the captain can make sense out of it. Damned if I can. He says they keep the boat under the wharf. Run it under the wharf at night, and that they can't get it out again until the tide goes out tomorrow."

"Under the wharf? A boat? What is this?" He was now speaking to the lieutenant. "Do they operate some kind of aquatic motorcycles?"

"Something like that," the lieutenant said. "You've seen them—the boats. Launches, camouflaged and all. Dashing up and down the harbor. You've seen them. They do that all day and sleep in the gutters here all night."

"Oh," the captain said. "I thought those boats were ship commanders' launches. You mean to tell me they use officers just to—"

"I don't know," the lieutenant said. "Maybe they use them to fetch hot water from one ship to another. Or buns. Or maybe to go back and forth fast when they forget napkins or something."

"Nonsense," the captain said. He looked at the English boy again.

"That's what they do," the lieutenant said. "Town's lousy with them all night long. Gutters full, and their M. P.'s carting them away in batches, like nursemaids in a park. Maybe the French give them the launches to get them out of the gutters during the day."

"Oh," the captain said, "I see." But it was clear that he didn't see, wasn't listening, didn't believe what he did hear. He looked at the English boy. "Well, you can't leave him here in that shape," he said.

Again the English boy tried to pull himself together. "Quite all right, 'sure you," he said glassily, his voice pleasant, cheerful almost, quite courteous. "Used to it. Confounded rough *pavé*, though. Should force French do something about it. Visiting lads jolly well deserve decent field to play on, what?"

"And he was jolly well using all of it too," the policeman said savagely. "He must think he's a one-man team, maybe."

At that moment a fifth man came up. He was a British

military policeman. "Nah then," he said. "What's this? What's this?" Then he saw the American's shoulder bars. He saluted. At the sound of his voice the English boy turned, swaying, peering.

"Oh, hullo, Albert," he said.

"Nah then, Mr. Hope," the British policeman said. He said to the American policeman, over his shoulder: "What is it this time?"

"Likely nothing," the American said. "The way you guys run a war. But I'm a stranger here. Here. Take him."

"What is this, corporal?" the captain said. "What was he doing?"

"He won't call it nothing," the American policeman said, jerking his head at the British policeman. "He'll just call it a thrush or a robin or something. I turn into this street about three blocks back a while ago, and I find it blocked with a line of trucks going up from the docks, and the drivers all hollering ahead what the hell the trouble is. So I come on, and I find it is about three blocks of them, blocking the cross streets too; and I come on to the head of it where the trouble is, and I find about a dozen of the drivers out in front, hold-ing a caucus or something in the middle of the street, and I come up and I say, 'What's going on here?' and they leave me through and I find this egg here laying—"

"Yer talking about one of His Majesty's officers, my man," the British policeman said.

"Watch yourself, corporal," the captain said. "And you found this officer—"

"He had done gone to bed in the middle of the street, with an empty basket for a pillow. Laying there with his hands under his head and his knees crossed, arguing with them about whether he ought to get up and move or not. He said that the trucks could turn back and go around by another street, but that he couldn't use any other street, because this street was his."

"His street?"

The English boy had listened, interested, pleasant. "Billet, you see," he said. "Must have order, even in war emergency. Billet by lot. This street mine; no poaching, eh? Next street Jamie Wutherspoon's. But trucks can go by that street because Jamie not using it yet. Not in bed yet. Insomnia. Knew so. Told them. Trucks go that way. See now?"

"Was that it, corporal?" the captain said.

"He told you. He wouldn't get up. He just laid there, arguing with them. He was telling one of them to go somewhere and bring back a copy of their articles of war—"

"King's Regulations; yes," the captain said.

"—and see if the book said whether he had the right of way, or the trucks. And then I got him up, and then the captain come along. And that's all. And with the captain's permission I'll now hand him over to His Majesty's wet nur—"

"That'll do, corporal," the captain said. "You can go. I'll see to this." The policeman saluted and went on. The British policeman was now supporting the English boy. "Can't you take him home?" the captain said. "Where are their quarters?"

"I don't rightly know, sir, if they have quarters or not. We—I usually see them about the pubs until daylight. They don't seem to use quarters."

"You mean, they really aren't off of ships?"

"Well, sir, they might be ships, in a manner of speaking. But a man would have to be a bit sleepier than him to sleep in one of them."

"I see," the captain said. He looked at the policeman. "What kind of boats are they?"

This time the policeman's voice was immediate, final and completely inflectionless. It was like a closed door. "I don't rightly know, sir."

"Oh," the captain said. "Quite. Well, he's in no shape to stay about pubs until daylight this time."

"Perhaps I can find him a bit of a pub with a back table,

where he can sleep," the policeman said. But the captain was
not listening. He was looking across the street, where the
lights of another cafe fell across the pavement. The English
boy yawned terrifically, as a child does, his mouth pink and
frankly gaped as a child's.

The captain turned to the policeman:

"Would you mind stepping across there and asking for
Captain Bogard's driver? I'll take care of Mr. Hope."

The policeman departed. The captain now supported the
English boy, his hand beneath the other's arm. Again the
boy yawned like a weary child. "Steady," the captain said.
"The car will be here in a minute."

"Right," the English boy said through the yawn.

II

Once in the car, he went to sleep immediately with the
peaceful suddenness of babies, sitting between the two
Americans. But though the aerodrome was only thirty minutes away, he was awake when they arrived, apparently quite
fresh, and asking for whisky. When they entered the mess he
appeared quite sober, only blinking a little in the lighted
room, in his raked cap and his awry-buttoned pea-jacket and
a soiled silk muffler, embroidered with a club insignia which
Bogard recognized to have come from a famous preparatory
school, twisted about his throat.

"Ah," he said, his voice fresh, clear now, not blurred, quite
cheerful, quite loud, so that the others in the room turned
and looked at him. "Jolly. Whisky, what?" He went straight
as a bird dog to the bar in the corner, the lieutenant following. Bogard had turned and gone on to the other end of the
room, where five men sat about a card table.

"What's he admiral of?" one said.

"Of the whole Scotch navy, when I found him," Bogard
said.

Another looked up. "Oh, I thought I'd seen him in town."
He looked at the guest. "Maybe it's because he was on his

feet that I didn't recognize him when he came in. You usually
see them lying down in the gutter."

"Oh," the first said. He, too, looked around. "Is he one of
those guys?"

"Sure. You've seen them. Sitting on the curb, you know,
with a couple of limey M. P.'s hauling at their arms."

"Yes. I've seen them," the other said. They all looked at
the English boy. He stood at the bar, talking, his voice loud,
cheerful. "They all look like him too," the speaker said.
"About seventeen or eighteen. They run those little boats
that are always dashing in and out."

"Is that what they do?" a third said. "You mean, there's a
male marine auxiliary to the Waacs? Good Lord, I sure made
a mistake when I enlisted. But this war never was advertised
right."

"I don't know," Bogard said. "I guess they do more than
just ride around."

But they were not listening to him. They were looking at
the guest. "They run by clock," the first said. "You can see
the condition of one of them after sunset and almost tell
what time it is. But what I don't see is, how a man that's in
that shape at one o'clock every morning can even see a
battleship the next day."

"Maybe when they have a message to send out to a ship,"
another said, "they just make duplicates and line the launches
up and point them toward the ship and give each one a
duplicate of the message and let them go. And the ones that
miss the ship just cruise around the harbor until they hit
a dock somewhere."

"It must be more than that," Bogard said.

He was about to say something else, but at that moment
the guest turned from the bar and approached, carrying a
glass. He walked steadily enough, but his color was high and
his eyes were bright, and he was talking, loud, cheerful, as
he came up.

"I say. Won't you chaps join—" He ceased. He seemed to

remark something; he was looking at their breasts. "Oh, I say. You fly. All of you. Oh, good gad! Find it jolly, eh?"

"Yes," somebody said. "Jolly."

"But dangerous, what?"

"A little faster than tennis," another said. The guest looked at him, bright, affable, intent.

Another said quickly, "Bogard says you command a vessel."

"Hardly a vessel. Thanks, though. And not command. Ronnie does that. Ranks me a bit. Age."

"Ronnie?"

"Yes. Nice. Good egg. Old, though. Stickler."

"Stickler?"

"Frightful. You'd not believe it. Whenever we sight smoke and I have the glass, he sheers away. Keeps the ship hull down all the while. No beaver then. Had me two down a fortnight yesterday."

The Americans glanced at one another. "No beaver?"

"We play it. With basket masts, you see. See a basket mast. Beaver! One up. The Ergenstrasse doesn't count any more, though."

The men about the table looked at one another. Bogard spoke. "I see. When you or Ronnie see a ship with basket masts, you get a beaver on the other. I see. What is the Ergenstrasse?"

"She's German. Interned. Tramp steamer. Foremast rigged so it looks something like a basket mast. Booms, cables, I dare say. I didn't think it looked very much like a basket mast, myself. But Ronnie said yes. Called it one day. Then one day they shifted her across the basin and I called her on Ronnie. So we decided to not count her any more. See now, eh?"

"Oh," the one who had made the tennis remark said, "I see. You and Ronnie run about in the launch, playing beaver. H'm'm. That's nice. Did you ever pl—"

"Jerry," Bogard said. The guest had not moved. He

looked down at the speaker, still smiling, his eyes quite wide.

The speaker still looked at the guest. "Has yours and Ronnie's boat got a yellow stern?"

"A yellow stern?" the English boy said. He had quit smiling, but his face was still pleasant.

"I thought that maybe when the boats had two captains, they might paint the sterns yellow or something."

"Oh," the guest said. "Burt and Reeves aren't officers."

"Burt and Reeves," the other said, in a musing tone. "So they go, too. Do they play beaver too?"

"Jerry," Bogard said. The other looked at him. Bogard jerked his head a little. "Come over here." The other rose. They went aside. "Lay off of him," Bogard said. "I mean it, now. He's just a kid. When you were that age, how much sense did you have? Just about enough to get to chapel on time."

"My country hadn't been at war going on four years, though," Jerry said. "Here we are, spending our money and getting shot at by the clock, and it's not even our fight, and these limeys that would have been goose-stepping twelve months now if it hadn't been——"

"Shut it," Bogard said. "You sound like a Liberty Loan."

"——taking it like it was a fair or something. 'Jolly.'" His voice was now falsetto, lilting. "'But dangerous, what?'"

"Sh-h-h-h," Bogard said.

"I'd like to catch him and his Ronnie out in the harbor, just once. Any harbor. London's. I wouldn't want anything but a Jenny, either. Jenny? Hell, I'd take a bicycle and a pair of water wings! I'll show him some war."

"Well, you lay off him now. He'll be gone soon."

"What are you going to do with him?"

"I'm going to take him along this morning. Let him have Harper's place out front. He says he can handle a Lewis. Says they have one on the boat. Something he was telling me —about how he once shot out a channel-marker light at seven hundred yards."

"Well, that's your business. Maybe he can beat you."

"Beat me?"

"Playing beaver. And then you can take on Ronnie."

"I'll show him some 'war, anyway," Bogard said. He looked at the guest. "His people have been in it three years now, and he seems to take it like a sophomore in town for the big game." He looked at Jerry again. "But you lay off him now."

As they approached the table, the guest's voice was loud and cheerful: ". . . if he got the glasses first, he would go in close and look, but when I got them first, he'd sheer off where I couldn't see anything but the smoke. Frightful stickler. Frightful. But Ergenstrasse not counting any more. And if you make a mistake and call her, you lose two beaver from your score. If Ronnie were only to forget and call her we'd be even."

### III

At two o'clock the English boy was still talking, his voice bright, innocent and cheerful. He was telling them how Switzerland had been spoiled by 1914, and instead of the vacation which his father had promised him for his sixteenth birthday, when that birthday came he and his tutor had had to do with Wales. But that he and the tutor had got pretty high and that he dared to say—with all due respect to any present who might have had the advantage of Switzerland, of course—that one could see probably as far from Wales as from Switzerland. "Perspire as much and breathe as hard, anyway," he added. And about him the Americans sat, a little hard-bitten, a little sober, somewhat older, listening to him with a kind of cold astonishment. They had been getting up for some time now and going out and returning in flying clothes, carrying helmets and goggles. An orderly entered with a tray of coffee cups, and the guest realized that for some time now he had been hearing engines in the darkness outside.

At last Bogard rose. "Come along," he said. "We'll get your togs." When they emerged from the mess, the sound of the engines was quite loud—an idling thunder. In alignment along the invisible tarmac was a vague rank of short banks of flickering blue-green fire suspended apparently in mid-air. They crossed the aerodrome to Bogard's quarters, where the lieutenant, McGinnis, sat on a cot fastening his flying boots. Bogard reached down a Sidcott suit and threw it across the cot. "Put this on," he said.

"Will I need all this?" the guest said. "Shall we be gone that long?"

"Probably," Bogard said. "Better use it. Cold upstairs."

The guest picked up the suit. "I say," he said. "I say. Ronnie and I have a do ourselves, tomor—today. Do you think Ronnie won't mind if I am a bit late? Might not wait for me."

"We'll be back before teatime," McGinnis said. He seemed quite busy with his boot. "Promise you." The English boy looked at him.

"What time should you be back?" Bogard said.

"Oh, well," the English boy said, "I dare say it will be all right. They let Ronnie say when to go, anyway. He'll wait for me if I should be a bit late."

"He'll wait," Bogard said. "Get your suit on."

"Right," the other said. They helped him into the suit. "Never been up before," he said, chattily, pleasantly. "Dare say you can see farther than from mountains, eh?"

"See more, anyway," McGinnis said. "You'll like it."

"Oh, rather. If Ronnie only waits for me. Lark. But dangerous, isn't it?"

"Go on," McGinnis said. "You're kidding me."

"Shut your trap, Mac," Bogard said. "Come along. Want some more coffee?" He looked at the guest, but McGinnis answered:

"No. Got something better than coffee. Coffee makes such a confounded stain on the wings."

"On the wings?" the English boy said. "Why coffee on the wings?"

"Stow it, I said, Mac," Bogard said. "Come along."

They recrossed the aerodrome, approaching the muttering banks of flame. When they drew near, the guest began to discern the shape, the outlines, of the Handley-Page. It looked like a Pullman coach run upslanted aground into the skeleton of the first floor of an incomplete skyscraper. The guest looked at it quietly.

"It's larger than a cruiser," he said in his bright, interested voice. "I say, you know. This doesn't fly in one lump. You can't pull my leg. Seen them before. It comes in two parts: Captain Bogard and me in one; Mac and 'nother chap in other. What?"

"No," McGinnis said. Bogard had vanished. "It all goes up in one lump. Big lark, eh? Buzzard, what?"

"Buzzard?" the guest murmured. "Oh, I say. A cruiser. Flying. I say, now."

"And listen," McGinnis said. His hand came forth; something cold fumbled against the hand of the English boy—a bottle. "When you feel yourself getting sick, see? Take a pull at it."

"Oh, shall I get sick?"

"Sure. We all do. Part of flying. This will stop it. But if it doesn't. See?"

"What? Quite. What?"

"Not overside. Don't spew it overside."

"Not overside?"

"It'll blow back in Bogy's and my face. Can't see. Bingo. Finished. See?"

"Oh, quite. What shall I do with it?" Their voices were quiet, brief, grave as conspirators.

"Just duck your head and let her go."

"Oh, quite."

Bogard returned. "Show him how to get into the front pit, will you?" he said. McGinnis led the way through the trap.

Forward, rising to the slant of the fuselage, the passage narrowed; a man would need to crawl.

"Crawl in there and keep going," McGinnis said.

"It looks like a dog kennel," the guest said.

"Doesn't it, though?" McGinnis agreed cheerfully. "Cut along with you." Stooping, he could hear the other scuttling forward. "You'll find a Lewis gun up there, like as not," he said into the tunnel.

The voice of the guest came back: "Found it."

"The gunnery sergeant will be along in a minute and show you if it is loaded."

"It's loaded," the guest said; almost on the heels of his words the gun fired, a brief staccato burst. There were shouts, the loudest from the ground beneath the nose of the aeroplane. "It's quite all right," the English boy's voice said. "I pointed it west before I let it off. Nothing back there but Marine office and your brigade headquarters. Ronnie and I always do this before we go anywhere. Sorry if I was too soon. Oh, by the way," he added, "my name's Claude. Don't think I mentioned it."

On the ground, Bogard and two other officers stood. They had come up running. "Fired it west," one said. "How in hell does he know which way is west?"

"He's a sailor," the other said. "You forgot that."

"He seems to be a machine gunner too," Bogard said.

"Let's hope he doesn't forget that," the first said.

IV

NEVERTHELESS, Bogard kept an eye on the silhouetted head rising from the round gunpit in the nose ten feet ahead of him. "He did work that gun, though," he said to McGinnis beside him. "He even put the drum on himself, didn't he?"

"Yes," McGinnis said. "If he just doesn't forget and think that that gun is him and his tutor looking around from a Welsh alp."

"Maybe I should not have brought him," Bogard said. Mc-

Ginnis didn't answer. Bogard jockeyed the wheel a little. Ahead, in the gunner's pit, the guest's head moved this way and that continuously, looking. "We'll get there and unload and haul air for home," Bogard said. "Maybe in the dark— Confound it, it would be a shame for his country to be in this mess for four years and him not even to see a gun pointed in his direction."

"He'll see one tonight if he don't keep his head in," McGinnis said.

But the boy did not do that. Not even when they had reached the objective and McGinnis had crawled down to the bomb toggles. And even when the searchlights found them and Bogard signaled to the other machines and dived, the two engines snarling full speed into and through the bursting shells, he could see the boy's face in the searchlight's glare, leaned far overside, coming sharply out as a spotlighted face on a stage, with an expression upon it of childlike interest and delight. "But he's firing that Lewis," Bogard thought. "Straight too"; nosing the machine farther down, watching the pinpoint swing into the sights, his right hand lifted, waiting to drop into McGinnis' sight. He dropped his hand; above the noise of the engines he seemed to hear the click and whistle of the released bombs as the machine freed of the weight, shot zooming in a long upward bounce that carried it for an instant out of the light. Then he was pretty busy for a time, coming into and through the shells again, shooting athwart another beam that caught and held long enough for him to see the English boy leaning far over the side, looking back and down past the right wing, the undercarriage. "Maybe he's read about it somewhere," Bogard thought, turning, looking back to pick up the rest of the flight.

Then it was all over, the darkness cool and empty and peaceful and almost quiet, with only the steady sound of the engines. McGinnis climbed back into the office, and standing up in his seat, he fired the colored pistol this time and stood for a moment longer, looking backward toward where the searchlights still probed and sabered. He sat down again.

"O.K.," he said. "I counted all four of them. Let's haul air." Then he looked forward. "What's become of the King's Own? You didn't hang him onto a bomb release, did you?" Bogard looked. The forward pit was empty. It was in dim silhouette again now, against the stars, but there was nothing there now save the gun. "No," McGinnis said; "there he is. See? Leaning overside. Dammit, I told him not to spew it! There he comes back." The guest's head came into view again. But again it sank out of sight.

"He's coming back," Bogard said. "Stop him. Tell him we're going to have every squadron in the Hun Channel group on top of us in thirty minutes."

McGinnis swung himself down and stooped at the entrance to the passage. "Get back!" he shouted. The other was almost out; they squatted so, face to face like two dogs, shouting at one another above the noise of the still-unthrottled engines on either side of the fabric walls. The English boy's voice was thin and high.

"Bomb!" he shrieked.

"Yes," McGinnis shouted, "they were bombs! We gave them hell! Get back, I tell you! Have every Hun in France on us in ten minutes! Get back to your gun!"

Again the boy's voice came, high, faint above the noise: "Bomb! All right?"

"Yes! Yes! All right. Back to your gun, damn you!"

McGinnis climbed back into the office. "He went back. Want me to take her awhile?"

"All right," Bogard said. He passed McGinnis the wheel. "Ease her back some. I'd just as soon it was daylight when they come down on us."

"Right," McGinnis said. He moved the wheel suddenly. "What's the matter with that right wing?" he said. "Watch it. . . . See? I'm flying on the right aileron and a little rudder. Feel it."

Bogard took the wheel a moment. "I didn't notice that. Wire somewhere, I guess. I didn't think any of those shells were that close. Watch her, though."

"Right," McGinnis said. "And so you are going with him on his boat tomorrow—today."

"Yes. I promised him. Confound it, you can't hurt a kid, you know."

"Why don't you take Collier along, with his mandolin? Then you could sail around and sing."

"I promised him," Bogard said. "Get that wing up a little."

"Right," McGinnis said.

Thirty minutes later it was beginning to be dawn; the sky was gray. Presently McGinnis said: "Well, here they come. Look at them! They look like mosquitoes in September. I hope he don't get worked up now and think he's playing beaver. If he does he'll just be one down to Ronnie, provided the devil has a beard. . . . Want the wheel?"

## V

AT EIGHT o'clock the beach, the Channel, was beneath them. Throttled back, the machine drifted down as Bogard ruddered it gently into the Channel wind. His face was strained, a little tired.

McGinnis looked tired, too, and he needed a shave.

"What do you guess he is looking at now?" he said. For again the English boy was leaning over the right side of the cockpit, looking backward and downward past the right wing.

"I don't know," Bogard said. "Maybe bullet holes." He blasted the port engine. "Must have the riggers—"

"He could see some closer than that," McGinnis said. "I'll swear I saw tracer going into his back at one time. Or maybe it's the ocean he's looking at. But he must have seen that when he came over from England." Then Bogard leveled off; the nose rose sharply, the sand, the curling tide edge fled alongside. Yet still the English boy hung far overside, looking backward and downward at something beneath the right wing, his face rapt, with utter and childlike interest. Until the machine was completely stopped he continued to do so. Then he ducked down, and in the abrupt silence of the engines they could hear him crawling in the passage. He emerged just as the two pilots climbed stiffly down from the office, his face bright, eager; his voice high, excited.

"Oh, I say! Oh, good gad! What a chap! What a judge of distance! If Ronnie could only have seen! Oh, good gad! Or maybe they aren't like ours—don't load themselves as soon as the air strikes them."

The Americans looked at him. "What don't what?" Mc-Ginnis said.

"The bomb. It was magnificent; I say, I shan't forget it. Oh, I say, you know! It was splendid!"

After a while McGinnis said, "The bomb?" in a fainting voice. Then the two pilots glared at each other; they said in unison: "That right wing!" Then as one they clawed down through the trap and, with the guest at their heels, they ran around the machine and looked beneath the right wing. The bomb, suspended by its tail, hung straight down like a plumb bob beside the right wheel, its tip just touching the sand. And parallel with the wheel track was the long delicate line in the sand where its ultimate tip had dragged. Behind them the English boy's voice was high, clear, childlike:

"Frightened, myself. Tried to tell you. But realized you knew your business better than I. Skill. Marvelous. Oh, I say, I shan't forget it."

## VI

A MARINE with a bayoneted rifle passed Bogard onto the wharf and directed him to the boat. The wharf was empty, and he didn't even see the boat until he approached the edge of the wharf and looked directly down into it and upon the backs of two stooping men in greasy dungarees, who rose and glanced briefly at him and stooped again.

It was about thirty feet long and about three feet wide. It was painted with gray-green camouflage. It was quarter-decked forward, with two blunt, raked exhaust stacks. "Good Lord," Bogard thought, "if all that deck is engine—" Just aft the deck was the control seat; he saw a big wheel, an instrument panel. Rising to a height of about a foot above the freeboard, and running from the stern forward to where the deck began, and continuing on across the after edge of the deck and thence back down the other gunwale to the stern, was a solid screen, also camouflaged, which inclosed the boat save for the width of the stern, which was open. Facing the steersman's seat like an eye was a hole in the screen about eight inches in diameter. And looking down into the long, narrow, still, vicious shape, he saw a machine gun swiveled at the stern, and he looked at the low screen—including which the whole vessel did not sit much more than a yard above water level—with its single empty forward-staring eye, and he thought quietly: "It's steel. It's made of steel." And his face was quite sober, quite thoughtful, and he drew his trench coat about him and buttoned it, as though he were getting cold.

He heard steps behind him and turned. But it was only an orderly from the aerodrome, accompanied by the marine with the rifle. The orderly was carrying a largish bundle wrapped in paper.

"From Lieutenant McGinnis to the captain," the orderly said.

Bogard took the bundle. The orderly and the marine retreated. He opened the bundle. It contained some objects and a scrawled note. The objects were a new yellow silk sofa cushion and a Japanese parasol, obviously borrowed, and a comb and a roll of toilet paper. The note said:

Couldn't find a camera anywhere and Collier wouldn't let me have his mandolin. But maybe Ronnie can play on the comb.

MAC.

Bogard looked at the objects. But his face was still quite thoughtful, quite grave. He rewrapped the things and carried the bundle on up the wharf a way and dropped it quietly into the water.

As he returned toward the invisible boat he saw two men approaching. He recognized the boy at once—tall, slender, already talking, voluble, his head bent a little toward his shorter companion, who plodded along beside him, hands in pockets, smoking a pipe. The boy still wore the pea-coat beneath a flapping oilskin, but in place of the rakish and casual cap he now wore an infantryman's soiled Balaclava helmet, with, floating behind him as though upon the sound of his voice, a curtainlike piece of cloth almost as long as a burnous.

"Hullo, there!" he cried, still a hundred yards away.

But it was the second man that Bogard was watching, thinking to himself that he had never in his life seen a more curious figure. There was something stolid about the very shape of his hunched shoulders, his slightly down-looking face. He was a head shorter than the other. His face was ruddy, too, but its mold was of a profound gravity that was almost dour. It was the face of a man of twenty who has been for a year trying, even while asleep, to look twenty-one. He wore a high-necked sweater and dungaree slacks; above this a leather jacket; and above this a soiled naval officer's warmer that reached almost to his heels and which had one shoulder strap missing and not one remaining button at all. On his head was a plaid fore-and-aft deer stalker's cap, tied on by a narrow scarf brought across and down, hiding his ears, and then wrapped once about his throat and knotted with a hangman's noose beneath his left ear. It was unbelievably soiled, and with his hands elbow-deep in his pockets and his hunched shoulders and his bent head, he looked like someone's grandmother hanged, say, for a witch. Clamped upside down between his teeth was a short brier pipe.

"Here he is!" the boy cried. "This is Ronnie. Captain Bogard."

"How are you?" Bogard said. He extended his hand. The other said no word, but his hand came forth, limp. It was quite cold, but it was hard, calloused. But he said no word; he just glanced briefly at Bogard and then away. But in that instant Bogard caught something in the look, something strange—a flicker; a kind of covert and curious respect, something like a boy of fifteen looking at a circus trapezist.

But he said no word. He ducked on; Bogard watched him drop from sight over the wharf edge as though he had jumped feet first into the sea. He remarked now that the engines in the invisible boat were running.

"We might get aboard too," the boy said. He started toward the boat, then he stopped. He touched Bogard's arm. "Yonder!" he hissed. "See?" His voice was thin with excitement.

"What?" Bogard also whispered; automatically he looked backward and upward, after old habit. The other was gripping his arm and pointing across the harbor.

"There! Over there. The Ergenstrasse. They have shifted her again." Across the harbor lay an ancient, rusting, sway-backed hulk. It was small and nondescript, and, remembering, Bogard saw that the foremast was a strange mess of cables and booms, resembling—allowing for a great deal of license or looseness of imagery—a basket mast. Beside him the boy was almost chortling. "Do you think that Ronnie noticed?" he hissed. "Do you?"

"I don't know," Bogard said.

"Oh, good gad! If he should glance up and call her before he notices, we'll be even. Oh, good gad! But come along." He went on; he was still chortling. "Careful," he said. "Frightful ladder."

He descended first, the two men in the boat rising and saluting. Ronnie had disappeared, save for his backside, which now filled a small hatch leading forward beneath the deck. Bogard descended gingerly.

"Good Lord," he said. "Do you have to climb up and down this every day?"

"Frightful, isn't it?" the other said, in his happy voice. "But you know yourself. Try to run a war with makeshifts, then wonder why it takes so long." The narrow hull slid and surged, even with Bogard's added weight. "Sits right on top, you see," the boy said. "Would float on a lawn, in a heavy dew. Goes right over them like a bit of paper."

"It does?" Bogard said.

"Oh, absolutely. That's why, you see." Bogard didn't see, but he was too busy letting himself gingerly down to a sitting posture. There were no thwarts; no seats save a long, thick, cylindrical ridge which ran along the bottom of the boat from the driver's seat to the stern. Ronnie had backed into sight. He now sat behind the wheel, bent over the instrument panel. But when he glanced back over his shoulder he did not speak. His face was merely interrogatory. Across his face there was now a long smudge of grease. The boy's face was empty, too, now.

"Right," he said. He looked forward, where one of the seamen had gone. "Ready forward?" he said.

"Aye, sir," the seaman said.

The other seaman was at the stern line. "Ready aft?"

"Aye, sir."

"Cast off." The boat sheered away, purring, a boiling of water under the stern. The boy looked down at Bogard. "Silly business. Do it shipshape, though. Can't tell when silly fourstriper—" His face changed again, immediate, solicitous. "I say. Will you be warm? I never thought to fetch—"

"I'll be all right," Bogard said. But the other was already taking off his oilskin. "No, no," Bogard said. "I won't take it."

"You'll tell me if you get cold?"

"Yes. Sure." He was looking down at the cylinder on which he sat. It was a half cylinder—that is, like the hot-water tank to some Gargantuan stove, sliced down the middle and bolted, open side down, to the floor plates. It was twenty feet long and more than two feet thick. Its top rose as high as the gunwales and between it and the hull on either side was just room enough for a man to place his feet to walk.

"That's Muriel," the boy said.

"Muriel?"

"Yes. The one before that was Agatha. After my aunt. The first one Ronnie and I had was Alice in Wonderland. Ronnie and I were the White Rabbit. Jolly, eh?"

"Oh, you and Ronnie have had three, have you?"

"Oh, yes," the boy said. He leaned down. "He didn't notice," he whispered. His face was again bright, gleeful. "When we come back," he said. "You watch."

"Oh," Bogard said. "The Ergenstrasse." He looked astern, and then he thought: "Good Lord! We must be going—traveling." He looked out now, broadside, and saw the harbor line fleeing past, and he thought to himself that the boat was well-nigh moving at the speed at which the Handley-Page flew, left the ground. They were beginning to bound now, even in the sheltered water, from one wave crest to the next with a distinct shock. His hand still rested on the cylinder on which he sat. He looked down at it again, following it from where it seemed to emerge beneath Ronnie's seat, to where it beveled into the stern. "It's the air in here, I suppose," he said.

"The what?" the boy said.

"The air. Stored up in here. That makes the boat ride high."

"Oh, yes. I dare say. Very likely. I hadn't thought about it." He came forward, his burnous whipping in the wind, and sat down beside Bogard. Their heads were below the top of the screen.

Astern the harbor fled, diminishing, sinking into the sea. The boat had begun to lift now, swooping forward and down, shocking almost stationary for a moment, then lifting and swooping again; a gout of spray came aboard over the bows like a flung shovelful of shot. "I wish you'd take this coat," the boy said.

Bogard didn't answer. He looked around at the bright face. "We're outside, aren't we?" he said quietly.

"Yes. . . . Do take it, won't you?"

"Thanks, no. I'll be all right.•We won't be long, anyway, I guess."

"No. We'll turn soon. It won't be so bad then."

"Yes. I'll be all right when we turn." Then they did turn. The motion became easier. That is, the boat didn't bang head-on, shuddering, into the swells. They came up beneath now, and the boat fled with increased speed, with a long, sickening, yawning motion, first to one side and then the other. But it fled on, and Bogard looked astern with that same soberness with which he had first looked down into the boat. "We're going east now," he said.

"With just a spot of north," the boy said. "Makes her ride a bit better, what?"

"Yes," Bogard said. Astern there was nothing now save empty sea and the delicate needlelike cant of the machine gun against the boiling and slewing wake, and the two seamen crouching quietly in the stern. "Yes. It's easier." Then he said: "How far do we go?"

The boy leaned closer. He moved closer. His voice was happy, confidential, proud, though lowered a little: "It's Ronnie's show. He thought of it. Not that I wouldn't have, in time. Gratitude and all that. But he's the older, you see. Thinks fast. Courtesy, *noblesse oblige*—all that. Thought of it soon as I told him this morning. I said, 'Oh, I say, I've been there. I've seen it'; and he said, 'Not flying'; and I said, 'Strewth'; and he said, 'How far? No lying now'; and I said, 'Oh, far. Tremendous. Gone all night'; and he said, 'Flying all night. That must have been to Berlin'; and I said, 'I don't know. I dare say'; and he thought. I could see him thinking. Because he is the older, you see. More experience in courtesy, right thing. And he said, 'Berlin. No fun to that chap, dashing out and back with us.' And he thought and I waited, and I said, 'But we can't take him to Berlin. Too far. Don't know the way, either'; and he said—fast, like a shot—said, 'But there's Kiel'; and I knew—"

"What?" Bogard said. Without moving, his whole body sprang. "Kiel? In this?"

"Absolutely. Ronnie thought of it. Smart, even if he is a stickler. Said at once, 'Zeebrugge no show at all for that chap. Must do best we can for him. Berlin,' Ronnie said. 'My gad! Berlin.'"

"Listen," Bogard said. He had turned now, facing the other, his face quite grave. "What is this boat for?"

"For?"

"What does it do?" Then, knowing beforehand the answer to his own question, he said, putting his hand on the cylinder: "What is this in here? A torpedo, isn't it?"

"I thought you knew," the boy said.

"No," Bogard said. "I didn't know." His voice seemed to reach him from a distance, dry, cricketlike: "How do you fire it?"

"Fire it?"

"How do you get it out of the boat? When that hatch was open a while ago I could see the engines. They were right in front of the end of this tube."

"Oh," the boy said. "You pull a gadget there and the torpedo drops out astern. As soon as the screw touches the water it begins to turn, and then the torpedo is ready, loaded. Then all you have to do is turn the boat quickly and the torpedo goes on."

"You mean—" Bogard said. After a moment his voice obeyed him again. "You mean you aim the torpedo with the boat and release it and it starts moving, and you turn the boat out of the way and the torpedo passes through the same water that the boat just vacated?"

"Knew you'd catch on," the boy said. "Told Ronnie so.

Airman. Tamer than yours, though. But can't be helped.
Best we can do, just on water. But knew you'd catch on."

"Listen," Bogard said. His voice sounded to him quite
calm. The boat fled on, yawing over the swells. He sat quite
motionless. It seemed to him that he could hear himself
talking to himself: "Go on. Ask him. Ask him what? Ask
him how close to the ship do you have to be before you
fire. . . . Listen," he said, in that calm voice. "Now, you
tell Ronnie, you see. You just tell him—just say—" He could
feel his voice ratting off on him again, so he stopped it. He
sat quite motionless, waiting for it to come back; the boy
leaning now, looking at his face. Again the boy's voice was
solicitous:

"I say. You're not feeling well. These confounded shallow
boats."

"It's not that," Bogard said. "I just—Do your orders say
Kiel?"

"Oh, no. They let Ronnie say. Just so we bring the boat
back. This is for you. Gratitude. Ronnie's idea. Tame, after
flying. But if you'd rather, eh?"

"Yes, some place closer. You see, I—"

"Quite. I see. No vacations in wartime. I'll tell Ronnie."
He went forward. Bogard did not move. The boat fled in
long, slewing swoops. Bogard looked quietly astern, at the
scudding sea, the sky.

"My God!" he thought. "Can you beat it? Can you beat
it?"

The boy came back; Bogard turned to him a face the color
of dirty paper. "All right now," the boy said. "Not Kiel.
Nearer place, hunting probably just as good. Ronnie says he
knows you will understand." He was tugging at his pocket.
He brought out a bottle. "Here. Haven't forgot last night.
Do the same for you. Good for the stomach, eh?"

Bogard drank, gulping—a big one. He extended the bottle, but the boy refused. "Never touch it on duty," he said.
"Not like you chaps. Tame here."

The boat fled on. The sun was already down the west. But Bogard had lost all count of time, of distance. Ahead he could see white seas through the round eye opposite Ronnie's face, and Ronnie's hand on the wheel and the granitelike jut of his profiled jaw and the dead upside-down pipe. The boat fled on.

Then the boy leaned and touched his shoulder. He half rose. The boy was pointing. The sun was reddish; against it, outside them and about two miles away, a vessel—a trawler, it looked like—at anchor swung a tall mast.

"Lightship!" the boy shouted. "Theirs." Ahead Bogard could see a low, flat mole—the entrance to a harbor. "Channel!" the boy shouted. He swept his arm in both directions. "Mines!" His voice swept back on the wind. "Place filthy with them. All sides. Beneath us too. Lark, eh?"

VII

Against the mole a fair surf was beating. Running before the seas now, the boat seemed to leap from one roller to the next; in the intervals while the screw was in the air the engine seemed to be trying to tear itself out by the roots. But it did not slow; when it passed the end of the mole the boat seemed to be standing almost erect on its rudder, like a sailfish. The mole was a mile away. From the end of it little faint lights began to flicker like fireflies. The boy leaned. "Down," he said. "Machine guns. Might stop a stray."

"What do I do?" Bogard shouted. "What can I do?"

"Stout fellow! Give them hell, what? Knew you'd like it!"

Crouching, Bogard looked up at the boy, his face wild. "I can handle the machine gun!"

"No need," the boy shouted back. "Give them first innings. Sporting. Visitors, eh?" He was looking forward. "There she is. See?" They were in the harbor now, the basin opening before them. Anchored in the channel was a big freighter. Painted midships of the hull was a huge Argentine flag. "Must get back to stations!" the boy shouted down to him.

Then at that moment Ronnie spoke for the first time. The boat was hurtling along now in smoother water. Its speed did not slacken and Ronnie did not turn his head when he spoke. He just swung his jutting jaw and the clamped cold pipe a little, and said from the side of his mouth a single word:

"Beaver."

The boy, stooped over what he had called his gadget, jerked up, his expression astonished and outraged. Bogard also looked forward and saw Ronnie's arm pointing to starboard. It was a light cruiser at anchor a mile away. She had basket masts, and as he looked a gun flashed from her after turret. "Oh, damn!" the boy cried. "Oh, you putt! Oh, confound you, Ronnie! Now I'm three down!" But he had already stooped again over his gadget, his face bright and empty and alert again; not sober; just calm, waiting. Again Bogard looked forward and felt the boat pivot on its rudder and head directly for the freighter at terrific speed, Ronnie now with one hand on the wheel and the other lifted and extended at the height of his head.

But it seemed to Bogard that the hand would never drop. He crouched, not sitting, watching with a kind of quiet horror the painted flag increase like a moving picture of a locomotive taken from between the rails. Again the gun crashed from the cruiser behind them, and the freighter fired point-blank at them from its poop. Bogard heard neither shot.

"Man, man!" he shouted. "For God's sake!"

Ronnie's hand dropped. Again the boat spun on its rudder. Bogard saw the bow rise, pivoting; he expected the hull to slam broadside on into the ship. But it didn't. It shot off on a long tangent. He was waiting for it to make a wide sweep, heading seaward, putting the freighter astern, and he thought of the cruiser again. "Get a broadside, this time, once we clear the freighter," he thought. Then he remembered the freighter, the torpedo, and he looked back

toward the freighter to watch the torpedo strike, and saw to
his horror that the boat was now bearing down on the
freighter again, in a skidding turn. Like a man in a dream,
he watched himself rush down upon the ship and shoot
past under her counter, still skidding, close enough to see the
faces on her decks. "They missed and they are going to run
down the torpedo and catch it and shoot it again," he thought
idiotically.

So the boy had to touch his shoulder before he knew he
was behind him. The boy's voice was quite calm: "Under
Ronnie's seat there. A bit of a crank handle. If you'll just
hand it to me—"

He found the crank. He passed it back; he was thinking
dreamily: "Mac would say they had a telephone on board."
But he didn't look at once to see what the boy was doing
with it, for in that still and peaceful horror he was watching
Ronnie, the cold pipe rigid in his jaw, hurling the boat at top
speed round and round the freighter, so near that he could
see the rivets in the plates. Then he looked aft, his face
wild, importunate, and he saw what the boy was doing with
the crank. He had fitted it into what was obviously a small
windlass low on one flank of the tube near the head. He
glanced up and saw Bogard's face. "Didn't go that time!"
he shouted cheerfully.

"Go?" Bogard shouted. "It didn't— The torpedo—"

The boy and one of the seamen were quite busy, stooping
over the windlass and the tube. "No. Clumsy. Always happening. Should think clever chaps like engineers— Happens, though. Draw her in and try her again."

"But the nose, the cap!" Bogard shouted. "It's still in the
tube, isn't it? It's all right, isn't it?"

"Absolutely. But it's working now. Loaded. Screw's
started turning. Get it back and drop it clear. If we should
stop or slow up it would overtake us. Drive back into the
tube. Bingo! What?"

Bogard was on his feet now, turned, braced to the terrific

merry-go-round of the boat. High above them the freighter seemed to be spinning on her heel like a trick picture in the movies. "Let me have that winch!" he cried.

"Steady!" the boy said. "Mustn't draw her back too fast. Jam her into the head of the tube ourselves. Same bingo! Best let us. Every cobbler to his last, what?"

"Oh, quite," Bogard said. "Oh, absolutely." It was as if someone else was using his mouth. He leaned, braced, his hands on the cold tube, beside the others. He was hot inside, but his outside was cold. He could feel all his flesh jerking with cold as he watched the blunt, grained hand of the seaman turning the windlass in short, easy, inch-long arcs, while at the head of the tube the boy bent, tapping the cylinder with a spanner, lightly, his head turned with listening delicate and deliberate as a watchmaker. The boat rushed on in those furious, slewing turns. Bogard saw a long, drooping thread loop down from somebody's mouth, between his hands, and he found that the thread came from his own mouth.

He didn't hear the boy speak, nor notice when he stood up. He just felt the boat straighten out, flinging him to his knees beside the tube. The seaman had gone back to the stern and the boy stooped again over his gadget. Bogard knelt now, quite sick. He did not feel the boat when it swung again, nor hear the gun from the cruiser which had not dared to fire and the freighter which had not been able to fire, firing again. He did not feel anything at all when he saw the huge, painted flag directly ahead and increasing with locomotive speed, and Ronnie's lifted hand drop. But this time he knew that the torpedo was gone; in pivoting and spinning this time the whole boat seemed to leave the water; he saw the bow of the boat shoot skyward like the nose of a pursuit ship going into a wingover. Then his outraged stomach denied him. He saw neither the geyser nor heard the detonation as he sprawled over the tube. He felt only a hand grasp him by the slack of his coat, and the voice of one of the seamen: "Steady all, sir. I've got you."

## VIII

A VOICE roused him, a hand. He was half sitting in the narrow starboard runway, half lying across the tube. He had been there for quite a while; quite a while ago he had felt someone spread a garment over him. But he had not raised his head. "I'm all right," he had said. "You keep it."

"Don't need it," the boy said. "Going home now."

"I'm sorry I—" Bogard said.

"Quite. Confounded shallow boats. Turn any stomach until you get used to them. Ronnie and I both, at first. Each time. You wouldn't believe it. Believe human stomach hold so much. Here." It was the bottle. "Good drink. Take enormous one. Good for stomach."

Bogard drank. Soon he did feel better, warmer. When the hand touched him later, he found that he had been asleep.

It was the boy again. The pea-coat was too small for him; shrunken, perhaps. Below the cuffs his long, slender, girl's wrists were blue with cold. Then Bogard realized what the garment was that had been laid over him. But before Bogard could speak, the boy leaned down, whispering; his face was gleeful: "He didn't notice!"

"What?"

"Ergenstrasse! He didn't notice that they had shifted her. Gad, I'd be just one down, then." He watched Bogard's face with bright, eager eyes. "Beaver, you know. I say. Feeling better, eh?"

"Yes," Bogard said, "I am."

"He didn't notice at all. Oh, gad! Oh, Jove!"

Bogard rose and sat on the tube. The entrance to the harbor was just ahead; the boat had slowed a little. It was just dusk. He said quietly: "Does this often happen?" The boy looked at him. Bogard touched the tube. "This. Failing to go out."

"Oh, yes. Why they put the windlass on them. That was later. Made first boat; whole thing blew up one day. So put on windlass."

"But it happens sometimes, even now? I mean, sometimes they blow up, even with the windlass?"

"Well, can't say, of course. Boats go out. Not come back. Possible. Not ever know, of course. Not heard of one captured yet, though. Possible. Not to us, though. Not yet."

"Yes," Bogard said. "Yes." They entered the harbor, the boat moving still fast, but throttled now and smooth, across the dusk-filled basin. Again the boy leaned down, his voice gleeful.

"Not a word, now!" he hissed. "Steady all!" He stood up; he raised his voice: "I say, Ronnie." Ronnie did not turn his head, but Bogard could tell that he was listening. "That Argentine ship was amusing, eh? In there. How do you suppose it got past us here? Might have stopped here as well. French would buy the wheat." He paused, diabolical—Machiavelli with the face of a strayed angel. "I say. How long has it been since we had a strange ship in here? Been months, eh?" Again he leaned, hissing. "Watch, now!" But Bogard could not see Ronnie's head move at all. "He's looking, though!" the boy whispered, breathed. And Ronnie was looking, though his head had not moved at all. Then there came into view, in silhouette against the dusk-filled sky, the vague, basket-like shape of the interned vessel's foremast. At once Ronnie's arm rose, pointing; again he spoke without turning his head, out of the side of his mouth, past the cold, clamped pipe, a single word:

"Beaver."

The boy moved like a released spring, like a heeled dog freed. "Oh, damn you!" he cried. "Oh, you putt! It's the Ergenstrasse! Oh, confound you! I'm just one down now!" He had stepped in one stride completely over Bogard, and he now leaned down over Ronnie. "What?" The boat was slowing in toward the wharf, the engine idle. "Aren't I, Ronnie? Just one down now?"

The boat drifted in; the seaman had again crawled forward onto the deck. Ronnie spoke for the third and last time. 'Right," he said.

## IX

"I want," Bogard said, "a case of Scotch. The best we've got. And fix it up good. It's to go to town. And I want a responsible man to deliver it." The responsible man came. "This is for a child," Bogard said, indicating the package. "You'll find him in the Street of the Twelve Hours, somewhere near the Café Twelve Hours. He'll be in the gutter. You'll know him. A child about six feet long. Any English M. P. will show him to you. If he is asleep, don't wake him. Just sit there and wait until he wakes up. Then give him this. Tell him it is from Captain Bogard."

## X

ABOUT a month later a copy of the English Gazette which had strayed onto an American aerodrome carried the following item in the casualty lists:

Missing: Torpedo Boat XOOI. Midshipmen R. Boyce Smith and L. C. W. Hope, R. N. R., Boatswain's Mate Burt and Able Seaman Reeves, Channel Fleet, Light Torpedo Division. Failed to return from coast patrol duty.

Shortly after that the American Air Service headquarters also issued a bulletin:

For extraordinary valor over and beyond the routine of duty, Captain H. S. Bogard, with his crew, composed of Second Lieutenant Darrel McGinnis and Aviation Gunners Watts and Harper, on a daylight raid and without scout protection, destroyed with bombs an ammunition depot several

miles behind the enemy's lines. From here, beset by enemy
aircraft in superior numbers, these men proceeded with
what bombs remained to the enemy's corps headquarters at
Blank and partially demolished this château, and then returned safely without loss of a man.

And regarding which exploit, it might have added, had it
failed and had Captain Bogard come out of it alive, he would
have been immediately and thoroughly court-martialed.

Carrying his remaining two bombs, he had dived the
Handley-Page at the château where the generals sat at lunch,
until McGinnis, at the toggles below him, began to shout at
him, before he ever signaled. He didn't signal until he could
discern separately the slate tiles of the roof. Then his hand
dropped and he zoomed, and he held the aeroplane so, in its
wild snarl, his lips parted, his breath hissing, thinking: "God!
God! If they were all there—all the generals, the admirals,
the presidents and the kings—theirs, ours—all of them."

# THE OLD DEMON
### by Pearl S. Buck

OLD Mrs. Wang knew of course that there was a war. Everybody had known for a long time that there was war going on and that Japanese were killing Chinese. But still it was not real and no more than hearsay since none of the Wangs had been killed. The Village of Three Mile Wangs on the flat banks of the Yellow River, which was old Mrs. Wang's clan village, had never even seen a Japanese. This was how they came to be talking about Japanese at all.

It was evening and early summer, and after her supper Mrs. Wang had climbed the dike steps, as she did every day, to see how high the river had risen. She was much more afraid of the river than of the Japanese. She knew what the river would do. And one by one the villagers had followed her up the dike, and now they stood staring down at the malicious yellow water, curling along like a lot of snakes, and biting at the high dike banks.

"I never saw it as high as this so early," Mrs. Wang said. She sat down on a bamboo stool that her grandson, Little Pig, had brought for her, and spat into the water.

"It's worse than the Japanese, this old devil of a river," Little Pig said recklessly.

"Fool!" Mrs. Wang said quickly. "The river god will hear you. Talk about something else."

So they had gone on talking about the Japanese. . . . How, for instance, asked Wang, the baker, who was old Mrs. Wang's nephew twice removed, would they know the Japanese when they saw them?

Mrs. Wang at this point said positively, "You'll know them. I once saw a foreigner. He was taller than the eaves of my house and he had mud-colored hair and eyes the color of a fish's eyes. Anyone who does not look like us—that is a Japanese."

Everybody listened to her since she was the oldest woman in the village and whatever she said settled something.

Then Little Pig spoke up in his disconcerting way. "You can't see them, Grandmother. They hide up in the sky in airplanes."

Mrs. Wang did not answer immediately. Once she would have said positively, "I shall not believe in an airplane until I see it." But so many things had been true which she had not believed—the Empress, for instance, whom she had not believed dead, was dead. The Republic, again, she had not believed in because she did not know what it was. She still did not know, but they had said for a long time there had been one. So now she merely stared quietly about the dike where they all sat around her. It was very pleasant and cool, and she felt nothing mattered if the river did not rise to flood.

"I don't believe in the Japanese," she said flatly.

They laughed at her a little, but no one spoke. Someone lit her pipe—it was Little Pig's wife, who was her favorite, and she smoked it.

"Sing, Little Pig!" someone called.

So Little Pig began to sing an old song in a high, quavering voice, and old Mrs. Wang listened and forgot the Japanese. The evening was beautiful, the sky so clear and still that the willows overhanging the dike were reflected even in the muddy water. Everything was at peace. The thirty-odd houses which made up the village straggled along beneath them. Nothing could break this peace. After all, the Japanese were only human beings.

"I doubt those airplanes," she said mildly to Little Pig when he stopped singing.

But without answering her, he went on to another song.

Year in and year out she had spent the summer evenings

like this on the dike. The first time she was seventeen and a bride, and her husband had shouted to her to come out of the house and up the dike, and she had come, blushing and twisting her hands together, to hide among the women while the men roared at her and made jokes about her. All the same, they had liked her. "A pretty piece of meat in your bowl," they had said to her husband. "Feet a trifle big," he had answered deprecatingly. But she could see he was pleased, and so gradually her shyness went away.

He, poor man, had been drowned in a flood when he was still young. And it had taken her years to get him prayed out of Buddhist purgatory. Finally she had grown tired of it, what with the child and the land all on her back, and so when the priest said coaxingly, "Another ten pieces of silver and he'll be out entirely," she asked, "What's he got in there yet?"

"Only his right hand," the priest said, encouraging her.

Well, then, her patience broke. Ten dollars! It would feed them for the winter. Besides, she had had to hire labor for her share of repairing the dike, too, so there would be no more floods.

"If it's only one hand, he can pull himself out," she said firmly.

She often wondered if he had, poor silly fellow. As like as not, she had often thought gloomily in the night, he was still lying there, waiting for her to do something about it. That was the sort of man he was. Well, some day, perhaps, when Little Pig's wife had had the first baby safely and she had a little extra, she might go back to finish him out of purgatory. There was no real hurry, though. . . .

"Grandmother, you must go in," Little Pig's wife's soft voice said. "There is a mist rising from the river now that the sun is gone."

"Yes, I suppose I must," old Mrs. Wang agreed. She gazed at the river a moment. That river—it was full of good and evil together. It would water the fields when it was curbed and checked, but then if an inch were allowed it, it

crashed through like a roaring dragon. That was how her
husband had been swept away—careless, he was, about his
bit of the dike. He was always going to mend it, always
going to pile more earth on top of it, and then in a night the
river rose and broke through. He had run out of the house,
and she had climbed on the roof with the child and had saved
herself and it while he was drowned. Well, they had pushed
the river back again behind its dikes, and it had stayed there
this time. Every day she herself walked up and down the
length of the dike for which the village was responsible and
examined it. The men laughed and said, "If anything is
wrong with the dikes, Granny will tell us."

It had never occurred to any of them to move the village
away from the river. The Wangs had lived there for generations, and some had always escaped the floods and had
fought the river more fiercely than ever afterward.

Little Pig suddenly stopped singing.

"The moon is coming up!" he cried. "That's not good.
Airplanes come out on moonlight nights."

"Where do you learn all this about airplanes?" old Mrs.
Wang exclaimed. "It is tiresome to me," she added, so
severely that no one spoke. In this silence, leaning upon the
arm of Little Pig's wife, she descended slowly the earthen
steps which led down into the village, using her long pipe in
the other hand as a walking stick. Behind her the villagers
came down, one by one, to bed. No one moved before she did,
but none stayed long after her.

And in her own bed at last, behind the blue cotton mosquito
curtains which Little Pig's wife fastened securely, she fell
peacefully asleep. She had lain awake a little while thinking
about the Japanese and wondering why they wanted to fight.
Only very coarse persons wanted wars. In her mind she saw
large coarse persons. If they came one must wheedle them,
she thought, invite them to drink tea, and explain to them,
reasonably—only why should they come to a peaceful farm-
ing village . . . ?

So she was not in the least prepared for Little Pig's wife screaming at her that the Japanese had come. She sat up in bed muttering, "The tea bowls—the tea—"

"Grandmother, there's no time!" Little Pig's wife screamed. "They're here—they're here!"

"Where?" old Mrs. Wang cried, now awake.

"In the sky!" Little Pig's wife wailed.

They had all run out at that, into the clear early dawn, and gazed up. There, like wild geese flying in autumn, were great birdlike shapes.

"But what are they?" old Mrs. Wang cried.

And then, like a silver egg dropping, something drifted straight down and fell at the far end of the village in a field. A fountain of earth flew up, and they all ran to see it. There was a hole thirty feet across, as big as a pond. They were so astonished they could not speak, and then, before anyone could say anything, another and another egg began to fall and everybody was running, running . . .

Everybody, that is, but Mrs. Wang. When Little Pig's wife seized her hand to drag her along, old Mrs. Wang pulled away and sat down against the bank of the dike.

"I can't run," she remarked. "I haven't run in seventy years, since before my feet were bound. You go on. Where's Little Pig?" She looked around. Little Pig was already gone. "Like his grandfather," she remarked, "always the first to run."

But Little Pig's wife would not leave her, not, that is, until old Mrs. Wang reminded her that it was her duty.

"If Little Pig is dead," she said, "then it is necessary that his son be born alive." And when the girl still hesitated, she struck at her gently with her pipe. "Go on—go on," she exclaimed.

So unwillingly, because now they could scarcely hear each other speak for the roar of the dipping planes, Little Pig's wife went on with the others.

By now, although only a few minutes had passed, the village was in ruins and the straw roofs and wooden beams were blazing. Everybody was gone. As they passed they had shrieked at old Mrs. Wang to come on, and she had called back pleasantly:

"I'm coming—I'm coming!"

But she did not go. She sat quite alone watching now what was an extraordinary spectacle. For soon other planes came, from where she did not know, but they attacked the first ones. The sun came up over the fields of ripening wheat, and in the clear summery air the planes wheeled and darted and spat at each other. When this was over, she thought, she would go back into the village and see if anything was left. Here and there a wall stood, supporting a roof. She could not see her own house from here. But she was not unused to war. Once bandits had looted their village, and houses had been burned then, too. Well, now it had happened again. Burning houses one could see often, but not this darting silvery shining battle in the air. She understood none of it—not what those things were, nor how they stayed up in the sky. She simply sat, growing hungry, and watching.

"I'd like to see one close," she said aloud. And at that moment, as though in answer, one of them pointed suddenly downward, and, wheeling and twisting as though it were wounded, it fell head down in a field which Little Pig had ploughed only yesterday for soybeans. And in an instant the sky was empty again, and there was only this wounded thing on the ground and herself.

She hoisted herself carefully from the earth. At her age she need be afraid of nothing. She could, she decided, go and see what it was. So, leaning on her bamboo pipe, she made her way slowly across the fields. Behind her in the sudden stillness two or three village dogs appeared and followed, creeping close to her in their terror. When they drew near to the fallen plane, they barked furiously. Then she hit them with her pipe.

"Be quiet," she scolded, "there's already been noise enough to split my ears!"

She tapped the airplane.

"Metal," she told the dogs. "Silver, doubtless," she added. Melted up, it would make them all rich.

She walked around it, examining it closely. What made it fly? It seemed dead. Nothing moved or made a sound within it. Then, coming to the side to which it tipped, she saw a young man in it, slumped into a heap in a little seat. The dogs growled, but she struck at them again and they fell back.

"Are you dead?" she inquired politely.

The young man moved a little at her voice, but did not speak. She drew nearer and peered into the hole in which he sat. His side was bleeding.

"Wounded!" she exclaimed. She took his wrist. It was warm, but inert, and when she let it go, it dropped against the side of the hole. She stared at him. He had black hair and a dark skin like a Chinese and still he did not look like a Chinese.

"He must be a Southerner," she thought. Well, the chief thing was, he was alive.

"You had better come out," she remarked. "I'll put some herb plaster on your side."

The young man muttered something dully.

"What did you say?" she asked. But he did not say it again.

"I am still quite strong," she decided after a moment. So she reached in and seized him about the waist and pulled him out slowly, panting a good deal. Fortunately he was rather a little fellow and very light. When she had him on the ground, he seemed to find his feet; and he stood shakily and clung to her, and she held him up.

"Now if you can walk to my house," she said, "I'll see if it is there."

Then he said something, quite clearly. She listened and

could not understand a word of it. She pulled away from him and stared.

"What's that?" she asked.

He pointed at the dogs. They were standing growling, their ruffs up. Then he spoke again, and as he spoke he crumpled to the ground. The dogs fell on him, so that she had to beat them off with her hands.

"Get away!" she shouted. "Who told *you* to kill him?"

And then, when they had slunk back, she heaved him somehow onto her back; and, trembling, half carrying, half pulling, she dragged him to the ruined village and laid him in the street while she went to find her house, taking the dogs with her.

Her house was quite gone. She found the place easily enough. This was where it should be, opposite the water gate into the dike. She had always watched that gate herself. Miraculously it was not injured now, nor was the dike broken. It would be easy enough to rebuild the house. Only, for the present, it was gone.

So she went back to the young man. He was lying as she had left him, propped against the dike, panting and very pale. He had opened his coat and he had a little bag from which he was taking out strips of cloth and a bottle of something. And again he spoke, and again she understood nothing. Then he made signs and she saw it was water he wanted, so she took up a broken pot from one of many blown about the street, and, going up the dike, she filled it with river water and brought it down again and washed his wound, and she tore off the strips he made from the rolls of bandaging. He knew how to put the cloth over the gaping wound and he made signs to her, and she followed these signs. All the time he was trying to tell her something, but she could understand nothing.

"You must be from the South, sir," she said. It was easy to see that he had education. He looked very clever. "I have heard your language is different from ours." She laughed a little to put him at his ease, but he only stared at her somberly with dull eyes. So she said brightly, "Now if I could find something for us to eat, it would be nice."

He did not answer. Indeed he lay back, panting still more heavily, and stared into space as though she had not spoken.

"You would be better with food," she went on. "And so would I," she added. She was beginning to feel unbearably hungry.

It occurred to her that in Wang, the baker's, shop there might be some bread. Even if it were dusty with fallen mortar, it would still be bread. She would go and see. But before she went she moved the soldier a little so that he lay in the edge of shadow cast by a willow tree that grew in the bank of the dike. Then she went to the baker's shop. The dogs were gone.

The baker's shop was, like everything else, in ruins. No one was there. At first she saw nothing but the mass of crumpled earthen walls. But then she remembered that the oven was just inside the door, and the door frame still stood erect, supporting one end of the roof. She stood in this frame, and, running her hand in underneath the fallen roof inside, she felt the wooden cover of the iron caldron. Under this there might be steamed bread. She worked her arm delicately and carefully in. It took quite a long time, but, even so, clouds of lime and dust almost choked her. Nevertheless she was right. She squeezed her hand under the cover and felt the firm smooth skin of the big steamed bread rolls, and one by one she drew out four.

"It's hard to kill an old thing like me," she remarked cheerfully to no one, and she began to eat one of the rolls as she walked back. If she had a bit of garlic and a bowl of tea—but one couldn't have everything in these times.

It was at this moment that she heard voices. When she came in sight of the soldier, she saw surrounding him a crowd of other soldiers, who had apparently come from nowhere. They were staring down at the wounded soldier, whose eyes were now closed.

"Where did you get this Japanese, Old Mother?" they shouted at her.

"What Japanese?" she asked, coming to them.

"This one!" they shouted.

"Is he a Japanese?" she cried in the greatest astonishment. "But he looks like us—his eyes are black, his skin—"

"Japanese!" one of them shouted at her.

"Well," she said quietly, "he dropped out of the sky."

"Give me that bread!" another shouted.

"Take it," she said, "all except this one for him."

"A Japanese monkey eat good bread?" the soldier shouted.

"I suppose he is hungry also," old Mrs. Wang replied. She began to dislike these men. But then, she had always disliked soldiers.

"I wish you would go away," she said. "What are you doing here? Our village has always been peaceful."

"It certainly looks very peaceful now," one of the men said, grinning, "as peaceful as a grave. Do you know who did that, Old Mother? The Japanese!"

"I suppose so," she agreed. Then she asked, "Why? That's what I don't understand."

"Why? Because they want our land, that's why!"

"Our land!" she repeated. "Why, they can't have our land!"

"Never!" they shouted.

But all this time while they were talking and chewing the bread they had divided among themselves, they were watching the eastern horizon.

"Why do you keep looking east?" old Mrs. Wang now asked.

"The Japanese are coming from there," the man replied who had taken the bread.

"Are you running away from them?" she asked, surprised.

"There are only a handful of us," he said apologetically.

"We were left to guard a village—Pao An, in the county of—"

"I know that village," old Mrs. Wang interrupted. "You needn't tell me. I was a girl there. How is the old Pao who keeps the teashop in the main street? He's my brother."

"Everybody is dead there," the man replied. "The Japanese have taken it—a great army of men came with their foreign guns and tanks, so what could we do?"

"Of course, only run," she agreed. Nevertheless she felt dazed and sick. So he was dead, that one brother she had left! She was now the last of her father's family.

But the soldiers were straggling away again leaving her alone.

"They'll be coming, those little black dwarfs," they were saying. "We'd best go on."

Nevertheless, one lingered a moment, the one who had taken the bread, to stare down at the young wounded man, who lay with his eyes shut, not having moved at all.

"Is he dead?" he inquired. Then, before Mrs. Wang could answer, he pulled a short knife out of his belt. "Dead or not, I'll give him a punch or two with this—"

But old Mrs. Wang pushed his arm away.

"No, you won't," she said with authority. "If he is dead, then there is no use in sending him into purgatory all in pieces. I am a good Buddhist myself."

The man laughed. "Oh well, he is dead," he answered; and then, seeing his comrades already at a distance, he ran after them.

A Japanese, was he? Old Mrs. Wang, left alone with this inert figure, looked at him tentatively. He was very young, she could see, now that his eyes were closed. His hand, limp in unconsciousness, looked like a boy's hand, unformed and still growing. She felt his wrist but could discern no pulse. She leaned over him and held to his lips the half of her roll which she had not eaten.

"Eat," she said very loudly and distinctly. "Bread!"

But there was no answer. Evidently he was dead. He must have died while she was getting the bread out of the oven.

There was nothing to do then but to finish the bread herself. And when that was done, she wondered if she ought not to follow after Little Pig and his wife and all the villagers. The sun was mounting and it was growing hot. If she were going, she had better go. But first she would climb the dike and see what the direction was. They had gone straight west, and as far as eye could look westward was a great plain. She might even see a good-sized crowd miles away. Anyway, she could see the next village, and they might all be there.

So she climbed the dike slowly, getting very hot. There was a slight breeze on top of the dike and it felt good. She was shocked to see the river very near the top of the dike. Why, it had risen in the last hour!

"You old demon!" she said severely. Let the river god hear it if he liked. He was evil, that he was—so to threaten flood when there had been all this other trouble.

She stooped and bathed her cheeks and her wrists. The water was quite cold, as though with fresh rains somewhere. Then she stood up and gazed around her. To the west there was nothing except in the far distance the soldiers still half-running, and beyond them the blur of the next village, which stood on a long rise of ground. She had better set out for that village. Doubtless Little Pig and his wife were there waiting for her.

Just as she was about to climb down and start out, she saw something on the eastern horizon. It was at first only an immense cloud of dust. But, as she stared at it, very quickly it became a lot of black dots and shining spots. Then she saw what it was. It was a lot of men—an army. Instantly she knew what army.

"That's the Japanese," she thought. Yes, above them were the buzzing silver planes. They circled about, seeming to search for someone.

"I don't know who you're looking for," she muttered,

"unless it's me and Little Pig and his wife. We're the only ones left. You've already killed my brother Pao."

She had almost forgotten that Pao was dead. Now she remembered it acutely. He had such a nice shop—always clean, and the tea good and the best meat dumplings to be had and the price always the same. Pao was a good man. Besides, what about his wife and his seven children? Doubtless they were all killed, too. Now these Japanese were looking for her. It occurred to her that on the dike she could easily be seen. So she clambered hastily down.

It was when she was about half way down that she thought of the water gate. This old river—it had been a curse to them since time began. Why should it not make up a little now for all the wickedness it had done? It was plotting wickedness again, trying to steal over its banks. Well, why not? She wavered a moment. It was a pity, of course, that the young dead Japanese would be swept into the flood. He was a nice-looking boy, and she had saved him from being stabbed. It was not quite the same as saving his life, of course, but still it was a little the same. If he had been alive, he would have been saved. She went over to him and tugged at him until he lay well near the top of the bank. Then she went down again.

She knew perfectly how to open the water gate. Any child knew how to open the sluice for crops. But she knew also how to swing open the whole gate. The question was, could she open it quickly enough to get out of the way?

"I'm only one old woman," she muttered. She hesitated a second more. Well, it would be a pity not to see what sort of a baby Little Pig's wife would have, but one could not see everything. She had seen a great deal in this life. There was an end to what one could see, anyway.

She glanced again to the east. There were the Japanese coming across the plain. They were a long clear line of black, dotted with thousands of glittering points. If she opened this gate, the impetuous water would roar toward them, rushing into the plains, rolling into a wide lake, drowning them, maybe. Certainly they could not keep on marching nearer and nearer to her and to Little Pig and his wife who were waiting for her. Well, Little Pig and his wife—they would wonder about her—but they would never dream of this. It would make a good story—she would have enjoyed telling it.

She turned resolutely to the gate. Well, some people fought with airplanes and some with guns, but you could fight with a river, too, if it were a wicked one like this one. She wrenched out a huge wooden pin. It was slippery with silvery green moss. The rill of water burst into a strong jet. When she wrenched one more pin, the rest would give way themselves. She began pulling at it, and felt it slip a little from its hole.

"I might be able to get myself out of purgatory with this," she thought, "and maybe they'll let me have that old man of mine, too. What's a hand of his to all this? Then we'll—"

The pin slipped away suddenly, and the gate burst flat against her and knocked her breath away. She had only time to gasp, to the river:

"Come on, you old demon!"

Then she felt it seize her and lift her up to the sky. It was beneath her and around her. It rolled her joyfully hither and thither, and then, holding her close and enfolded, it went rushing against the enemy.

# THE RED PONY
*by John Steinbeck*

### I. THE GIFT

AT DAYBREAK Billy Buck emerged from the bunkhouse and stood for a moment on the porch looking up at the sky. He was a broad, bandy-legged little man with a walrus mustache, with square hands, puffed and muscled on the palms. His eyes were a contemplative, watery gray and the hair which protruded from under his Stetson hat was spiky and weathered. Billy was still stuffing his shirt into his blue jeans as he stood on the porch. He unbuckled his belt and tightened it again. The belt showed, by the worn shiny places opposite each hole, the gradual increase of Billy's middle over a period of years. When he had seen to the weather, Billy cleared each nostril by holding its mate closed with his forefinger and blowing fiercely. Then he walked down to the barn, rubbing his hands together. He curried and brushed two saddle horses in the stalls, talking quietly to them all the time; and he had hardly finished when the iron triangle started ringing at the ranch house. Billy stuck the brush and currycomb together and laid them on the rail, and went up to breakfast. His action had been so deliberate and yet so wasteless of time that he came to the house while Mrs. Tiflin was still ringing the triangle. She nodded her gray head to him and withdrew into the kitchen. Billy Buck sat down on the steps, because he was a cow-hand, and it wouldn't be fitting that he should go first into the dining room. He heard Mr. Tiflin in the house, stamping his feet into his boots.

The high jangling note of the triangle put the boy Jody in motion. He was only a little boy, ten years old, with hair like dusty yellow grass and with shy polite gray eyes, and with a mouth that worked when he thought. The triangle picked him up out of sleep. It didn't occur to him to disobey the harsh note. He never had: no one he knew ever had. He brushed the tangled hair out of his eyes and skinned his nightgown off. In a moment he was dressed—blue chambray shirt and overalls. It was late in the summer, so of course there were no shoes to bother with. In the kitchen he waited until his mother got from in front of the sink and went back to the stove. Then he washed himself and brushed back his wet hair with his fingers. His mother turned sharply on him as he left the sink. Jody looked shyly away.

"I've got to cut your hair before long," his mother said. "Breakfast's on the table. Go on in, so Billy can come."

Jody sat at the long table which was covered with white oilcloth washed through to the fabric in some places. The fried eggs lay in rows on their platter. Jody took three eggs on his plate and followed with three thick slices of crisp bacon. He carefully scraped a spot of blood from one of the egg yolks.

Billy Buck clumped in. "That won't hurt you," Billy explained. "That's only a sign the rooster leaves."

Jody's tall stern father came in then and Jody knew from the noise on the floor that he was wearing boots, but he looked under the table anyway, to make sure. His father turned off the oil lamp over the table, for plenty of morning light now came through the windows.

Jody did not ask where his father and Billy Buck were riding that day, but he wished he might go along. His father was a disciplinarian. Jody obeyed him in everything without questions of any kind. Now, Carl Tiflin sat down and reached for the egg platter.

"Got the cows ready to go, Billy?" he asked.

"In the lower corral," Billy said. "I could just as well take them in alone."

"Sure you could. But a man needs company. Besides your throat gets pretty dry." Carl Tiflin was jovial this morning.

Jody's mother put her head in the door. "What time do you think to be back, Carl?"

"I can't tell. I've got to see some men in Salinas. Might be gone till dark."

The eggs and coffee and big biscuits disappeared rapidly. Jody followed the two men out of the house. He watched them mount their horses and drive six old milk cows out of the corral and start over the hill toward Salinas. They were going to sell the old cows to the butcher.

When they had disappeared over the crown of the ridge Jody walked up the hill in back of the house. The dogs trotted around the house corner hunching their shoulders and grinning horribly with pleasure. Jody patted their heads—Doubletree Mutt with the big thick tail and yellow eyes, and Smasher, the shepherd, who had killed a coyote and lost an ear in doing it. Smasher's one good ear stood up higher than a collie's ear should. Billy Buck said that always happened. After the frenzied greeting the dogs lowered their noses to the ground in a businesslike way and went ahead, looking back now and then to make sure that the boy was coming. They walked up through the chicken yard and saw the quail eating with the chickens. Smasher chased the chickens a little to keep in practice in case there should ever be sheep to herd. Jody continued on through the large vegetable patch where the green corn was higher than his head. The cow-pumpkins were green and small yet. He went on to the sagebrush line where the cold spring ran out of its pipe and fell into a round wooden tub. He leaned over and drank close to the green mossy wood where the water tasted best. Then he turned and looked back on the ranch, on the low, whitewashed house girded with red geraniums, and on the long bunkhouse by the cypress tree where Billy Buck lived alone. Jody could see the great black kettle under the cypress tree. That was where the pigs were scalded. The sun was coming over the ridge now, glaring on the whitewash of the houses and barns, making the wet grass blaze softly. Behind him, in the tall sagebrush, the birds were scampering on the ground, making a great noise among the dry leaves; the squirrels piped shrilly on the side-hills. Jody looked along at the far buildings. He felt an uncertainty in the air, a feeling of change and of loss and of the gain of new and unfamiliar things. Over the hillside two big black buzzards sailed low to the ground and their shadows slipped smoothly and quickly ahead of them. Some animal had died in the vicinity. Jody knew it. It might be a cow or it might be the remains of a rabbit. The buzzards overlooked nothing. Jody hated them as all decent things hate them, but they could not be hurt because they made away with carrion.

After a while the boy sauntered down hill again. The dogs had long ago given him up and gone into the brush to do things in their own way. Back through the vegetable garden he went, and he paused for a moment to smash a green muskmelon with his heel, but he was not happy about it. It was a bad thing to do, he knew perfectly well. He kicked dirt over the ruined melon to conceal it.

Back at the house his mother bent over his rough hands, inspecting his fingers and nails. It did little good to start him clean to school, for too many things could happen on the way. She sighed over the black cracks on his fingers, and then gave him his books and his lunch and started him on the mile walk to school. She noticed that his mouth was working a good deal this morning.

Jody started his journey. He filled his pockets with little pieces of white quartz that lay in the road, and every so often he took a shot at a bird or at some rabbit that had stayed sunning itself in the road too long. At the crossroads over the bridge he met two friends and the three of them walked to school together, making ridiculous strides and being rather silly. School had just opened two weeks before. There was still a spirit of revolt among the pupils.

It was four o'clock in the afternoon when Jody topped the hill and looked down on the ranch again. He looked for the saddle horses, but the corral was empty. His father was not back yet. He went slowly, then, toward the afternoon chores. At the ranch house, he found his mother sitting on the porch, mending socks.

"There's two doughnuts in the kitchen for you," she said. Jody slid to the kitchen, and returned with half of one of the doughnuts already eaten and his mouth full. His mother asked him what he had learned in school that day, but she didn't listen to his doughnut-muffled answer. She interrupted, "Jody, tonight see you fill the wood-box clear full. Last night you crossed the sticks and it wasn't only about half full. Lay the sticks flat tonight. And Jody, some of the hens are hiding eggs, or else the dogs are eating them. Look about in the grass and see if you can find any nests."

Jody, still eating, went out and did his chores. He saw the quail come down to eat with the chickens when he threw out the grain. For some reason his father was proud to have them come. He never allowed any shooting near the house for fear the quail might go away.

When the wood-box was full, Jody took his twenty-two rifle up to the cold spring at the brush line. He drank again and then aimed the gun at all manner of things, at rocks, at birds on the wing, at the big black pig kettle under the cypress tree, but he didn't shoot, for he had no cartridges and wouldn't have until he was twelve. If his father had seen him aim the rifle in the direction of the house he would have put the cartridges off another year. Jody remembered this and did not point the rifle down the hill again. Two years was enough to wait for cartridges. Nearly all of his father's presents were given with reservations which hampered their value somewhat. It was good discipline.

The supper waited until dark for his father to return. When at last he came in with Billy Buck, Jody could smell the delicious brandy on their breaths. Inwardly he rejoiced, for his father sometimes talked to him when he smelled of brandy, sometimes even told things he had done in the wild days when he was a boy.

After supper, Jody sat by the fireplace and his shy polite eyes sought the room corners, and he waited for his father to tell what it was he contained, for Jody knew he had news of some sort. But he was disappointed. His father pointed a stern finger at him.

"You'd better go to bed, Jody. I'm going to need you in the morning."

That wasn't so bad. Jody liked to do things he had to do as long as they weren't routine things. He looked at the floor and his mouth worked out a question before he spoke it. "What are we going to do in the morning, kill a pig?" he asked softly.

"Never you mind. You better get to bed."

When the door was closed behind him, Jody heard his father and Billy Buck chuckling and he knew it was a joke of some kind. And later, when he lay in bed, trying to make words out of the murmurs in the other room, he heard his father protest, "But, Ruth, I didn't give much for him."

Jody heard the hoot-owls hunting mice down by the barn, and he heard a fruit tree limb tap-tapping against the house. A cow was lowing when he went to sleep.

When the triangle sounded in the morning, Jody dressed more quickly even than usual. In the kitchen, while he washed his face and combed back his hair, his mother addressed him irritably. "Don't you go out until you get a good breakfast in you."

He went into the dining room and sat at the long white table. He took a steaming hotcake from the platter, arranged two fried eggs on it, covered them with another hotcake and squashed the whole thing with his fork.

His father and Billy Buck came in. Jody knew from the sound on the floor that both of them were wearing flat-heeled

shoes, but he peered under the table to make sure. His father
turned off the oil lamp, for the day had arrived, and he looked
stern and disciplinary, but Billy Buck didn't look at Jody
at all. He avoided the shy questioning eyes of the boy and
soaked a whole piece of toast in his coffee.

Carl Tiflin said crossly, "You come with us after breakfast!"

Jody had trouble with his food then, for he felt a kind of
doom in the air. After Billy had tilted his saucer and drained
the coffee which had slopped into it, and had wiped his hands
on his jeans, the two men stood up from the table and went
out into the morning light together, and Jody respectfully
followed a little behind them. He tried to keep his mind
from running ahead, tried to keep it absolutely motionless.

His mother called, "Carl! Don't you let it keep him from
school."

They marched past the cypress, where a singletree hung
from a limb to butcher the pigs on, and past the black iron
kettle, so it was not a pig killing. The sun shone over the hill
and threw long, dark shadows of the trees and buildings.
They crossed a stubble-field to shortcut to the barn. Jody's
father unhooked the door and they went in. They had been
walking toward the sun on the way down. The barn was
black as night in contrast and warm from the hay and from
the beasts. Jody's father moved over toward the one box
stall. "Come here!" he ordered. Jody could begin to see
things now. He looked into the box stall and then stepped
back quickly.

A red pony colt was looking at him out of the stall. Its
tense ears were forward and a light of disobedience was in
its eyes. Its coat was rough and thick as an airedale's fur
and its mane was long and tangled. Jody's throat collapsed
in on itself and cut his breath short.

"He needs a good currying," his father said, "and if I ever
hear of you not feeding him or leaving his stall dirty, I'll
sell him off in a minute."

Jody couldn't bear to look at the pony's eyes any more. He gazed down at his hands for a moment, and he asked very shyly, "Mine?" No one answered him. He put his hand out toward the pony. Its gray nose came close, sniffing loudly, and then the lips drew back and the strong teeth closed on Jody's fingers. The pony shook its head up and down and seemed to laugh with amusement. Jody regarded his bruised fingers. "Well," he said with pride—"Well, I guess he can bite all right." The two men laughed, somewhat in relief. Carl Tiflin went out of the barn and walked up a side-hill to be by himself, for he was embarrassed, but Billy Buck stayed. It was easier to talk to Billy Buck. Jody asked again —"Mine?"

Billy became professional in tone. "Sure! That is, if you look out for him and break him right. I'll show you how. He's just a colt. You can't ride him for some time."

Jody put out his bruised hand again, and this time the red pony let his nose be rubbed. "I ought to have a carrot," Jody said. "Where'd we get him, Billy?"

"Bought him at a sheriff's auction," Billy explained. "A show went broke in Salinas and had debts. The sheriff was selling off their stuff."

The pony stretched out his nose and shook the forelock from his wild eyes. Jody stroked the nose a little. He said softly, "There isn't a—saddle?"

Billy Buck laughed. "I'd forgot. Come along."

In the harness room he lifted down a little saddle of red morocco leather. "It's just a show saddle," Billy Buck said disparagingly. "It isn't practical for the brush, but it was cheap at the sale."

Jody couldn't trust himself to look at the saddle either, and he couldn't speak at all. He brushed the shining red leather with his fingertips, and after a long time he said, "It'll look pretty on him though." He thought of the grandest and prettiest things he knew. "If he hasn't a name already, I think I'll call him Gabilan Mountains," he said.

Billy Buck knew how he felt. "It's a pretty long name. Why don't you just call him Gabilan? That means hawk. That would be a fine name for him." Billy felt glad. "If you will collect tail hair, I might be able to make a hair rope for you sometime. You could use it for a hackamore."

Jody wanted to go back to the box stall. "Could I lead him to school, do you think—to show the kids?"

But Billy shook his head. "He's not even halter-broke yet. We had a time getting him here. Had to almost drag him. You better be starting for school though."

"I'll bring the kids to see him here this afternoon," Jody said.

Six boys came over the hill half an hour early that afternoon, running hard, their heads down, their forearms working, their breath whistling. They swept by the house and cut across the stubble-field to the barn. And then they stood self-consciously before the pony, and then they looked at Jody with eyes in which there was a new admiration and a new respect. Before today Jody had been a boy, dressed in overalls and a blue shirt—quieter than most, even suspected of being a little cowardly. And now he was different. Out of a thousand centuries they drew the ancient admiration of the footman for the horseman. They knew instinctively that a man on a horse is spiritually as well as physically bigger than a man on foot. They knew that Jody had been miraculously lifted out of equality with them, and had been placed over them. Gabilan put his head out of the stall and sniffed them.

"Why'n't you ride him?" the boys cried. "Why'n't you braid his tail with ribbons like in the fair?" "When you going to ride him?"

Jody's courage was up. He too felt the superiority of the horseman. "He's not old enough. Nobody can ride him for a long time. I'm going to train him on the long halter. Billy Buck is going to show me how."

"Well, can't we even lead him around a little?"

"He isn't even halter-broke," Jody said. He wanted to be completely alone when he took the pony out the first time. "Come and see the saddle."

They were speechless at the red morocco saddle, completely shocked out of comment. "It isn't much use in the brush," Jody explained. "It'll look pretty on him though. Maybe I'll ride bareback when I go into the brush."

"How you going to rope a cow without a saddle horn?"

"Maybe I'll get another saddle for every day. My father might want me to help him with the stock." He let them feel the red saddle, and showed them the brass chain throat-latch on the bridle and the big brass buttons at each temple where the headstall and brow band crossed. The whole thing was too wonderful. They had to go away after a little while, and each boy, in his mind, searched among his possessions for a bribe worthy of offering in return for a ride on the red pony when the time should come.

Jody was glad when they had gone. He took brush and currycomb from the wall, took down the barrier of the box stall and stepped cautiously in. The pony's eyes glittered, and he edged around into kicking position. But Jody touched him on the shoulder and rubbed his high arched neck as he had always seen Billy Buck do, and he crooned, "So-o-o Boy," in a deep voice. The pony gradually relaxed his tenseness. Jody curried and brushed until a pile of dead hair lay in the stall and until the pony's coat had taken on a deep red shine. Each time he finished he thought it might have been done better. He braided the mane into a dozen little pigtails, and he braided the forelock, and then he undid them and brushed the hair out straight again.

Jody did not hear his mother enter the barn. She was angry when she came, but when she looked in at the pony and at Jody working over him, she felt a curious pride rise up in her. "Have you forgot the wood-box?" she asked gently.

"It's not far off from dark and there's not a stick of wood in the house, and the chickens aren't fed."

Jody quickly put up his tools. "I forgot, ma'am."

"Well, after this do your chores first. Then you won't forget. I expect you'll forget lots of things now if I don't keep an eye on you."

"Can I have carrots from the garden for him, ma'am?"

She had to think about that. "Oh—I guess so, if you only take the big tough ones."

"Carrots keep the coat good," he said, and again she felt the curious rush of pride.

Jody never waited for the triangle to get him out of bed after the coming of the pony. It became his habit to creep out of bed even before his mother was awake, to slip into his clothes and to go quietly down to the barn to see Gabilan. In the gray quiet mornings when the land and the brush and the houses and the trees were silver-gray and black like a photograph negative, he stole toward the barn, past the sleeping stones and the sleeping cypress tree. The turkeys, roosting in the tree out of coyotes' reach, clicked drowsily. The fields glowed with a gray frost-like light and in the dew the tracks of rabbits and of field mice stood out sharply. The good dogs came stiffly out of their little houses, hackles up and deep growls in their throats. Then they caught Jody's scent, and their stiff tails rose up and waved a greeting—Doubletree Mutt with the big thick tail, and Smasher, the incipient shepherd—then went lazily back to their warm beds.

It was a strange time and a mysterious journey, to Jody—an extension of a dream. When he first had the pony he liked to torture himself during the trip by thinking Gabilan would not be in his stall, and worse, would never have been there. And he had other delicious little self-induced pains. He thought how the rats had gnawed ragged holes in the red saddle, and how the mice had nibbled Gabilan's tail until it was stringy and thin. He usually ran the last little way to the barn. He unlatched the rusty hasp of the barn door and stepped in, and no matter how quietly he opened the door, Gabilan was always looking at him over the barrier of the box stall and Gabilan whinnied softly and stamped his front foot, and his eyes had big sparks of red fire in them like oakwood embers.

Sometimes, if the work horses were to be used that day, Jody found Billy Buck in the barn harnessing and currying. Billy stood with him and looked long at Gabilan and he told Jody a great many things about horses. He explained that they were terribly afraid for their feet, so that one must make a practice of lifting the legs and patting the hoofs and ankles to remove their terror. He told Jody how horses love conversation. He must talk to the pony all the time, and tell him the reasons for everything. Billy wasn't sure a horse could understand everything that was said to him, but it was impossible to say how much was understood. A horse never kicked up a fuss if some one he liked explained things to him. Billy could give examples, too. He had known, for instance, a horse nearly dead beat with fatigue to perk up when told it was only a little farther to his destination. And he had known a horse paralyzed with fright to come out of it when his rider told him what it was that was frightening him. While he talked in the mornings, Billy Buck cut twenty or thirty straws into neat three-inch lengths and stuck them into his hatband. Then during the whole day, if he wanted to pick his teeth or merely to chew on something, he had only to reach up for one of them.

Jody listened carefully, for he knew and the whole country knew that Billy Buck was a fine hand with horses. Billy's own horse was a stringy cayuse with a hammer head, but he nearly always won the first prizes at the stock trials. Billy could rope a steer, take a double half-hitch about the horn with his riata, and dismount, and his horse would play the steer as an angler plays a fish, keeping a tight rope until the steer was down or beaten.

Every morning, after Jody had curried and brushed the pony, he let down the barrier of the stall, and Gabilan thrust past him and raced down the barn and into the corral. Around and around he galloped, and sometimes he jumped forward and landed on stiff legs. He stood quivering, stiff ears forward, eyes rolling so that the whites showed, pretending to be frightened. At last he walked snorting to the water-trough and buried his nose in the water up to the nostrils. Jody was proud then, for he knew that was the way to judge a horse. Poor horses only touched their lips to the water, but a fine spirited beast put his whole nose and mouth under, and only left room to breathe.

Then Jody stood and watched the pony, and he saw things he had never noticed about any other horse, the sleek, sliding flank muscles and the cords of the buttocks, which flexed like a closing fist, and the shine the sun put on the red coat. Having seen horses all his life, Jody had never looked at them very closely before. But now he noticed the moving ears which gave expression and even inflection of expression to the face. The pony talked with his ears. You could tell exactly how he felt about everything by the way his ears pointed. Sometimes they were stiff and upright and sometimes lax and sagging. They went back when he was angry or fearful, and forward when he was anxious and curious and pleased; and their exact position indicated which emotion he had.

Billy Buck kept his word. In the early fall the training began. First there was the halter-breaking, and that was the hardest because it was the first thing. Jody held a carrot and coaxed and promised and pulled on the rope. The pony set his feet like a burro when he felt the strain. But before long he learned. Jody walked all over the ranch leading him. Gradually he took to dropping the rope until the pony followed him unled wherever he went.

And then came the training on the long halter. That was slower work. Jody stood in the middle of a circle, holding the long halter. He clucked with his tongue and the pony started to walk in a big circle, held in by the long rope. He clucked again to make the pony trot, and again to make him gallop. Around and around Gabilan went thundering and enjoying it immensely. Then he called, "Whoa," and the pony stopped. It was not long until Gabilan was perfect at it. But in many ways he was a bad pony. He bit Jody in the pants and stomped on Jody's feet. Now and then his ears went back and he aimed a tremendous kick at the boy. Every time he did one of these bad things, Gabilan settled back and seemed to laugh to himself.

Billy Buck worked at the hair rope in the evenings before the fireplace. Jody collected tail hair in a bag, and he sat and watched Billy slowly constructing the rope, twisting a few hairs to make a string and rolling two strings together for a cord, and then braiding a number of cords to make the rope. Billy rolled the finished rope on the floor under his foot to make it round and hard.

The long halter work rapidly approached perfection. Jody's father, watching the pony stop and start and trot and gallop, was a little bothered by it.

"He's getting to be almost a trick pony," he complained. "I don't like trick horses. It takes all the—dignity out of a horse to make him do tricks. Why, a trick horse is kind of like an actor—no dignity, no character of his own." And his father said, "I guess you better be getting him used to the saddle pretty soon."

Jody rushed for the harness-room. For some time he had been riding the saddle on a sawhorse. He changed the stirrup length over and over, and could never get it just right. Sometimes, mounted on the sawhorse in the harness-room, with collars and hames and tugs hung all about him, Jody rode out beyond the room. He carried his rifle across the pommel. He saw fields go flying by; and he heard the beat of the galloping hoofs.

It was a ticklish job, saddling the pony the first time. Gabilan hunched and reared and threw the saddle off before the cinch could be tightened. It had to be replaced again and again until at last the pony let it stay. And the cinching was difficult, too. Day by day Jody tightened the girth a little more until at last the pony didn't mind the saddle at all.

Then there was the bridle. Billy explained how to use a stick of licorice for a bit until Gabilan was used to having something in his mouth. Billy explained, "Of course we could force-break him to everything, but he wouldn't be as good a horse if we did. He'd always be a little bit afraid, and he wouldn't mind because he wanted to."

The first time the pony wore the bridle he whipped his head about and worked his tongue against the bit until the blood oozed from the corners of his mouth. He tried to rub the headstall off on the manger. His ears pivoted about and his eyes turned red with fear and with general rambunctiousness. Jody rejoiced, for he knew that only a mean-souled horse does not resent training.

And Jody trembled when he thought of the time when he would first sit in the saddle. The pony would probably throw him off. There was no disgrace in that. The disgrace would come if he did not get right up and mount again. Sometimes he dreamed that he lay in the dirt and cried and couldn't make himself mount again. The shame of the dream lasted until the middle of the day.

Gabilan was growing fast. Already he had lost the long-leggedness of the colt; his mane was getting longer and blacker. Under the constant currying and brushing his coat lay as smooth and gleaming as orange-red lacquer. Jody oiled the hoofs and kept them carefully trimmed so they would not crack.

The hair rope was nearly finished. Jody's father gave him an old pair of spurs and bent in the side bars and cut down the strap and took up the chainlets until they fitted. And then one day Carl Tiflin said:

"The pony's growing faster than I thought. I guess you can ride him by Thanksgiving. Think you can stick on?"

"I don't know," Jody said shyly. Thanksgiving was only three weeks off. He hoped it wouldn't rain, for rain would spot the red saddle.

Gabilan knew and liked Jody by now. He nickered when Jody came across the stubble-field, and in the pasture he came running when his master whistled for him. There was always a carrot for him every time.

Billy Buck gave him riding instructions over and over. "Now when you get up there, just grab tight with your knees and keep your hands away from the saddle, and if you get throwed, don't let that stop you. No matter how good a man is, there's always some horse can pitch him. You just climb up again before he gets to feeling smart about it. Pretty soon, he won't throw you no more, and pretty soon he *can't* throw you no more. That's the way to do it."

"I hope it don't rain before," Jody said.

"Why not? Don't want to get throwed in the mud?"

That was partly it, and also he was afraid that in the flurry of bucking Gabilan might slip and fall on him and break his leg or his hip. He had seen that happen to men before, had seen how they writhed on the ground like squashed bugs, and he was afraid of it.

He practiced on the sawhorse how he would hold the reins in his left hand and a hat in his right hand. If he kept his hands thus busy, he couldn't grab the horn if he felt himself going off. He didn't like to think of what would happen if he did grab the horn. Perhaps his father and Billy Buck would never speak to him again, they would be so ashamed. The news would get about and his mother would be ashamed too. And in the school yard—it was too awful to contemplate.

He began putting his weight in a stirrup when Gabilan was saddled, but he didn't throw his leg over the pony's back. That was forbidden until Thanksgiving.

Every afternoon he put the red saddle on the pony and cinched it tight. The pony was learning already to fill his stomach out unnaturally large while the cinching was going on, and then to let it down when the straps were fixed. Sometimes Jody led him up to the brush line and let him drink from the round green tub, and sometimes he led him up through the stubble-field to the hilltop from which it was possible to see the white town of Salinas and the geometric fields of the great valley, and the oak trees clipped by the sheep. Now and then they broke through the brush and came to little cleared circles so hedged in that the world was gone and only the sky and the circle of brush were left from the old life. Gabilan liked these trips and showed it by keeping his head very high and by quivering his nostrils with interest. When the two came back from an expedition they smelled of the sweet sage they had forced through.

Time dragged on toward Thanksgiving, but winter came fast. The clouds swept down and hung all day over the land and brushed the hilltops, and the winds blew shrilly at night. All day the dry oak leaves drifted down from the trees until they covered the ground, and yet the trees were unchanged.

Jody had wished it might not rain before Thanksgiving, but it did. The brown earth turned dark and the trees glistened. The cut ends of the stubble turned black with mildew; the haystacks grayed from exposure to the damp, and on the roofs the moss, which had been all summer as gray as lizards, turned a brilliant yellow-green. During the week of rain, Jody kept the pony in the box stall out of the dampness, except for a little time after school when he took him out for exercise and to drink at the water-trough in the upper corral. Not once did Gabilan get wet.

The wet weather continued until little new grass appeared. Jody walked to school dressed in a slicker and short rubber boots. At length one morning the sun came out brightly. Jody,

at his work in the box stall, said to Billy Buck, "Maybe I'll
leave Gabilan in the corral when I go to school today."

"Be good for him to be out in the sun," Billy assured him.
"No animal likes to be cooped up too long. Your father and
me are going back on the hill to clean the leaves out of the
spring." Billy nodded and picked his teeth with one of his
little straws.

"If the rain comes, though—" Jody suggested.

"Not likely to rain today. She's rained herself out." Billy
pulled up his sleeves and snapped his arm bands. "If it comes
on to rain—why a little rain don't hurt a horse."

"Well, if it does come on to rain, you put him in, will you,
Billy? I'm scared he might get cold so I couldn't ride him
when the time comes."

"Oh sure! I'll watch out for him if we get back in time. But
it won't rain today."

And so Jody, when he went to school, left Gabilan standing
out in the corral.

Billy Buck wasn't wrong about many things. He couldn't
be. But he was wrong about the weather that day, for a little
after noon the clouds pushed over the hills and the rain began
to pour down. Jody heard it start on the schoolhouse roof.
He considered holding up one finger for permission to go to
the outhouse and, once outside, running for home to put
the pony in. Punishment would be prompt both at school
and at home. He gave it up and took ease from Billy's assurance that rain couldn't hurt a horse. When school was finally
out, he hurried home through the dark rain. The banks at
the sides of the road spouted little jets of muddy water. The
rain slanted and swirled under a cold and gusty wind. Jody
dog-trotted home, slopping through the gravelly mud of the
road.

From the top of the ridge he could see Gabilan standing
miserably in the corral. The red coat was almost black, and
streaked with water. He stood head down with his rump to
the rain and wind. Jody arrived running and threw open the

barn door and led the wet pony in by his forelock. Then he found a gunny sack and rubbed the soaked hair and rubbed the legs and ankles. Gabilan stood patiently, but he trembled in gusts like the wind.

When he had dried the pony as well as he could, Jody went up to the house and brought hot water down to the barn and soaked the grain in it. Gabilan was not very hungry. He nibbled at the hot mash, but he was not very much interested in it, and he still shivered now and then. A little steam rose from his damp back.

It was almost dark when Billy Buck and Carl Tiflin came home. "When the rain started we put up at Ben Herche's place, and the rain never let up all afternoon," Carl Tiflin explained. Jody looked reproachfully at Billy Buck and Billy felt guilty.

"You said it wouldn't rain," Jody accused him.

Billy looked away. "It's hard to tell, this time of year," he said, but his excuse was lame. He had no right to be fallible, and he knew it.

"The pony got wet, got soaked through."

"Did you dry him off?"

"I rubbed him with a sack and I gave him hot grain."

Billy nodded in agreement.

"Do you think he'll take cold, Billy?"

"A little rain never hurt anything," Billy assured him.

Jody's father joined the conversation then and lectured the boy a little. "A horse," he said, "isn't any lap-dog kind of thing." Carl Tiflin hated weakness and sickness, and he held a violent contempt for helplessness.

Jody's mother put a platter of steaks on the table and boiled potatoes and boiled squash, which clouded the room with their steam. They sat down to eat. Carl Tiflin still grumbled about weakness put into animals and men by too much coddling.

Billy Buck felt bad about his mistake. "Did you blanket him?" he asked.

"No. I couldn't find any blanket. I laid some sacks over his back."

"We'll go down and cover him up after we eat, then." Billy felt better about it then. When Jody's father had gone in to the fire and his mother was washing dishes, Billy found and lighted a lantern. He and Jody walked through the mud to the barn. The barn was dark and warm and sweet. The horses still munched their evening hay. "You hold the lantern!" Billy ordered. And he felt the pony's legs and tested the heat of the flanks. He put his cheek against the pony's gray muzzle and then he rolled up the eyelids to look at the eyeballs and he lifted the lips to see the gums, and he put his fingers inside the ears. "He don't seem so chipper," Billy said. "I'll give him a rub-down."

Then Billy found a sack and rubbed the pony's legs violently and he rubbed the chest and the withers. Gabilan was strangely spiritless. He submitted patiently to the rubbing. At last Billy brought an old cotton comforter from the saddle-room, and threw it over the pony's back and tied it at neck and chest with string.

"Now he'll be all right in the morning," Billy said.

Jody's mother looked up when he got back to the house. "You're late up from bed," she said. She held his chin in her hand and brushed the tangled hair out of his eyes and she said, "Don't worry about the pony. He'll be all right. Billy's as good as any horse doctor in the country."

Jody hadn't known she could see his worry. He pulled gently away from her and knelt down in front of the fireplace until it burned his stomach. He scorched himself through and then went in to bed, but it was a hard thing to go to sleep. He awakened after what seemed a long time. The room was dark but there was a grayness in the window like that which precedes the dawn. He got up and found his overalls and searched for the legs, and then the clock in the other room struck two. He laid his clothes down and got back into bed. It was broad daylight when he awakened again. For the first time he had slept through the ringing of the triangle. He leaped up, flung on his clothes and went out of the door still buttoning his shirt. His mother looked after him for a moment and then went quietly back to her work. Her eyes were brooding and kind. Now and then her mouth smiled a little but without changing her eyes at all.

Jody ran on toward the barn. Halfway there he heard the sound he dreaded, the hollow rasping cough of a horse. He broke into a sprint then. In the barn he found Billy Buck with the pony. Billy was rubbing its legs with his strong thick hands. He looked up and smiled gaily. "He just took a little cold," Billy said. "We'll have him out of it in a couple of days."

Jody looked at the pony's face. The eyes were half closed and the lids thick and dry. In the eye corners a crust of hard mucus stuck. Gabilan's ears hung loosely sideways and his head was low. Jody put out his hand, but the pony did not move close to it. He coughed again and his whole body constricted with the effort. A little stream of fluid ran from his nostrils.

Jody looked back at Billy Buck. "He's awful sick, Billy."

"Just a little cold, like I said," Billy insisted. "You go get some breakfast and then go back to school. I'll take care of him."

"But you might have to do something else. You might leave him."

"No, I won't. I won't leave him at all. Tomorrow's Saturday. Then you can stay with him all day." Billy had failed again, and he felt bad about it. He had to cure the pony now.

Jody walked up to the house and took his place listlessly at the table. The eggs and bacon were cold and greasy, but he didn't notice it. He ate his usual amount. He didn't even ask to stay home from school. His mother pushed his hair back when she took his plate. "Billy'll take care of the pony," she assured him.

He moped through the whole day at school. He couldn't answer any questions nor read any words. He couldn't even tell anyone the pony was sick, for that might make him sicker. And when school was finally out he started home in dread. He walked slowly and let the other boys leave him. He wished he might continue walking and never arrive at the ranch.

Billy was in the barn, as he had promised, and the pony was worse. His eyes were almost closed now, and his breath whistled shrilly past an obstruction in his nose. A film covered that part of the eyes that was visible at all. It was doubtful whether the pony could see any more. Now and then he snorted, to clear his nose, and by the action seemed to plug it tighter. Jody looked dispiritedly at the pony's coat. The hair lay rough and unkempt and seemed to have lost all of its old luster. Billy stood quietly beside the stall. Jody hated to ask, but he had to know.

"Billy, is he—is he going to get well?"

Billy put his fingers between the bars under the pony's jaw and felt about. "Feel here," he said and he guided Jody's fingers to a large lump under the jaw. "When that gets bigger, I'll open it up and then he'll get better."

Jody looked quickly away, for he had heard about that lump. "What is the matter with him?"

Billy didn't want to answer, but he had to. He couldn't be wrong three times. "Strangles," he said shortly, "but don't you worry about that. I'll pull him out of it. I've seen them get well when they were worse than Gabilan is. I'm going to steam him now. You can help."

"Yes," Jody said miserably. He followed Billy into the grain room and watched him make the steaming bag ready. It was a long canvas nose bag with straps to go over a horse's ears. Billy filled it one-third full of bran and then he added a couple of handfuls of dried hops. On top of the dry substance he poured a little carbolic acid and a little turpentine.

"I'll be mixing it all up while you run to the house for a kettle of boiling water," Billy said.

When Jody came back with the steaming kettle, Billy buckled the straps over Gabilan's head and fitted the bag tightly around his nose. Then through a little hole in the side of the bag he poured the boiling water on the mixture. The pony started away as a cloud of strong steam rose up, but then the soothing fumes crept through his nose and into his lungs, and the sharp steam began to clear out the nasal passages. He breathed loudly. His legs trembled in an ague, and his eyes closed against the biting cloud. Billy poured in more water and kept the steam rising for fifteen minutes. At last he set down the kettle and took the bag from Gabilan's nose. The pony looked better. He breathed freely, and his eyes were open wider than they had been.

"See how good it makes him feel," Billy said. "Now we'll wrap him up in the blanket again. Maybe he'll be nearly well by morning."

"I'll stay with him tonight," Jody suggested.

"No. Don't you do it. I'll bring my blankets down here and put them in the hay. You can stay tomorrow and steam him if he needs it."

The evening was falling when they went to the house for their supper. Jody didn't even realize that someone else had fed the chickens and filled the wood-box. He walked up past the house to the dark brush line and took a drink of water from the tub. The spring water was so cold that it stung his mouth and drove a shiver through him. The sky above the hills was still light. He saw a hawk flying so high that it caught the sun on its breast and shone like a spark. Two blackbirds were driving him down the sky, glittering as they attacked their enemy. In the west, the clouds were moving in to rain again.

Jody's father didn't speak at all while the family ate supper, but after Billy Buck had taken his blankets and gone to sleep in the barn, Carl Tiflin built a high fire in the fireplace and told stories. He told about the wild man who ran naked through the country and had a tail and ears like a horse, and he told about the rabbit-cats of Moro Cojo that hopped into the trees for birds. He revived the famous Maxwell brothers who found a vein of gold and hid the traces of it so carefully that they could never find it again.

Jody sat with his chin in his hands; his mouth worked nervously and his father gradually became aware that he wasn't listening very carefully. "Isn't that funny?" he asked.

Jody laughed politely and said, "Yes, sir." His father was angry and hurt, then. He didn't tell any more stories. After a while, Jody took a lantern and went down to the barn. Billy Buck was asleep in the hay, and, except that his breath rasped a little in his lungs, the pony seemed to be much better. Jody stayed a little while, running his fingers over the red rough coat, and then he took up the lantern and went back to the house. When he was in bed, his mother came into the room.

"Have you enough covers on? It's getting winter."

"Yes, ma'am."

"Well, get some rest tonight." She hesitated to go out, stood uncertainly. "The pony will be all right," she said.

Jody was tired. He went to sleep quickly and didn't awaken until dawn. The triangle sounded, and Billy Buck came up from the barn before Jody could get out of the house.

"How is he?" Jody demanded.

Billy always wolfed his breakfast. "Pretty good. I'm going to open that lump this morning. Then he'll be better maybe."

After breakfast, Billy got out his best knife, one with a needle point. He whetted the shining blade a long time on a little carborundum stone. He tried the point and the blade again and again on his calloused thumb-ball, and at last he tried it on his upper lip.

On the way to the barn, Jody noticed how the young grass was up and how the stubble was melting day by day into the new green crop of volunteer. It was a cold sunny morning.

As soon as he saw the pony, Jody knew he was worse. His eyes were closed and sealed shut with dried mucus. His head hung so low that his nose almost touched the straw of his bed. There was a little groan in each breath, a deep-seated, patient groan.

Billy lifted the weak head and made a quick slash with the knife. Jody saw the yellow pus run out. He held up the head while Billy swabbed out the wound with weak carbolic acid salve.

"Now he'll feel better," Billy assured him. "That yellow poison is what makes him sick."

Jody looked unbelieving at Billy Buck. "He's awful sick."

Billy thought a long time what to say. He nearly tossed off a careless assurance, but he saved himself in time. "Yes, he's pretty sick," he said at last. "I've seen worse ones get well. If he doesn't get pneumonia, we'll pull him through. You stay with him. If he gets worse, you can come and get me."

For a long time after Billy went away, Jody stood beside the pony, stroking him behind the ears. The pony didn't flip his head the way he had done when he was well. The groaning in his breathing was becoming more hollow.

Doubletree Mutt looked into the barn, his big tail waving provocatively, and Jody was so incensed at his health that he found a hard black clod on the floor and deliberately threw it. Doubletree Mutt went yelping away to nurse a bruised paw.

In the middle of the morning, Billy Buck came back and made another steam bag. Jody watched to see whether the pony improved this time as he had before. His breathing eased a little, but he did not raise his head.

The Saturday dragged on. Late in the afternoon Jody went to the house and brought his bedding down and made up a place to sleep in the hay. He didn't ask permission. He knew from the way his mother looked at him that she would let him do almost anything. That night he left a lantern

burning on a wire over the box stall. Billy had told him to
rub the pony's legs every little while.

At nine o'clock the wind sprang up and howled around the
barn. And in spite of his worry, Jody grew sleepy. He got
into his blankets and went to sleep, but the breathy groans of
the pony sounded in his dreams. And in his sleep he heard
a crashing noise which went on and on until it awakened
him. The wind was rushing through the barn. He sprang
up and looked down the lane of stalls. The barn door had
blown open, and the pony was gone.

He caught the lantern and ran outside into the gale, and
he saw Gabilan weakly shambling away into the darkness,
head down, legs working slowly and mechanically. When
Jody ran up and caught him by the forelock, he allowed
himself to be led back and put into his stall. His groans
were louder, and a fierce whistling came from his nose.
Jody didn't sleep any more then. The hissing of the pony's
breath grew louder and sharper.

He was glad when Billy Buck came in at dawn. Billy
looked for a time at the pony as though he had never seen
him before. He felt the ears and flanks. "Jody," he said,
"I've got to do something you won't want to see. You run
up to the house for a while."

Jody grabbed him fiercely by the forearm. "You're not
going to shoot him?"

Billy patted his hand. "No. I'm going to open a little hole
in his windpipe so he can breathe. His nose is filled up. When
he gets well, we'll put a little brass button in the hole for
him to breath through."

Jody couldn't have gone away if he had wanted to. It was
awful to see the red hide cut, but infinitely more terrible to
know it was being cut and not to see it. "I'll stay right here,"
he said bitterly. "You sure you got to?"

"Yes. I'm sure. If you stay, you can hold his head. If it
doesn't make you sick, that is."

The fine knife came out again and was whetted again just

as carefully as it had been the first time. Jody held the pony's head up and the throat taut, while Billy felt up and down for the right place. Jody sobbed once as the bright knife point disappeared into the throat. The pony plunged weakly away and then stood still, trembling violently. The blood ran thickly out and up the knife and across Billy's hand and into his shirtsleeve. The sure square hand sawed out a round hole in the flesh, and the breath came bursting out of the hole, throwing a fine spray of blood. With the rush of oxygen, the pony took a sudden strength. He lashed out with his hind feet and tried to rear, but Jody held his head down while Billy mopped the new wound with carbolic salve. It was a good job. The blood stopped flowing and the air puffed out the hole and sucked it in regularly with a little bubbling noise.

The rain brought in by the night wind began to fall on the barn roof. Then the triangle rang for breakfast. "You go up and eat while I wait," Billy said. "We've got to keep this hole from plugging up."

Jody walked slowly out of the barn. He was too dispirited to tell Billy how the barn door had blown open and let the pony out. He emerged into the wet gray morning and sloshed up to the house, taking a perverse pleasure in splashing through all the puddles. His mother fed him and put dry clothes on. She didn't question him. She seemed to know he couldn't answer questions. But when he was ready to go back to the barn she brought him a pan of steaming meal. "Give him this," she said.

But Jody did not take the pan. He said, "He won't eat anything," and ran out of the house. At the barn, Billy showed him how to fix a ball of cotton on a stick, with which to swab out the breathing hole when it became clogged with mucus.

Jody's father walked into the barn and stood with them in front of the stall. At length he turned to the boy. "Hadn't you better come with me? I'm going to drive over the hill."

Jody shook his head. "You better come on, out of this," his father insisted.

Billy turned on him angrily. "Let him alone. It's his pony, isn't it?"

Carl Tiflin walked away without saying another word. His feelings were badly hurt.

All morning Jody kept the wound open and the air passing in and out freely. At noon the pony lay wearily down on his side and stretched his nose out.

Billy came back. "If you're going to stay with him tonight, you better take a little nap," he said. Jody went absently out of the barn. The sky had cleared to a hard thin blue. Everywhere the birds were busy with worms that had come to the damp surface of the ground.

Jody walked to the brush line and sat on the edge of the mossy tub. He looked down at the house and at the old bunkhouse and at the dark cypress tree. The place was familiar, but curiously changed. It wasn't itself any more, but a frame for things that were happening. A cold wind blew out of the east now, signifying that the rain was over for a little while. At his feet Jody could see the little arms of new weeds spreading out over the ground. In the mud about the spring were thousands of quail tracks.

Doubletree Mutt came sideways and embarrassed up through the vegetable patch, and Jody, remembering how he had thrown the clod, put his arm about the dog's neck and kissed him on his wide black nose. Doubletree Mutt sat still, as though he knew some solemn thing was happening. His big tail slapped the ground gravely. Jody pulled a swollen tick out of Mutt's neck and popped it dead between his thumb-nails. It was a nasty thing. He washed his hands in the cold spring water.

Except for the steady swish of the wind, the farm was very quiet. Jody knew his mother wouldn't mind if he didn't go in to eat his lunch. After a little while he went slowly back to the barn. Mutt crept into his own little house and whined softly to himself for a long time.

Billy Buck stood up from the box and surrendered the cotton swab. The pony still lay on his side and the wound in his throat bellowsed in and out. When Jody saw how dry and dead the hair looked, he knew at last that there was no hope for the pony. He had seen the dead hair before on dogs cows, and it was a sure sign. He sat heavily on the box and let down the barrier of the box stall. For a long time he kept his eyes on the moving wound, and at last he dozed, and the afternoon passed quickly. Just before dark his mother brought a deep dish of stew and left it for him and went away. Jody ate a little of it, and, when it was dark, he set the lantern on the floor by the pony's head so he could watch the wound and keep it open. And he dozed again until the night chill awakened him. The wind was blowing fiercely, bringing the north cold with it. Jody brought a blanket from his bed in the hay and wrapped himself in it. Gabilan's breathing was quiet at last; the hole in his throat moved gently. The owls flew through the hayloft, shrieking and looking for mice. Jody put his hands down on his head and slept. In his sleep he was aware that the wind had increased. He heard it slamming about the barn.

It was daylight when he awakened. The barn door had swung open. The pony was gone. He sprang up and ran out into the morning light.

The pony's tracks were plain enough, dragging through the frost-like dew on the young grass, tired tracks with little lines between them where the hoofs had dragged. They headed for the brush line halfway up the ridge. Jody broke into a run and followed them. The sun shone on the sharp white quartz that stuck through the ground here and there. As he followed the plain trail, a shadow cut across in front of him. He looked up and saw a high circle of black buzzards, and the slowly revolving circle dropped lower and

lower. The solemn birds soon disappeared over the ridge.
Jody ran faster then, forced on by panic and rage. The trail
entered the brush at last and followed a winding route among
the tall sage bushes.

At the top of the ridge Jody was winded. He paused, puff-
ing noisily. The blood pounded in his ears. Then he saw
what he was looking for. Below, in one of the little clearings
in the brush, lay the red pony. In the distance, Jody could see
the legs moving slowly and convulsively. And in a circle
around him stood the buzzards, waiting for the moment of
death they know so well.

Jody leaped forward and plunged down the hill. The wet
ground muffled his steps and the brush hid him. When he
arrived, it was all over. The first buzzard sat on the pony's
head and its beak had just risen dripping with dark eye fluid.
Jody plunged into the circle like a cat. The black brother-
hood arose in a cloud, but the big one on the pony's head was
too late. As it hopped along to take off, Jody caught its wing
tip and pulled it down. It was nearly as big as he was. The
free wing crashed into his face with the force of a club, but
he hung on. The claws fastened on his leg and the wing
elbows battered his head on either side. Jody groped blindly
with his free hand. His fingers found the neck of the struggling bird. The red eyes looked into his face, calm and fear-
less and fierce; the naked head turned from side to side. Then
the beak opened and vomited a stream of putrefied fluid.
Jody brought up his knee and fell on the great bird. He held
the neck to the ground with one hand while his other found
a piece of sharp white quartz. The first blow broke the beak
sideways and black blood spurted from the twisted, leathery
mouth corners. He struck again and missed. The red fear-
less eyes still looked at him, impersonal and unafraid and
detached. He struck again and again, until the buzzard lay
dead, until its head was a red pulp. He was still beating the
dead bird when Billy Buck pulled him off and held him
tightly to calm his shaking.

Carl Tiflin wiped the blood from the boy's face with a red bandana. Jody was limp and quiet now. His father moved the buzzard with his toe. "Jody," he explained, "the buzzard didn't kill the pony. Don't you know that?"

"I know it," Jody said wearily.

It was Billy Buck who was angry. He had lifted Jody in his arms, and had turned to carry him home. But he turned back on Carl Tiflin. "'Course he knows it," Billy said furiously, "Jesus Christ! man, can't you see how he'd feel about it?"

## II. THE GREAT MOUNTAINS

IN THE humming heat of a midsummer afternoon the little boy Jody listlessly looked about the ranch for something to do. He had been to the barn, had thrown rocks at the swallows' nests under the eaves until every one of the little mud houses broke open and dropped its lining of straw and dirty feathers. Then at the ranch house he baited a rat trap with stale cheese and set it where Doubletree Mutt, that good big dog, would get his nose snapped. Jody was not moved by an impulse of cruelty; he was bored with the long hot afternoon. Doubletree Mutt put his stupid nose in the trap and got it smacked, and shrieked with agony and limped away with blood on his nostrils. No matter where he was hurt, Mutt limped. It was just a way he had. Once when he was young, Mutt got caught in a coyote trap, and always after that he limped, even when he was scolded.

When Mutt yelped, Jody's mother called from inside the house, "Jody! Stop torturing that dog and find something to do."

Jody felt mean then, so he threw a rock at Mutt. Then he took his slingshot from the porch and walked up toward the brush line to try to kill a bird. It was a good slingshot, with store-bought rubbers, but while Jody had often shot at birds, he had never hit one. He walked up through the vegetable patch, kicking his bare toes into the dust. And on the way he found the perfect slingshot stone, round and slightly flattened and heavy enough to carry through the air. He fitted it into the leather pouch of his weapon and proceeded to the brush line. His eyes narrowed, his mouth worked strenuously; for the first time that afternoon he was intent. In the shade of the sagebrush the little birds were working, scratching in the leaves, flying restlessly a few feet and scratching again. Jody pulled back the rubbers of the sling and advanced cautiously. One little thrush paused and looked at him and crouched, ready to fly. Jody sidled nearer, moving one foot slowly after the other. When he was twenty feet away, he carefully raised the sling and aimed. The stone whizzed; the thrush started up and flew right into it. And down the little bird went with a broken head. Jody ran to it and picked it up.

"Well, I got you," he said.

The bird looked much smaller dead than it had alive. Jody felt a little mean pain in his stomach, so he took out his pocket-knife and cut off the bird's head. Then he disemboweled it, and took off its wings; and finally he threw all the pieces into the brush. He didn't care about the bird, or its life, but he knew what older people would say if they had seen him kill it; he was ashamed because of their potential opinion. He decided to forget the whole thing as quickly as he could, and never to mention it.

The hills were dry at this season, and the wild grass was golden, but where the spring-pipe filled the round tub and the tub spilled over, there lay a stretch of fine green grass, deep and sweet and moist. Jody drank from the mossy tub and washed the bird's blood from his hands in cold water. Then he lay on his back in the grass and looked up at the dumpling summer clouds. By closing one eye and destroying perspective he brought them down within reach so that he could put up his fingers and stroke them. He helped the gentle wind push them down the sky; it seemed to him that they went faster for his help. One fat white cloud he helped clear to the mountain rims and pressed it firmly over, out of sight. Jody wondered what it was seeing, then. He sat up, the better to look at the great mountains where they went piling back, growing darker and more savage until they finished with one jagged ridge, high up against the west. Curious secret mountains; he thought of the little he knew about them.

"What's on the other side?" he asked his father once.

"More mountains, I guess. Why?"

"And on the other side of them?"

"More mountains. Why?"

"More mountains on and on?"

"Well, no. At last you come to the ocean."

"But what's in the mountains?"

"Just cliffs and brush and rocks and dryness."

"Were you ever there?"

"No."

"Has anybody ever been there?"

"A few people, I guess. It's dangerous, with cliffs and things. Why, I've read there's more unexplored country in the mountains of Monterey County than any place in the United States." His father seemed proud that this should be so.

"And at last the ocean?"

"At last the ocean."

"But," the boy insisted, "but in between? No one knows?"

"Oh, a few people do, I guess. But there's nothing there to get. And not much water. Just rocks and cliffs and grease-wood. Why?"

"It would be good to go."

"What for? There's nothing there."

Jody knew something was there, something very wonderful because it wasn't known, something secret and mysterious. He could feel within himself that this was so. He said to his mother, "Do you know what's in the big mountains?"

She looked at him and then back at the ferocious range, and she said, "Only the bear, I guess."

"What bear?"

"Why the one that went over the mountain to see what he could see."

Jody questioned Billy Buck, the ranch hand, about the possibility of ancient cities lost in the mountains, but Billy agreed with Jody's father.

"It ain't likely," Billy said. "There'd be nothing to eat unless a kind of people that can eat rocks live there."

That was all the information Jody ever got, and it made the mountains dear to him, and terrible. He thought often of the miles of ridge after ridge until at last there was the sea. When the peaks were pink in the morning they invited him among them: and when the sun had gone over the edge in the evening and the mountains were a purple-like despair, then Jody was afraid of them; then they were so impersonal and aloof that their very imperturbability was a threat.

Now he turned his head toward the mountains of the east, the Gabilans, and they were jolly mountains, with hill ranches in their creases, and with pine trees growing on the crests. People lived there, and battles had been fought against the Mexicans on the slopes. He looked back for an instant at the Great Ones and shivered a little at the contrast. The foothill cup of the home ranch below him was sunny and safe. The house gleamed with white light and the barn was brown and warm. The red cows on the farther hill ate their way slowly toward the north. Even the dark cypress tree by the bunkhouse was usual and safe. The chickens scratched about in the dust of the farmyard with quick waltzing steps.

Then a moving figure caught Jody's eye. A man walked slowly over the brow of the hill, on the road from Salinas, and he was headed toward the house. Jody stood up and moved down toward the house too, for if someone was coming, he wanted to be there to see. By the time the boy had got to the house the walking man was only halfway down the road, a lean man, very straight in the shoulders. Jody could tell he was old only because his heels struck the ground with hard jerks. As he approached nearer, Jody saw that he was dressed in blue jeans and in a coat of the same material. He wore clodhopper shoes and an old flat-brimmed Stetson hat. Over his shoulder he carried a gunny sack, lumpy and full. In a few moments he had trudged close enough so that his face could be seen. And his face was as dark as dried beef. A mustache, blue-white against the dark skin, hovered over his mouth, and his hair was white, too, where it showed at his neck. The skin of his face had shrunk back against the skull until it defined bone, not flesh, and made the nose and chin seem sharp and fragile. The eyes were large and deep and dark, with eyelids stretched tightly over them. Irises and pupils were one, and very black, but the eyeballs were brown. There were no wrinkles in the face at all. This old man wore a blue denim coat buttoned to the throat with brass buttons, as all men do who wear no shirts. Out of the sleeves came strong bony wrists and hands gnarled and knotted and hard as peach branches. The nails were flat and blunt and shiny.

The old man drew close to the gate and swung down his sack when he confronted Jody. His lips fluttered a little and a soft impersonal voice came from between them.

"Do you live here?"

Jody was embarrassed. He turned and looked at the house, and he turned back and looked toward the barn where his father and Billy Buck were. "Yes," he said, when no help came from either direction.

"I have come back," the old man said. "I am Gitano, and I have come back."

Jody could not take all this responsibility. He turned abruptly, and ran into the house for help, and the screen door banged after him. His mother was in the kitchen poking out the clogged holes of a colander with a hairpin, and biting her lower lip with concentration.

"It's an old man," Jody cried excitedly. "It's an old *paisano* man, and he says he's come back."

His mother put down the colander and stuck the hairpin behind the sink board. "What's the matter now?" she asked patiently.

"It's an old man outside. Come on out."

"Well, what does he want?" She untied the strings of her apron and smoothed her hair with her fingers.

"I don't know. He came walking."

His mother smoothed down her dress and went out, and Jody followed her. Gitano had not moved.

"Yes?" Mrs. Tiflin asked.

Gitano took off his old black hat and held it with both hands in front of him. He repeated, "I am Gitano, and I have come back."

"Come back? Back where?"

Gitano's whole straight body leaned forward a little. His right hand described the circle of the hills, the sloping fields and the mountains, and ended at his hat again. "Back to the rancho. I was born here, and my father, too."

"Here?" she demanded. "This isn't an old place."

"No, there," he said, pointing to the western ridge. "On the other side there, in a house that is gone."

At last she understood. "The old 'dobe that's washed almost away, you mean?"

"Yes, *señora*. When the rancho broke up they put no more lime on the 'dobe, and the rains washed it down."

Jody's mother was silent for a little, and curious homesick thoughts ran through her mind, but quickly she cleared them out. "And what do you want here now, Gitano?"

"I will stay here," he said quietly, "until I die."

"But we don't need an extra man here."

"I cannot work hard any more, *señora*. I can milk a cow, feed chickens, cut a little wood; no more. I will stay here."

He indicated the sack on the ground beside him. "Here are my things."

She turned to Jody. "Run down to the barn and call your father."

Jody dashed away, and he returned with Carl Tiflin and Billy Buck behind him. The old man was standing as he had been, but he was resting now. His whole body had sagged into a timeless repose.

"What is it?" Carl Tiflin asked. "What's Jody so excited about?"

Mrs. Tiflin motioned to the old man. "He wants to stay here. He wants to do a little work and stay here."

"Well, we can't have him. We don't need any more men. He's too old. Billy does everything we need."

They had been talking over him as though he did not exist, and now, suddenly, they both hesitated and looked at Gitano and were embarrassed.

He cleared his throat. "I am too old to work. I come back where I was born."

"You weren't born here," Carl said sharply.

"No. In the 'dobe house over the hill. It was all one rancho before you came."

"In the mud house that's all melted down?"

"Yes. I and my father. I will stay here now on the rancho."

"I tell you you won't stay," Carl said angrily. "I don't need an old man. This isn't a big ranch. I can't afford food and doctor bills for an old man. You must have relatives and friends. Go to them. It is like begging to come to strangers."

"I was born here," Gitano said patiently and inflexibly.

Carl Tiflin didn't like to be cruel, but he felt he must. "You can eat here tonight," he said. "You can sleep in the little room of the old bunkhouse. We'll give you your breakfast in the morning, and then you'll have to go along. Go to your friends. Don't come to die with strangers."

Gitano put on his black hat and stooped for the sack. "Here are my things," he said.

Carl turned away. "Come on, Billy, we'll finish down at the barn. Jody, show him the little room in the bunkhouse."

He and Billy turned back toward the barn. Mrs. Tiflin went into the house, saying over her shoulder, "I'll send some blankets down."

Gitano looked questioningly at Jody. "I'll show you where it is," Jody said.

There was a cot with a shuck mattress, an apple box holding a tin lantern, and a backless rocking-chair in the little room of the bunkhouse. Gitano laid his sack carefully on the floor and sat down on the bed. Jody stood shyly in the room, hesitating to go. At last he said:

"Did you come out of the big mountains?"

Gitano shook his head slowly. "No, I worked down the Salinas Valley."

The afternoon thought would not let Jody go. "Did you ever go into the big mountains back there?"

The old dark eyes grew fixed, and their light turned inward on the years that were living in Gitano's head. "Once— when I was a little boy. I went with my father."

"Way back, clear into the mountains?"

"Yes."

"What was there?" Jody cried. "Did you see any people or any houses?"

"No."

"Well, what was there?"

Gitano's eyes remained inward. A little wrinkled strain came between his brows.

"What did you see in there?" Jody repeated.

"I don't know," Gitano said. "I don't remember."

"Was it terrible and dry?"

"I don't remember."

In his excitement, Jody had lost his shyness. "Don't you remember anything about it?"

Gitano's mouth opened for a word, and remained open

while his brain sought the word. "I think it was quiet—I think it was nice."

Gitano's eyes seemed to have found something back in the years, for they grew soft and a little smile seemed to come and go in them.

"Didn't you ever go back in the mountains again?" Jody insisted.

"No."

"Didn't you ever want to?"

But now Gitano's face became impatient. "No," he said in a tone that told Jody he didn't want to talk about it any more. The boy was held by a curious fascination. He didn't want to go away from Gitano. His shyness returned.

"Would you like to come down to the barn and see the stock?" he asked.

Gitano stood up and put on his hat and prepared to follow.

It was almost evening now. They stood near the watering trough while the horses sauntered in from the hillsides for an evening drink. Gitano rested his big twisted hands on the top rail of the fence. Five horses came down and drank, and then stood about, nibbling at the dirt or rubbing their sides against the polished wood of the fence. Long after they had finished drinking an old horse appeared over the brow of the hill and came painfully down. It had long yellow teeth; its hoofs were flat and sharp as spades, and its ribs and hip-bones jutted out under its skin. It hobbled up to the trough and drank water with a loud sucking noise.

"That's old Easter," Jody explained. "That's the first horse my father ever had. He's thirty years old." He looked up into Gitano's old eyes for some response.

"No good any more," Gitano said.

Jody's father and Billy Buck came out of the barn and walked over.

"Too old to work," Gitano repeated. "Just eats and pretty soon dies."

Carl Tiflin caught the last words. He hated his brutality toward old Gitano, and so he became brutal again.

"It's a shame not to shoot Easter," he said. "It'd save him a lot of pains and rheumatism." He looked secretly at Gitano, to see whether he noticed the parallel, but the big bony hands did not move, nor did the dark eyes turn from the horse. "Old things ought to be put out of their misery," Jody's father went on. "One shot, a big noise, one big pain in the head maybe, and that's all. That's better than stiffness and sore teeth."

Billy Buck broke in. "They got a right to rest after they worked all of their life. Maybe they like to just walk around."

Carl had been looking steadily at the skinny horse. "You can't imagine now what Easter used to look like," he said softly. "High neck, deep chest, fine barrel. He could jump a five-bar gate in stride. I won a flat race on him when I was fifteen years old. I could of got two hundred dollars for him any time. You wouldn't think how pretty he was." He checked himself, for he hated softness. "But he ought to be shot now," he said.

"He's got a right to rest," Billy Buck insisted.

Jody's father had a humorous thought. He turned to Gitano. "If ham and eggs grew on a side-hill I'd turn you out to pasture too," he said. "But I can't afford to pasture you in my kitchen."

He laughed to Billy Buck about it as they went on toward the house. "Be a good thing for all of us if ham and eggs grew on the side-hills."

Jody knew how his father was probing for a place to hurt in Gitano. He had been probed often. His father knew every place in the boy where a word would fester.

"He's only talking," Jody said. "He didn't mean it about shooting Easter. He likes Easter. That was the first horse he ever owned."

The sun sank behind the high mountains as they stood

there, and the ranch was hushed. Gitano seemed to be more
at home in the evening. He made a curious sharp sound with
his lips and stretched one of his hands over the fence. Old
Easter moved stiffly to him, and Gitano rubbed the lean neck
under the mane.

"You like him?" Jody asked softly.

"Yes—but he's no damn good."

The triangle sounded at the ranch house. "That's supper,"
Jody cried. "Come on up to supper."

As they walked up toward the house Jody noticed again
that Gitano's body was as straight as that of a young man.
Only by a jerkiness in his movements and by the scuffling of
his heels could it be seen that he was old.

The turkeys were flying heavily into the lower branches of
the cypress tree by the bunkhouse. A fat sleek ranch cat
walked across the road carrying a rat so large that its tail
dragged on the ground. The quail on the side-hills were still
sounding the clear water call.

Jody and Gitano came to the back steps and Mrs. Tiflin
looked out through the screen door at them.

"Come running, Jody. Come in to supper, Gitano."

Carl and Billy Buck had started to eat at the long oilcloth-
covered table. Jody slipped into his chair without moving it,
but Gitano stood holding his hat until Carl looked up and
said, "Sit down, sit down. You might as well get your belly
full before you go on." Carl was afraid he might relent and
let the old man stay, and so he continued to remind himself
that this couldn't be.

Gitano laid his hat on the floor and diffidently sat down.
He wouldn't reach for food. Carl had to pass it to him.
"Here, fill yourself up." Gitano ate very slowly, cutting tiny
pieces of meat and arranging little pats of mashed potato
on his plate.

The situation would not stop worrying Carl Tiflin.
"Haven't you got any relatives in this part of the country?"
he asked.

Gitano answered with some pride,"My brother-in-law is in Monterey. I have cousins there, too."

"Well, you can go and live there, then."

"I was born here," Gitano said in gentle rebuke.

Jody's mother came in from the kitchen, carrying a large bowl of tapioca pudding.

Carl chuckled to her, "Did I tell you what I said to him? I said if ham and eggs grew on the side-hills I'd put him out to pasture, like old Easter."

Gitano stared unmoved at his plate.

"It's too bad he can't stay," said Mrs. Tiflin.

"Now don't you start anything," Carl said crossly.

When they had finished eating, Carl and Billy Buck and Jody went into the living room to sit for a while, but Gitano, without a word of farewell or thanks, walked through the kitchen and out the back door. Jody sat and secretly watched his father. He knew how mean his father felt.

"This country's full of these old *paisanos*," Carl said to Billy Buck.

"They're damn good men," Billy defended them. "They can work older than white men. I saw one of them a hundred and five years old, and he could still ride a horse. You don't see any white men as old as Gitano walking twenty or thirty miles."

"Oh, they're tough, all right," Carl agreed. "Say, are you standing up for him too? Listen, Billy," he explained, "I'm having a hard enough time keeping this ranch out of the Bank of Italy without taking on anybody else to feed. You know that, Billy."

"Sure, I know," said Billy. "If you was rich, it'd be different."

"That's right, and it isn't like he didn't have relatives to go to. A brother-in-law and cousins right in Monterey. Why should I worry about him?"

Jody sat quietly listening, and he seemed to hear Gitano's gentle voice and its unanswerable, "I was born here." Gitano was mysterious like the mountains. There were ranges back as far as you could see, but behind the last range piled up against the sky there was a great unknown country. And Gitano was an old man, until you got to the dull dark eyes. And in behind them was some unknown thing. He didn't ever say enough to let you guess what was inside, under the eyes. Jody felt himself irresistibly drawn toward the bunkhouse. He slipped from his chair while his father was talking and he went out the door without making a sound.

The night was very dark and far-off noises carried in clearly. The hamebells of a wood team sounded from way over the hill on the country road. Jody picked his way across the dark yard. He could see a light through the window of the little room of the bunkhouse. Because the night was secret he walked quietly up to the window and peered in. Gitano sat in the rocking-chair and his back was toward the window. His right arm moved slowly back and forth in front of him. Jody pushed the door open and walked in. Gitano jerked upright and, seizing a piece of deerskin, he tried to throw it over the thing in his lap, but the skin slipped away. Jody stood overwhelmed by the thing in Gitano's hand, a lean and lovely rapier with a golden basket hilt. The blade was like a thin ray of dark light. The hilt was pierced and intricately carved.

"What is it?" Jody demanded.

Gitano only looked at him with resentful eyes, and he picked up the fallen deerskin and firmly wrapped the beautiful blade in it.

Jody put out his hand. "Can't I see it?"

Gitano's eyes smoldered angrily and he shook his head.

"Where'd you get it? Where'd it come from?"

Now Gitano regarded him profoundly, as though he pondered. "I got it from my father."

"Well, where'd he get it?"

Gitano looked down at the long deerskin parcel in his hand. "I don' know."

"Didn't he ever tell you?"

"No."

"What do you do with it?"

Gitano looked slightly surprised. "Nothing. I just keep it."

"Can't I see it again?"

The old man slowly unwrapped the shining blade and let the lamplight slip along it for a moment. Then he wrapped it up again. "You go now. I want to go to bed." He blew out the lamp almost before Jody had closed the door.

As he went back toward the house, Jody knew one thing more sharply than he had ever known anything. He must never tell anyone about the rapier. It would be a dreadful thing to tell anyone about it, for it would destroy some fragile structure of truth. It was a truth that might be shattered by division.

On the way across the dark yard Jody passed Billy Buck. "They're wondering where you are," Billy said.

Jody slipped into the living room, and his father turned to him. "Where have you been?"

"I just went out to see if I caught any rats in my new trap."

"It's time you went to bed," his father said.

Jody was first at the breakfast table in the morning. Then his father came in, and last, Billy Buck. Mrs. Tiflin looked in from the kitchen.

"Where's the old man, Billy?" she asked.

"I guess he's out walking," Billy said. "I looked in his room and he wasn't there."

"Maybe he started early to Monterey," said Carl. "It's a long walk."

"No," Billy explained. "His sack is in the little room."

After breakfast Jody walked down to the bunkhouse. Flies

were flashing about in the sunshine. The ranch seemed especially quiet this morning. When he was sure no one was watching him, Jody went into the little room, and looked into Gitano's sack. An extra pair of long cotton underwear was there, an extra pair of jeans and three pairs of worn socks. Nothing else was in the sack. A sharp loneliness fell on Jody. He walked slowly back toward the house. His father stood on the porch talking to Mrs. Tiflin.

"I guess old Easter's dead at last," he said. "I didn't see him come down to water with the other horses."

In the middle of the morning Jess Taylor from the ridge ranch rode down.

"You didn't sell that old gray crowbait of yours, did you, Carl?"

"No, of course not. Why?"

"Well," Jess said. "I was out this morning early, and I saw a funny thing. I saw an old man on an old horse, no saddle, only a piece of rope for a bridle. He wasn't on the road at all. He was cutting right up straight through the brush. I think he had a gun. At least I saw something shine in his hand."

"That's old Gitano," Carl Tiflin said. "I'll see if any of my guns are missing." He stepped into the house for a second. "Nope, all here. Which way was he heading, Jess?"

"Well, that's the funny thing. He was heading straight back into the mountains."

Carl laughed. "They never get too old to steal," he said. "I guess he just stole old Easter."

"Want to go after him, Carl?"

"Hell, no, just save me burying that horse. I wonder where he got the gun. I wonder what he wants back there."

Jody walked up through the vegetable patch, toward the brush line. He looked searchingly at the towering mountains —ridge after ridge after ridge until at last there was the ocean. For a moment he thought he could see a black speck crawling up the farthest ridge. Jody thought of the rapier

and of Gitano. And he thought of the great mountains. A
longing caressed him, and it was so sharp that he wanted to
cry to get it out of his breast. He lay down in the green grass
near the round tub at the brush line. He covered his eyes
with his crossed arms and lay there a long time, and he was
full of a nameless sorrow.

### III.   THE PROMISE

In a mid-afternoon of spring, the little boy Jody walked
martially along the brush-lined road toward his home ranch.
Banging his knee against the golden lard bucket he used for
school lunch, he contrived a good bass drum, while his tongue
fluttered sharply against his teeth to fill in snare drums and
occasional trumpets. Some time back the other members of
the squad that walked so smartly from the school had turned
into the various little canyons and taken the wagon roads to
their own home ranches. Now Jody marched seemingly
alone, with high-lifted knees and pounding feet; but behind
him there was a phantom army with great flags and swords,
silent but deadly.

The afternoon was green and gold with spring. Underneath the spread branches of the oaks the plants grew pale
and tall, and on the hills the feed was smooth and thick. The
sagebrushes shone with new silver leaves and the oaks wore
hoods of golden green. Over the hills there hung such a green
odor that the horses on the flats galloped madly, and then
stopped, wondering; lambs, and even old sheep jumped in
the air unexpectedly and landed on stiff legs, and went on
eating; young clumsy calves butted their heads together and
drew back and butted again.

As the gray and silent army marched past, led by Jody,
the animals stopped their feeding and their play and watched
it go by.

Suddenly Jody stopped. The gray army halted, bewildered
and nervous. Jody went down on his knees. The army stood
in long uneasy ranks for a moment, and then, with a soft

sigh of sorrow, rose up in a faint gray mist and disappeared. Jody had seen the thorny crown of a horny-toad moving under the dust of the road. His grimy hand went out and grasped the spiked halo and held firmly while the little beast struggled. Then Jody turned the horny-toad over, exposing its pale gold stomach. With a gentle forefinger he stroked the throat and chest until the horny-toad relaxed, until its eyes closed and it lay languorous and asleep.

Jody opened his lunch pail and deposited the first game inside. He moved on now, his knees bent slightly, his shoulders crouched; his bare feet were wise and silent. In his right hand there was a long gray rifle. The brush along the road stirred restively under a new and unexpected population of gray tigers and gray bears. The hunting was very good, for by the time Jody reached the fork of the road where the mail box stood on a post, he had captured two more horny-toads, four little grass lizards, a blue snake, sixteen yellow-winged grasshoppers and a brown damp newt from under a rock. This assortment scrabbled unhappily against the tin of the lunch bucket.

At the road fork the rifle evaporated and the tigers and bears melted from the hillsides. Even the moist and uncomfortable creatures in the lunch pail ceased to exist, for the little red metal flag was up on the mail box, signifying that some postal matter was inside. Jody set his pail on the ground and opened the letter box. There was a Montgomery Ward catalogue and a copy of the *Salinas Weekly Journal*. He slammed the box, picked up his lunch pail and trotted over the ridge and down into the cup of the ranch. Past the barn he ran, and past the used-up haystack and the bunkhouse and the cypress tree. He banged through the front screen door of the ranch house calling, "Ma'am, ma'am, there's a catalogue."

Mrs. Tiflin was in the kitchen spooning clabbered milk into a cotton bag. She put down her work and rinsed her hands under the tap. "Here in the kitchen, Jody. Here I am."

He ran in and clattered his lunch pail on the sink. "Here it is. Can I open the catalogue, ma'am?"

Mrs. Tiflin took up the spoon again and went back to her cottage cheese. "Don't lose it, Jody. Your father will want to see it." She scraped the last of the milk into the bag. "Oh, Jody, your father wants to see you before you go to your chores." She waved a cruising fly from the cheese bag.

Jody closed the new catalogue in alarm. "Ma'am?"

"Why don't you ever listen? I say your father wants to see you."

The boy laid the catalogue gently on the sink board. "Do you—is it something I did?"

Mrs. Tiflin laughed. "Always a bad conscience. What did you do?"

"Nothing, ma'am," he said lamely. But he couldn't remember, and besides it was impossible to know what action might later be construed as a crime.

His mother hung the full bag on a nail where it could drip into the sink. "He just said he wanted to see you when you got home. He's somewhere down by the barn."

Jody turned and went out the back door. Hearing his mother open the lunch pail and then gasp with rage, a memory stabbed him and he trotted away toward the barn, conscientiously not hearing the angry voice that called him from the house.

Carl Tiflin and Billy Buck, the ranch hand, stood against the lower pasture fence. Each man rested one foot on the lowest bar and both elbows on the top bar. They were talking slowly and aimlessly. In the pasture half a dozen horses nibbled contentedly at the sweet grass. The mare, Nellie, stood backed up against the gate, rubbing her buttocks on the heavy post.

Jody sidled uneasily near. He dragged one foot to give an impression of great innocence and nonchalance. When he arrived beside the men he put one foot on the lowest fence rail, rested his elbows on the second bar and looked into the pasture too. The two men glanced sideways at him.

"I wanted to see you," Carl said in the stern tone he reserved for children and animals.

"Yes, sir," said Jody guiltily.

"Billy, here, says you took good care of the pony before it died."

No punishment was in the air. Jody grew bolder. "Yes, sir, I did."

"Billy says you have a good patient hand with horses."

Jody felt a sudden warm friendliness for the ranch hand.

Billy put in, "He trained that pony as good as anybody I ever seen."

Then Carl Tiflin came gradually to the point. "If you could have another horse would you work for it?"

Jody shivered. "Yes, sir."

"Well, look here, then. Billy says the best way for you to be a good hand with horses is to raise a colt."

"It's the *only* good way," Billy interrupted.

"Now, look here, Jody," continued Carl. "Jess Taylor, up to the ridge ranch, has a fair stallion, but it'll cost five dollars. I'll put up the money, but you'll have to work it out all summer. Will you do that?"

Jody felt that his insides were shriveling. "Yes, sir," he said softly.

"And no complaining? And no forgetting when you're told to do something?"

"Yes, sir."

"Well, all right, then. Tomorrow morning you take Nellie up to the ridge ranch and get her bred. You'll have to take care of her, too, till she throws the colt."

"Yes, sir."

"You better get to the chickens and the wood now."

Jody slid away. In passing behind Billy Buck he very

nearly put out his hand to touch the blue-jeaned legs. His shoulders swayed a little with maturity and importance.

He went to his work with unprecedented seriousness. This night he did not dump the can of grain to the chickens so that they had to leap over each other and struggle to get it. No, he spread the wheat so far and so carefully that the hens couldn't find some of it at all. And in the house, after listening to his mother's despair over boys who filled their lunch pails with slimy, suffocated reptiles, and bugs, he promised never to do it again. Indeed, Jody felt that all such foolishness was lost in the past. He was far too grown up ever to put horny-toads in his lunch pail any more. He carried in so much wood and built such a high structure with it that his mother walked in fear of an avalanche of oak. When he was done, when he had gathered eggs that had remained hidden for weeks, Jody walked down again past the cypress tree, and past the bunkhouse toward the pasture. A fat warty toad that looked out at him from under the watering-trough had no emotional effect on him at all.

Carl Tiflin and Billy Buck were not in sight, but from a metallic ringing on the other side of the barn Jody knew that Billy Buck was just starting to milk a cow.

The other horses were eating toward the upper end of the pasture, but Nellie continued to rub herself nervously against the post. Jody walked slowly near, saying, "So, girl, so-o, Nellie." The mare's ears went back naughtily and her lips drew away from her yellow teeth. She turned her head around; her eyes were glazed and mad. Jody climbed to the top of the fence and hung his feet over and looked paternally down on the mare.

The evening hovered while he sat there. Bats and night-hawks flicked about. Billy Buck, walking toward the house carrying a full milk bucket, saw Jody and stopped. "It's a long time to wait," he said gently. "You'll get awful tired waiting."

"No, I won't, Billy. How long will it be?"

"Nearly a year."

"Well, I won't get tired."

The triangle at the house rang stridently. Jody climbed down from the fence and walked to supper beside Billy Buck. He even put out his hand and took hold of the milk bucket to help carry it.

The next morning after breakfast Carl Tiflin folded a five-dollar bill in a piece of newspaper and pinned the package in the bib pocket of Jody's overalls. Billy Buck haltered the mare Nellie and led her out of the pasture.

"Be careful now," he warned. "Hold her up short here so she can't bite you. She's crazy as a coot."

Jody took hold of the halter leather itself and started up the hill toward the ridge ranch with Nellie skittering and jerking behind him. In the pasturage along the road the wild oat heads were just clearing their scabbards. The warm morning sun shone on Jody's back so sweetly that he was forced to take a serious, stiff-legged hop now and then in spite of his maturity. On the fences the shiny blackbirds with red epaulets clicked their dry call. The meadowlarks sang like water, and the wild doves, concealed among the bursting leaves of the oaks, made a sound of restrained grieving. In the fields the rabbits sat sunning themselves, with only their forked ears showing above the grass heads.

After an hour of steady uphill walking, Jody turned into a narrow road that led up a steeper hill to the ridge ranch. He could see the red roof of the barn sticking up above the oak trees, and he could hear a dog barking unemotionally near the house.

Suddenly Nellie jerked back and nearly freed herself. From the direction of the barn Jody heard a shrill whistling scream and a splintering of wood, and then a man's voice shouting. Nellie reared and whinnied. When Jody held to the halter rope she ran at him with bared teeth. He dropped his hold and scuttled out of the way, into the brush. The high scream came from the oaks again, and Nellie answered it.

With hoofs battering the ground the stallion appeared and charged down the hill trailing a broken halter rope. His eyes glittered feverishly. His stiff, erected nostrils were as red as flame. His black, sleek hide shone in the sunlight. The stallion came on so fast that he couldn't stop when he reached the mare. Nellie's ears went back; she whirled and kicked at him as he went by. The stallion spun around and reared. He struck the mare with his front hoof, and while she staggered under the blow, his teeth raked her neck and drew an ooze of blood.

Instantly Nellie's mood changed. She became coquettishly feminine. She nibbled his arched neck with her lips. She edged around and rubbed her shoulder against his shoulder. Jody stood half-hidden in the brush and watched. He heard the step of a horse behind him, but before he could turn, a hand caught him by the overall straps and lifted him off the ground. Jess Taylor sat the boy behind him on the horse.

"You might have got killed," he said. "Sundog's a mean devil sometimes. He busted his rope and went right through a gate."

Jody sat quietly, but in a moment he cried, "He'll hurt her, he'll kill her. Get him away!"

Jess chuckled. "She'll be all right. Maybe you'd better climb off and go up to the house for a little. You could get maybe a piece of pie up there."

But Jody shook his head. "She's mine, and the colt's going to be mine. I'm going to raise it up."

Jess nodded. "Yes, that's a good thing. Carl has good sense sometimes."

In a little while the danger was over. Jess lifted Jody down and then caught the stallion by its broken halter rope. And he rode ahead, while Jody followed, leading Nellie.

It was only after he had unpinned and handed over the five dollars, and after he had eaten two pieces of pie, that Jody started for home again. And Nellie followed docilely after him. She was so quiet that Jody climbed on a stump and rode her most of the way home.

The five dollars his father had advanced reduced Jody to peonage for the whole late spring and summer. When the hay was cut he drove a rake. He led the horse that pulled on the Jackson-fork tackle, and when the baler came he drove the circling horse that put pressure on the bales. In addition, Carl Tiflin taught him to milk and put a cow under his care, so that a new chore was added night and morning.

The bay mare Nellie quickly grew complacent. As she walked about the yellowing hillsides or worked at easy tasks, her lips were curled in a perpetual fatuous smile. She moved slowly, with the calm importance of an empress. When she was put to a team, she pulled steadily and unemotionally. Jody went to see her every day. He studied her with critical eyes and saw no change whatever.

One afternoon Billy Buck leaned the many-tined manure fork against the barn wall. He loosened his belt and tucked in his shirt-tail and tightened the belt again. He picked one of the little straws from his hat-band and put it in the corner of his mouth. Jody, who was helping Doubletree Mutt, the big serious dog, to dig out a gopher, straightened up as the ranch hand sauntered out of the barn.

"Let's go up and have a look at Nellie," Billy suggested.

Instantly Jody fell into step with him. Doubletree Mutt watched them over his shoulder; then he dug furiously, growled, sounded little sharp yelps to indicate that the gopher was practically caught. When he looked over his shoulder again, and saw that neither Jody nor Billy was interested, he climbed reluctantly out of the hole and followed them up the hill.

The wild oats were ripening. Every head bent sharply under its load of grain, and the grass was dry enough so that it made a swishing sound as Jody and Billy stepped through it. Halfway up the hill they could see Nellie and the iron-gray gelding, Pete, nibbling the heads from the wild oats. When they approached, Nellie looked at them and backed her ears and bobbed her head up and down rebelliously. Billy walked to her and put his hand under her mane and patted her neck, until her ears came forward again and she nibbled delicately at his shirt.

Jody asked, "Do you think she's really going to have a colt?"

Billy rolled the lids back from the mare's eyes with his thumb and forefinger. He felt the lower lip and fingered the black, leathery teats. "I wouldn't be surprised," he said.

"Well, she isn't changed at all. It's three months gone."

Billy rubbed the mare's flat forehead with his knuckle while she grunted with pleasure. "I told you you'd get tired waiting. It'll be five months more before you can even see a sign, and it'll be at least eight months more before she throws the colt, about next January."

Jody sighed deeply. "It's a long time, isn't it?"

"And then it'll be about two years more before you can ride."

Jody cried out in despair, "I'll be grown up."

"Yep, you'll be an old man," said Billy.

"What color do you think the colt'll be?"

"Why, you can't ever tell. The stud is black and the dam is bay. Colt might be black or bay or gray or dappled. You can't tell. Sometimes a black dam might have a white colt."

"Well, I hope it's black, and a stallion."

"If it's a stallion, we'll have to geld it. Your father wouldn't let you have a stallion."

"Maybe he would," Jody said. "I could train him not to be mean."

Billy pursed his lips, and the little straw that had been in the corner of his mouth rolled down to the center. "You can't ever trust a stallion," he said critically. "They're mostly fighting and making trouble. Sometimes when they're feeling funny they won't work. They make the mares uneasy and kick hell out of the geldings. Your father wouldn't let you keep a stallion."

Nellie sauntered away, nibbling the drying grass. Jody skinned the grain from a grass stem and threw the handful into the air, so that each pointed, feathered seed sailed out like a dart. "Tell me how it'll be, Billy. Is it like when the cows have calves?"

"Just about. Mares are a little more sensitive. Sometimes you have to be there to help the mare. And sometimes if it's wrong you have to—" he paused.

"Have to what, Billy?"

"Have to tear the colt to pieces to get it out, or the mare'll die."

"But it won't be that way this time, will it, Billy?"

"Oh, no. Nellie's thrown good colts."

"Can I be there, Billy? Will you be certain to call me? It's my colt."

"Sure, I'll call you. Of course I will."

"Tell me how it'll be."

"Why, you've seen the cows calving. It's almost the same. The mare starts groaning and stretching, and then, if it's a good right birth, the head and forefeet come out, and the front hoofs kick a hole just the way the calves do. And the colt starts to breathe. It's good to be there, 'cause if its feet aren't right maybe he can't break the sac, and then he might smother."

Jody whipped his leg with a bunch of grass. "We'll have to be there, then, won't we?"

"Oh, we'll be there, all right."

They turned and walked slowly down the hill toward the barn. Jody was tortured with a thing he had to say, although he didn't want to. "Billy," he began miserably, "Billy, you won't let anything happen to the colt, will you?"

And Billy knew he was thinking of the red pony, Gabilan, and of how it died of strangles. Billy knew he had been infallible before that, and now he was capable of failure. This knowledge made Billy much less sure of himself than he had been. "I can't tell," he said roughly. "All sorts of things might happen, and they wouldn't be my fault. I can't do everything." He felt bad about his lost prestige, and so he said, meanly, "I'll do everything I know, but I won't promise anything. Nellie's a good mare. She's thrown good colts before. She ought to this time." And he walked away from Jody and went into the saddle-room beside the barn, for his feelings were hurt.

Jody traveled often to the brushline behind the house. A rusty iron pipe ran a thin stream of spring water into an old green tub. Where the water spilled over and sank into the ground there was a patch of perpetually green grass. Even when the hills were brown and baked in the summer that little patch was green. The water whined softly into the trough all the year round. This place had grown to be a centerpoint for Jody. When he had been punished the cool green grass and the singing water soothed him. When he had been mean the biting acid of meanness left him at the brushline. When he sat in the grass and listened to the purling stream, the barriers set up in his mind by the stern day went down to ruin.

On the other hand, the black cypress tree by the bunkhouse was as repulsive as the water-tub was dear; for to this tree all the pigs came, sooner or later, to be slaughtered. Pig killing was fascinating, with the screaming and the blood, but it made Jody's heart beat so fast that it hurt him. After the pigs were scalded in the big iron tripod kettle and their skins were scraped and white, Jody had to go to the water-tub to sit in the grass until his heart grew quiet. The water-tub and the black cypress were opposites and enemies.

When Billy left him and walked angrily away, Jody turned up toward the house. He thought of Nellie as he walked, and of the little colt. Then suddenly he saw that he was under the black cypress, under the very singletree where the

pigs were hung. He brushed his dry-grass hair off his forehead and hurried on. It seemed to him an unlucky thing to
be thinking of his colt in the very slaughter place, especially
after what Billy had said. To counteract any evil result of
that bad conjunction he walked quickly past the ranch house,
through the chicken yard, through the vegetable patch, until
he came at last to the brushline.

He sat down in the green grass. The trilling water sounded
in his ears. He looked over the farm buildings and across at
the round hills, rich and yellow with grain. He could see
Nellie feeding on the slope. As usual the water place elimi-
nated time and distance. Jody saw a black, long-legged colt,
butting against Nellie's flanks, demanding milk. And then he
saw himself breaking a large colt to halter. All in a few moments the colt grew to be a magnificent animal, deep of chest,
with a neck as high and arched as a sea-horse's neck, with a
tail that tongued and rippled like black flame. This horse
was terrible to everyone but Jody. In the schoolyard the boys
begged rides, and Jody smilingly agreed. But no sooner were
they mounted than the black demon pitched them off. Why,
that was his name, Black Demon! For a moment the trilling
water and the grass and the sunshine came back, and
then . . .

Sometimes in the night the ranch people, safe in their
beds, heard a roar of hoofs go by. They said, "It's Jody, on
Demon. He's helping out the sheriff again." And then . . .

The golden dust filled the air in the arena at the Salinas
Rodeo. The announcer called the roping contests. When Jody
rode the black horse to the starting chute the other con-
testants shrugged and gave up first place, for it was well
known that Jody and Demon could rope and throw and tie
a steer a great deal quicker than any roping team of two
men could. Jody was not a boy any more, and Demon was
not a horse. The two together were one glorious individual.
And then . . .

The President wrote a letter and asked them to help catch

a bandit in Washington. Jody settled himself comfortably in
the grass. The little stream of water whined into the mossy
tub.

The year passed slowly on. Time after time Jody gave up
his colt for lost. No change had taken place in Nellie. Carl
Tiflin still drove her to a light cart, and she pulled on a hay
rake and worked the Jackson-fork tackle when the hay was
being put into the barn.

The summer passed, and the warm bright autumn. And
then the frantic morning winds began to twist along the
ground, and a chill came into the air, and the poison oak
turned red. One morning in September, when he had finished his breakfast, Jody's mother called him into the kitchen.
She was pouring boiling water into a bucket full of dry
midlings and stirring the materials to a steaming paste.

"Yes, ma'am?" Jody asked.

"Watch how I do it. You'll have to do it after this every
other morning."

"Well, what is it?"

"Why, it's warm mash for Nellie. It'll keep her in good
shape."

Jody rubbed his forehead with a knuckle. "Is she all
right?" he asked timidly.

Mrs. Tiflin put down the kettle and stirred the mash with
a wooden paddle. "Of course she's all right, only you've got
to take better care of her from now on. Here, take this breakfast out to her!"

Jody seized the bucket and ran, down past the bunkhouse,
past the barn, with the heavy bucket banging against his
knees. He found Nellie playing with the water in the trough,
pushing waves and tossing her head so that the water slopped
out on the ground.

Jody climbed the fence and set the bucket of steaming
mash beside her. Then he stepped back to look at her. And
she was changed. Her stomach was swollen. When she
moved, her feet touched the ground gently. She buried her

nose in the bucket and gobbled the hot breakfast. And when she had finished and had pushed the bucket around the ground with her nose a little, she stepped quietly over to Jody and rubbed her cheek against him.

Billy Buck came out of the saddle-room and walked over. "Starts fast when it starts, doesn't it?"

"Did it come all at once?"

"Oh, no, you just stopped looking for a while." He pulled her head around toward Jody. "She's goin' to be nice, too. See how nice her eyes are! Some mares get mean, but when they turn nice, they just love everything." Nellie slipped her head under Billy's arm and rubbed her neck up and down between his arm and his side. "You better treat her awful nice now," Billy said.

"How long will it be?" Jody demanded breathlessly.

The man counted in whispers on his fingers. "About three months," he said aloud. "You can't tell exactly. Sometimes it's eleven months to the day, but it might be two weeks early, or a month late, without hurting anything."

Jody looked hard at the ground. "Billy," he began nervously, "Billy, you'll call me when it's getting born, won't you? You'll let me be there, won't you?"

Billy bit the tip of Nellie's ear with his front teeth. "Carl says he wants you to start right at the start. That's the only way to learn. Nobody can tell you anything. Like my old man did with me about the saddle blanket. He was a government packer when I was your size, and I helped him some. One day I left a wrinkle in my saddle blanket and made a saddle-sore. My old man didn't give me hell at all. But the next morning he saddled me up with a forty-pound stock saddle. I had to lead my horse and carry that saddle over a whole damn mountain in the sun. It darn near killed me, but I never left no wrinkles in a blanket again. I couldn't. I never in my life since then put on a blanket but I felt that saddle on my back."

Jody reached up a hand and took hold of Nellie's mane.

"You'll tell me what to do about everything, won't you? I guess you know everything about horses, don't you?"

Billy laughed. "Why, I'm half horse myself, you see," he said. "My ma died when I was born, and being my old man was a government packer in the mountains, and no cows around most of the time, why he just gave me mostly mare's milk." He continued seriously, "And horses know that. Don't you know it, Nellie?"

The mare turned her head and looked full into his eyes for a moment, and this is a thing horses practically never do. Billy was proud and sure of himself now. He boasted a little. "I'll see you get a good colt. I'll start you right. And if you do like I say, you'll have the best horse in the county."

That made Jody feel warm and proud, too; so proud that when he went back to the house he bowed his legs and swayed his shoulders as horsemen do. And he whispered, "Whoa, you Black Demon, you! Steady down there and keep your feet on the ground."

The winter fell sharply. A few preliminary gusty showers, and then a strong steady rain. The hills lost their straw color and blackened under the water, and the winter streams scrambled noisily down the canyons. The mushrooms and puffballs popped up and the new grass started before Christmas.

But this year Christmas was not the central day to Jody. Some undetermined time in January had become the axis day around which the months swung. When the rains fell, he put Nellie in a box stall and fed her warm food every morning and curried her and brushed her.

The mare was swelling so greatly that Jody became alarmed. "She'll pop wide open," he said to Billy.

Billy laid his strong square hand against Nellie's swollen abdomen. "Feel here," he said quietly. "You can feel it move. I guess it would surprise you if there were twin colts."

"You don't think so?" Jody cried. "You don't think it will be twins, do you, Billy?"

"No, I don't, but it does happen, sometimes."

During the first two weeks of January it rained steadily. Jody spent most of his time, when he wasn't in school, in the box stall with Nellie. Twenty times a day he put his hand on her stomach to feel the colt move. Nellie became more and more gentle and friendly to him. She rubbed her nose on him. She whinnied softly when he walked into the barn.

Carl Tiflin came to the barn with Jody one day. He looked admiringly at the groomed bay coat, and he felt the firm flesh over ribs and shoulders. "You've done a good job," he said to Jody. And this was the greatest praise he knew how to give. Jody was tight with pride for hours afterward.

The fifteenth of January came, and the colt was not born. And the twentieth came; a lump of fear began to form in Jody's stomach. "Is it all right?" he demanded of Billy.

"Oh, sure."

And again, "Are you sure it's going to be all right?"

Billy stroked the mare's neck. She swayed her head uneasily. "I told you it wasn't always the same time, Jody. You just have to wait."

When the end of the month arrived with no birth, Jody grew frantic. Nellie was so big that her breath came heavily, and her ears were close together and straight up, as though her head ached. Jody's sleep grew restless, and his dreams confused.

On the night of the second of February he awakened crying. His mother called to him, "Jody, you're dreaming. Wake up and start over again."

But Jody was filled with terror and desolation. He lay quietly a few moments, waiting for his mother to go back to sleep, and then he slipped his clothes on, and crept out in his bare feet.

The night was black and thick. A little misting rain fell. The cypress tree and the bunkhouse loomed and then dropped back into the mist. The barn door screeched as he opened it, a thing it never did in the daytime. Jody went to the rack and found a lantern and a tin box of matches. He lighted the wick and walked down the long straw-covered aisle to Nellie's stall. She was standing up. Her whole body weaved from side to side. Jody called to her, "So, Nellie, so-o, Nellie," but she did not stop her swaying nor look around. When he stepped into the stall and touched her on the shoulder she shivered under his hand. Then Billy Buck's voice came from the hayloft right above the stall.

"Jody, what are you doing?"

Jody started back and turned miserable eyes up toward the nest where Billy was lying in the hay. "Is she all right, do you think?"

"Why, sure, I think so."

"You won't let anything happen, Billy, you're sure you won't?"

Billy growled down at him, "I told you I'd call you, and I will. Now you get back to bed and stop worrying that mare. She's got enough to do without you worrying her."

Jody cringed, for he had never heard Billy speak in such a tone. "I only thought I'd come and see," he said. "I woke up."

Billy softened a little then. "Well, you get to bed. I don't want you bothering her. I told you I'd get you a good colt. Get along now."

Jody walked slowly out of the barn. He blew out the lantern and set it in the rack. The blackness of the night, and the chilled mist struck him and enfolded him. He wished he believed everything Billy said as he had before the pony died. It was a moment before his eyes, blinded by the feeble lantern-flame, could make any form of the darkness. The damp ground chilled his bare feet. At the cypress tree the roosting turkeys chattered a little in alarm, and the two good dogs responded to their duty and came charging out, barking to frighten away the coyotes they thought were prowling under the tree.

As he crept through the kitchen, Jody stumbled over a chair. Carl called from his bedroom, "Who's there? What's the matter there?"

And Mrs. Tiflin said sleepily, "What's the matter, Carl?"

The next second Carl came out of the bedroom carrying a candle, and found Jody before he could get into bed. "What are you doing out?"

Jody turned shyly away. "I was down to see the mare."

For a moment anger at being awakened fought with approval in Jody's father. "Listen," he said, finally, "there's not a man in this country that knows more about colts than Billy. You leave it to him."

Words burst out of Jody's mouth. "But the pony died—"

"Don't you go blaming that on him," Carl said sternly. "If Billy can't save a horse, it can't be saved."

Mrs. Tiflin called, "Make him clean his feet and go to bed, Carl. He'll be sleepy all day tomorrow."

It seemed to Jody that he had just closed his eyes to try to go to sleep when he was shaken violently by the shoulder. Billy Buck stood beside him, holding a lantern in his hand. "Get up," he said. "Hurry up." He turned and walked quickly out of the room.

Mrs. Tiflin called, "What's the matter? Is that you, Billy?"

"Yes, ma'am."

"Is Nellie ready?"

"Yes, ma'am."

"All right, I'll get up and heat some water in case you need it."

Jody jumped into his clothes so quickly that he was out the back door before Billy's swinging lantern was halfway to the barn. There was a rim of dawn on the mountain-tops, but no light had penetrated into the cup of the ranch yet. Jody ran frantically after the lantern and caught up to Billy

just as he reached the barn. Billy hung the lantern to a nail
on the stall-side and took off his blue denim coat. Jody saw
that he wore only a sleeveless shirt under it.

Nellie was standing rigid and stiff. While they watched,
she crouched. Her whole body was wrung with a spasm. The
spasm passed. But in a few moments it started over again,
and passed.

Billy muttered nervously, "There's something wrong."
His bare hand disappeared. "Oh, Jesus," he said. "It's
wrong."

The spasm came again, and this time Billy strained, and
the muscles stood out on his arm and shoulder. He heaved
strongly, his forehead beaded with perspiration. Nellie cried
with pain. Billy was muttering, "It's wrong. I can't turn it.
It's way wrong. It's turned all around wrong."

He glared wildly toward Jody. And then his fingers made
a careful, careful diagnosis. His cheeks were growing tight
and gray. He looked for a long questioning minute at Jody
standing back of the stall. Then Billy stepped to the rack
under the manure window and picked up a horseshoe hammer with his wet right hand.

"Go outside, Jody," he said.

The boy stood still and stared dully at him.

"Go outside, I tell you. It'll be too late."

Jody didn't move.

Then Billy walked quickly to Nellie's head. He cried,
"Turn your face away, damn you, turn your face."

This time Jody obeyed. His head turned sideways. He
heard Billy whispering hoarsely in the stall. And then he
heard a hollow crunch of bone. Nellie chuckled shrilly. Jody
looked back in time to see the hammer rise and fall again on
the flat forehead. Then Nellie fell heavily to her side and
quivered for a moment.

Billy jumped to the swollen stomach; his big pocket-knife
was in his hand. He lifted the skin and drove the knife in.
He sawed and ripped at the tough belly. The air filled with

the sick odor of warm living entrails. The other horses reared back against their halter chains and squealed and kicked.

Billy dropped the knife. Both of his arms plunged into the terrible ragged hole and dragged out a big, white, dripping bundle. His teeth tore a hole in the covering. A little black head appeared through the tear, and little slick, wet ears. A gurgling breath was drawn, and then another. Billy shucked off the sac and found his knife and cut the string. For a moment he held the little black colt in his arms and looked at it. And then he walked slowly over and laid it in the straw at Jody's feet.

Billy's face and arms and chest were dripping red. His body shivered and his teeth chattered. His voice was gone; he spoke in a throaty whisper. "There's your colt. I promised. And there it is. I had to do it—had to." He stopped and looked over his shoulder into the box stall. "Go get hot water and a sponge," he whispered. "Wash him and dry him the way his mother would. You'll have to feed him by hand. But there's your colt, the way I promised."

Jody stared stupidly at the wet, panting foal. It stretched out its chin and tried to raise its head. Its blank eyes were navy blue.

"God damn you," Billy shouted, "will you go now for the water? *Will you go?*"

Then Jody turned and trotted out of the barn into the dawn. He ached from his throat to his stomach. His legs were stiff and heavy. He tried to be glad because of the colt, but the bloody face, and the haunted, tired eyes of Billy Buck hung in the air ahead of him.

# Biographical Notes

## JOSEPH CONRAD *(1857-1924)*

JOSEPH CONRAD was born at Berdichev in the Ukraine, of Polish parents. Though born in a country with no sea coast, he felt the call of the sea, and shipped as a sailor on the first vessel he could find. One of his voyages ultimately brought him to England, where he settled and eventually became a British citizen in 1886.

His first novel, *Almayer's Folly*, appeared in 1895. Bear in mind that Conrad was already thirty-eight years old— and that English, after all, was an alien tongue to him. Yet with *Nostromo, Lord Jim, Victory,* and a dozen other masterly novels, Joseph Conrad established himself indisputably as the greatest writer of sea stories in the English language. His books are particularly popular in America, and first editions of his early works fetch fabulous prices. Conrad spent the last years of his life in Kent, and there he died in 1924. He is buried in Canterbury. *Heart of Darkness* is the longest and most memorable of the stories contained in the volume called *Youth*.

## JOHN GALSWORTHY *(1867-1933)*

*The Forsyte Saga,* of course, towers far above any other of John Galsworthy's works, but he is also the author of many other fine novels and plays. His writings are possibly the clearest picture future generations will get of England in its heyday—the comfortable, secure, smug era that preceded the World War—and his most notable plays, *The Silver Box, Strife, Justice, The Skin Game,* and *Loyalties,* throw a penetrating light on some of the evils and injustices that lurked just under the surface of those placid late Victorian and Edwardian days. John Galsworthy was born at Coombe, in Surrey, and educated at Harrow and New College, Oxford. He lived to enjoy a universal acclaim that is rarely bestowed on literary figures, being awarded the Nobel Prize in 1932 and honorary doctorates from Oxford, Cambridge, and five other universities. The *Apple-Tree* is reprinted from *Caravan*. Some day a genius in Hollywood is going to discover this beautiful story and make a couple of million dollars out of it.

## DAVID HERBERT LAWRENCE *(1885-1930)*

D. H. Lawrence, dead, has been the subject of bitter controversy by his intimates and a score of petty writers bent on exploiting their memories of him. Alive, his tormented pilgrimage in the world was a constant quest for health and a feverish devotion to his writings. He was born in Eastwood, Nottinghamshire, the son of an impoverished coal miner, and began life as a school teacher. His first venture as a novelist was *The White Peacock,* published in 1911. Two years later came his masterpiece, *Sons and Lovers. The Rainbow,* in 1915, was declared obscene, and an entire edition destroyed by court order. Harassed by illness and shortage of funds, Lawrence wandered through Europe, Australia, and America, where he lived awhile at Taos, New Mexico. In 1928, the private publication of *Lady Chatterley's Lover* provoked another storm. It was only in 1959 with the now-famous decision of the United States District Court for the Southern District of New York that an unexpurgated edition of *Chatterley* could be freely published and distributed. *The Prussian Officer* is the title story of his finest collection of shorter tales.

## KATHERINE MANSFIELD *(1888-1923)*

KATHERINE MANSFIELD was born in Wellington, New Zealand. At an early age she was sent to England and was educated at Queen's College, London. Her first story appeared in *The Lone Hand* when the author was nine, but only three of her books were published during her lifetime. Four came later, with her letters and journals. Among her works the best known are *Bliss, The Garden Party, The Doves' Nest, The Little Girl,* and *Aloe.* Katherine Mansfield has taken her place as one of the greatest short story writers of modern times. *Miss Brill* is from *The Garden Party.*

## WILLIAM SOMERSET MAUGHAM *(1874-1965)*

WILLIAM SOMERSET MAUGHAM was born in Paris, France. He was educated in King's School at Canterbury and the University of Heidelberg. He studied medicine and received his degree at St. Thomas's Hospital in London but never practiced. His first novel, *Liza of Lambeth,* appeared in 1897. Maugham's reputation was made with *Of Human Bondage, The Moon and Sixpence, Cakes and Ale,* and his very successful plays, *Our Betters* and *The Circle.* Many of his short stories have been adapted for television and motion pictures and are collected in *The Trembling of a Leaf, On a Chinese Screen, Ashenden,* and other volumes. He has also published two excellent collections of poetry and prose, *The Traveller's Library* and *Tellers of Tales,* and an autobiography, *Summing Up.* Mr. Maugham spent the last years of his life in France and Switzerland in an effort to improve his health. *The Letter* is here reprinted from *The Casuarina Tree.*

### ERNEST HEMINGWAY *(1899-1961)*

ERNEST HEMINGWAY's reputation as one of the leading American writers of the twentieth century rests squarely on his three fine novels, *The Sun Also Rises, A Farewell to Arms,* and *For Whom the Bell Tolls,* but his short stories are no less admired and acclaimed. *The Snows of Kilimanjaro,* reprinted here, is one of his best.

Hemingway was born in Illinois. His father was a country doctor, and Hemingway accompanied him on many of his rounds (see his first book of stories, *In Our Time*). Just before the First World War, he served as a reporter on the *Kansas City Star,* but soon after the outbreak of hostilities he enlisted in an American ambulance unit. He served with conspicuous bravery on the Italian front, where he was seriously wounded. After the Armistice, he became a foreign correspondent in Paris and there devoted himself to the writing that eventually made him an international celebrity. His brusque, highly individual style became the model for a horde of imitators; publishers began hailing one new hopeful after another as "another Ernest Hemingway." He did something to American fiction from which it has never quite recovered.

In 1952, Hemingway published *The Old Man and the Sea* which won the Pulitzer Prize. He was awarded the Nobel Prize for literature in 1954. His last book—the sketches of Paris in the '20's under the title *A Moveable Feast*—was posthumously published in 1964.

### WILLA CATHER *(1873-1947)*

WILLA CATHER was born in Virginia and moved in the 1880's to Nebraska. She attended the University of Nebraska, then taught in Pittsburgh, and came to New York later to do editorial work with *McClure's Magazine.* Very early in Miss Cather's career Sarah Orne Jewett advised her to write "truthfully and simply" about her own subject matter. And Miss Cather followed that admonition closely in her most successful books—*My Antonia,* in which she recorded impressions of the early years of her life in Nebraska, and *Death Comes for the Archbishop,* her masterpiece.

Miss Cather has not written many short stories. Those that are collected, notably the volume *Youth and the Bright Medusa,* though well written, are not as consistently fine as her novels. But a few of them do stand out—*A Wagner Matinee, The Sculptor's Funeral,* and *Paul's Case.* And perhaps one should also mention *Death in the Desert.*

In the story *Paul's Case,* Miss Cather records what must have been, in essence, an experience encountered while she was teaching English in Pittsburgh. The subject matter is pathological, and it would be merely another case history, except for the creative imagination that has taken the facts and fused them into a story that is illuminating and sympathetic and profound.

## SHERWOOD ANDERSON *(1876-1941)*

SHERWOOD ANDERSON was born in Ohio, moved to Chicago, then to New York, and finally to Virginia where he edited two newspapers, one Republican and the other Democratic. Newspaper work in a small town fulfilled a lifelong ambition of being "in close and constant touch with every phase of life in an American community every day of the year." This is the theme so beautifully personified in his best-known volume, *Winesburg, Ohio.*

Anderson never subscribed to the "pattern theory"; he was a born teller of tales, and his chief gift was his depth of insight into his characters and, in his best work, the simplicity and clarity of his prose. *I'm a Fool* is one of the memorable stories in *Horses and Men*.


## RING LARDNER *(1885-1933)*

RING LARDNER was born in 1885 at Niles, Michigan. He was educated at the Armour Institute of Technology in Chicago; was a reporter on the South Bend, Ind., *Times* for two years; and for four years he did newspaper work in Chicago, St. Louis, and New York. During this period he gained a wide audience as a gifted and original writer on sports. But with the publication of his *You Know Me, Al,* about the time of the First World War, it was evident that this sports writer was more than a sports reporter— that there was a creative imagination at work. With the appearance of further stories, he gained steadily in reputation, until even the "highbrow" critics acclaimed him as a master in his own 'genre'.

More perhaps than any contemporary American writer he caught the flavor of American speech and of various American types of character. Some of his stories dealing with baseball players are masterpieces of their kind. At his best he is a humorist of the highest order. And like Mark Twain and other humorous writers there is a deep undercurrent of sadness and satire as well as a sense of tragedy underlying some of his work. *Haircut* is an example of the latter quality, and is the usual nomination of conscientious anthologists.

## WILLIAM FAULKNER *(1897-1962)*

THE VALUE and significance of William Faulkner's work
has aroused as much controversy as that of any other contemporary writer. For years his work was unjustly neglected and damned by critics for its involved style and
preoccupation with the lives of decadent, neurotic people
in the South. However, soon after World War II a tremendous revival of interest established his best novels
among the greatest and most lasting of any in American
literature.

Faulkner was born in New Albany, Mississippi, but
moved to Oxford when he was about five. In 1918 he enlisted in the Royal Air Force in Canada, but the Armistice
interrupted his training, and he returned home and enrolled
at the University of Mississippi for a brief period. His
first novel, *Soldiers' Pay,* was published in 1926.

Of Faulkner's nineteen novels *The Sound and the Fury,
Sanctuary, Absalom, Absalom!, Light in August,* and his
last work, *The Reivers* are perhaps the most admired.
*Turn About,* reprinted in this volume, was made into one
of the most successful motion pictures ever screened. With
the possible exception of *A Rose For Emily,* it is Faulkner's best known short story.

## PEARL S. BUCK *(1892-1973)*

PEARL BUCK was born in Hillsboro, West Virginia, and
educated at Randolph-Macon Woman's College. In 1921
she became a teacher in Nanking, China, and in the next
ten years acquired the vast knowledge and love for the
Chinese people that she subsequently poured into her
Pulitzer Prize novel, *The Good Earth,* and a host of other
distinguished books. Stories like *The Old Demon,* reprinted
here, gave the American public an insight into the Japanese

mentality as well and into their mode of warfare long before Pearl Harbor. In fact, it is not too much to say that if proper heed had been paid to her words, there might never have been a Pearl Harbor tragedy. In recent years, Pearl Buck worked tirelessly for the welfare of displaced children of American soldiers and Asian mothers, and published in 1966 an account of her work with these children under the title *For Spacious Skies*. Pearl Buck is the only American woman to have won the Nobel Prize for literature.

## JOHN STEINBECK *(1902-1968)*

JOHN STEINBECK was born in Salinas, California, where he began the close association with workingmen and farmers reflected so clearly in his novels. After intermittent attendance at Stanford, he headed for New York. One of his jobs there was carrying bricks for the construction of Madison Square Garden.

Steinbeck's first novel, *Cup of Gold,* appeared in 1929, but it was not until 1935 with *Tortilla Flat* and its sympathetic depiction of Monterey *paisanos* that his work caught the public fancy. Many of his greatest novels, *Of Mice and Men,* his masterpiece *The Grapes of Wrath, Cannery Row,* and others have taken Salinas or a similar landscape as their setting. His most recent books are *The Winter of Our Discontent,* a novel, and *Travels with Charley in Search of America,* a perceptive and charming journal of a trip through America with the author's French poodle. Steinbeck was awarded the Nobel Prize for literature in 1962—the seventh American so honored.

*The Red Pony,* one of the most beautiful stories of our time, appeared originally in a volume published in 1938 under the title of *The Long Valley.*